FARO
AND THE
ROYALS

ALANNA KNIGHT

FARO AND THE ROYALS

The Bull Slayers
The Missing Duchess
The Final Enemy

BLACK & WHITE PUBLISHING

This omnibus edition first published 2005
by Black & White Publishing Ltd
99 Giles Street, Edinburgh, EH6 6BZ

ISBN 1 84502 045 6

Printed and bound by Creative Print and Design,
Ebbw Vale, Wales

THE
BULL
SLAYERS
1874

For Chris and Lucie

I

'It will be our secret...'

As Detective Inspector Jeremy Faro walked briskly away from the Palace of Holyroodhouse, the Queen's words echoed through his footsteps.

'It will be our secret, Inspector Faro.' And stretching out a small white hand, still girlish despite her increasing bulk, she had beamed on him.

There was no encouraging or polite smile from Faro as he returned the letter. He was reeling from the words he had just read. Momentarily speechless, watching her fold and replace in a drawer what might be damning evidence, enough to hang an ordinary man in a court of law, he gasped out: 'Your Majesty – would it not be, er, advisable perhaps to destroy that?'

The Queen was very small, and neither Faro nor anyone else was permitted to sit in the Royal Presence. It would never have occurred to her to be this thoughtful, that a chair might be welcome to one of her loyal subjects who walked considerable distances each day.

Although Faro towered over her by more than a foot, she was not in the least intimidated since she froze statesmen twice as big as herself on any day of the week.

'We take it that you are not indicating that His Royal Highness is in any way involved in this unfortunate affair,' she said sternly.

Faro was doing exactly that, but thought better of it. He shook his head, in a valiant attempt to banish the ghastly realisation taking shape as the Queen's glance changed to one of icy displeasure calculated to demolish even a senior detective of the Edinburgh City Police. If looks could have killed...

The imperial hand moved in a gesture of airy dismissal.

'You have our permission to withdraw, sir.'

As Faro bowed himself out of her presence, followed by that ferocious glare, she added: 'His Royal Highness is quite innocent. Oh yes, entirely innocent, we expect you understand that.'

Faro didn't understand in the slightest, after the condemnation he had just read. Bewildered and with that sharp reprimand ringing in his ears as the footman closed the door on the Royal Presence, he marched smartly past equerries, attendants and various hangers-on hopeful of achieving an audience.

Moments later he emerged thankfully into the frivolous breeze of Holyrood Gardens.

'Sir... Follow me, if you please.'

A breathless footman waving frantically indicated that the Royal Command was still in operation. As Faro was wondering what further nonsense Her Majesty had in mind, he was led into the equally intimidating presence of her Prime Minister, with whom it must be confessed Inspector Faro had never been on the best of terms.

Ushered into Mr Gladstone's sanctuary, he noted that gentleman consulting his watch in the urgent manner of one who suspects that every waiting second is diminishing his not inconsiderable bank balance. And that those who wasted his time would find themselves in deep trouble.

At Faro's approach the gold watch was closed with a snap and returned to the Prime Minister's breast pocket.

'Further to your interview with Her Majesty, I must impress upon you the importance of your assignation. That on no account must you involve or invoke the Edinburgh Police. And that includes your Superintendent. Absolute confidentiality is vital. Do I make myself clear?'

'So Her Majesty has given me to understand. That is precisely why I am to go incognito.'

'A new role for you.' Gladstone's thin-lipped smile was mirthless. 'Her Majesty may have neglected, er, omitted to inform you of two paintings at Elrigg she is keen to possess?'

Without waiting for Faro's response, he continued: 'One is of His Royal Highness the Prince of Wales with a wild bull from the Elrigg cattle herd, shot on a previous visit. Her Majesty is very keen to have it for Balmoral. Painted by Landseer, of course. The other painting is of the state visit of King George the Fourth to Edinburgh. The Family is very sentimental about such connections and His Royal Highness has informed his mother how it reminds him of his late father. Hence her interest,' he added with a knife-like smirk.

While Faro was considering a tactful response and how anyone with reasonable eyesight could see any likeness between such dissimilar men, Mr Gladstone came rapidly to the point.

'Unfortunately His Royal Highness discovered on his recent visit that the two paintings had disappeared from the Castle. Stolen, he was told. No one knew quite how or when.'

He sighed heavily. 'We expect that you will do your best to recover these two items and acquire them for Her Majesty. This part of your, er, duty is, I need not tell you,' he added, heading Faro to the door, 'of a most secret nature.'

Secret, indeed. Her Majesty's childlike greed regarding possessions, especially paintings for her ever-growing collection, was as well known as her childlike delight in secrets. Regarding possessions, however, few were ever bought, most were acquired – demanded from their owners who, according to Her Majesty, had been 'pleased and honoured' to hand them over to her.

The Elriggs, however, had forestalled her. Even as the Prime Minister spoke, Faro had already put together one or two ideas of where they might be found. Knowing human nature, he did not envisage any problem in solving this particular mystery, the easiest part of his assignment.

Much more serious was the Prince's possible involvement in the mysterious death of his equerry, Sir Archie Elrigg. Faro, who had total recall where documents were concerned, found himself seeing again the letter Bertie had written to his mother, a damning but oddly boyish epistle, stressing the very unfortunate coincidence that on an earlier visit to Elrigg, a fellow guest, an actor, had also met with a fatal accident while they were out riding together.

'It was not *my* fault, Mama.' There was a whining note of schoolboy complaint as if such communications were regular and betrayed a desperate anxiety to get in his excuses before the headmaster's report had a chance to raise the parental wrath.

Presumably Her Majesty's anxiety was capable of innocent interpretation, as a fond mother's desire to protect her firstborn and to prove to herself that the future King of England had nothing at all to do with the extraordinary coincidence of two fatal accidents during his visits to Elrigg. Her particular concern was his equerry's unfortunate end, an almost desperate anxiety to prove to all who knew him the impossibility that Bertie could be guilty of the eighth deadly sin for the English gentleman: cowardice. Bertie had left an injured comrade to face the enemy, in this case a wild bull.

Such monstrous accusations had destroyed many a noble family. Less exalted men than princes had been forced by an unforgiving society to take the 'decent way out' while loading a conveniently inefficient shotgun.

Redemption was the name of that particular game. But in a royal house, there existed an even more sinister motive: the anxiety of a ruling monarch whose reprobate son's conduct failed to live up to the high moral standards implanted on the unwholesome Georgian society at her coronation. Such standards, admirable for the nation, were totally ignored by the heir to the throne as he lusted after yet another actress or society beauty.

Nor could his mother forgive or forget that his affair with actress Nellie Clifton while at Cambridge University had contributed to the premature death of her beloved Albert and her long and bitter widowhood.

In a poignant letter announcing his visit (and carelessly abandoned in Bertie's rooms at Madingley Hall), Prince Albert had written: 'You are the cause of the greatest pain I have ever felt in my life. You must not, you dare not be lost. The consequences for the country, for the world, would be too dreadful.'

But Bertie remained unrepentant, an unwilling student who stated publicly that he 'preferred men to books and women to either'.

After her husband's death, the Queen wrote that she never could or would look at their son without a shudder. Her hopes for his marriage in 1863 to Princess Alexandra of Denmark – 'one of those sweet creatures' (she wrote) 'who seem to come from the skies to help and bless poor mortals' – were doomed to disappointment as the bridegroom soon demonstrated an easy ability to accommodate a wife as well as a succession of mistresses.

Faro felt sympathetic; knowing a great deal more than would ever be made public about His Royal Highness's 'scrapes', he could understand Her Majesty's concern about the future of Britain.

'If he succeeds, he will spend his life in one whirl of amusements. There is a very strong feeling against the frivolity of society, everyone comments upon my simplicity.'

Simplicity was admirable, Faro thought, remembering her words, but cowardice never. For if coward Bertie was leaving one man – his equerry – to be gored to death by a wild bull, how in heaven's name would he deal with the future of whole regiments of soldiers and the glory that was the ever-expanding British Empire?

Faro sighed. As for understanding, he was certain of only one thing, that he was being asked, or rather commanded, to divert the course of justice if necessary on what might well turn out to be yet another royal scandal involving the future King.

It was a hopeless investigation with a trail long cold, Sir Archie dead and buried, while the Queen had taken some time to decide whether or not she should take the Prime Minister's advice regarding her son's letter.

The situation was by no means unique. In the past, Royal persons had been revealed as suspiciously close to fatal accidents. The pages of history books were littered with prime examples. But such knowledge offered little consolation to the man whose unpleasant job was to throw a bucket of whitewash over the sordid business at Elrigg. Especially a man whose instinct for justice was equally as unyielding as his sovereign's moral code.

'There'll be a knighthood in it for you,' smirked Superintendent McIntosh, who had been eagerly awaiting the outcome of Faro's summons to the Palace of Holyroodhouse. In the unhappy position of following instructions in the form of a Royal Command that his chief detective was to be granted leave of absence to undertake a personal and confidential mission for Her Majesty, he tried with difficulty to conceal his curiosity.

Regarding Faro narrowly, he signed the paper releasing him from duty. The Inspector had done it all before many times, of course, protecting Her Majesty and the Realm, but never with such secrecy. What were things coming to when a superintendent of highest character and spotless record could not be trusted with such confidential information?

'Thank you, sir,' said Faro. 'I'll be back as soon as I can.'

'Do that,' was all that McIntosh could say in the circumstances. 'Do you need anyone – McQuinn, perhaps? I could spare him.'

'That's very good of you, sir, but that would be complicated.'

'In what way? I mean, you will be in Edinburgh, of course?'

Faro shook his head. 'No, not even in Scotland.'

McIntosh's eyebrows disappeared into his hairline.

'I won't be far away, though, just over the border, only a day's ride. And now, sir, if you'll excuse me.'

Nodding agreement, a very puzzled McIntosh went to the window and watched Faro leave the building and head across the High Street, as if such action might reveal some indication of his plans.

With a sigh he returned to his desk. Borders, eh. Then this could not be a police matter, hence his own exclusion from the details. Besides, the English police had very different ideas of how the law should be administered and were, as far as he was concerned, a race apart.

No doubt time would reveal all.

Faro, however, hoped most fervently that it would not as he walked rapidly homewards through the crowded, odorous High Street and emerged at last in the quiet villa quarters of Newington.

All around him Edinburgh blossomed, touched with the gentle splendour of Maytime. Arthur's Seat, proud and majestic, bloomed richly under the gold of broom while roadside hedgerows and gardens beguiled him with the scent of hawthorn blossom, of meadowsweet and delicate wild irises marching in sedate regiments shaded by mighty trees.

He breathed deeply. The warm breeze and gentle sunlight carried sweet odours of new grass and distant peat fires.

Approaching the tree-lined avenue leading to Sheridan Place with its handsome Georgian houses, he observed his housekeeper, Mrs Brook, industriously polishing the brass plate outside the home he shared with his stepson: DR VINCENT B. LAURIE, FAMILY PHYSICIAN, to which a new name, DR STEPHEN BALFOUR, had been added recently, a partner to accommodate the growing practice in this ever-expanding suburb of prosperous merchants.

Mrs Brook looked up at his approach. 'This is a grand day to be alive, sir,' she said cheerfully.

'It is indeed, Mrs Brook.'

Alive, he thought grimly as the sudden cool darkness of the interior hallway engulfed him and he climbed the stairs to his study. Beyond the window the distant Pentland Hills glowed in the late sunlight. This room containing all his books, his most precious possessions, had never looked more desirable, more comfortable and protective. And he sighed, with an ominous feeling that there might be precious few days like this in the immediate future.

As far as he was concerned, for 'incognito' read ' Royal spy' and he winced at having to conceal his identity. Once a policeman, always a policeman.

That he was incapable of successfully wearing any other disguise was a possibility that Her Majesty obviously had not taken into consideration.

He shuddered as a sudden vision of the Tower of London loomed before him. He had seen gloomy and alarming lithographs of its grim interior and, considering its bloody and dreadful history, it was one place he had no desire to visit either outside or in.

What if he discovered that the Prince of Wales was guilty of worse than cowardice. What then?

The Queen's displeasure for a mission failed and a scandal might at best merit discreet exile to the Colonies, or at worst a rather splendid civic funeral financed by Edinburgh City Police.

Such were his sour thoughts as he prepared to assume the new role necessary for what promised to be a most trying investigation. Given a straight choice, he would have taken on an Edinburgh murder any day.

2

'A pity you are no actor,' said Dr Vincent Laurie, who sympathised with his stepfather's present predicament.

For the sake of his two young daughters, Rose and Emily, living in Orkney with their grandmother, Faro realised that he must disregard the Royal Command to the extent of taking a member of his family into his confidence. In case a similar fate awaited him in Elrigg and he too was victim of a mysterious fatal accident.

And who better to be trusted with the details of his secret mission than his stepson, whose quick thinking had on many occasions saved his life?

'Elrigg Castle?' said Vince. 'Sir Archie Elrigg's place – equerry to the Prince of Wales, was he not?' Wide-eyed, he looked at Faro. 'The one who has just been gored to death by a bull? A bit about in the paper few weeks ago. Didn't you read it?'

Faro shook his head rather irritably. He had been particularly busy chasing a notorious villain, a fact that seemed to have escaped his stepson's memory. As he gently reminded him, Vince shook his head.

'The wild cattle are notorious. I seem to remember there was a similar accident in the papers a while back. An actor – Philip Gray. Entertaining guests with monologues from Shakespeare. Remember we saw him in *Hamlet* at the theatre...'

As Faro listened, he wondered if the actor had also been the Prince's rival for a lady's love. From the few veiled hints Her Majesty had vouchsafed in this sorry tale – hints that were all he had in the way of clues – he guessed that Bertie was more than a little interest in the laird's wife, Lady Elrigg, the former actress Miss Poppy Lynne.

Such knowledge was enough to support the theory that Bertie was following the usual pattern of his seductions. Fancy a married lady and, providing the social stratum was correct, the first step on the road to her bed was to appoint her husband as equerry. Next, suggest a weekend shooting party; grouse, deer, wild cattle, nothing on wing or hoof was safe from His

Royal Highness's attentions. If the lady was willing and the mansion large enough to conceal indiscretions, the husband was more often than not only too honoured at enjoying Royal patronage to care about being cuckolded.

There were scores of such stories, at least one a year, but for Bertie, Royal sportsman, the thrill was in the kill. Once the lady had succumbed to his arms, the Royal eyes soon wandered. An expensive piece of jewellery for the lady, a knighthood and a bit more land for the husband and there the *affaire* ended. When next the ex-lovers came face to face, a chilly bow of polite acknowledgement was all the lady could reasonably expect to receive for services rendered.

Bertie was always very discreet. Having the husband meet with a particularly nasty accident while his Royal person was on the premises, to say nothing of the publicity such a story might invoke, was clearly most embarrassing.

'What happened exactly?' Vince asked curiously.

'At the moment all I have are some vague theories,' said Faro with a sigh. 'Doubtless I'll have more to tell you when I get back.'

'Wish I could come with you.'

'So do I.'

'Wait a minute. Elrigg's quite near Wooler, isn't it?'

When Faro nodded agreement, Vince said triumphantly, 'I might just be ale to look in, see how you're getting on...'

The prospect of Vince's presence on any investigation was immensely cheering. Appearances were deceptive, none more than in his stepson's case. Bright curls and a boyishly handsome countenance innocent of guile disguised a keen brain, austere and analytical. Slighter in build than Faro, he was also capable of swift and often deadly movement when danger threatened.

'The Gilchrists have a great aunt who lives near Flodden,' Vince continued. 'She's celebrating her birthday on Saturday and Livvy has hinted once or twice,' he added shyly, 'that Great-Aunt would like to meet me and of course, I would love to see the countryside.'

Faro smiled. He had great hopes of Olivia Gilchrist, for this relationship had lasted the best part of a year, much longer than his stepson's usual run of disastrously short-lived courtships. Indeed, he had even developed a sentimental tendency to picture her fondly as Vince's future wife.

The two young people were eminently well suited. Olivia had brains as well as good looks and infinite patience, all excellent qualities for a doctor's wife. There was only one problem that concerned him deeply. Since leaving school she had been tied to her mother's invalid cousin, who had brought up Olivia and her twin brother Owen from the age of ten after their missionary parents had died of cholera in India.

When the hitherto strong and active Cousin Edith had been suddenly struck down in late middle age with a mysterious paralysis, Olivia immediately assumed the mantle of dutiful surrogate daughter, self-appointed nurse and companion. Vince assured Faro she did not find this arduous in the least since the two were devoted to each other, with a common love of books and music.

However admirable, such devotion was also the one impediment to his stepson's possible matrimonial intentions. And Faro was forced to accept Vince's claim that this was merely a very dear friendship. Owen and he had been at medical college together and the trio enjoyed a pleasant friendship with no desire for change.

'What precisely are you supposed to be doing at Elrigg?'

'Investigating the disappearance of two paintings the Queen wishes to acquire for her collection...'

At the end of his description of the paintings, Faro added helpfully: 'I might take along a magnifying glass, check over their vast collection. Who knows what I might come up with?' he ended cheerfully.

Vince wasn't convinced. 'A bit thin as excuses go, don't you think?'

'I couldn't have agreed more.' Faro sighed.

'And hardly enough reason for an extended visit.'

'I can take my time about it. I can use your imminent visit as a good reason for lingering in the area, taking a few extra days' holiday. Why not?'

Vince frowned. 'That's all very well but it doesn't guarantee you unlimited access to Elrigg Castle. Besides, you don't know the first thing about art, Stepfather,' he added sternly.

'I know that. Have you any better suggestions?'

Vince was silent. 'Couldn't they have dreamed up something a bit more convincing for your visit, some more plausible excuse?'

'Perhaps Her Majesty isn't rich on imagination – I expect Mr Gladstone had a hand in this one and as far as he is concerned a Royal Command refuses to recognise the impossible. It's all part of the divine right of kings.'

Vince looked at him. 'Of course, the main reason is this so-called accident to Elrigg, I can see that. But why is the Queen so concerned – apart from the anxiety of having the future King of England branded as coward?' he added cheerfully. 'I dare say he'd outlive that one. Royal subjects have short memories, especially for a prince who is also a leader of society.'

'True. But there is a complication. A difference of opinion between Bertie and his equerry – overheard – angry words in front of the whole castle before they rode out together alone. And only one came back,' he added grimly.

'Bertie?'

'Precisely. He said Elrigg had taken a bad fall from his horse. Help had been summoned on his way back to the castle, the local constable alerted. But when they arrived on the scene, Sir Archie was dead. Not from the fall. Someone had carelessly left a gate open and he had been gored by a bull.'

'Well, that sounds feasible.'

'Except that this was not the first time. On his previous visit to Elrigg, there was a similar incident with a fellow guest –'

'Wait a minute. You aren't saying that he was there when Philip Gray died?'

'I am.'

Vince whistled. 'What a very unfortunate coincidence.'

And at Faro's expression, he said slowly, 'You don't surely think he had a hand in it?'

'There was a quarrel certainly – both times.' And Faro frowned again, seeing the damning words of the Prince's letter to his mother.

'In Gray's case, he and Bertie had been playing at cards – for high stakes. Bertie doesn't like to lose and tempers ran high, there were hints at – certain irregularities –'

'Cheating, you mean.'

'Precisely.'

'Gray had a reputation as a gambler,' Vince put in. 'It was well known, I heard about it when he was in Edinburgh...'

Ignoring the interruption, Faro continued, 'The two went out alone next morning – Elrigg asked to be excused, indisposed with a bout of toothache. Bertie returned alone. Gray's horse meanwhile had bolted into the high pasture – the domain of the wild cattle. When he didn't return to the castle a search party went out and he was found, gored to death by one of the wild bulls.'

'Very unfortunate. This quarrel between Bertie and Elrigg – what was it about?'

'I have no idea.'

Vince rubbed his chin thoughtfully. 'So you think there is a possible link between the two?'

Faro sighed. 'All I know is guesswork. Gray was young, handsome, adored by the ladies. Perhaps he was also anxious to enjoy Lady Elrigg's favours.'

'A rival, you mean.' Vince sat up in his chair. 'Good Lord – you don't think –'

'I'm trying hard not to – until I know a great deal more, Vince. This is, after all, circumstantial evidence.'

'Yes, it is. And not very good at that, Stepfather. I can't seriously imagine the heir to the throne killing off his rivals for a lady's favours. After all, with the pick of the field at his disposal, so to speak, would he really care about one more or less drifting towards his bed? As for sullying his hands with murder, surely he has enough influence to discreetly engage someone to do the dire deed for him?'

'Not with his already damaged reputation, Vince.'

'Blackmail, you mean?'

'Precisely. Think of the blackmail potential if the coincidence of these two deaths were made public.'

Vince thought for a moment. 'True. We're in a far from happy position regarding the monarchy. I know he is not popular with his mother's less illustrious subjects, despite that leader-of-society role.'

As Vince spoke, Faro remembered the Queen's comment: 'If he ever becomes king, he will find all these friends most inconvenient.'

'Running away from an embarrassing situation is a long way from murder, Stepfather,' Vince reminded him.

'Then why didn't he wait for Sir Archie to be brought back home instead of immediately leaving the castle?'

'He did that? How do you know?'

'Because he said so in his letter to the Queen. That was what was worrying him. That he might be thought a coward because he gathered up his entourage. And left immediately.'

'Cut short his visit, you mean?'

'Precisely. "I thought it best to withdraw" – his own words.'

'But he didn't realise that Sir Archie was dead, did he?'

'He might have waited to find out.' And Faro remembered again the whining tones of the spoilt schoolboy. 'Try as hard as I can, Vince lad, this doesn't sound to me like the behaviour of an innocent man.'

'Perhaps the business with the actor made him nervous – it was an appalling coincidence after all.'

Faro looked at him sharply. 'I'm no great believer in coincidences, Vince, and this was altogether too strange. No, it won't do, lad. Think about it. Put yourself in those royal shoes. How would you – or any decent fellow – have reacted had you gone riding with another guest – even one you didn't care for – when you saw him thrown and injured?'

Vince frowned. 'Lacking medical knowledge, I'd have tried to make him comfortable before tearing back for help. And I'd have gone back to direct the rescue party to the spot.'

'Exactly. You wouldn't have rushed back so carelessly that you left the gates open with an injured man lying there and wild cattle in the vicinity.'

Vince shook his head. 'Not unless...'

'Unless? You see the doubt. Now you realise what we're dealing with.'

Vince sighed. 'No doubt Bertie will tell you a convincing story. Settle all your fears.'

'I'm afraid not. As you well know, the first place we look for a murderer is within the family circle or close friends, or known enemies, but this is one occasion when I am not allowed to interview the prime suspect.'

'Not allowed – I don't see –'

'Of course you don't. I have been expressly told by Her Majesty that His Royal Highness is not to be interviewed and no mention of his name is to be made. He wishes it kept secret that he was ever at Elrigg at the time of his equerry's death.'

Vince's mouth twisted in distaste. 'All this rather bears out Bradlaugh's scandalous letter, doesn't it?'

The Prince of Wales was twenty-seven in 1868, his behaviour already notorious, when the radical Member of Parliament's sentiments were made public. He wrote, 'This present Prince should never dishonour his country by becoming its King... neither his intelligence nor his virtues entitle him to occupy the throne.'

Vince shook his head. 'I don't envy you this one, Stepfather. A good clean murder would be much more your style.'

As Faro agreed with him, the future of what lay in wait at Elrigg was very fortunately veiled.

3

Faro's chief regret as he prepared for a hurried departure from Edinburgh was that he had no time to acquaint himself with the brief of a successful art valuer and investigator. His acquaintance with art was limited to sojourns in the National Gallery as a refuge from the rain or to rest his feet.

His fondness for the Gallery had begun more than twenty years earlier in 1850, when, as a young constable, one of his first assignments had been in the Royal Escort party.

The Prince Consort, turning sharply after the ceremony of laying the foundation stone, momentarily lost his balance. Faro sprang forward, dignity was restored and he was thanked with a warm handshake, a kind word and gentle smile. This was Faro's first encounter with the Royal Family and in one of his weird intuitive flashes he saw a great deal into the character of Prince Albert.

Now, as he headed towards Waverley Station, he wished time had been available to acquire some additional facts about wild cattle. His present rudimentary knowledge was limited to the Highland variety whose menacing horns had cast a terrifying shadow over his childhood holidays with his Aunt Isa on Deeside.

He was still subject to nightmares involving heart-thumping chases which now coloured his mental pictures of the Elrigg herd and he resolved to keep the animals at a safe distance since he disliked all cattle, his distrust extending to the allegedly docile and domestic varieties, such as the dairy cows being led across the meadow past the railway track.

And so, armed with scant knowledge of painters and almost none of cattle, Inspector Faro boarded the south-bound train and prepared to emerge at Belford Station transformed into Jeremy Faro, art valuer and insurance investigator.

He had a particular fondness for trains. Had his mind been free from anxiety, he would have enjoyed this opportunity to stare idly out of the window and welcome those inspired avenues of thought that often helped him solve his most difficult cases.

On occasions when the compartment was shared with other passengers, he indulged in a silent game of Observation and Deduction. Sifting through the minute details of their wearing apparel, gestures and habits, he would produce evidence of their stations in life and their reasons for boarding that particular train.

As a boy, Vince had been introduced to this novel game and had found it both an admirable and often hilarious way of passing many an otherwise tedious winter journey.

Today, however, Faro was offered no such diversions. Consumed by anxiety at the prospect ahead, his assumed role was as uncomfortable as an ill-fitting overcoat. Everything seemed to be wrong with it and his misgivings refused to be distracted by the passing countryside.

For once, the beauty of a late-spring day failed to beguile him and he was left quite unmoved by the soft green grass and radiant meadows of the East Lothian landscape. Glimpses of the North Sea, notorious for winter storms, now stretched out to embrace a cloudless horizon radiantly blue and setting forth gentle waves to lap golden beaches with a froth of lace. He remembered his mother's favourite saying: 'God's in his heaven, all's right with the world.'

Had he ever entertained such noble and simple faith, it would certainly have been destroyed by many years of dealing with hardened criminals in a world where neither the guilty nor the innocent were certain of being rewarded by their just deserts.

Earlier dealings with the monarchy had taught him that failure was tantamount to treason in royal eyes and, as for what lay ahead, this might well prove to be the last chapter in his long and faithful employment with the Edinburgh City Police.

If the future King of England was a murderer, or at best, a coward, capable of manslaughter, then Detective Inspector Faro was expendable and his distinguished career would be abruptly and quietly brought to a close.

Trying to shake aside his gloomy thoughts, he realised that his most urgent consideration was how to convince Elrigg Castle of his bogus identity. Perhaps that would be hardest of all, suspecting as he did that his sober dress was inappropriate for anyone connected with the art world.

Catching a glimpse of his reflection in the window, he considered the craggy high-cheekboned face which betrayed his Viking ancestry, the once bright fair hair still thick but now touched with silver.

He sighed. A tall athletic body and deepset watchful eyes told him that his disguise was incomplete. He looked what he was – a policeman, a man of action more accustomed to criminal-catching than browsing idly among valuable paintings.

His dismal preoccupation was interrupted as the train was leaving Berwick Station. Suddenly a porter threw open the door and thrust a young woman into the compartment. Breathless, she threw a coin into the man's hand and as the train gathered speed sat down on the seat opposite.

Faro's sympathetic smile and murmur – 'Well done, well done,' – was dismissed in a single scornful glance.

As the newcomer withdrew a book from her valise and proceeded to read with deep concentration, her attitude presented Faro was a unique opportunity of trying out his Observation game.

Glad of some diversion from his melancholy thoughts, he decided cheerfully that this one was not too difficult. The lady had not come far, for she carried little luggage, only one small travelling bag. Her numerous veils and scarves worn over a cloak of waterproof material indicated that she was used to and prepared for all weathers.

This was confirmed by the condition of her boots, sturdy footwear with scuffed toes, which had seen a great deal of rough walking. She retained hat and gloves so he had no means of seeing hair colour nor of identifying her marital status.

A veiled bonnet concealed most of her face from all but occasional glimpses and her slim figure suggested that she was probably in her early thirties. There Faro knew he was on shaky territory, the first to confess he usually erred on the side of gallantry where ladies' ages were concerned.

He studied her carefully. Even in the simple matter of reading there was something purposeful and decisive about the way she turned the pages. Here was no nervous, unsure female unused to travelling alone and about to visit a sick relative. She did not look in the least anxious but, suddenly aware of his scrutiny, she looked up from her book and fixed him with a fierce stare.

Embarrassed, he hastily pretended to sleep while continuing to observe, through half-closed eyes, her reflection conveniently provided by the compartment window.

When the train arrived at his destination, he was surprised to see the chilly lady push open the door ahead of him, spring lightly along the platform and claim the hiring cab which Faro soon discovered was the only vehicle the station provided.

One long road disappeared westwards into the hills. According to his map, in that direction lay Elrigg and he leaped forward: 'We are possibly heading in the same direction, madam.'

Head averted, she did not seem to hear him.

He persisted. 'May I be permitted to share your carriage, we appear –'

But before he could explain further, she cut him short with a withering look. 'And where might you be going?'

'To the Elrigg Arms.'

'That is not my destination, I'm afraid. Drive on, if you please,' she instructed the coachman and left Faro standing, staring indignantly after the departing carriage.

Patience was not one of the few virtues he was inclined to boast about and he paced the empty platform angrily, stamping his feet both to relieve his feelings and to keep them warm in the thirty minutes before the cab returned.

He would have been surprised indeed to know that the lady had an ability to observe and deduce that equalled his own.

But for a quite different reason.

She had summed him up accurately as a man without vanity, a man who needed none of the accoutrements of fine clothes and superficial elegance to add false lustre to what nature had given him. And that, she knew from bitter experience, made him all the more dangerous.

Bypassing that strongly male but admittedly attractive and appealing countenance, the straight, slightly hooked nose and the wide-set eyes that, shuddering, she thought resembled those of a bird of prey, she had immediately decided on his identity.

He was a policeman.

A breed of man she hated and feared. One she had learned to recognise, distrust and at all costs avoid.

4

The hiring cab returned to the station, collected Faro and the horses set off again at a brisk pace on their uphill climb.

When at last a church spire and a huddle of houses indicated a surprisingly modern town, the coachman pointed with his whip: 'Wooler, sir.'

Faro had heard of Wooler as one of the baronies into which Northumberland was divided after the Norman Conquest. In the twelfth century a rich and prosperous centre of the woollen industry, three centuries later it had borne the full brunt of the Border Wars, with only a hilly mound, a rickle of stones, to mark those turbulent times.

The houses in the main street were newly built and as Wooler disappeared from view the coachman said: 'Almost destroyed by a fire about ten years back, 1862 it was, sir. Second time in less than two hundred years. Eve the church over there, see, rebuilt in 1863.'

A short distance from Wooler and the countryside changed dramatically. It was no longer soft and undulating as in front of them rose hills of grimmer aspect. Wild moorland, great crags and huge boulders were the legacy of some ice age when the world was still young.

Now only a few spindly hawthorns, taking what shelter they could find, suggested that it had seen little in the way of human footsteps or endeavour.

He was acutely aware that he was in an alien land.

Used to the protection of city streets, Faro regarded the scene around him. This was an ancient battlefield which stretched from the Solway Firth to the North Sea, the Debatable Land of history, and he was right in the middle of it.

As if all those ancient bloodthirsty ballads still lived, their battle cries still throbbing to the long and terrible violence that had soaked these hills and moors in blood. For this was the ring in which the champions of England and Scotland clashed arms, some armoured in splendour, proud and valiant, their clansmen running alongside, fighting loyally beside their Border barons.

Here the victors robbed, slaughtered and made an end without quarter on either side.

The ballads told it wrong. Many a battle had been lost not by defeat, but by raggle-taggle soldiers who seized the chance of pillage while their skins were still intact. While hungry mouths and empty stomachs awaited their homecoming with the spoils of war, there was no room for sentimental loyalty to lost causes.

To add to Faro's sombre thoughts, the radiant day disappeared to be replaced by clouds hiding the sun. Now he was aware of boulders that moved. A tide of woolly sheep, followed by a shepherd and his dog, signalled a not far distant civilisation.

There was something else too: mile upon mile of fences bordered the narrow road.

'We're in the domain of the wild cattle, sir,' the coachman replied to his question. 'They don't like us and we don't like them.'

'Dangerous, are they?'

The coachman laughed uproariously at this naïve question.

'Kill you as soon as look at you, sir. I dare say they feel they have the right to it – the right of way, as you may say. Seeing they were here long before the Romans came. They've seen the killing times come and go – and many a fight that's gone badly for both sides.'

'Could the cattle not have been moved?' he asked.

The coachman thought this was even more humorous than his last question.

'I wouldn't like to try any of that sir. Wouldn't want their horns in my backside – begging your pardon, sir. Besides, His Lordship says it's best not to interfere with nature...' He stopped suddenly, remembering that His Lordship had also lost out in the end.

As the road descended once more, Faro felt that the legends and the ballads had never said half enough. They only skimmed the surface of a brutal reality.

The men this land had once supported had lived by the law of the jungle, the same law that saw the survival of the wild cattle hadn't worked for them.

While his beloved Shakespeare was penning the most exquisite prose the world had ever known, or perhaps ever would know, paving the way to an enlightened culture that would last for centuries still unborn, while Elizabethan seamen kept the might of Spain at bay, the monarchs of Scotland and England had emerged from the darkness of the Middle Ages to live in a fair approximation of luxury and culture.

But both were helpless to rule their borders or the men who lived on them. A race apart, their laws were made and their swords wielded by tribal leaders who would have seemed outmoded in the Roman Empire. They were intent on only one thing: blood feuds, the perennial excuse to annihilate one another.

Not all were peasants, or smallholders, or cattle rustlers. Some were educated gentlemen; a few were peers of the realm. All had in common that they were fighting men of great resource to whom the crafty arts of theft, raid, ambush and sudden death were inborn talents. Men born not with a silver spoon in their mouths but with a steel sword in their hands, the only language they or their enemies understood.

Now time had obliterated all evidence of their savage rule, ancient cruelties and swift death were replaced by a breeze warm and soft about Faro's face. Had this been a social call at Elrigg Castle, he would have looked forward to such a prospect with considerable enjoyment.

Aware that they had travelled for some distance and that in an ever-changing skyscape the blue was being overtaken by a steel-like grey, Faro considered how he might tactfully ask the coachman if they were indeed heading in the right direction: 'Is this all the Elrigg estate?'

The coachman pointed to the hilly horizon: 'You'll see the trees first, sir. His Lordship's grandfather was very liberal with trees, planted them everywhere as a protection against the prevailing wind.' And pointing with his whip: 'Look, sir, over yonder.'

The skyline opposite was dominated by a ring of stones. At first glance they looked like the wasted torsos of women petrified in some forgotten dance to gods older than history.

'The headless women, they call them hereabouts,' the driver grinned.

'How charming.'

'You wouldn't say that, sir, at dead at night if you heard them crying.'

'Crying?'

'Aye, sir, that's right. Crying. When the wind's in the right direction,' he added matter-of-factly at Faro's disbelieving expression. 'Acts like organ pipes, though there's others prefer to believe differently.'

His story was cut short by a sudden flurry of rain. As Faro put up his umbrella provided for such an emergency, he was reassured that their destination was almost in sight.

Moments later he was relieved to see a church tower reaching into the sky, followed by a cluster of ancient houses and a twisting ribbon of river. On a hill overlooking the only street, a flag flew from battlements, hinting at the castle which had dominated Elrigg long before the present parkland hid it from the curious.

The Elrigg Arms was a coaching inn of ancient vintage. Time and natural subsidence had thrust its upper storey out of alignment with the lower walls, which also leaned gently but precariously over the paved road.

Instructing the coachman that he would shortly be continuing his journey to the castle, Faro saw his luggage carried into the inn and gave the man a pint of ale for his trouble.

Never willing to waste time on eating, a fact that Vince deplored since it added to his stepfather's tendency to digestive problems, Faro emerged twenty minutes later, reinforced by a rather heavy slice of pie and a dram of whisky.

The coachman sensing gentry and a larger tip, respectfully tucked a travelling rug about his knees as they resumed their journey. A half-mile up the steep road some dense trees gave way to iron gates and a lodge, which, by its air of neglect and overgrown garden, was unoccupied.

As they sped up the drive, Faro saw that Elrigg Castle was no Gothic edifice, in the current architectural fashion for the romantic but comfortable baronial hall that the Queen had made so popular at Balmoral. Protection from the elements by parkland had been a necessary and wise investment.

Here was the stark realism of a Border peel tower, an oblong castle house belonging to sterner days when the beasts were kept on the ground floor and in times of stress and danger (which was probably every other Thursday) the inhabitants were rushed in through that high door and the ladder raised so that they could be relatively safe from marauders.

A serious attempt might be made to burn down the tower, but although the laird and his clan would get very uncomfortable underfoot in the process, it was difficult to burn through a solid stone floor. Besides cattle and movable goods were of most interest to raiders, plus any females who happened to be wandering about and could also be carried off.

In the late sixteenth century when the Border was settling down to more peaceful activities, buildings were inclining to comfort first, with a projecting porch and staircase on the outside, three storeyed with small, square headed windows, a ridged roof and embattled parapet.

The tower's original stout doorway, no longer under threat, had been tamed into masquerading as a large and handsome window, replacing arrow slits which were now merely picturesque reminders of harsher times.

Ancient oaks now sheltered sheep and a few shy deer who melted into the trees at the carriage's approach. The medieval theme, however, was continued in a field with an archery course from which a young couple had just emerged. Armed with bows and arrows, they were leading their horses through the trees in the direction of the castle.

But they were in no hurry to reach their destination and Faro smiled indulgently. They made an attractive sight; the young man, tall and fair, put his arm about his companion's shoulder and said something that pleased her. Faro heard her laughter and as she threw back her head, a gesture that sent her bonnet flying and her light hair rippling over her shoulders.

The young man joined in this peal of merriment, and, leaning over, the girl put out a hand and, patting his cheek, gazed tenderly into his eyes. A moment later they were gone.

Who were they? Dark riding attire did not necessarily indicate mourning relatives. But there was a quality of intimacy about the pair and their mocking laughter that remained with Faro, striking that first incongruous note of warning regarding the house so recently bereaved.

5

As the carriage rounded the drive, Faro saw another building crouching alongside the tower, invisible from the drive. Someone had attempted to turn bleak tower into homely mansion by the addition of two storeys, a few windows, a good sprinkling of ivy and not much imagination.

It was set around a square courtyard to house stables and servants, and Faro suspected that it had never seen an architect's plans but had been thrown together by an enthusiastic laird directing an army of loyal tenants who were even less sure of what was required of them. Dwarfed by the original castle, it would have presented no difficulties for any aspiring brigand or determined Border raider.

Faro climbed the steps to the main door, where an ancient butler asked his business and ushered him somewhat breathlessly up a wide stone staircase, considerably worn, not only by many generations of human feet but doubtless by processions of horses and sundry animals.

'If you wait in here, sir, I will see if Her Ladyship is able to receive you.'

Faro looked around. This then was the Great Hall. A stone fireplace stood at each end, massive enough to have comfortably roasted an ox. The high, vaulted ceiling was of rough stone, as were the walls with sconces for illumination by burning brands or torches. At one end a raised stone dais, for this was the scene of the barony courts where the Elriggs dispensed justice.

And everywhere, suspended if by magic, a legion of ragged flags from which all colour and delineation had long since vanished. Tributes, he guessed, to every battle that warrior Elriggs of former glory had borne triumphantly from the field.

The sound of light footsteps on stone announced the arrival of Her Ladyship. Her sudden presence was as if the sun had come down to earth.

Later, Faro remembered his quick intake of breath at her radiance. Honey-coloured hair, richly dressed, eyes startlingly blue in a flawless complexion, all enhanced by a jet-encrusted black-velvet gown, which he later described to Vince as fittingly medieval in design.

Expecting the ex-actress to put on a decent performance of Sorrowing Widow, he found instead that he was bowing over the hand of one of the young riders he had seen dallying in the grounds, a young woman who exuded warmth and laughter.

When she spoke her voice was resonant with a marvellous cadence, the lyrical quality of pure music. He thought how beautifully she might have played Shakespeare's heroines. She held out hands untouched by that chilly hall, so soft and welcoming that he found himself clinging to them longer than politeness dictated.

The heavy words of condolence he had rehearsed faded. As he stammered them out, she smiled and, as if aware of his embarrassment, she patted his arm gently, as one would offer a small child a gesture of consolation.

'Thank you, sir. I shall miss Archie. He was a kind man.' And, as if that was her last word on the subject, 'I am sure you would like tea, or perhaps something a little stronger. It is a cold, tedious journey from the railway station.'

A tall, thin maid with the same colourless anonymity as the butler appeared silently and put down a tray set for the ritual of afternoon tea.

Faro, invited to sit down opposite Lady Elrigg, prepared to leave the talking to her. A shrewd detective, he knew from experience, can learn a lot about character from apparent irrelevancies. People give much away in trivialities, if one is sharp enough to observe. Gestures too can be revealing.

She talked fondly about the countryside, deplored the weather, loved springtime. There was nothing there for Faro who watched as he listened and had to bite his lip on what he was best at – asking questions.

Suddenly the door opened and the young man, her archery companion, strode in. Faro did not miss the frowning glance the two exchanged, a warning from Lady Elrigg could not have been more clearly expressed if the words had been shouted across the room.

Then smiling, calm, she was introducing Faro to the newcomer.

'This is Mark, Archie's stepson.'

'My mother was an Elrigg cousin,' Mark explained.

As they shook hands, Faro realised that not only were the years between the two less than a decade but also that they brought into that bleak cold hall a substantial aura of affection and intimacy, which they made no attempt to conceal.

If this was illicit love, was that devotion strong enough for murder? Oh yes, Faro knew it was. He had learned through twenty-five years of criminal cases, that love was the strongest of human passions, one ruthlessly to stamp out ties of blood and duty. From the dawn of history man had been fully aware of its potential long before Cain destroyed his brother Abel.

Frowning, Lady Elrigg handed Mark the card which had been hastily printed for Faro in Edinburgh.

'Mr Faro's here about the missing pictures, Mark,' she added rather loudly with a slight emphasis on the words.

Mark opened his mouth but, before he could speak, she said, still smiling: 'Archie apparently told the insurance assessors – this gentleman's people – that the pictures were missing.'

And to Faro: 'This is all rather a surprise to us.'

It was indeed, thought Faro, for Mark continued to look not only surprised but quite dumbfounded.

Taking up the theme of the missing paintings and hoping to sound businesslike and convincing, Faro had a very nasty moment as Mark, studying the card, looked at his stepmother and said sharply: 'He never mentioned any insurance people to me.'

Lady Elrigg shook her head and smiled at Faro. She did not seem in the least perturbed that the paintings had not yet been recovered and her manner of indifference confirmed Faro's own growing suspicion.

'I can show you the place where they used to hang, if you like. There is still a mark on the wall.' She laughed as he and Mark followed her upstairs into the dining room with its massive refectory table stretching the entire length of the room.

As they entered, from every wall the faces of ancestral Elriggs glared down at them. Expressions of arrogance, suspicion, mild astonishment and rarely any degree of pleasure suggested that the steely-eyed gazes of these ancient warlords might have set the digestion of sensitive diners at a disadvantage.

'Over here.' Lady Elrigg pointed to the space between several sporting prints of indifferent merit and two large unhappy landscapes suggesting that Northumberland existed in the eternal gloom shed by a forest of Caledonian pines.

Faro pursed his lips obligingly and stared at the blank wall in what he hoped was the manner of an insurance assessor giving his subject deep and earnest thought and doing a careful assessment by a process of mental arithmetic.

Poppy Elrigg helped him out. 'I can't help you, I'm afraid I know absolutely nothing about paintings, valuable or otherwise. The one of old King George was of historic importance, I expect, but he was such a clown – all that ridiculous tartan on such a figure.' Her giggle was infectious, looking from one to the other, inviting them to abandon their sober expressions and join in her mirth.

When they continued to watch her, solemn as owls, she added, 'I suppose the one of the Prince of Wales with his foot on one of our wild bulls could possibly be of some value, of course – to anyone who had a personal concern.'

Faro looked at her quickly. Did she know of the Queen's interest?

Again she shrugged, a dismissive but elegant gesture. 'If a painting or an ornament is pretty and it pleases me, whether it cost a few pence or a few thousand pounds, well, that's all I care about. But Archie was different. Valuable things were his domain. He was so knowledgeable, a great collector. We have attics full of the weirdest assortment that took his fancy from every place he visited, I imagine, all over the world.'

Pausing, she smiled at them, her sidelong glance impish. 'He couldn't resist beautiful things.' Her lip curled gently as, pretty as any picture, she added slowly, 'And he was prepared to pay a great deal for what he wanted, you know. One could say beauty was an obsession with him.'

She gave Faro a slightly arch glance, daring him to come to his own conclusions about that strange marriage and turning from the empty spaces about them, she laughed again, that echoing sound at once carefree and infectious and totally inappropriate for a wife so recently bereaved.

Unhampered by her voluminous skirts, she walked quickly ahead of them, long-legged and graceful, moving her hands in light gestures as she talked. She was, thought Faro admiringly, a sheer delight for any man to watch.

'The police were notified, I expect Archie told them, or you wouldn't be here,' she said, her quick glance demanding confirmation.

As he nodded vaguely, Mark muttered agreement. 'Yes, of course. Talk to them.' He sounded suddenly eager, relieved to shed any responsibility for the pictures' disappearance.

When his stepmother said nothing, leading the way towards the great hall, he fell into step after them mutely. But glancing suspiciously at Faro his manner was loyally protective, indication that should this strange man threaten her in any way, he was ready to spring to her assistance.

Suddenly apologetic, Poppy Elrigg turned to Faro: 'We should have made more of it, I know, but then... the accident – you know...' Her voice trailed off.

'The very next day. Put everything else right out of our minds,' said Mark with a glance of stern reproach in Faro's direction as Lady Elrigg took out a lace handkerchief and sniffed into it dutifully.

Faro, watching the touching scene, murmured sympathetically and prepared to take his leave.

'I shall be staying at the Elrigg Arms for several days, while my inquiries continue. My stepson is arriving at the end of the week, we plan to spend a few days walking. Presumably my business will be finished by then.'

The two listened to him glumly, their faces expressionless, their minds clearly elsewhere.

He had to go. There was nothing else for it. He could hardly expect to be invited to supper. A mourning widow, that lace handkerchief being twisted in delicate fingers was a reproach, a reminder of her grief which provided a very good excuse for terminating the interview.

In a last stab at politeness, she smiled wanly, offering the pony trap to take him back to his hotel.

He declined, saying that he preferred to walk. Their relief at his departure was so obvious he guessed that they were even less happy in their roles of grieving kin than he was at presenting himself as a noteworthy and really reliable insurance assessor of valuable works of art.

Walking briskly down the drive, he went carefully over the scene he had just left. What evidence, if any, had been revealed during that brief meeting?

First, and most important, he had seen enough to know that Sir Archie had left no grieving spouse and that some powerful emotion existed between his stepson and his young widow.

As for the paintings, their disappearance during the Prince's visit confirmed Faro's earlier suspicions. Poppy Elrigg's statement that her late husband was obsessive about possessions had a certain kinship with the childlike greed that was one of the Queen's characteristics. As far as Her Majesty was concerned, merely to comment, to enthuse aloud, was to demand.

Did her son also believe in the divine right of kings to their subjects' good and chattels? Was he on the wrong track and had the Prince's quarrel with his equerry been a wrangle over two paintings of indifferent merit but of sentimental value to Her Majesty?

Most important of all, what was the relationship between the Prince and Lady Elrigg? He would need to know a great deal more about the stage that had reached before he could set the scene with accuracy. One would have imagined that the recent Mordaunt divorce might have given the Prince reason for caution, especially when he was named in Sir Charles's petition against his twenty-one-year-old wife. Lady Mordaunt had thereupon tearfully confessed that she had 'done wrong with the Prince of Wales and others, often and in open day'.

The press had leaped with joy upon such a scandal and the Prince's letters had been printed in *The Times*. There were many prepared to read very diligently between the lines of what appeared to be simple gossipy letters and come to conclusions that did little to enhance the Royal reputation.

Faro sighed. In common with that other less fortunate royal family, the Bourbons, it seemed that the Saxe-Coburgs learned nothing and forgot nothing.

6

The supper room at the Elrigg Arms sported ancient oak beams, dark panelling and a regiment of antlers as well as an assortment of glass-entombed tiny animals. Their bright eyes followed Faro as he walked across a floor on which only the sturdiest of tables could rest all four legs at the one time.

A cheerfully cracking log fire shed a glow of welcoming hospitality but any hopes Faro had of meeting fellow diners inclined to local gossip were doomed to failure. The two gentlemen who shared one end of the oak refectory table greeted him politely and hastily resumed a conversation that revealed them as business acquaintances travelling north to Edinburgh.

Another diner entered. The chilly lady from Faro's railway encounter. As her presence suggested she was also staying at the inn, he felt a resurgence of indignation that she had deliberately left him standing on the station platform when they might have shared the only hiring carriage.

Her brief acknowledgement of his cold bow declined admission of any earlier meeting. Firmly opening the book she carried indicated to her fellow diners that she intended keeping her own counsel.

Despite her formidable attitude, the lamplit table revealed what veils and scarves kept hidden, an abundance of dark auburn hair and slanting green eyes, which suggested in her less disagreeable moments capabilities of appeal, even enticement.

Observing the secret glances exchanged by the two other gentlemen, Faro decided that such looks might encourage the attentions of predatory males and that her chilly reception was perhaps a necessity for a female travelling alone.

As the plates were passed round he observed ink-stained fingernails. An artist or some clerkly occupation, school teacher or governess? Even as he pondered, she wasted no time over eating but tackled each course in a hearty businesslike manner, far from the polite toying with food in public that characterised genteel members of her sex. Eager to be gone, with a murmured excuse she rose from the table so abruptly that the capacious leather bag she carried slid to the floor and disgorged a quantity of papers.

As Faro helped her to retrieve them, they were snatched from his hands, with hardly a word of thanks. He sat back in his chair and realised that he had been correct in his suspicions. Such rudeness, however, was inexcusable. He hoped he had seen the last of this formidable travelling lady as he devoted his attention to the increased buzz of voices that issued from the public bar.

There might be valuable information to be obtained regarding his mission by mingling with the tenants and he carried though his pint of ale.

A few farmers were playing cards and although his greeting was politely received, by no stretch of imagination could it be called encouraging. It was neither as warm nor even as mildly curious as the flurry of tail-wagging the scent of a stranger stirred among their farm dogs.

He patted a few heads and distributed liberal 'good fellow's but this failed to play him into their owners' confidences. Resolutely they devoted themselves again to their game, having called their fraternising animals sternly to order.

Refusing to be daunted, Faro threw in some cheerful remarks about good weather, to be greeted by grunts and at most a few disbelieving headshakes. He had almost given up hope of any success and was about to retreat to his room when the door opened.

The man who entered was clad in an indescribably dirty, voluminous greatcoat which contained more than his large frame and Faro realised he was face-to-face with the local poacher. The huge garment wrapped tent-like about him was composed of inside pockets large enough comfortably to stow away a variety of game birds and small animals for the pot and, by the smell of it, included an interesting range of fish.

Faro's greeting to the newcomer was cordially but toothlessly received, its warmth strengthened by the offer of a jug of ale. The poacher's eyes glistened and he responded cheerfully to Faro's careful overtures about the weather for the time of year.

'Travelling in this area are you, sir?'

'Briefly,' said Faro.

'Fisherman, are you?'

'Alas, no.'

The poacher regarded him, head on side. 'Naught much for a gentleman to do, to fill in his time, like.'

Refusing to be drawn and hoping to direct the conversation towards the castle, Faro asked: 'I presume there is much casual employment hereabouts during the shooting season?'

'Just for the young lads, the beaters. But I'd never let one of my lads go – dead dangerous it is, those high-nosed gentry are awful shots,' he added confidentially. 'Few years back, there was one killed...'

'What are you going on about, Will Duffy?' The enquiry came sharply from the barman who had edged his mopping-up activities on the counter a shade nearer. 'That was an accident,' he said sharply to Faro. 'Such things do happen.'

'Mebbe,' was the poacher's reply. 'Mebbe like the horns over yonder.' So saying he nodded towards a bull's head among the decapitated trophies adorning one wall.

Caring little for the present bloodthirsty fashion in wall decoration, Faro had given this evidence of sporting skill scant attention. Now he observed for the first time that the splendid white bull's head lacked horns.

'You probably know more than most what happened to them,' the barman said heavily to Duffy, who thereupon leaned across the counter, his fists bunched in a threatening manner: 'Are you saying that I pinched them, Bowden?'

'It wouldn't be the first time something had gone amissing from my walls...'

Duffy stood up to his full height, bulging pockets giving him monumental stature.

'Are you accusing me?' he said in menacing fashion.

Faro and the other drinkers stood by, fascinated by what promised to be a fists-up between barman and poacher, men of equal height and weight.

'Duffy!' At that moment the door behind them was flung open and an elderly man with the look of a prosperous farmer glared in. 'Gossiping again, are you? Am I to wait all night while you fill yourself with drink?'

'Coming, sir.'

The poacher, suddenly deflated, tipped Faro an embarrassed wink and allowed himself to be meekly led away.

'When did this happen?' Faro asked Bowden, nodding towards the bull's head.

'A while back. Duffy can't keep his hands off anything that might fetch a few pennies.' And, refusing to be drawn into any further conversation with a stranger, the barman returned to polishing the counter as if his life depended on a shining, stain-free surface.

Faro's bedroom boasted a cheery fire and a large four-poster bed, plus the uneven floor of antiquity which creaked at every step. His door added to this orchestra of rheumatic boards. Testing the bed gingerly, he was pleased to find that the mattress was of a more modern vintage than the faded velvet canopy and ragged, brocade curtains.

Drawing the oil lamp closer, he took out his notebook and logged the day's events, ending: 'Wild bull's horns missing from public bar. Duffy might know something about the Elriggs and be willing to talk for a fee? Talk to him again!'

He slept well that night and awoke to the appetising smell of ham and eggs. He was relieved to find that his digestion was not hampered by the presence of the chilly lady at the breakfast table, and ten o'clock was striking on the church clock as he walked down the main street.

Between the post office and barber's shop, a one-time cottage bore on its window the words POLICE STATION. A narrow hallway ended in a door with a heavy bolt and a heavily barred square cut out of the central panel. It might serve as an imposing warning to the local inhabitants, but Faro doubted whether it had ever held a criminal with violent inclinations and uncongenial habits.

Opening the door marked ENQUIRIES, PLEASE ENTER, he stepped into what had once been the parlour. A large desk sat uneasily against one wall while a wooden form opposite offered uncomfortable seats for inquirers.

The constable on duty had the healthy look of an elderly countryman who has had a good life: white-haired, apple-cheeked and overweight. He nodded in reply to Faro's question and pointed to the closed door.

'It's Sergeant Yarrow you'll be wanting, sir. He has a visitor – if you'll just take a seat.'

Pondering on the hierarchy of two policemen in charge of a village station, Faro heard men's voices raised angrily from behind the half-glassed door on the other side of the room.

'You'd better do something about it, then.' The first voice was cultured, authoritative.

'I'm doing all I can –' The second voice was slow, weary.

'Which isn't half good enough. I demand permission to excavate the site,' was the reply.

'I cannot grant that. You know perfectly well it was refused by your late uncle –'

'Who is happily no longer with us,' said the first man, cutting short the weary man's shocked exclamation. 'It was just his pig-headedness after all, his sense of possession. Scared that I might find a treasure trove or some such nonsense. And, dammit, on what is, if there was any justice left in this country, my own land after all.'

'Look, sir,' there was an attempt at mollification in the other speaker's voice. 'Not a bit of use going on like this. I know you have a right to feel resentment, but the police can't help you here. It's lawyers – good ones – you're needing.'

'Lawyers, you say. I've wasted years trying to prove my inheritance. I've lived in a cramped, damp cottage when my rightful place should have been up there – in the castle. Damn you, man, you know all this, you know how unjust he's been, but you're on his side. He bought the law just as he bought everything else.'

The other man's protest was cut short by a sound suspiciously like a fist thumping a table followed by a crash.

The constable regarded Faro nervously, suspected this scene was making a bad impression and decided to intervene. Taking the law into his own hands, he marched to the closed door and rapped loudly on it.

'Visitor to see you, Sergeant.'

The door opened and, with a final curse, a young man exploded into the office and vanished out of the hallway.

'I seem to have come at an awkward time,' said Faro, aware that his words were a masterpiece of understatement.

Sergeant Yarrow did not rise to greet him. Perhaps this was due to the vexation caused by the angry young man's hasty exit, but Faro felt that his reception was less than cordial.

Closer to Faro in age than the constable at the desk, he did not look nearly as fit. There was nothing of the rosy-cheeked countryman about his sallow complexion and heavily lined face. Only his eyes were remarkable, a bright pale blue with the iris clearly defined.

As Faro introduced himself in his assumed role, he realised that the sergeant must once have possessed outstanding good looks with such eyes and black curling hair, now thin and grey.

Even as he wondered what suffering had brought about this premature ageing, with a weary sigh Yarrow began impatiently rustling the papers on his desk, his gesture indicating that such callers as Mr Jeremy Faro were wasting his time.

Put out by his attitude, Faro was almost tempted to reveal his true identity but thought better of it instantly. The whole point of his mission was to remain incognito. An insurance investigator was within his rights to interview the policeman who had examined the deceased after the accident and talk to the doctor who had signed the death certificate.

'Was there a coroner's inquest?'

Yarrow stared at him. 'Of course. A verdict of accidental death was recorded. You had better talk to Constable Dewar about it,' he added sharply, eyeing his piles of paper as if straining to get back to really important business. 'He has all the details and can let you see the statements.'

So saying, the sergeant stood up to speed this tiresome time-wasting enquirer on his way. As he walked across the floor, Faro observed that he was lame and that the effort cost him some discomfort.

He decided he would like to know a lot more about the Elrigg police and their curious hierarchy.

7

Constable Dewar's reception of Mr Jeremy Faro, insurance assessor, was considerably more encouraging than that of Sergeant Yarrow. His eyes brightened, his eagerness to be helpful confirmed Faro's suspicions of a daily round with nothing more exciting than stranded animals or pursuit of the local poacher.

Faro produced an official-looking notebook and said he wished to be taken to the scene of Sir Archie Elrigg's demise. Dewar regarded this activity with nervous anxiety. His eyes widened on being informed that this was the usual procedure when violent death was involved to which there had been no witnesses.

'Coroner said there were no suspicious circumstances, if that's what you're inferring, sir. And he is His Lordship's cousin,' Dewar added indignantly, his tone implying that such an eminent member of the family could not be in question on points of law.

'Besides,' he continued, 'I'd have never thought the family would need things like insurance, what with all their wealth. Death insurances seem to be only for common folk like us.' With a sigh, he added, 'Aye well, ye live and learn.'

'We do indeed. The site of the accident – is it far?'

'No, sir, but we can drive there.' Dewar stood up. 'If you'll follow me.'

The police vehicle turned out to be a pony trap. As they jogged up the hill at a leisurely pace, with an ancient horse who, Faro decided, would be as inept as the constable at pursuing a fleeing criminal, he used the opportunity to satisfy his curiosity regarding the Elrigg constabulary.

'Do you see a great deal of crime?'

Dewar laughed merrily at such a ridiculous idea. 'What – here? Not on your life. The local poacher keeps us busy and that's about all.'

'I should have imagined that an experienced constable like yourself would be all that was needed to keep order.'

'Indeed that was the case. Sergeant Yarrow came to us from the Metropolitan Police Force a few years back. Very badly shot up in one of their murder hunts. Cornered the villains, single-handed. Got an award for it,' he added proudly, 'but he was finished for active service.'

Dewar sighed. 'End of a promising career. Refused to retire. Asked for a quiet country posting up north, where he came from. His Lordship thought highly of him although he was appointed by the Northumberland Constabulary.'

'Isn't that the usual procedure?' Faro asked.

Dewar shook his head. 'His Lordship has the last word, makes the decisions. Only right and proper, since it is his property we are looking after. However, the Sergeant was personally recommended by the Chief Constable, who is kin to Sir Archie.'

Before Faro could comment, Dewar continued. 'Old wounds plague him a bit, poor fellow. But he's a good just man, well liked and respected by everyone.'

And a good man to have around, thought Faro, if it's a murder we're investigating. An experienced officer I can trust should an emergency arise.

They had reached the summit of the hill where the landscape was once more dominated by the weird stone circle.

Faro pointed to it. 'Interesting?'

'The headless women, sir,' said Dewar.

'I can see the reason for that. They look like sawn-off torsos.'

'Some say they were Celtic princesses, five sisters. Decapitated by the Romans and turned into stone.' Dewar chuckled. 'You should hear them crying, sir. When the wind's in the north, it echoes through the gulleys and channels. Makes your blood run cold to hear it.'

Faro looked back towards the village nestling peaceful and serene at the base of the hill. Smoke from its peat fires climbed wraithlike into the still air.

Constable Dewar smiled at him. 'Folk hereabouts believe the old superstition that the headless women are calling for vengeance.'

Between the standing stones and the road a line of trees marched sharply downwards to a grass-covered plateau.

'That's the old hillfort, sir,' said Dewar. 'Just below – see, there's the wild cattle.'

Distant white shapes grazed peacefully about three hundred yards and one substantial fence away as Faro descended from the pony trap whose ancient horse was being sympathetically patted by Dewar.

'Out of breath, old fellow? You take a good rest now.'

What would Superintendent McIntosh make of the Elrigg Police and their archaic mode of transport, thought Faro, used to the swift well-trained horses of the Edinburgh City Police, drawing the police carriage as it rattled across the cobblestones of the High Street, striking fear into the hearts of its citizens as it carried the guilty to justice?

Following Dewar to the site of the accident, keeping a watchful eye on the empty, bleak pastureland that lay between the cattle and the safety of the road they had just left, he was relieved to set foot inside the only shelter offered, a tiny copse of birch trees and bushes.

'The Elrigg shooting parties go mainly for game birds, foxes and the like,' the constable explained. 'Occasionally the guests are allowed to kill some of the wild cattle, if numbers have to be kept down, that is.'

Safe within the copse, Faro breathed again.

'They look just like an ordinary herd of cows,' he said.

Dewar nodded. 'You don't see many all-white herds, sir. When you get closer you'll see they're very different, smaller than our beef and dairy cattle. And with those horns,' he laughed, 'a lot more dangerous.'

Suddenly sober, remembering their mission, he said quietly: 'This is where I found His Lordship. There's the gate that was left open. That's how the beast got in at him.'

'A moment, Constable. Can we back to the beginning, if you please? Two gentlemen out riding, one of them is thrown by his horse. His companion suspects he is badly injured, goes for help...'

As he spoke, Faro's brief examination of the gate revealed a sturdy heavy iron latch which could hardly have been left open accidentally. Except by someone leaving in too much of a panic to check that it was closed, he thought grimly.

'Am I correct, so far?'

Dewar grinned. 'You are, sir. As luck would have it Sergeant Yarrow and I were out riding on duty together that day. We need the horses when we have a lot of ground to cover during the shoot. We are expected to keep an eye on things. The Sergeant being lame and I'm not a young man any more, we both move fairly slowly on foot.'

'You usually accompany a shooting party?'

'That's correct, sir. Oversee it, in case of accidents.'

'But there wasn't a shooting party that day?'

Dewar looked uncomfortable. 'No, but there had been earlier that week. You see, at the Castle they were entertaining a very special guest, an important gentleman.' He went on hurriedly before Faro could ask if he knew this important gentleman's identity. 'We had also been warned to keep a lookout for those two valuable paintings that went missing.'

Faro had no wish to be diverted from the circumstances of Archie's death. He had already decided that there had been no burglary at the castle. And that the paintings had been conveniently stored away by the Elriggs themselves, safe from Her Majesty's acquisitiveness.

'Did you witness the accident by any chance?'

'No. But we were just a short distance away – over there, on the pastureland when the gentleman rode over to us. He was in a dreadful state. A real panic. Said he was going for help.'

'Were the cattle about?'

'Oh yes, they were grazing. Just like today.'

'And you rode among them?'

'Not quite among them, sir, that would be asking for trouble. We kept at a safe distance and if you're on horseback they don't attack. Seems as if they only see the horses and don't consider other four-footed creatures as their enemies. It's odd because they don't seem aware of the men on their backs.'

'And what happened then?'

'Sergeant Yarrow told me to ride like the devil for the doctor and bring back the pony trap from the station in case he needed it to carry Sir Archie back if he was badly injured. He'd stay with him, meantime, see if there was anything he could do to help.'

'How long did all this take?'

Dewar shook his head. 'I didn't take much notice of the time to tell truth, sir. I was a bit flustered – His Lordship injured and all that. We're not used to crises like that. I suppose we thought of Sir Archie as being immortal. A bit like God. And he wasn't the sort that accidents happen to, could ride like the wind, drunk or sober.'

He was silent for a moment. 'I had to tell Her Ladyship and get old Clarence ready for the pony trap.' He sucked his lip, calculating. 'I'd reckon I was nearly an hour at least. When I got back Dr Brand was already there with Sergeant Yarrow. And I knew, just by looking at their faces, that it was too late.'

Dewar stopped and glanced at Faro who was studying the ground curiously. 'Is there something wrong, sir?'

'Has there been much rain since the accident?'

Dewar clearly thought this an odd question. 'Not more than a few showers, sir. We're having a dry spell.'

Kneeling down, Faro examined the ground, ran the soil though his fingers, but any evidence had long since returned to dust. A few weeks was enough to obliterate the churned-up mud which might have preserved evidence of two riders side by side, and even of a charging animal.

Dewar watched, too polite to ask the burning questions brought about by such strange behaviour.

Faro straightened up, smiled at him. 'Footprints and horses' hoofs, sharp and clear, can tell us a lot. Did you notice anything unusual?'

And when Dewar looked merely puzzled, Faro pointed: 'About the ground, I mean.'

Dewar thought for a moment. 'Odd that you should ask, sir.' And rubbing his chin thoughtfully, 'When I came back with the others, I walked around –' He grinned. 'Just the policeman in me, sir. Can't help that. And when the doctor said that Sir Archie had been gored, I wondered about the bull's hoofprints.'

'There were some?'

'No, sir, that's what was odd. There weren't any. Nothing to indicate the churned-up ground a great heavy angry beast would make charging down on someone.'

'Did you point it out to Sergeant Yarrow?'

Dewar looked embarrassed. 'Yes, I did. But he wasn't impressed. I don't blame him,' he added hastily. 'He's a city policeman really, and they don't see things like country folk born and bred. Besides,' he added reluctantly, 'he does make a bit of fun of me, says I'm always on the lookout, hoping for a crime but that I'd never recognise one if it stared me in the face.'

His voice was sad, then he laughed. 'He's probably right, sir. Crimes are the last thing he wants. And you can understand that, after all he's been through, he values a peaceful life above all things. Not like me, I've never had much chance of real crime,' he added in tones of wistful regret.

Faro smiled. Such reaction fitted in with Yarrow's relaxed attitude to crime; however, if Dewar's observations were correct, the omission of hoofprints should have perturbed him considerably. He said consolingly: 'Well, you were quite right to bring it to Sergeant Yarrow' s attention, even the smallest thing can be of importance.'

'I could have been wrong. I admit that. The rescue party from the castle with horses and the like would have covered up any other tracks.'

He paused, looking back towards the village, remembering. 'I told Her Ladyship. She was very upset and there was a great deal of bustle in the house. Maids rushing this way and that. The other gentleman, the one with the beard, that had been riding with His Lordship, he was leaving. He seemed to be in a great hurry.'

Dewar shook his head, at a loss to know how to continue but with condemnation in every line of his face. 'A very important guest, he was,' he said heavily. Again he hesitated, aware that Faro was a stranger, then he continued: 'As you maybe know, sir, His Lordship is – was – equerry to the Prince of Wales. You'd have thought in the circumstances he'd have waited...'

His lip curled scornfully, indicating more than any words, his contempt for this very important guest who did not even stay long enough to see Sir Archie carried home, to comfort his bereaved family and respectfully see him laid to rest.

Did Dewar know the identity of the bearded gentleman? It was quite outside the strict purpose of police procedure laid down for the protection of royalty for the local police not to be informed of the Prince's incognito. It indicated that the Northumberland Constabulary treated such visitors much more casually than the Edinburgh City Police, where royalty brought safety measures to a fever pitch of activity.

Presumably Sergeant Yarrow had been lulled into a false sense of security by the Chief Constable being kin to the laird and subscribed to the view that in this remote village outside time, where the Elriggs ruled supreme, assassins and murderers never lurked.

8

As he followed Constable Dewar across the field, Faro noticed on the other side of the copse an area roped off on the raised plateau with evidence of an archaeological dig.

'That's Mr Hector Elrigg's domain,' Dewar told him.

Faro looked at him. 'Another Elrigg?'

'Sir Archie's nephew,' said Dewar, and continued, 'the old hillfort was built long before the Romans came – or anyone else for that matter. Except the cattle, of course – they were roaming about long before men set foot in the Cheviots. Mr Hector's been digging there for years. I think he's hoping for buried treasure...

'Claims that all this is rightly his, that his father was tricked out of his inheritance. Not to put too fine a point on it, sir, it was all wine, women and gambling with Mr Malcolm, the young Master of Elrigg. He was not a good man,' said Dewar reluctantly, 'and he'd have gone to prison and the estate sold, if it hadn't been for Mr Archie, his younger brother.

'Mr Archie was completely different. As he didn't expect to inherit the title he'd gone off and built up a fine shipping line in Newcastle. He paid off all of his brother's debts, but Mr Archie was a keen businessman and the price was high – Elrigg was to be turned over to him – and his heirs.

'No one believed that Mr Malcolm would agree to such terms, but agree he did. He signed the document, took a boat out at Almouth and was never seen again. Mr Hector feels bitter about it. A man can understand that. Having to lose his rightful inheritance, in payment of his father's sins.'

As the village came in sight, Dewar asked: 'Where shall I set you down, sir?'

'I'll come back with you, if I may, and have a word with Sergeant Yarrow.'

'As you please, sir.'

'What can I do for you, Mr Faro?'

Sergeant Yarrow smiled, his greeting friendly and, as he indicated a seat opposite, Faro decided that their first meeting must have taken him at a bad moment, his calm ruffled by the stormy interview with Hector Elrigg.

'Has Dewar been helpful?'

'Indeed he has. We have just returned from the site of the accident.'

Yarrow nodded. 'And he gave you a report on what happened?'

'He did. There are just a few questions which you might be able to answer, sir.' Faro paused and Yarrow nodded agreement.

'Of course, I'll be glad to help, if I can.'

'Sir Archie was already dead when you reached him?'

'Alas, yes, I was too late.'

'What did you think when you examined the body, Sergeant?'

'That he hadn't been lying there very long. Perhaps half an hour. After sending Dewar off for help, I didn't reach the copse as fast as I intended. My damned horse went lame and I had to lead her the last part – very cautiously I can tell you, with the cattle roaming about.

'Fortunately I knew exactly where to find him. The copse is the only bit of shelter this side of the hill. But the gentleman's directions were very precise, considering the state he was in. White as a sheet and very upset he was. Almost in tears.'

He sighed. 'Alas, by the time I got there, it was too late. There was no sign of Sir Archie's horse. The cattle – they were grazing nearby – and someone, presumably the gentleman in his panic, had left the gate open.'

'And you think a bull had been attracted by the noise and had charged the man on the ground?'

Even as Faro said the words, he found such a statement most unlikely. The beast, he thought, was more likely to have been scared off.

'You see, sir, the old bull, the king bull, would be enraged by the blood, they smell blood – and fear, too, so I'm told.'

'Blood? I didn't know Sir Archie was bleeding.'

Yarrow shook his head. 'Not His Lordship's blood – his own. Dewar probably mentioned that there had been a shoot earlier in the week. It happens from time to time when guests who want a shoot come to the castle. It was the same procedure as in olden times, until lately. Like a hunt in the Middle Ages.'

'What do they use? Bows and arrows?' Faro asked in amazement.

'That's right, sir. And crossbows. And everyone comes, a regular festival with a feast afterwards. A notice goes up that a wild bull will be killed on a certain day. The men – and some of the women too – come on horse and foot and then the horsemen ride off the bull that's the intended target.'

'Ride him off?'

'Yes, try and get him away from the rest of the herd. And when he stands at bay, the chief marksman, usually His Lordship or the most honoured guest, dismounts and fires the arrow. That goes on until the old bull succumbs. You can imagine that the old fellow gets wilder and wilder, in pain as he is.'

'I can imagine,' said Faro sourly.

Yarrow gave him a quick glance. 'I – see you don't approve, sir. No more than I do. I'm a town man myself but in the country these traditions are hard to break. Everyone comes along who is capable of shooting an arrow, even little bairns. The Elrigg family are born to it. Experts – Mr Hector and Mr Mark were trained from when they could first hold a bow.'

He paused and smiled proudly. 'Everyone is encouraged to take up the local sport and I'm now quite a good marksman myself, so is Dewar. But I prefer to stick to the archery field. We'll be having our annual contest – for the Golden Arrow – next week.'

'Really? With the castle in mourning?'

'Her Ladyship's decision. She said Sir Archie would have wanted everything to go on as normal. He would have wished to have the contest and not disappoint all the tenants.'

'That was very far seeing of her,' said Faro as he wondered at her motives.

'Come if you can. You'll be most welcome. The proceeds go to the Elriggs' favourite charities.'

'I doubt whether I'll be here then. With all these arrows flying about it might be a dangerous pastime for an observer.'

Yarrow frowned. 'The bull slaying was – for some. Not always fatal but like the ones used in the Spanish bullfights, they could turn very nasty. And that was when Sir Archie's grandfather decided most humanely that the beast should be finished off by rifle fire.'

'And that was what happened last week?'

'Yes. But some of them are not very good on the guns...'

He was silent, frowning before he continued: 'They thought they wounded one, but not the king bull. They were probably wrong and if His Lordship wasn't dead in the fall, and struggling to get to the road, the bull might have seen and set about him with his horns. It looked to me like that was the case –'

'What makes you think that?'

'He was gored in the back.' He shrugged away the unpleasant picture. 'And that was the end of him.'

Again he fell silent, his face bleak, his expression harsh with suffering. And Faro remembered that Yarrow had been seen many deaths and had almost lost his own life.

'Did you see anyone else in the area – who could have helped perhaps?'

Yarrow regarded him curiously. 'Not in the immediate vicinity,' he said heavily.

'But near enough?' said Faro eagerly.

He looked away. 'Hector Elrigg, Sir Archie's nephew. You – almost – met when you came to the station,' he added with a wry grimace. 'When I found Sir Archie, Hector was working at the hillfort.' He drew a deep breath. 'I shouted to him for help...'

'And ...' said Faro softly.

Yarrow gave him a glance of desperate appeal. 'Look, there is probably nothing in this at all. I just didn't care for his attitude. He was rather flippant about the whole thing. A downright refusal, sir, that's what I got from Hector Elrigg,' he added in shocked tones.

'From what you heard when you arrived earlier on, you'll realise he's a difficult sort of young devil, but I try to be fair-minded. And I'm certainly not suggesting that Hector seriously wished his uncle dead or would have tried to bring it about. Not at all.'

Wondering whether he should have revealed his true identity to Yarrow, Faro returned to the inn. In the empty bar he had a good look at the bull's magnificent de-horned head and decided that in life he must have been an ugly customer to face.

No doubt the Prince, despite his readiness to mow down everything in sight on a shoot, completely lost his nerve when he was unarmed – and left the gate open in his hasty retreat.

And Faro would have given much to know more about that quarrel between the Prince and his equerry, the reasons for which he had delicately omitted in his letter to the Queen. Had Poppy Elrigg been the reason, or had the Prince lost at cards?

Whatever the quarrel, it had been serious enough for him to cut short his visit to Elrigg. Was his anxiety to escape scandal or blackmail the only reason why he had been reported as 'abroad' and unable to attend the funeral of his equerry?

But Faro now had another strand leading into the labyrinth.

Yarrow's revelations regarding Sir Archie's nephew, who was also in the vicinity, had posed yet another question over the events of that day.

As he made notes of his interviews with the local police, Faro was left with an uneasy feeling of something he had missed. Something of vital importance. And what began as a personal command from Her Majesty, to prove for her anxious pride that her son, the future King of England, was not a coward, was already showing unmistakable signs of developing into a worse scandal.

Murder.

As he walked briskly in the direction of the castle to talk again to the devoted couple who had been his prime suspects, Lady Elrigg and her stepson Mark, Faro was already adding one other name. That of Hector Elrigg.

Even as he did so, he realised his behaviour was one of habit. But it was also quite out of order and he must not give in to temptation but merely regard it as an exercise in detection to fill in the few days before Vince's arrival, an investigation dictated by personal curiosity and the challenge set by a long-buried victim, no clues and some very vague suspects.

If murder was involved then he had no rights beyond turning over any evidence he found to Sergeant Yarrow, who would doubtless stir himself out of the torpor of Elrigg village and its feudal system and, remembering his old skills, do an efficient job of seeing justice done.

As for himself, he must return to Edinburgh, report to Her Majesty that her son was guiltless – of cowardice. She need never know that he had narrowly escaped being involved in a murder inquiry, much more difficult to live down for a future King of England than a divorce scandal.

9

Later that morning, Faro was retracing his steps along the Castle drive. He was in no very good temper, for it had been a wasted journey. The ancient butler had informed him quite firmly that there was no one at home and, in terms that suggested shocked effrontery, no, he had not the least idea when Her Ladyship and Mr Mark might be expected to return.

The weather too fitted Faro's mood of exasperation. How on earth did one bring any possible criminal investigation to a satisfying conclusion in such circumstances as he faced at Elrigg? Small wonder policemen like Dewar and Yarrow were only too glad to accept 'accidental death' and close the inquiries as fast as possible.

Rounding up suspects over a wide area, much less trying to interview them, faced with ancient retainers like the Castle butler, was a daunting prospect for even the most experienced detective.

Police procedure in Edinburgh's Central Office, well documented and with carriages on hand, had never seemed more agreeable to Faro as he walked past the archery field, the scene of the Elriggs' medieval pursuits.

He quickened his steps as, on both sides of the drive, storm-tossed rhododendrons shivered and swayed in the rising wind. If those swift-gathering rain clouds broke, he reckoned he was in for a thorough soaking long before he reached the inn.

Seconds later, the warning patter of heavy raindrops on the trees above his head had him running towards the gate lodge. But the wooden porch he hoped would offer temporary shelter was already leaking badly.

As he leaned back against the door, it yielded to his touch. Presumably the cottage was not empty after all and, anxious not to alarm the occupants, he applied his hand to the brass knocker. When there was no response, he stepped inside.

A woman's voice from upstairs greeted his entrance.

'Go through to the kitchen. The back door won't close properly and the cupboard door has jammed. I'll be with you in a minute.'

Faro did as he was bid. The cottage obviously had not been lived in for some time. It felt damp and unwelcoming; the furniture stood shrouded in attitudes of neglect that he felt often characterised inanimate objects in deserted houses.

In the kitchen, a fire recently lit crackled feebly and a book lying open beside provisions scattered on the table suggested a new tenant had taken possession.

Insatiably curious about other people's reading matter, from which Faro believed there might be much to be gained in the matter of observation and deduction, he picked it up and read:

> We hear every day of murders committed in the country. Brutal and treacherous murder; slow, protracted agonies from poisons administered by some kindred hand; sudden and violent deaths by cruel blows, inflicted with a stake cut from some spreading oak, whose every shadow promised – Peace. In the country of which I write, I have been shown a meadow in which, on a quiet summer Sunday evening, a young farmer murdered the girl who loved and trusted him; and yet, even now, with the stain of that foul deed upon it, the aspect of the spot is – Peace. No species of crime has ever been committed in the worst rookeries of the Seven Dials that has not been also done in the face of that rustic calm which still, in spite of all, we look on with a tender, half-mournful yearning, and associate with – Peace.

The passage was heavily underscored, the word 'Elrigg?' written in the margin. But what surprised Faro most of all was its title: *Lady Audley's Secret*. Written by Mary Elizabeth Braddon in the 1860s, it belonged to the category of 'Sensation' novels, whereby authors came by their plots from real-life murders and sensational crimes reported in the newspapers.

'Have you found the problem?' called the voice from upstairs, obviously wondering at his silence.

'I believe so,' Faro called and tackling the back door discovered the cause to be rusted hinges. Such a domestic challenge was always calculated to put him on his mettle, as his housekeeper Mrs Brook was well aware.

On a shelf beside the kitchen dresser, he found what he was

looking for, an oil can. A liberal application soon had the offending door working nicely again and, encouraged by this success, he was turning his attention to the cupboard door when light footsteps in the passage announce the occupier's approach.

'There are some other jobs you might tackle now that you've deigned to put in an appearance.'

Half turning his head in the gloom, with sinking heart Faro recognised the acid tones of the chilly lady who he had fondly imagined was now travelling far from Elrigg.

She was not a prepossessing sight, her abundant hair tied loosely in a scarf and clad in a capacious and none-too-clean apron. She regarded him curiously.

'So, you are the new factor. Well, well,' she added as if surprised by the discovery. 'They said you might look in.'

Indignant, Faro stood up and drew himself to his full height. Unperturbed, she looked him over and taking in every detail of his appearance she said: 'Or am I mistaken? Is it the new gardener, you are?'

This was too much for even Faro. Notoriously uncaring in sartorial matters, he decided that although his clothes were by no means new, they did not merit such an outrageous assumption.

'No, madam,' he said coldly. 'I am neither gardener nor factor. I happened to be passing on my way from the Castle when the rain began – I was simply taking shelter –'

'Spying –' she interrupted, pointing a finger at him.

'I beg your pardon?'

'Spying,' she repeated accusingly. 'Of course, you're a policeman.'

Taken aback, he stared at her. 'What makes you think –?'

'Oh, don't bother to deny it. I saw you going into the police station this morning. I guessed right, didn't I?' she demanded triumphantly. 'You're here about Sir Archie?'

Faro remained speechless as she continued: 'You'll get no help from Constable Dewar, I'm afraid. He's not very good at his job. Or that poor doomed fellow Yarrow, who's in charge –'

'What makes you say he's doomed?'

She looked at him strangely. 'I just know such things. I can see them written in people's faces.'

'Indeed. Psychic, are you?' he said mockingly.

She shrugged. 'Sometimes. I know things. I get flashes about people. Like you – like policemen,' she added sourly.

With the kitchen table between them, they glared at each other, adversaries poised in anticipation of the next move.

Finally, she gave way, and with a shrug walked over to the back door. Opening and closing it a few times, she nodded and said grudgingly: 'You did a good job, I'll say that for you. Thanks. I didn't feel very secure or very comfortable with it open to the four winds.'

'So you're a town lady?'

'Ye-es. How did –?'

'Country folk don't lock doors.'

'*Touché.*' For the first time she smiled, an expression, Faro admitted reluctantly, that quite transformed her face.

As he walked towards the front door, she said: 'What about the cupboard then?'

Faro looked at her and went over to the offending door. A vigorous tug and it responded. Turning, he gave her a grin of satisfaction. 'That's all it needed.'

'I see,' she said slowly. 'Brute strength! That was the answer.'

Faro merely nodded and preparing to take his leave, he asked: 'How long have you been living here?'

'Oh, about a month – on and off. I come and go.'

'You're not from these parts, are you?'

'Neither are you,' she said sharply.

Again Faro was taken aback, but before he could reply she said: 'I'm Irish. I took you for a Scot at first, but your accent isn't quite right.'

Faro smiled. 'That's very perceptive of you. I'm from Orkney.'

She opened the door. 'I've never been there.'

On the doorstep he turned. 'Are you staying here long?'

'Depends,' she said suspiciously.

Faro was about to ask 'On what?' As if reading his thoughts, she added: 'Depends on when my money runs out.' Poking her head out, she looked at the sky and dismissed him with the words: 'The rain's stopped. You can go now.'

As he stepped outside, she said, 'Name's Imogen Crowe.'

'Pleased to meet you, Miss Crowe,' he said, feeling hypocritical.

'How do you know I'm "Miss"?' she demanded.

'That's easy.' He pointed to her hand. 'No ring.'

And as he walked away, she called, 'What's your name?'

'Faro. Jeremy Faro.'

'Is that Sergeant or just plain Constable Faro?'

'Just plain Mister will do nicely. I'm an insurance assessor,' he said acidly, in time to see a grin of mocking disbelief on her face as she banged the door behind him too quickly for politeness.

Going over that brief conversation, he didn't even give her credit for guessing he was a policeman, although that was extraordinary. He must take more care in future. There might be others about Elrigg as sharp as Miss Crowe, but he doubted that.

He didn't like her. He had no logical reason except hurt male pride and something about her that quite illogically nettled him. And almost angrily he shook his head, in an attempt to dismiss her completely from his thoughts.

At the inn a letter from Vince awaited him. 'Have managed to get an invitation to Miss Gilchrist's eightieth birthday celebration. Arriving with Owen and Olivia on Saturday. Plan to take an extra couple of days off, give Balfour a chance to become better acquainted with the patients! If you're not too busy with crime, I'd appreciate the opportunity of some decent tramping about, go to Hexham and walk the Roman Wall.'

Faro groaned. Vince never considered distances, while he became less agreeably aware that his feet, like his teeth, were not what they had been twenty-five years ago when the young lad from Orkney, Constable Jeremy Faro, had joined the Edinburgh City Police. To wear and tear of the damage done by years of ill-fitting boots, time had added sundry injuries acquired during many an altercation with villains.

Old stab and gun wounds to various parts of his body still plagued his extremely robust frame. Sore feet were more easily dealt with. He had found a temporary cure, and liked nothing better than pleasurably soaking them in a basin of warm soapy water which Mrs Brook sympathetically provided for him after supper. With a pipe of tobacco and a book propped before him, he was quite addicted to this secret vice. Such bliss – as he wriggled his toes, his joy was complete.

He preferred not to think of that other bane of his life. Toothache. That too was becoming more frequent, although he was consoled by the dental surgeon on his good fortune in having all his front teeth, top and bottom, and most of his back molars in fine condition (the result of good heredity and rare indulgence in sweet things).

Vince found his attitude extraordinary. That a brave man who fearlessly faced death and injuries inflicted by violent criminals would suffer any agony rather than the inevitable extraction of an aching tooth. As for Faro, he seldom considered the miraculous human machine that carried him through day after relentless day, except when it threw out an occasional warning that chasing criminals had a definitely ageing effect.

Pride, however, forbade any dwelling at length on his personal weaknesses of foot and mouth to his young stepson. After all, a man in his early forties wasn't all that old. There were politicians and a monarch ruling the country who were much older than himself, not to mention policemen still walking the beat. Men like Constable Dewar.

Over a pint of ale and a game pie in the almost deserted dining room of the inn, Faro returned to Sir Archie's fatal accident – or was it murder? Glancing over the notes of his interview with Lady Elrigg and Mark, he had reached certain conclusions which might be significant.

Dewar had been helpful in filling in some of the background details and Faro was now almost certain that no wounded bull had been involved and that horns, stolen earlier from the inn's public bar, were the murder weapon, inflicting the fatal wound to lead the doctor and the two local policemen away from the truth, that Sir Archie had met his death at the hands of some person or persons as yet unknown.

He decided that a talk to the village doctor was his next step but, perhaps of greater importance, a visit to the angry young nephew Hector whose excavations of the hillfort were within sight of the copse where his uncle had died.

In weather unreliable from hour to hour, vacillating from warm sunshine to driving rain, he set forth from the inn wrapped about temporarily in the splendour of an afternoon when the world held its breath.

Here was a day that had never heard of grey skies, of storms and cruel winds as it basked in the dazzling greens and innocent white blossom of a May morning. A lark blissfully hurled its triumphant song into a sky of celestial blue as he quickened his steps up the road.

To reach the hillfort he had to cross a strip of open pasture, domain of the wild cattle, and, leaving the road, he opened the gate cautiously, breathing freely again when he saw they were far up the hill. But even at that distance he felt naked and vulnerable, for they ceased grazing and fixed their eyes on him, all heads suddenly turned in his direction, as if they were well aware of his unease.

Hurrying towards the hillfort, he realised this was another wasted journey. There was no sign of Hector Elrigg, although his absence provided a chance to inspect the excavations more closely. He was not sure what he hoped to find, but it offered no helpful clues to the solution of the mystery.

Changing direction, he walked rapidly to the shelter of the trees across the deserted field, where he again examined the spot where Dewar had found Elrigg. Apart from a few broken branches the ground had healed and there was nothing to connect murder with that fatal misadventure.

Enjoying the warm sunshine on his back, he sat down on a large stone to enjoy a pipe. The crumbling wall beside him was part of a winter pen to give the sheep shelter. Looking round idly, he noticed what appeared to be the tip of a broken branch sticking out between the stones.

A sharp tug released it from its anchor. No branch emerged but the singly stiletto-sharp horn of a bull. He gazed at it triumphantly. He had not the slightest doubt that what he held as once part of the pair stolen from the inn.

The murder weapon.

He examined it more closely: the ominous dark stain on the tip could be dried blood. Deciding this evidence might be useful and not wishing to be seen with it in his possession, he tucked it up his jacket sleeve for a closer inspection later.

Emerging from the copse, his back was now turned towards the cattle but the trees concealed him from their gaze. He was not consoled for although there were no animals visible except for a few grazing sheep, his mind dwelt nervously on fences and open gates.

Not only the king bull was dangerous, he realised, but a young and skittish male, moving apart from the herd and for reasons of its own, of a possible homicidal disposition, could be equally damaging when on the rampage.

He walked quickly in the direction of the road and, conscious of the lack of any shelter, glanced back frequently over his shoulder. Alert at every sound, he found himself reliving that moment in his childhood near his aunt's Deeside croft more than thirty years ago.

How terrifyingly the ground had shaken under his feet at the thunderous charge, the snort of rage as the great red shaggy beast hurtled towards him through the mist.

He knew how narrowly he had escaped death that morning and, for years afterwards, he had awakened screaming with the smell of the enraged Highland bull's hot breath on his neck, its murderous sharp horns at his heels...

Shuddering from remembrance, he was within sight of the gate leading to the road when the chill gathering about his shoulders was not from fear but from a black sky replacing what had been cloudless sunshine minutes ago.

The next moment the cloud burst overhead and hailstones pelted down on him. He began to run...

Thunder rattled across the sky, shaking the hills and, almost within safety and the fenced road, he heard the ground echoing with the monstrous sound of hoofs...

IO

The beast pounding towards Faro along the road was no wild bull, merely a rather stout horse and trap bearing an elderly gentleman sheltering under a large umbrella.

'Whoa!' And stopping alongside, he leaned out. 'Care for a lift?'

'I would be most grateful.'

As Faro climbed in, the man who was clad in a handsome tweed greatcoat handed him a waterproof cape. 'Keep the worst of the rain off you, although I dare say it'll pass over in a minute.'

Even as he spoke, the sun came out again, scudding across the field, and the angry clouds were swept away, their rain sheets now lying heavily to the east.

'That's that,' said the man, closing the umbrella. 'I'm Dr Brand, by the way.'

An unexpected stroke of luck, Faro thought, as the doctor continued: 'Saw you crossing the field. Out walking, were you?' Acquainted with everyone in the village, he was obviously curious about this stranger and it was in Faro's own interest to enlighten him.

'Oh, I see. An insurance assessor. Of course,' the doctor nodded sympathetically, 'the family can take no chances.'

'I suppose you examined Sir Archie,' said Faro tentatively.

'I did indeed. Nothing I could do by that time. Clearly an accident. Gored by one of the cattle. Such things do happen. We do have the very occasional accident,' he added apologetically.

'I remember reading something about an earlier incident in the newspapers,' said Faro encouragingly. 'A young fellow staying at the castle, was it not?'

The doctor nodded. 'An actor. Philip Gray, you may have seen him on the stage in Edinburgh. I only heard his Shakespearean monologues one evening at the Castle. But I was most impressed.'

'You attended him when he was injured?'

'I examined his body, if that's what you mean,' said the doctor grimly. 'Death by misadventure. His horse had thrown him, he had a fractured skull. Of course, he had no right to be in the grazing pastures at all. Guests are always warned that the cattle are dangerous.'

'But he had ignored the warning?'

The doctor sighed. 'I understood that the, er, guest he was out riding with had dared him to venture out and bring back the horns from a beast the shooting party had wounded earlier that week.'

'Not a very sensible thing to do from all accounts,' Faro volunteered.

'As he soon found out,' said the doctor grimly. 'You know what these young fellows are like, must prove themselves. Sense of honour and all that nonsense. The beast wasn't too badly wounded to charge him and gore him to death.' He shook his head. 'It's this damned archaic system to blame. Sportsmen they call themselves. Rounding up the beasts and choosing their target. All of them having a go at it with their arrows first. Shouldn't be allowed. One man, one bullet – that's the humane way.'

He paused and sighed. 'The poor lad made it to the copse over there, same place they found Elrigg.'

'An odd coincidence?'

Dr Brand ignored his interruption. 'Elrigg might have survived: he had severe but not fatal neck and head injuries sustained in the fall and was probably unconscious.'

He paused like a man who had a lot more to say on that subject but had remembered in time that his passenger was a stranger. He shrugged. 'Perhaps he never regained consciousness when the cow got him. One can only hope so, anyway.'

'Cow? I thought only the bulls were dangerous.'

The doctor smiled. 'The cow is just as dangerous if she has just dropped a calf. This is the time of year and they often choose a sheltered place, away from the herd. Like the copse. There'd been a stalking party out from the castle the day before the accident, it was deer and birds they were interested in but that would make a cow very nervous.

'That's my theory, anyway. These animals have their own laws, far older and wiser than man's. I was brought up on a farm. We were used to taking in newborn orphaned animals and raising them by hand. Tried it once when I first came here. Found this newborn calf, abandoned or orphaned, I thought. It was getting dark, a freezing cold night, so I wrapped it in a blanket hoping to keep it alive till next day when I'd see if its mother had come back for it.'

He paused and sighed deeply. 'I was young and idealistic then, couldn't bear the thought of an animal suffering. I soon learned my lesson,' he added harshly.

'Did she charge you too?'

'No. But when I went back the next day to see how the wee creature was,' he shuddered, 'there was nothing left of it but a few bones and bits of skin. But the hoofmarks were visible where it had lain. Looked as if there had been a stampede and it had been trampled into the earth. Their sense of smell is acute and if a calf is handled by a human the other animals detect the smell and kill it.'

'But surely –'

'I know what you're going to say, but you're quite wrong. I had made the crucial mistake of humans interfering with wild creatures. I had mismanaged my rescue attempt and turned the calf into an alien from the herd. They had their own ways of dealing with that,' he added grimly.

'Make no mistake about these animals. They are quite unique, they have a society evolved though hundreds – perhaps thousands of years. The herd is under complete control of one beast. Only the fittest and the strongest in the herd ever becomes king bull. And during the two or three years until he is successfully challenged and defeated in combat by a younger rival, he reigns supreme and sires all the calves that are born.'

As he talked, he let the reins go slack and the horse, finding this an agreeable change of pace, ambled slowly along.

'I've been fascinated by their behaviour for years. I've watched them, through a telescope – from my house over there,' he added pointing to the east of the village. 'Once I saw a young bull come out of the herd, it was the bellowing that drew me. I saw him pawing the ground, the old bull doing likewise. They charged – and this time it was a fight to the death.'

'You say they've been here for thousands of years – where did they come from?'

'No one can answer that. Bones which might belong to them have been found in the hillfort, so they provided meat for prehistoric man. At one time they were thought to be related to the Highland cattle, a sort of albino relative. But that has been disproved.'

'How have they managed to survive without inbreeding with other domestic cattle?'

'Because they've never been domestic. It's possible that being white they were regarded as sacred – kept for some ancient religious ritual. They've never been known to throw a coloured or even partly coloured calf. As for their survival, who knows? It is against all the odds since the cows are poor breeders, suckle their calves for long periods. Nature's way of preventing the herd increasing rapidly.'

'I'm surprised that they survived the moss troopers and the Border reivers. I understood they carried off everything they could lay their hands on.'

Dr Brand laughed. 'Aye, what they laid hands on, right enough. But there was no hope of laying hands on these beasts and driving them back across the border. Much too wild and fierce to be treated like the ordinary domestic variety.'

Turning, he looked back towards the hill. 'I'd advise you to take great care about walking across these fields. I was quite alarmed when I saw you. Someone should have warned you. Where are you staying?' When Faro told him, he nodded. 'I shall have a severe word with him, have a notice posted in very large letters.'

Pausing, he regarded Faro sharply. 'I don't think you are taking me seriously, sir.'

'I am, doctor, I am indeed.'

'Make no mistake about it. These animals are extremely dangerous. And they have perception beyond what we humans understand.' Shading his eyes, the doctor pointed with his whip. 'I don't suppose you've been here long enough to observe that they never take their eyes off any humans in the vicinity. We are under constant surveillance. There is always one animal watching, on guard, somewhere,' he added with an uneasy laugh.

'So you think there might have been a calf in the vicinity that Sir Archie didn't know about?'

'It certainly wasn't a wounded king bull, anyway. Saw him large as life grazing with the herd the next day. Besides the horns – the goring injury, I mean – they hadn't penetrated deep enough for a really angry charging bull. Makes a nasty mess, I can tell you. But this was just one hole, quite neat, just an inch or two deep.'

'Is that so?' said Faro thoughtfully. According to Constable Dewar there had been no hoofmarks of a charging animal either. 'You had no doubts about the cause of the death when you signed the death certificate?'

'None at all. The coroner's inquest was a mere waste of time. Death by misadventure, there couldn't be any other verdict in the circumstances. I'll let you have his report if you need it for your firm. And if you're interested in the cattle, there's some old documents in the Castle library, I'm sure Lady Elrigg would let you see them.'

The road narrowed steeply and they were passing by the tiny Saxon church with its graveyard, deep in primroses and wood anemones. A blackbird sang on one of the tombstones, the feathers on its throat fluttering, its piercing sweetness a eulogy to an awakening world.

Faro sighed. 'Gives you hope, doesn't it? I wouldn't mind lying here to all eternity with a requiem like that every spring.'

At his side the doctor had raised his top hat to reveal a mane of silver hair and lapsed into a reverent silence. 'Spring's a sad time for some people, for the ones who are left.'

'I understand, sir, only too well.' Noting the doctor's grief-stricken expression, Faro remembered that his Lizzie had died with their newborn son beside her on a June morning eight years ago. 'To lose one's partner in life...' He paused. 'Your wife, sir?' he said gently.

'Lost her long ago,' was the bitter response. 'God only knows what sky her bones lie under. It was my daughter I lost. My dearest only child.' His voice broke and, geeing up the pony, he drove fast into the village, his lips a tight line of misery, while at his side Faro cursed his own lack of tact.

Setting him down at the inn, Dr Brand spoke again. 'You must forgive my outburst, sir, to you a stranger, quite unforgivable.'

'It is I who must apologise, sir. But I do know something of the loss you have suffered. A child dying –'

'Dying. She didn't die. She could have been alive today, she was seventeen with all the world before her. She didn't die. She was murdered.'

At Faro's shocked expression, he jabbed a finger in the direction of the Castle. 'And they killed her.'

II

As Faro entered the inn, Bowden ceased the polishing of the counter long enough to say: 'Duffy has been looking for you, Mr Faro.'

'Are you sure it was me?'

'You're the insurance mannie, aren't you?'

'Did he say what he wanted?'

'Not my business to ask, sir. But knowing Duffy I'd say there was money involved. Wouldn't you, gentlemen?'

Bowden grinned at Yarrow and Dewar. About to depart, they paused long enough to give Faro a decidedly searching glance. It suggested that they also suspected he might be involved in some of the poacher's dubious activities.

'He said he'll see you when he comes in for his pint of ale later on,' said Bowden as Faro made his way towards his room.

What could the poacher want with him? Faro was curious and hopeful too. From his vast experience of the criminal world, he did not doubt that this new turn of events indicated information was for sale.

Beyond his window was a pageant of undulating hills, cloudless skies. Trees moved in slow ecstasy to their burden of soft breeze and birdsong, a scene characteristic of any gentle sleepy village that one could hardly credit with violence. Even the ivy-clad walls of its ancient cottages seemed to have grown naturally out of the tranquil earth rather than the stones hewed by men.

A traveller passing though *en route* for Scotland would think nothing ever happened here, that time had passed it by, but Faro was aware of the elements of passion that lurked behind such quiet exteriors and that this was a more elemental world than the one he had left a short time ago in Edinburgh. With total recall he saw again the words written by Mary Elizabeth Braddon:

> We hear every day of murders committed in the country... No species of crime has ever been

committed in the worst rookeries of the Seven Dials that has not been also done in the face of that rustic calm...

Words that Imogen Crowe had heavily underscored. She had written 'Elrigg?' beside them. Why?

Do not be fooled, Jeremy Faro, he told himself as he considered his evidence so far.

Philip Gray had been riding with the Prince. They had quarrelled when the Prince accused him of cheating at cards. Bertie had returned alone. Later, when the actor's horse came in riderless, a search party found him gored to death.

Sir Archie had met his death in suspiciously similar circumstances. Two men dying in identical place and manner, months apart, after quarrels with the same illustrious guest, hinted not merely at coincidence, but at murder.

If only the trail was still warm. Any clues regarding Gray's death by misadventure had vanished beneath last year's fallen autumn leaves and for the last four weeks Sir Archie had rested in his grave.

The Prince had been the last to see both men alive and Faro remembered grimly the letter Her Majesty had shown him.

He wished he had been allowed to make a copy of it for a more careful study of the schoolboy pleading: 'Don't blame me. It wasn't my fault, Mama.'

Her son's innocence was all he had to prove. Murder in this case was not his business.

If only he could leave it at that...

From the valise under his bed, Faro withdrew the bull's horn. Weighing it in his hands, he knew how Sir Archie had been murdered. Almost as if he had been present, a silent witness, he could conjure up the exact picture of Elrigg's last moments.

The horn had been broken off from the pair stolen from the public bar downstairs.

Archery was the local sport and it would not have needed an expert marksman to realise that although it could not be fired with any accuracy from a crossbow, it presented a splendid potential as a murder weapon. By a piece of good fortune his opportunity came when he found his victim semi-conscious and unable to rise from the ground.

Faro frowned. That posed a question. It had to be someone who was in the area at the time and witnessed the accident. It might have been that Sir Archie was still alive when the first of the rescue party arrived, perhaps one of the tenants alerted by Constable Dewar on his way through the village. For a man with a grievance, a unique opportunity of settling an old score.

Once the deed was done, the murderer withdrew the horn and thrust it into the wall, where with luck he hoped it would never be noticed.

With circumstances of Philip Gray's death still fresh in everyone's mind, the possibility of foul play had never occurred. Neither Yarrow nor Dewar had thought to search the copse for evidence, indeed the constable's observation regarding the lack of hoofmarks had been mockingly dismissed.

Faro regarded the bull's horn thoughtfully. The question now was who had reached Sir Archie ahead of Yarrow and Dr Brand.

The only person he could safely eliminate was Lady Elrigg who had remained at the Castle. In a state of shock as befitted the newly widowed.

He knew nothing of any relationship with the young actor but he recalled vividly his first sight of Lady Elrigg and Mark leaving the archery field together. Had there been a sinister quality to their careless laughter?

Although Elrigg would be Mark's some day, did he see himself as a young knight ready to dare all – even murder – for the stepmother who could never be his wife?

Guilty lovers invariably provided the best motive for murder. From Biblical times to the present day that had been the case and Faro did not doubt it would continue until the final curtain descended on mankind. The male rivalry between the old and young was not unique. Just a mile away, that instinct for survival of the species was strong enough to drive young bulls to challenge the king for supremacy of the wild cattle herd.

The question was, did Lady Elrigg respond to Mark? If so, then she had the perfect reason for wishing to be rid of an elderly husband whose charm was limited to his bank account, especially when there was a fortune and a handsome, young and virile man to inherit it. If Poppy Lynne had married Elrigg only for his fortune and with his stepson conspired in his murder, then Faro would feel no sympathy for either of them.

Was she morally responsible for Gray's death too, enticing men to kill for her love? The more facts Faro unearthed, the less he liked the unpleasant picture that his imagination created. One did not have to dig too deeply below the surface to discover that Elrigg was a man who made many enemies. Known as well as unknown – as yet!

Of the known enemies, Hector Elrigg had the best reason of all. Over the years, a festering rage and resentment that he was morally the rightful heir. He also had the best vantage point for murder: witnessing the accident from the hillfort, seeing the Prince ride off and finding his hated uncle helpless, had he seized the chance for revenge?

With the bull's horn?

Faro shook his head. No, it wouldn't do. Hector might have stolen the horns, but it was unlikely he could have secreted them away for such a possibility. If they had been taken from the inn with such a plot in mind, then Sir Archie would have been lured to his death.

And it seemed highly unlikely that the future King of England could have dreamed up anything as subtle as the method used of diverting attention from his equerry's murder. Unless he had been the willing accomplice of Lady Elrigg. Would such a theory fit the Prince's panic-stricken retreat from the copse and his speedy departure from the Castle?

Faro doubted that. Bertie's constant fear of blackmail and his ready supply of mistresses made Poppy Elrigg in no way special or permanent. Merely one more dalliance, that was all.

Dismissing the Prince's role in his equerry's murder, Faro realised that anyone besides the poacher Duffy might have stolen the horns, hidden them away in the copse where they had been accidentally found by someone from the village with murder in mind – that local tenant with reason to hate the laird?

Someone like Dr Brand who blamed his daughter's death on the Elriggs. (What had happened? Constable Dewar would no doubt reveal the circumstances if asked.)

Recalling the earlier part of his conversation with the doctor, all Faro now knew for certain was that Elrigg had been unconscious but not fatally injured when the Prince – and his horse – bolted.

And that brought him sharply back to the reason for his presence at Elrigg. His main purpose was to obey the Royal Command and report back to Her Majesty that the Prince of Wales was innocent of cowardice. This he could do with confidence, for if the hidden bull's horn was the weapon used to end Sir Archie's life, then it was unlikely indeed that the Prince had been the murderer.

But instead of being satisfied that he had completed his mission and returning to Edinburgh, he realised he was following the habit of a lifetime of police investigation and allowing himself to be drawn into a mystery that it was not even his right to solve. If the entire population of Elrigg decided to kill each other off, or their laird, this was the business of the Northumberland Constabulary to assist Sergeant Yarrow and Constable Dewar by the appointment of a detective experienced in murder investigations.

The evidence of his own eyes was, apart from finding the probable murder weapon, only circumstantial. But he wished he could have known the exact location of the possible suspects at the time of Sir Archie's death.

Replacing the horn reluctantly, as if by holding it in his hands he might extract by supernatural means the identity of the murderer, he made a mental note to be firm with himself and concentrate on the history of Elrigg while he awaited Vince's arrival, meanwhile ignoring any grisly secrets of the past that were none of his business.

He would begin by having another look at the hillfort.

12

Hector Elrigg's greeting was cordial. In more leisurely circumstances than their first encounter in the police station, Faro saw that generations of Elrigg warriors had created the young man's strong physique and vital personality. A fighting man in the tradition of Harry Hotspur. Leaning on his spade, Hector said: 'Good day to you, sir. Interested in our old hillfort, are you?'

Faro murmured that he was and Hector nodded eagerly. Tapping the ground with his foot, he said: 'You're standing on the oldest part of Elrigg, it's been here since the dawn of history, when this entire area was covered with a vast forest and the inhabitants had just left their nomadic ways and decided to make places of settlement where they could trade, chat, make marriage contracts, worship – become a community.'

'Does your hillfort predate the wild cattle?'

Hector shook his head. 'Who can tell? Certainly the ancestors of our cattle would have provided meat for their spears. Come, walk round with me.'

As Faro followed him across the grassy mound, which was the size of a small field, only piles of stones and a few broken walls marked the spot that Hector told him lay within a circle of byroads.

'Once it rose to about five hundred feet, crowned with a camp for whoever made himself chief. Even in those days, there were men who had more physical strength, cunning and insight to come out on top as leaders.'

As they climbed up the slope, Hector said, 'Look back. This is a good time to be here, when the sun is sinking. See how it lights up the contours. Those parallel lines you see under the turf are cultivation terraces.'

And walking quickly ahead, he jumped on a large boulder and pointed back the way they had come.

'Those humps in the ground are the remains of hut circles, folds for cattle, and burial cairns.'

'Have you found anything interesting?'

'A few urn burials, amber necklaces, silver rings, and so forth.' He smiled. 'A liking for luxury and personal vanity is not news; the powerful and rich had jewellery and other ornaments, superior pottery and weapons. Power takes many forms but the display of one's riches was necessary and popular then, as a fine house, a carriage and horses are today. The secret of power for early man was their ability to use the landscape not only to survive but to produce a surplus that they could use to bargain and trade with, to buy slaves and most important to buy allegiance from chiefs to serve them.

'Of course, like everyone then and now, they mislaid and lost things, broke them or threw them away. Except that, as they didn't have much to lose, they left us enough to give us some idea of their lives. Their technology depended largely on flint – flint that could be smashed up, flaked and worked into tools of every variety – blades, scrapers and arrowheads. With the discovery of flint animals could be killed, eaten and their hides used for clothes, tents, waterbags.'

Hector paused and pointed to the skyline. 'You get the best view from the top of the hill yonder, worth the climb. The headless women. If you aren't afraid to go there.'

'The cattle, you mean.'

'No. Even the cattle are scared of them. It's the noise they make that scares them off. The presence of the old gods.'

Faro smiled.

'An unbeliever, eh? Well, take it from me, whatever you want to call that primeval force, it's worthy of respect. And fear. It can be very unnerving if you're up there in a rising wind. First it sounds as if the stones are sighing, then crying – that's when you want to run...'

'Has anyone tried to find the cause?'

'Oh, I know the cause,' said Hector cheerfully. 'Natural erosion has resulted in fluting and gulleys on the stones. The wind rushes through them rather like organ pipes. That's the scientific explanation, but try to persuade generations of the ignorant and superstitious that they are not the cries of Celtic princesses turned to stone. And when they scream then disaster will strike Elrigg.'

'Have you ever excavated the site?'

Hector's face darkened. 'I've tried to. I'm certain there is evidence to link the date of the stones with the hillfort, perhaps they were part of a religious ceremonial or the burial site of some important tribal chief. But I've been denied that right.'

He paused and regarded Faro suspiciously for the first time. 'Wait a moment. I have seen you before. At the police station.'

'That is so.'

When Faro did not offer any further explanation, Hector continued: 'Are you here to register for the archery contest?'

'Alas, no.'

'A pity. You have the look of a man who might be handy with weapons,' he said, surveying him candidly.

But Faro refused to be drawn.

Hector continued to regard him curiously. 'You seem remarkably well informed, sir. What exactly brings you to these parts?'

'Insurance business, alas.' Faro tried to sound casual. 'All rather boring, I'm afraid.'

'Connected with my late uncle, I presume.'

'Yes.'

'He was a bastard and he deserved to die. A few acres of his precious ground, a chance to discover the secret of the stones. That's all I've ever wanted, all I ever asked him for. He owed me a lot more than that – a damned lot more.'

He stopped, shrugged. 'I won't bore you with the details. It's a very long and sordid story. All I can tell you is that they're a rum lot up at the Castle.'

'In what way?'

Hector stared at the horizon. 'Oh, you know. The young and beautiful actress who marries an old man for his money. Brings one of her London actress friends with her as companion. Can't blame her insisting on that as part of the deal. Life would be pretty intolerable for her otherwise. But her friend, Miss Kent, I don't know how she sticks it. A far cry from the stage. Poppy must have made it worth her while – Miss Kent was never a great beauty with all the world and the Prince of Wales at her feet.'

He looked at Faro as he said it. So he knew the identity of the visitor at the time of Sir Archie's fatal accident. And as Faro listened and watched Hector's expression change to one of wistfulness, he realised that the nephew might also have a motive of jealousy, mesmerised by Poppy Elrigg too, although he might qualify only for one of 'all the world'.

'It would have made more sense for Mark to fall for the companion, wouldn't it?' Hector went on. 'But no, it's the stepma he wants. Miss Kent would have been much safer.'

'How safer?'

Hector laughed and, ignoring the question, he said: 'I've nothing against young Mark. Like the boy, I must say. We've always got along splendidly. I even gave him his first archery lessons. He saw me as a kind of latterday Robin Hood. Used to come and watch me dig when he came home from boarding school. He was intrigued by the possibilities of old graves and skeletons, the usual schoolboy preoccupation with buried treasure and that nonsense. I gave him a spade and a bit of encouragement.'

He smiled at the remembrance before adding: 'He didn't like his stepfather even then and their relationship didn't improve with time. Poppy's arrival was probably the last straw –'

And Faro wondered how much Mark's young life had been influenced by Hector's grudge against Sir Archie. He could well imagine the impressionable schoolboy with a case of hero worship for this romantic relative who searched ancient ruins for buried treasure.

Hector was eyeing him candidly. 'Insurance investigator, you say?' Without waiting for Faro's reply, he continued, 'If you'd been a policeman, I'd have said there are one or two who'll be mightily pleased that Uncle Archie got his just deserts. He killed a beater once. Drunk he was, should not have been in charge of a loaded shotgun. An accident, everyone covered up like mad. Young lad about twelve.'

'From these parts?'

'No. From Durham somewhere. He was staying with relations, farmers over Flodden way. Can't remember the details, illness in the family, something of the sort. An only child. Went to school here for a while and got on well with young Mark, the two of them used to come to the dig. His aunt and uncle were so upset by the tragedy they couldn't settle afterwards and moved away. Felt guilty, although it was none of their fault, poor souls.

'And then there's Dr Brand, his daughter drowned herself, suicide. Plenty would say she was driven to it.'

Faro recalled the doctor's words as Hector went on.

'She was a bright, clever girl, working for the summer on cataloguing family documents for my uncle. She left in a hurry. Rumour had it that she was pregnant – and the whispers were that it was Uncle Archie's bairn. Later it came out that the factor had been dallying with her. He'd been sacked for embezzlement, bolted for London before he could be arrested, leaving her in the lurch.'

He sighed. 'She walked into the ornamental lake by the walled garden. My uncle showed some finer feelings – or some remorse, by having the lake drained.'

'So all this will go to Mark now?'

Hector did not seem perturbed. 'That is so, since there is no issue, legitimate or otherwise. Mark's mother was ten years older than my uncle, plain but very wealthy. Nice woman, kind too. Coal owner's widow. There were no children. He was out of luck with Poppy too. Five years and no sign of an heir.'

A childless marriage, a barren wife. How often Faro had heard that. The bane of rich men and noble lairds with much to leave and desperate for a son to leave it to. Kings had murdered their queens and lords abandoned their ladies for just such a reason. In the new society even rich merchants keen to establish a dynasty had been known to be crafty and merciless in ridding themselves of a barren wife.

It remained one of the best of all possible motives for murder. If Poppy had been the victim instead of her husband.

Hector squinted up at the sky. 'We'll have rain soon. Must get on with things, unless you'd like a shot with a spade too.' And nodding towards a cottage half hidden by tress, 'I live over there. If you change your mind and feel like some healthy exercise any time.'

'I'll bear it in mind.' Faro pointed to the standing stones outlined against the sky. 'Meanwhile I think I'll brave the headless women.'

Hector grinned. 'Walk round the field unless you want an encounter with the farmer – an earful of his bellowing could be more scaring that our stone ladies' vocal qualities.'

Faro smiled. 'Constable Dewar warned me.'

Hector regarded him coolly. 'You don't look to me like a man who scares easily. What was it you said you were – an insurance assessor?'

And his accompanying laugh, with its note of disbelief, reminded Faro how thin his disguise was.

As he climbed the steep hill, the sun beat down straight into his eyes. The stones seemed to shiver in the glowing transparent light. Occasionally he stopped and shaded his eyes. Once or twice he could have sworn he saw a dark shadow move swiftly across his line of vision.

At last, following the rough path, he reached the perimeter of the circle. His mind far away, he almost leaped from his skin when a woman's face stared down at him.

Not stone, but flesh and blood with dark red hair and green eyes. A face as cold as the stones, whose response to his friendly greeting was to gather up her papers, tuck them swiftly into her valise and jump down the other side of the circle.

'Wait,' he called, 'I didn't mean to intrude. Don't let me disturb you.'

Whether she heard him or not, he couldn't tell, his efforts rewarded by her fleeing back, her hair flowing out like a burning bush behind her as she leaped through the stony field.

Obviously she feared an irate farmer less than himself, Faro thought. And watching her swift progress, half amused, half exasperated, he realised he had almost forgotten Imogen Crowe's existence.

About to retrace his steps, he noticed a slim book lying face downward where she had been sitting.

Glancing at the title, *The History of Civilisation*, he thrust it into his pocket, only mildly curious about this dramatic change in reading matter or what interesting mission his arrival had interrupted to cause her precipitate flight. He would hand in the book to the lodge sometime. A nuisance, and her own fault if she lost it. He turned his attention to the stones when he heard a cry.

A human cry…

13

The cry had issued not from the headless women behind him, but from the stony field.

Faro stared down from the perimeter of the circle. Imogen Crowe was lying on the ground about thirty yards away. She looked up, saw him and called: 'Help me, will you, please.'

What an irresistible invitation, he thought grimly and made his way carefully down the rough ground of the field.

'Are you hurt?' he asked, bending over her.

She struggled to sit up. 'Of course I'm hurt. I wouldn't call for help otherwise. My ankle, I think I've broken my bloody ankle. No, don't you touch it. Don't dare –'

And thrusting his hand away she seized her ankle between her hands and began to rub it vigorously, moaning a little as she did so. 'I twisted it on that bracken root. I just shot forward – and here I am.'

Faro stared down at her. 'You should have come up by the path at the edge of the field.'

'I did that.'

'Then why on earth didn't you go back the same way? Racing down the field like that...'

She shrugged and chose not to answer what was perfectly obvious and equally embarrassing: her eagerness to escape from him.

With a sigh, Faro looked down at her, held out his hands, still waiting to be thanked for his assistance: 'Can you stand?' he asked gently.

She stood up, wavered and with a cry would have fallen again but for Faro. She looked indignantly at his steadying hand on her arm as if she'd like to brush it off, given half a chance and a more reliable balance.

If only her damned ankle wasn't so sore. Now she had to rely on this wretched man. Nodding towards the still-distant road, she said, 'Help me down there, will you.'

'Of course.' And bending over, he picked her up bodily.

'What do you think you're doing?' she demanded angrily.

'Isn't that rather obvious, seeing that you are incapable of walking?'

'Put me down – at once.'

'As you wish,' Faro said coldly, setting her down so unceremoniously that she moaned, clutching her ankle as she tried to regain her balance.

'I – I can't.'

'Then will you allow me to assist you?' She put her arms around his neck and struggled no more as he carried her once more towards the stone circle.

'This isn't the way to the road.'

'I'm quite aware of that. But this is the way we are both going. The way we both came up. Unless you want us both to have twisted ankles – or worse. A broken neck might be the answer...'

She struggled in his arms. 'This is nonsense. Put me down. I'll manage.'

Faro stopped, and again set her on her feet. 'Listen to me. Either you do as I say or I will leave you to make your own damned way back to Elrigg. I don't care either way.'

She was silent, staring at the ground.

'Agreed?'

She nodded and, with a sigh, he said: 'Off we go then.'

Lifting her more carefully this time, he clambered up the last few yards very carefully. The terrain was strewn with smaller stones, boulders from the circle that had been eroded through the ages, washed by wind and weather down the field and were now barely but dangerously concealed by thick coarse grass.

'You shouldn't have taken it at a run. You could have hurt more than your ankle. Foolish creature.'

This expression was mild compared to what he wanted to say – and do – at that moment. She was behaving like a spoilt child and deserved more than a gentle reprimand. He pursed his lips grimly.

However, she was lighter than he had expected, small boned although she was quite tall. Bodily contact was not unpleasant, she was warm, sweet smelling, her hair resting against his cheek...

Damned woman. Damned woman, he muttered to himself and set her down rather more sharply than was kind on one of the flat stones within the circle. There, without a word of thanks, she began to moan and rub her injured ankle.

He pushed her hands aside. 'Let me look at it.'

Angrily, she thrust him away. 'No. Leave me alone. There's nothing you can do. Unless you're a doctor.' And wriggling her foot, she winced. 'It's probably just sprained a little. If I could rest for a few minutes.'

'Very well,' he said wearily. 'Let me know when you're ready to go down.'

She looked towards the road, distant beyond the stony field. 'How can I walk that far?'

He looked at her. 'I'll see if I can find a stick somewhere. You can use that. If not, I'll carry you. You're not very heavy.'

She darted him an angry glance. As if the whole episode was his fault.

Never had he met such a thankless, ungracious young woman and he walked quickly away before she could think of any ill-natured comment.

Leaving her with little hope of finding a branch for support, he was glad to escape from her and to concentrate on his reason for coming here in the first place. The view was breathtaking. The site commanded a magnificent landscape over the Cheviots, reaching out to touch the border with Scotland.

As for the five headless women, they were less forbidding at close quarters than seen from below. On closer examination the torso shapes were the result of natural erosion, confirming Hector Elrigg's theory that the fluting effect might well produce alarming sounds when the wind was in the right direction.

He made his way carefully through the nettles, which were their natural protective vegetation and whose roots had long ago hidden any significant details of what had been the purpose of their original builders.

Lost in thought, he was suddenly aware of Miss Crowe looking over his shoulder.

'You've been such a long time, I thought you'd gone without me,' she said anxiously, sounding so contrite and scared that, smiling kindly, he was able to bite back the words: As you richly deserved.

In no hurry to leave, he continued to look at the view, fascinated by the mystery of this strange prehistoric site.

As if reading his thoughts she said, 'Why were they put here?' – her voice a whisper as if they might be overheard, their presence resented by the ghosts of this ancient place. 'Do you have any idea? I mean, how they were carried up this steep hill?'

'They are questions to which we will never have proper answers, I'm afraid. No more than how the Pyramids of Egypt were built.'

Pointing towards a horizon where Scotland began: 'Defence? Was that what they had in mind?' she asked.

'Probably. A lookout post for the hillfort below.'

'It must have been more than that, surely. A lookout post wouldn't have lasted for thousands of years.' Caressing the outline of the nearest stone, she smiled. 'Could they have been Celtic princesses perhaps?'

Faro smiled. 'If you mean, is that winsome legend true, I can assure you of one thing. These stones had been well established for centuries, a landmark long before the Romans came.'

'Or before history was written.' She moved away from the stone, hobbling a little. 'I think I will be able to manage now – if I may take your arm.'

'Of course.' He helped her from the perimeter of the stones to the edge of the field. 'What brought you here?'

'Oh, I don't know. Natural curiosity. It's an intriguing story, one wants to believe that it's true. At least I'd like to. And I wanted to know why the village people were so afraid, why they avoid it.'

Leaning against the fence for support, she pointed towards the Eildon hills. 'Have you read Sir Walter Scott, by any chance?'

'Of course,' Faro replied. 'He is one of my heroes.'

She shook her head. 'A splendid writer, I give you that. Of romances. But he got it all wrong, didn't he?'

Faro looked at her, amazed at her perception. He had read all Scott's books eagerly, avidly, and realised the minute he set foot in Elrigg how far his hero was from the core of the truth.

'This is hardly the land of romance, of Gothic mystery as he portrayed it, don't you agree? You just have to be here a few hours to set that right.'

He found himself remembering that her choice of reading lay in the Sensation novels category, when he answered: 'You think the fairy tale of brave gallant Scot and sturdy Celt was a myth?'

'I most certainly do. As were his brave knights and beautiful maidens with high moral principles and dreams of chivalry. Men and women aren't like that. They're flesh and blood – weak creatures.'

'Not all flesh is weak,' he said stoutly.

'Don't tell me you believe all the ballads handed down from one generation to the next and from the heart of this nation's poetic soul. Can you be that innocent – or idealistic?'

She laughed and, before he could reply, she added solemnly: 'Scott was a Borderer himself, he must have known the truth, the terror and cruelty that he winced away from writing about. But he opted for the false name of romance to turn a blind eye on reality, on what really happened, and instead was content to present history as a kind of Arthurian legend.'

He knew it was true. Nothing was further from the reivers' thoughts than dying for their God and Queen or King.

'The patriotism Scott believed in never existed,' she said as if she read his thoughts. 'All they knew was the law of the jungle, of every man for himself and the devil take the hindmost. If patriotism of any kind existed, it was well down on their list of priorities.'

She pulled out a piece of grass from the fence and began to shred it. 'Patriotism that men die for – that's a different game, far removed from your fairy tales. Some of us know that only too well.'

He looked at her. The Irish accent she tried to suppress was stronger now, released by her passions.

'You are an authoress, are you not?'

She turned quickly to face him. 'How –'

'Ink stains on your fingernails, a valise full of papers –'

She held up her hand. 'I should have known – you being a policeman. Just my luck,' she murmured, turning away from him again.

'What brings you here?' he asked.

'What do you think? I'm writing a book, of course. One of your dreaded romances,' she said so mockingly he knew it to be a lie.

Staring at the horizon as though seeing a secret pageant of

weeping ghosts, her eyes widened. Suddenly she shivered. 'I've had enough of this place. Can we go down now?'

It was a slow, silent journey; step by tortuous step, she leaned heavily on his arm.

When at last they set foot on the road, she looked pale and exhausted. Faro looked at her anxiously. How was she to manage the long walk to the lodge? The alternative was to carry her.

'Listen,' she said. 'Someone's coming.'

A pony trap bustled round the bend in the road.

Dr Brand stopped, raised his hat, looked from one to the other, smiling.

Miss Crowe limped towards him.

'An accident? Dear, dear.'

As she explained, he was already helping her into the cart with Faro's assistance.

'You too, Mr Faro. You're lucky I was along the road. Called out to a difficult birth. Yes, yes, both well and doing fine now. I'll see Miss Crowe safely home, bind up that ankle. I'll set you down at the inn, sir.'

But Faro had spent enough time in Miss Crowe's uncomfortable company. She was impossible. He hadn't changed his original opinion of her and was left quite unmoved by the common bond they shared in his hero, Sir Walter Scott.

As they drove off he was seized by a fit of sneezing. Putting his hand in his greatcoat pocket for a handkerchief, he encountered Miss Crowe's book.

Waving it, he called after them, but they were too distant to heed him.

'Damn and blast,' he said, returning it to his pocket. He sneezed again.

14

Faro decided to visit the kirkyard. Vince might laugh at what he called his stepfather's morbid addiction but Faro found that such dalliance in the past had often saved him a considerable amount of walking. Many pieces of information could be gleaned and questions answered where there was no written evidence regarding past inhabitants.

As he walked his attention was drawn to a babble of shrill childish voices. It issued from the playground of the local school and indicated an earnest game of hopscotch.

The sound of a whistle blown by an elderly lady, grey-haired and pince-nezed, imposed immediate silence as the children swiftly formed a crocodile at the school door. Faro applauded the dominie's speedy control over forty or more pupils and he guessed that she had taught and disciplined, stern but kindly, at least two generations of Elrigg children.

Here was a contact worth following, he thought, as he continued on his way to the kirkyard where the lichened tombstones leaned at dangerous angles as if occupants rested uneasily in their graves. Surrounded by ancient cottages, it confirmed his awareness of being under observation. By now, his presence was known to the entire population, his identity a matter of tireless speculation. As, no doubt, was his appearance today with Miss Crowe, and equally distasteful as it might be to both, already interpreted as a budding romance.

At least he would prove them wrong, for, in the matter of Imogen Crowe, nothing was further from his thoughts as he concentrated on the task in hand.

Entering the church by the Norman door, he found himself facing a twelfth-century rounded chancel arch leading to the altar with its handsome rose window.

He knew enough about old churches to hazard a guess that Elrigg St Mary's with its square tower and narrow slit windows in the belfry tower had been built with defence as well as worship in mind, an additional place of security for the priest and worshippers to take refuge from raiders.

Never a religious man, Faro limited his appearances in the kirk of St Giles in Edinburgh to christenings, marriages and funerals but standing before the tiny altar surrounded by these ancient stones brought a feeling of peace and tranquillity, a sense of benediction.

If he had been a praying man, he would have seized the opportunity to beg for an audience, but he felt uncomfortable calling upon God's assistance when he was not a communicant of the Christian church. He looked up at the figure of Christ on the crucifix above the altar and, for one fanciful moment, it seemed that the Son of God's wry expression saw right through him and understood his problems very well indeed.

With a sigh, he wandered over to the stone effigies of the Elriggs who had dominated this piece of Northumberland for more than five hundred years. Elaborately carved and marbled, with a profusion of weeping angels, their tombs told him nothing and he wished, not for the first time, that he had with him his Sergeant, Danny McQuinn of the Edinburgh City Police.

He had never thought the Queen's mission would be simple, but the answers were turning out to be far more difficult than he had imagined. Living at the inn and carrying out inquiries at the Castle without proper authority to do so was fraught with frustrations. He felt that, as always when dealing with the aristocracy, the best clues were to be found in the servants' hall. But he could think of no good excuse for an insurance investigator to be closely questioning them regarding their mistress's behaviour.

This was the area in which McQuinn excelled. The boy who had left Ireland in the disastrous years after the potato famine had grown up to be a man of the people. There was no class barrier for Danny McQuinn. He could be relied upon to ferret out confidences that would never be given, tongue-tied and scared, in the awesome presence of a senior detective inspector. Servants felt at ease with McQuinn with his homely Irish wit, his charm with the humblest of maids, each one of whom he treated like a well-born lady. Such methods would be sure to find a way to get – and to keep – them talking.

Closing the church door behind him, Faro made his way slowly through the tombstones, reading the inscriptions.

'Good day to you, sir!'

The vicar, a tall figure in flowing black robes and white bands, hurried towards him.

'Perhaps I can help you, sir. Are you searching for someone in particular?'

As Faro murmured that he was just interested in old stones, Reverend Cairncross's natural curiosity about this stranger in their midst showed a disarmingly human side to the man of God whose ascetic face and lean frame were that of a medieval monk. His appearance suggested that he had been only recently removed from penning illuminated manuscripts in Melrose Abbey.

'You are, I believe, Mr – Faro – the insurance assessor?'

Thus confronted, Faro did not feel up to the direct lie. Yes, indeed, he was here in connection with Sir Archie's death.

That was strictly true.

Reverend Cairncross murmured sympathetically but the word 'death' had injected a sudden chill into his manner. The sudden tightening of his lips and his brooding gaze in the direction of the Castle hinted louder than any words that the Elriggs were not the most popular of his parishioners.

The uncomfortable silence between the two men was broken as a plump middle-aged woman appeared round the side of the church carrying a large basket.

She was introduced as Mrs Cairncross and Faro smiled. The bevy of children at her side indicated the danger of taking people at their face value. The priestly countenance, which suggested monastic celibacy, was gravely in error.

Mrs Cairncross greeted him warmly, talked kindly but anxiously about the weather. These civilities were interrupted as a young woman appeared from the direction of the church gate.

As she was introduced as 'our eldest daughter, Miss Harriet Cairncross', Faro noted that she had inherited her mother's comely looks and curves.

'Are you a bowman, by any chance, Mr Faro?' said Mrs Cairncross.

'Alas, no.'

'A pity,' said her husband, eyeing him narrowly. 'You have an excellent sturdy frame, strong about the shoulders –'

Mrs Cairncross interrupted laughingly, 'Alfred is a great enthusiast. He won the coveted Gold Arrow three years ago and has never forgotten it. I almost said it went to his head,' she giggled helplessly and Reverend Cairncross patted her arm affectionately.

'I can recommend archery to you, sir. A grand healthy relaxation and I tell myself much more in keeping with the Bible than guns.'

'Even if you are not an archer, sir, you must come to the fête in the church hall afterwards,' insisted Mrs Cairncross.

'Mr Faro is an insurance assessor, my dear. He is engaged at the Castle at present.'

Faro observed that the vicar's grip on his wife's arm tightened perceptibly. His words, spoken lightly but with a hint of warning, suddenly changed the scene from being warm and welcoming. It was as if a chill wind had blown over the little group. The daughter stepped back as if taking refuge, hiding behind her mother, and Faro's quick ears detected a strangled sob from the girl as her father bowed a dismissal in his direction.

Seizing her arm as if to restrain her from flight, his head close to hers, chiding or comforting, he propelled her in the direction of the manse.

Mrs Cairncross darted a helpless look at the pair of them, turned to Faro, opened her mouth as if to say something and, unable to think of anything to fit the occasion, turned on her heel and hurried after them.

Left standing, Faro regarded their swift departure thoughtfully. Curious behaviour indeed, remembering that warning tone clear as a bell as he was being introduced by the vicar to his wife and pretty daughter.

As he continued his perusal of the tombstones, he stored away in his excellent memory the picture of the consternation that the vicar's words 'at the Castle' had struck. A chord that the ominous words 'Detective Inspector Faro' normally aroused in those whose consciences trembled with guilt.

Now he wondered what the Cairncross family had to hide. Their reactions could hardly have been more dramatic had they known his real identity. The blight that mention of Elriggs or Castle brought into the most friendly and ordinary conversations was becoming uncomfortably familiar, swiftly changing listeners' attitudes from geniality to suspicious alertness, tense and watchful as the wild cattle on the hill.

Experienced as he was in the nuances of criminal attitudes, such strange behaviour fascinated him, as he wondered how many more village folk would be thrown into panic and consternation by the innocent announcement of his business at Elrigg.

Continuing his inspection of the gravestones, which was proving singularly uneventful, he was once again seized by a fit of sneezing. Aware of being tired and hoping this was not the prelude to a fever, he sat down on a rustic seat sheltered by the church wall.

Taking out his handkerchief, he encountered the book Miss Crowe had dropped. *The History of Civilisation* by Henry Thomas Buckle. A curious choice, he thought, for a young woman whose main reading was of the sensational kind. Opening it at the bookmarked page he read:

> Of all offences, it might well be supposed that the crime of murder is one of the most arbitrary and irregular. For when we consider that this, though generally the crowning act of a long career of vice, is often the immediate result of what seems a sudden impulse; <u>that when premeditated, its committal, even with the least change of impunity, requires a rare combination of favourable circumstances, for which the criminal will frequently wait; that he has thus to bide his time and look for opportunities he cannot control, that when the time has come his heart may fail him</u>, that the question whether or not he shall commit the crime may depend on a balance of conflicting motives, such as fear of the law, a dread of penalties held out by religion, the prickings of his own conscience, the apprehension of future remorse, the love of gain, jealousy, revenge, desperation; – when we put all these things together, there arises such a complication of causes, that we might reasonably despair of detecting any order or method in the result of those subtle and shifting agencies by which murder

is either caused or prevented. But now, how stands the fact. The fact is, that murder is committed with as much regularity, and bears as uniform a relation to certain known circumstances, as do the movements of the tides, and the rotations of the seasons.

Faro re-read the lines heavily underscored and, turning back the pages, read the owner's name on the flyleaf, so unexpected and disturbing that it set at naught all his evidence. With a sickening feeling of dismay he realised he might well have been following the wrong track.

15

Faro walked slowly down the main street, wrestling with the enormity of his new discovery. Constable Dewar had to hail him twice before he was aware of an interruption to his dismal thoughts.

The constable was off-duty, in his garden opposite the police station. With considerable effort Faro returned his greeting and paused to admire the neat array of daffodils.

Dewar smiled, indicating the rustic seat by the door.

'You're looking tired, sir. Rest yourself a while. Mrs Dewar'll bring us out a drink while we enjoy the sunshine.'

Faro needed no second invitation. As he sat down with a sigh of relief, Dewar said: 'Inquiries going well, sir?'

Faro shook his head. He didn't have McQuinn but in the circumstances Constable Dewar, who had lived in Elrigg for many years, might have convenient access to the kind of information he needed.

He sighed. 'Not very well, I'm afraid. I could do with your help, Constable.'

Dewar looked startled at the request. He regarded Faro indecisively, and then, squaring his shoulders, said firmly: 'I'll be straight with you, sir, although I don't think you're being straight with me.'

While Faro was thinking of a suitably evasive reply, he continued: 'I've been keeping an eye on your activities, sir.' He paused dramatically. 'You're a policeman yourself, aren't you?'

Taking Faro's silence as affirmation, he smiled triumphantly.

'You're either a policemen or you have been at some time in your life.'

At Faro's grudging admission, Dewar thumped his fists together with a crow of delight.

'Knew I was right all along, sir. Said so to Sergeant Yarrow. All he says is that if you wanted us to know that, then you'd tell us. And that I was to keep quiet about what I suspected.'

As Faro wondered anxiously how many others Dewar might have confided his suspicions to, the constable leaned forward and said earnestly: 'I am at your service, sir. You can rely on PC

Dewar. Born and bred in the place, there's nothing I don't know about the ways of folk hereabouts. Elrigg's an open book to me,' he added proudly.

Faro smiled vaguely.

'What is it exactly your lot sent you down to investigate?'

There seemed little to lose and much to gain by being honest with Dewar and Faro decided to reveal his true identity.

Dewar's eyes boggled. He whistled. 'Not *the* Inspector Faro. From the Edinburgh Police. Well, I never,' he said with an admiring glance. 'Why, every policeman from here to London has heard of you.'

And when Faro bowed modestly, Dewar's expression changed to one of shrewd intelligence.

'Then it must be something very important indeed that's brought you here. Not a couple of missing paintings or a death insurance, I'll be bound.'

Faro frowned. 'I take it that you are aware of who Sir Archie's companion was on the day of the accident?'

Dewar beamed. 'Bless you, sir, everyone is. Although we all pretend to go along with their incognitos. "Mr Osborne" – a lot of nonsense.'

'Tell me, is there much security attached to these visits?'

'Security!' Dewar laughed. 'At Elrigg? Bless your heart, no, sir. Sergeant Yarrow and I are required to ride at a discreet distance. This isn't London or Edinburgh, not like any big city. Just a token presence of the law, you understand, where royal visitors are concerned.

'We know all the people here, you see, and if there was any villain coming in with bad intent, well, he'd stand out like a sore thumb, sir. We'd be on to him before he had time to know what hit him.'

Even as Faro doubted that, he remembered his aunt's similar reaction to the Deeside inhabitants in the vicinity of Balmoral Castle.

'People think they are just strangers passing through and won't be noticed. They'd think differently if they knew how newcomers are a fascinating topic of speculation. Of course,' Dewar continued, tapping the side of his nose with his forefinger, 'we all know the real reason for the royal gentleman's visit, but enough said.'

And he closed his mouth firmly, loyal to Queen or Prince and Country.

'Where do you get your information from?' Faro asked.

'Servants, sir,' said Dewar cheerfully. 'The way the gentleman in question has to have a room nearby his, er, interest, if you get my meaning. So that he can come and go without embarrassment to either of them...'

Faro's eyes widened to think that matters arranged with such delicacy by discreet aristocratic hosts were in fact common village gossip.

Dewar paused and then, in a tone purposely diffident, 'Her Ladyship's a rum 'un, mind you.' And again he regarded Faro nervously and closed his mouth firmly in the way of a man who fears he has already said more than enough.

'How so?' Faro prodded him gently.

Dewar took a deep breath. 'Well, sir, the class she comes from, actresses and such like. Can't see one of her kind settling down to be a proper wife to His Lordship. Stands to reason, his family's one of the oldest in the land, older than any royalty.' With a shake of his head he added pityingly, 'Her so young, five years married and not a bairn, much less an heir. Just ain't natural.'

'Presumably Sir Archie wasn't worried by this?'

'You can never tell with that class of people, sir.'

'He does have an heir, I gather.'

'Yes, Mark, his first wife's son. But it's not the same, is it, sir?'

'I understood that they were close kin.'

'Yes.' Dewar sounded doubtful. 'The first Lady Elrigg was Sir Archie's cousin, so the lad had a right by blood. I was one of the witnesses to the will, sir, I tell you that in confidence. That in the event of the laird dying without issue, it would all go to Mark.'

Dewar frowned for a moment, before saying in the manner of one choosing his words carefully: 'It seems to me that Lady Elrigg isn't as grieved as is natural in the circumstances. Not like the example Her Majesty has set for widowed ladies. She's ordered mourning to be set aside and I hear tell that she and her companion have been heard playing the piano, singing comic songs. Now that's not nice.'

At Dewar's shocked expression Faro said gently: 'You mustn't forget that the two ladies are very young. At least having a companion who has known her for a long time must be a great help to Lady Elrigg at this time.'

'That's as maybe,' Dewar admitted grudgingly, 'But Miss Kent doesn't behave like a servant at all. Very grand with everyone in the village, too. Too good for the likes of us, you'd think. And it's time she was finding herself a man before it's too late...'

Faro felt a fleeting sympathy for Miss Kent at the village matchmaker's mercy as Dewar went on: 'Bowden tells me that one or two of his customers – young lads – have made, well, advances when she's been down on an errand. Nothing coarse or undesirable, you understand,' he added hastily, 'just friendly – a bit saucy like they are with the maids at the Castle. But this one just gives them a steely look, a frosty reply.

'What can you expect with stage folk?' He shook his head. 'Can't be doing with them. Mind you, I was sorry for that poor actor chap who had that nasty accident while staying at the Castle.'

'What kind of accident?' Faro asked innocently.

'Well, sir, it was all a bit mysterious, if you ask me. If it had happened anywhere else there would have been a full inquiry but here, well, it seemed to me that it was very hastily hushed up, the Chief Constable and the Coroner being close kin of Sir Archie –'

'Wait a moment,' Faro interrupted. 'You mean that there was something to hush up – like foul play?'

'Well,' said Dewar reluctantly, 'that's what I thought.'

'How so?'

Dewar shrugged. 'This actor arrives in the village and takes a room at the inn. He starts asking about Her Ladyship. Seems he was an old chum, they have been on the boards in London. Next thing we knew, he's cleared off in a carriage taking him to the Castle, to be the guest of the Elriggs, to entertain Mr Osbourne – on one of his visits. Must have been there for about a week, when he and Mr Osbourne went out riding together.'

He paused, frowning. 'Mr Osbourne came back alone, so we are told. They had parted company. No one took much notice of the fact that Mr Gray was missing at dinner that evening. It wasn't until next morning, when the maids discovered his bed hadn't been slept in, that the alarm was raised. The servants were a bit worried about that, especially the housekeeper, who thought he'd maybe gone off with the silver. You can never tell with that class of people, sir.

'We were alerted but we weren't permitted to question Mr Osbourne personally. All we had was what he told His Lordship, that he and Mr Gray had ridden as far as the pastureland at the edge of the estate and he, Mr Osbourne, was feeling tired and decided to return.

'That was all we had to go on. We set out and there he was, poor gentleman, lying dead in the copse beside the hillfort. He'd been gored by one of the wild cattle. There was no doubt about that. A dreadful accident. The Coroner and Sir Archie were all for having it cleared as quickly as possible. Didn't want it getting into the newspapers, with royalty involved.'

He looked at Faro. 'I've often thought that it was odd finding His Lordship in the same place. Died the same way too. A strange coincidence, don't you think?'

Faro made no comment, thinking that any other police than Elrigg would have thought it also suspicious enough to merit immediate investigation.

At that moment they were interrupted as Mrs Dewar came out of the house, drying her hands on her apron.

'Food's ready, Sandy.' And, seeing Faro, she smiled. 'Is this the gentleman you were telling me about?'

She bobbed a curtsy as they were introduced, looking very impressed. 'Won't you take a bite to eat with us, sir?'

'Aye, do that,' said Dewar. 'Jessie can beat the inn for anything they might produce. And it's steak pie –'

'Go on with you, Sandy,' said Mrs Dewar. 'Can't have Mr Faro expecting too much. It's all simple food.'

As they led the way into the house, he heard her murmur to her husband, 'He's younger than I thought he'd be. And my, isn't he handsome?'

16

Faro ate at the Dewars' kitchen table with its welcoming fire and even more welcoming smell of freshly baked pies. The vacant place opposite him was set for Sergeant Yarrow, the constable explained: 'We don't have many meals together. I go on duty when he comes off so that the station is manned during the day. He boards with us, has the spare room upstairs. House is too big for Jessie and me since the lads left the nest.'

'Came to look for a place of his own. But somehow he just stayed on and we've got used to having him.' Mrs Dewar looked round from piling extra potatoes on their plates. 'He's such a nice kind thoughtful man. Just like one of the family. More pie, Mr Faro?'

Faro declined the offer and Mrs Dewar continued: 'He's not a bit of trouble. He'd make a grand husband for some lucky lady, I tell him.'

Dewar laughed. 'Jessie's always trying to marry him off. There's no such thing as single blessedness for her.'

'A crime against nature, that's what it is, God never meant his creatures to live solitary lives,' Mrs Dewar protested.

'A bachelor, is he?' said Faro.

'Not him, more's the pity. His wife died around the time of his accident.'

'Aye, and he misses her. I often see him looking at her photograph when I take him in his tea,' sighed Mrs Dewar. 'I think he was glad to start a new life here, away from all the memories.'

Pausing, she looked across the table at Faro. 'Are you a married man yourself?'

Faro shook his head. 'Like your Sergeant, I'm a widower. My wife died in childbirth eight years ago.'

'How sad,' tut-tutted Mrs Dewar. 'You're all alone too, sir?'

'Not quite. I have two little girls living with their granny up in Orkney.'

'Orkney?' Mrs Dewar frowned. 'That's a fair distance from Edinburgh, isn't it?'

Faro smiled. 'It is indeed. But my wife was married before and I have a stepson living with me. He's a doctor.'

'That's nice for you. You'll have another spoonful of dumpling?'

'Yes, thank you, Mrs Dewar. That was absolutely delicious.'

As Mrs Dewar beamed, very liberal with the jam sauce, they heard the back door open.

'Talk of the devil,' said Dewar. 'That's the Sergeant now. I'll need to take over, Jessie,' he added, scraping his plate.

Faro wished he could have had a moment in private with Dewar to stress the need for secrecy. He didn't want the news of his real identity spread around Elrigg. However, such a hurried exit was impossible with a second helping of pudding uneaten on his plate.

Sergeant Yarrow's greeting was friendly and politely interested as he enquired about the progress of Faro's investigations. As Mrs Dewar made a great deal of fuss over him, he seemed to enjoy her attentions.

Faro mentioned that he had been to the kirkyard and Yarrow said: 'If you're interested in the history of Elrigg and the cattle, I have a book upstairs. You can borrow it if you like. It won't take you long to read.'

'What about your food, Sergeant?' Mrs Dewar sounded alarmed.

Yarrow smiled at her. 'That can wait a wee while, Mrs Dewar. I had a pint of ale at the inn so I won't starve.'

'You should be careful. Drinking isn't good for you. I hope you're taking the medicine that Dr Brand gave you.'

'Faithfully, Mrs Dewar.'

Faro looked at him quickly. His colour was bad, he looked like a sick man. And he found himself remembering Imogen Crowe's gloomy pronouncement.

'The Sergeant has one of the best views over Elrigg. A lovely room, it is,' said Mrs Dewar.

'Yes. My window looks directly towards the standing stones and if I take out my telescope, I can watch the cattle grazing. From a safe distance.'

'Why don't you show Mr Faro?'

When Yarrow frowned, Mrs Dewar said, 'No need to worry, it's all neat and tidy, not like the way you left it.'

Yarrow's smile was a little long-suffering as he nodded to Faro. 'Come along then.'

Faro followed him upstairs. The room with its bay window was very attractive, much lighter than the kitchen downstairs. He guessed that Yarrow strove to keep it as a man's domain despite his landlady's feminine touches of lace and vases of flowers.

Yarrow read his expression. 'They're very good to me. It's a relief to have a good working relationship with Dewar – makes life much easier.' He sighed. 'Too easy really. I didn't mean to stay with them year after year. Mrs Dewar spoils me, as you've probably observed.'

Faro was looking at the mantelpiece, dominated by three silver framed photographs. A wedding – a younger, handsome Yarrow in Metropolitan Police uniform with his pretty bride; a second photograph of the couple staring down at a baby and a third of Mrs Yarrow with a handsome curly-haired infant on her knee, smiling into the camera.

'What a beautiful child. Yours?' said Faro.

'Yes. But no more, alas.' Yarrow turned from the glass-fronted bookcase, his face expressionless. 'This is the book. No hurry, just leave it at the inn for me when you go –'

'Your food's getting cold, Sergeant!'

At Mrs Dewar's call upstairs, Faro smiled. 'I'll be on my way.' And he hurried downstairs through the kitchen, thanking Mrs Dewar for her kindness while she urged him to drop in any time.

'You'll be most welcome to share our little meal with us.'

He was not sorry to have missed eating at the Elrigg Arms in what would have been solitary splendour. A few farmers with their dogs occupied the bar and Bowden stopped him on his way up to his room. 'You've missed your visitor, sir.' At Faro's puzzled expression Bowden laughed. 'Aye, Jack Duffy. Called in to see you on the off-chance.'

'What did he want?'

'Wouldn't say. Just that he wanted a word with you. In a right old state he was, said it was urgent and where were you, and so forth. I told him I wasn't your keeper –'

'Did he leave a note?'

'A note, sir. Duffy can't write. There's nothing wrong with his sums though. He can certainly add up.' Bowden grinned. 'It was something important he wanted to get off his chest, that's for sure.' Bowden gave Faro a significant wink. 'And knowing Duffy, like I told you, I'd take any bet you like that it has to do with money.'

'Did he say when he'd be back?'

'Told me to tell you he'd be in at six again tomorrow evening. I was to tell you to be here because he had vital information to give you.'

Faro felt exasperated at having missed the poacher a second time. Was it no more than a ruse to extract money from a stranger by offering him some stolen booty, or did he know something vital about Sir Archie's death that he was willing to sell to the insurance mannie?

Later that afternoon, Faro set off for the Castle. On his way through the village, his conscience prompted him that he should send a postcard to his daughters in Orkney and write a long overdue letter to his mother.

Opposite the one church which catered for all Elrigg's spiritual needs was the one shop which catered for all their material ones, from food to farming implements.

Purchases in hand, Faro waited for some time behind a customer buying boiled sweets from a large selection of glass jars. Her choice involved a great deal of indecision.

Turning to him, she smiled apologetically and he recognised the elderly schoolteacher, whom the shopkeeper addressed very civilly as Miss Halliday.

'My apologies, sir, these are rewards for good conduct and good marks for my children. Yes, that will do nicely, thank you.' As she awaited the weighing out and summing up of pennies, she continued: 'Are you enjoying your visit? I observed you outside the school railings and deduced that, as you were not a parent and therefore known to me personally, you must be a visitor.'

'I am indeed,' Faro smiled inwardly. What splendid detectives these local people would have made. His strict rules of observation and deduction might well have been invented by them.

The teacher obviously expected some further enlightenment and Faro found it difficult to give the kind of response that the woman's shrewd and eager expression demanded. He still wore his recently acquired *persona* like an ill-fitting suit of clothes, about which he was becoming increasingly uncomfortable and self-conscious. A poor actor, he was certain that everyone in Elrigg had seen through his disguise and knew it for a lie.

'If you are staying for a while, perhaps you would care to come to our charity concert, the day after the Archery Contest? The children are performing well-known scenes from Shakespeare's plays and I can guarantee an evening of lively entertainment...'

As she warmed to her subject, waxing ecstatic about her small actors and actresses, Faro listened bleakly. How he dreaded and assiduously avoided amateur theatricals, the worst of all being school plays. His role of fond and indulgent parent had its limitations and he was thankful that his daughters Rose and Emily had never exhibited even hints of latent acting abilities.

Thanking Miss Halliday graciously but remaining vague about his immediate future in Elrigg, he made his escape.

Relying on his forged credentials and the fact that the further inquiries of an insurance investigator might be accepted as natural, Faro walked briskly towards the Castle.

At the lodge Imogen Crowe was at home, busily hanging curtains in the kitchen window. Pretending not to notice, and staring hard in the opposite direction, he hurried past, head down, eager to avoid any further communication with her.

An impossible woman.

17

The day was warm and sunny and Faro concentrated on what he was going to say to Lady Elrigg and her stepson. The aged butler opened the door and looked down his sharp nose at Faro. As usual he was left waiting on the doorstep for some time while the old man enquired as to who might be at home.

It was all very tiresome, thought Faro, his good nature evaporating rapidly as he wondered if his presence had been forgotten.

At last the door was reopened. 'Her Ladyship is not at home but Mr Mark is willing to see you.'

Faro was relieved to see Mark appear behind the butler at that moment.

'Good day to you, Mr Faro. Shall we stroll in the gardens?'

Faro smiled. Perhaps it was crediting the young man with too much subtlety to have realised that emotions are easier concealed strolling in a garden than sitting face to face across a table. And a much less unnerving experience.

'The paintings haven't turned up, I'm afraid,' Mark volunteered.

Faro would have been surprised if they had, having long since determined their fate.

'I suppose you have documents for us to sign?' Mark continued.

Faro hadn't thought of that.

'Sir Archie didn't tell me – as you know. All a bit of a shock, what happened.'

'I'm sorry. You were close to him?' Faro said boldly.

Mark shrugged. 'As close as anyone. He was good to me and I enjoyed better relations with him than most,' he added frankly. 'He could be a devil sometimes, you know, he believed in the old traditions of the gentry, tried to run Elrigg like a medieval warlord. He refused to believe that times were changing. He yearned for the old-style barony courts, with absolute power of life and death, the *droit de seigneur* – all that sort of thing. He liked the idea of summoning his tenants once a quarter – to dispense justice and administer punishment.'

They had reached the edge of the walled garden. Ahead of them stretched a large expanse of boggy, heavily weeded marshland, quite out of the keeping with the neat paths and well-trimmed garden.

'That was once an ornamental lake. We used to sail boats on it, have picnics. Then there was an accident, a girl drowned. Sir Archie wouldn't tolerate that sort of thing on his land. Had it drained. He was like that.'

'It must have been very distressing for you finding him that day –' Faro decided to pretend ignorance and the mild curiosity that might be expected of him regarding Sir Archie's death.

Mark shook his head. 'I didn't know what had happened until later. I was busy in the estate office. Something my stepfather wanted checked,' he continued swiftly. Then, looking at Faro, he said, 'We were used to him being unseated by his horse. He would arrive back on foot in a towering rage, out for blood.'

'That happened often?'

'Often enough. He had a passion for highly bred Arab horses, very expensive. He had to show them – like everyone else – that he was master. Used the whip cruelly at the breaking-in process –'

'He was riding alone, I take it?'

'No. As a matter of fact he had one of our guests with him.'

'And didn't this guest give the alarm?'

'Of course,' said Mark uncomfortably. 'Oh, there you are,' he called as Lady Elrigg and her companion Miss Kent emerged from the walled garden, the relief in his voice suggesting rescue from a particularly nasty situation. Faro bowed politely, greeted them cordially. While he listened to Mark explaining too brightly that Mr Faro was still busy with his inquiries about the paintings, he felt Lady Elrigg's smile was fixed and held no warmth.

But it was the companion who most interested him. This was their first meeting and he regarded her with considerable interest in the light of Constable Dewar's scathing remarks regarding her matrimonial chances.

Beatrice Kent was tall and thin with a sallow complexion,

the kind of anonymity that doomed actresses to character roles. Even in extreme youth he doubted whether she had ever been pretty enough for juvenile leads. She was no foil for her mistress's flamboyant beauty.

She was aware of his scrutiny and turned aside sharply. At her side Poppy Elrigg continued to smile, her composure unimpaired by this encounter with the insurance assessor. Only Miss Kent showed evidence of despair, her lips trembling, her eyes darting back and forth nervously from one to the other as if in some desperate mute appeal for help.

At last she touched Lady Elrigg's arm, the slightest gesture but enough communication for the two women to turn and look at him with expressions that left him in no doubt regarding his popularity. And had they been able to slip back into the shrubbery unobserved he guessed they would have withdrawn immediately.

Feeling that words of explanation were demanded of him, he said heartily: 'Just the usual procedures, you know.'

'In view of our unfortunate bereavement, I was reminding him –' Mark's voice held a note of pleading.

'I'm sure Mr Faro understands perfectly.' Lady Elrigg's brilliant smile in his direction was followed by a brisk nod to Mark. 'And now, if you'll excuse us. Come along, Mark,' she added as if he had some burning desire to remain. 'Beatrice and I were looking for you. There are estate matters urgently needing your attention, you know.'

The heir to Elrigg seemed in no great hurry to take over his duties either and Faro, detecting a hint of reproach and reprimand, regarded their rapid exit thoughtfully.

Lady Elrigg had been particularly anxious to remove Mark and, he felt sure, she would be very concerned about the particulars of their conversation.

At that moment, he decided that Mark was the most unlikely person to have murdered Sir Archie if he had found him unconscious in the spinney.

Unless he was lying in wait for just such a possibility, when he most certainly would have been seen in the vicinity by Yarrow or Dewar. Besides, from what Mark had told him, Faro felt the boy was more likely to have rushed to the scene and tried his best to resuscitate his stepfather.

Returning along the Castle drive, deep in his own thoughts, Faro stepped aside to make way for a rider leading a string of horses.

Greetings exchanged, Faro was admiring the mare with her new foal, when the lad said: 'You're the man from the insurance people. I thought I recognised you. I've seen you at the inn.'

'You were here the day of His Lordship's accident?'

'I was that,' said the lad as he dismounted. 'Mind you, I thought little of it at the time. His Lordship had frequent disagreements with the beasts. Often came off worst.'

He shook his head. 'I didn't realise he was hurt, especially as the other gentleman rode in, never mentioned it –'.

'This other gentleman. Who was he?'

The stable boy gave him a curious look. 'Very important he was sir, very confidential. We'd lose our jobs if we talked about him – gossiped and the like,' he said anxiously.

'Quite so. I just wondered why he hadn't waited and seen His Lordship home.'

'Can't say, sir. He rode in. I helped him dismount and he was very wet and in a tearing rage, I could see that. He ordered his carriage to be sent round immediately and stormed off to the house. We hadn't been told that he was leaving and of course there was the usual panic. I watched him leave with his servants, wondering about His Lordship. Wasn't like him not to be there to speed on the departing guest. Her Ladyship looked a bit flustered, apologetic like.'

'Was Mr Mark with her?'

'No. I didn't see him. When I got back to the stables, His Lordship's horse galloped in. I was alarmed. I realised His Lordship might have gone right up to the Castle not to be late for dinner. But that wasn't like him. It was still raining and getting dark. I chatted to the other lads and none of us liked the idea of him lying hurt out there, especially with the cattle roaming about, upset by a stalking party earlier on. And we'd been told there were some young calves just dropped.

'Then Constable Dewar rode in, told us about the accident,' He shrugged. 'When we got there it was too late. Sergeant Yarrow and Dr Brand were with him.'

'Anyone else?'

The stable lad thought. 'Aye. Mr Mark and Mr Hector were standing about and one or two of the estate folk. But there wasn't anything they could do.'

As Faro continued on his way, he made a mental picture of the scene in the copse. Mark, Hector and a few anonymous 'estate folk', any of whom could ride a horse and might have found Sir Archie lying injured. From what he had learned, all the tenants were expert archers. It didn't take much stretch of the imagination to realise that the bull's horn might be used as a murder weapon.

He considered the time factor. Although it took the best part of thirty minutes to walk briskly to the copse from the Castle, ten minutes on a swift mount was all that was required, taking well-known short cuts over fields and fences.

Luck had been with the murderer, since Sergeant Yarrow's arrival had been delayed by his horse going lame. A murderer who was clever – or desperate – who had discovered the bull's horns and realised the possibilities or re-enacting the death of the actor Philip Gray by blaming it on the wild cattle.

His thoughts were irresistibly drawn once more to Hector Elrigg. He could not dismiss him from his list of possible suspects. He spent most of his working days at the hillfort with the copse in clear view, his cottage less than a hundred yards away.

And Hector was an expert archer.

18

Deep in thought, Faro was halfway between the Castle drive and the village when the rain began. A few preliminary warning spots became a torrential downpour. Taking refuge in the only available shelter offered by a large but still leafless oak tree whose branches hung over the estate wall, he gazed longingly towards a cottage on the other side of the road.

Smoke issued from its chimney bringing the scent of a peat fire. Lamplight gleamed in its windows. Suddenly the door opened and a lady beckoned to him.

'Won't you come and take shelter, sir? It is only a shower, and it will soon pass...'

Faro recognised the schoolteacher Miss Halliday. And needing no second bidding, he raced across the intervening ground and followed her into the kitchen where a kettle whistled merrily on a large fire.

The room was well filled with bookshelves, every inch of wall covered by framed paintings, every foot of floor by sofas and soft-cushioned chairs. The hands of the needlewoman, either her own or those of her pupils, had been industriously employed through the years.

She pointed to the kettle. 'I was about to make myself a cup of tea when I looked out of the window, thinking my poor plants – how they would welcome a drink. And there you were, poor gentleman – getting absolutely drenched. Perhaps you would like a cup of tea while we try to dry you off.'

Faro insisted that he wasn't very wet, thanks to her timely intervention, but the tea would be most welcome.

As he introduced himself as Mr Faro, Miss Halliday smiled wordlessly and held out her hands for his coat. 'Wait a moment till I set a place for you at the table – oh yes, I insist,' she said and, indicating the papers she bundled on to the sideboard: 'Two of our little girls, sisters, have gone down with scarlet fever, poor dears. I have to fill these in for Sergeant Yarrow.' She sighed. 'I do hope we don't have to be quarantined and our little school closed.'

Faro murmured sympathetically as she set before him a plate of scones.

'By my cookery class,' she said proudly. 'They are quite excellent. Do try them.'

His initial misgivings were quickly set aside and he accepted a second helping.

She looked pleased. 'The dear children, all of them have their own special gift, there isn't one of them who doesn't shine at something. If they aren't clever at sums then they are usually very good with their hands. Do you have children, sir?'

Faro told her about Emily and Rose and she listened, smiling, and nodded sympathetically when she heard he was a widower.

'I can tell you are very proud of your daughters, a pity they cannot live in Edinburgh with you, but I think you have made the right decision, the countryside is a much better and safer choice for children to grow up in. Won't you came and sit by the fire?'

As he sank into a comfortable chair, he sighed. 'What a pretty house you have, Miss Halliday.' Noticing how some of her movements were slow and rheumatic, he added, 'Would it not be more convenient to live on the school house premises?'

She laughed. 'I know what you're thinking, Mr Faro, a big barn of a house for one elderly lady without any servants. But you see this has always been my home. I was born in this house, so were my parents and grandparents. It was a farmhouse in those days. Do you know, Sir Walter Scott once stayed here,' she added proudly. 'We have his letter.' And she pointed to a framed letter among the many watercolours.

'How fascinating, Miss Halliday. Why, Sir Walter is one of my heroes. I've read all his books.'

'And so have I. Well, he most likely sat on that very same chair you are occupying now, Mr Faro. Here you are –' and so saying she took down the letter. 'Read it – aloud, if you please, I love to hear his words.'

Touching through the glass that well-beloved handwriting which had brought so many hours of pleasure, Faro began:

Behold a letter from the mountain, for I am very snugly settled here in a farmer's house, about six miles from Wooler, in the very centre of the Cheviot Hills, in one of the wildest and most romantic situations... To

> add to my satisfaction we are midst places renowned
> by the feats of former days; each hill is crowned with
> a tower, or camp, or cairn; and in no situation can you
> be nearer more fields of battle. Out of the brooks with
> which these hills are intersected, we pull trouts of half
> a yard in length and we are in the very country of muir
> fowl. My uncle drinks the goat's whey here as I do ever
> since I understood it was brought to his bedside every
> morning at six by a very pretty dairy maid –

'Stop a moment, sir,' Miss Halliday interrupted, her face
gleaming with excitement. 'That dairy maid was my great-
grandmother. Sir Walter was only twenty years old when he
wrote that. He was still a law clerk in his father's office.'

She sighed happily. 'I like to think he might have been a little
in love with that pretty girl. I do beg your pardon, sir, please
continue.'

> All the day we shoot, fish, walk and ride; dine and sup
> on fish struggling from the stream, and the most
> delicious health-fed mutton, barn door fowls, pies,
> mild-cheese, etc. all in perfection: and so much
> simplicity resides among these hills that a pen, which
> could write at least, was not to be found about the
> house, though belonging to a considerable farmer, till
> I shot the crow with whose quill I write this epistle.

Miss Halliday sighed. 'Thank you, sir. I do love to hear a man's
voice read that letter, although I know every word of it. And
you did it so nicely.' And rehanging it, she added: 'I like to think
that perhaps he found his inspiration as a great author while
staying in this house. I have been very fortunate today.' She
smiled.

'Indeed?'

'Yes, I must confess that you are the second person who has
so indulged me. A young lady, Miss Crowe.' She shook her
head. 'A young lady of mystery, I might add. She comes and she
goes. Perhaps you have met her? She lives at the Castle lodge.'

'She occasionally takes meals at the inn where I am staying.'

'Does she really?' said Miss Halliday eagerly. 'And what do you think of her?'

'I really haven't paid her much attention, to be honest.'

As Miss Halliday refilled the teapot, Faro sensed that she was disappointed with his answer, and that she would have very much enjoyed a little speculative gossip about the mysterious Miss Crowe.

Faro, however, was more keenly interested in the treasures that surrounded him, the walls with their watercolours. Photographs too, for this new fashion had obviously seized Miss Halliday's enthusiasm.

There were several paintings of pretty young children and in place of honour an outstanding watercolour portrait of a handsome young boy who stared out at them with large enquiring eyes and a slight shy smile. He seemed ready to speak, his expression reminding Faro of someone he had met recently.

'One of your paintings, Miss Halliday?'

She clasped her hands in delight. 'Indeed yes, I'm glad you approve of my little painting.'

'A relation perhaps?'

He expected to be told that this was indeed a favourite nephew but instead she shook her head sadly.

'Merely a favourite pupil.' She sighed. 'Poor dear little Eric, he was at school a few years ago, and I must confess that he was exactly like the son I would have wished for had I ever married.'

She paused and Faro asked; 'Where is he now? Grown up and away, I expect.'

'If only that were so.' She bit her lip and turned away, near to tears and Faro guessed the answer before she spoke.

'He is dead, sir. Killed on the estate here, a most tragic accident. He was with the young beaters, when a gun that one of the party was loading misfired.'

She shook her head, her eyes tragic. 'We could hardly believe such a thing could happen. You can imagine how everyone felt, we were heartbroken – guilty even, for the boy was only a visitor but we were all fond of him, he had made so many friends. And, of course, we all blamed ourselves for not taking better care of him.'

Faro looked at her. Loyalty obviously demanded discretion and according to Hector Elrigg, the gun had been in the hands of Sir Archie who had been drunk at the time.

As he was leaving, he realised sadly that this handsome young boy who had won his way into her spinsterly heart and tragically died had been Miss Halliday's nearest encounter with motherhood.

But the person the boy reminded him of remained stubbornly obscure.

19

Six o'clock was wheezing from the inn's ancient clock as Faro sat down to his supper. The dining room was empty and he was pleased that he had the table to himself for his meeting with Duffy. He would put a pint of ale in front of the poacher just to loosen his tongue a little, with hopes that this eagerness for a meeting signalled enlightenment on the mystery of Sir Archie's last hours.

But his meal was finished, seven had struck with no sign of Duffy, and Faro returned to the bar where Bowden, polishing the counter with his usual eagerness, did not share his anxiety.

'Not the most reliable of chaps,' he said. 'If something better comes along, isn't that so, Sergeant?' he asked Yarrow who was seated at the far end of the counter.

Yarrow's smile indicated that Duffy was not one of his favourites. 'Care to join me, Mr Faro?'

Faro did so but with some diffidence since the bar was directly overlooked by a window. If Duffy chanced to look in and saw the insurance mannie chatting to the law in the shape of Yarrow, this might well scare him off.

As time passed in desultory talk with the Sergeant, Faro was certain this must have happened, despite his efforts to keep a watchful eye on the door.

At last Yarrow buttoned up his tunic and announced that he was back on duty. Faro was relieved to see him depart and with a final word to Bowden to let him know when Duffy arrived, he prepared to go up to his room.

The barman shook his head and looked at the clock. 'You'll not see him tonight, sir, he'll be busy about his own business by now. He'll have forgotten all about your arrangement and he'll be in as usual for his pint of ale at opening time tomorrow morning. If he's sober enough to walk, that it.'

Faro spent the rest of the evening making notes, bringing his log of the case up to date, carefully writing in dossiers of what he knew of the suspects, and of their movements.

Conscious that such an investigation had never been his responsibility and that he had no legal right to interfere, he threw down his pen at last.

The time had come to reveal his identity and confide his suspicions to Sergeant Yarrow. The rest was up to the Northumberland Constabulary who might well consider his observations of merely academic interest. If they felt there was not enough at this late date to follow his leads and reopen an inquiry into Sir Archie's death, he had done what he considered his moral duty.

When he undertook the Queen's Command regarding the future King of England, he had not expected to be landed with a murder case. In fact, the only conclusion he had reached was that the person least likely to have murdered Sir Archie was the Prince of Wales, despite his suspiciously hurried departure from Elrigg Castle.

Whether he had been guilty of that gravest of British sins, cowardice, could, however, be settled only by that most unsatisfactory of Scottish verdicts: 'Not proven'.

Faro slept badly that night, haunted by his old nightmare. Pursued by Highland cattle, the bull's hot breath on his heels as he ran, screaming...

He awoke screaming, but the bull's bellowing was merely the gentle lowing of the dairy cows on their way to milking.

Now fully awake, he was aware of sweeter sounds of birdsong that filled his open window. Shaking free from the web of nightmare, he washed and dressed for the day, aware that the weather beyond the window looked promising. He might as well make the most of this good fresh air before returning to the grime of Edinburgh's smoke-laden High Street and the Central Office of the City Police.

Concluding that dreams were contrary things signifying nothing, he tackled with promptitude the hearty breakfast set before him and contemplated Vince's imminent arrival.

Not for his stepson the train to Bedford and an undignified scramble for the only hiring carriage. Vince would arrive in style in the comfort of the Gilchrists' own carriage, since their family coachbuilding business had accommodated Midlothian's gentry for two generations.

In a decidedly cheerful frame of mind, Faro checked with Bowden that there was a vacant bedroom should Dr Vincent Laurie require it. Then he set off into the village in search of Sergeant Yarrow and a vague hope of buying a suitable birthday gift for the twins' great-aunt Gilchrist.

He had noted that the local shop, in addition to supplying everything from food to farming implements, also displayed in its window pretty lace caps with ribbon streamers, a fashion that the Queen had initiated and that widows and old ladies everywhere had eagerly adopted.

He was hesitating, undecided over the merits of a bewildering selection, when a voice at his elbow said: 'The one with more lace and less streamers, if it's for your mother. Sure, she'll like that, now.'

The Irish accent, the smiling face, was that of Imogen Crowe.

As he mumbled his thanks and handed the cap to the shopkeeper, she said: 'You'll not regret it. That's the one I'd have bought for my own mother. She'll be pleased too that it's good value. The rest are somewhat expensive,' she added in a whisper. 'And they won't launder as well.'

'I'm most grateful to you...'

But turning, he saw she had paid for her own purchases, which looked like a bag of groceries, and was leaving the shop.

What miracle had caused such a change of heart in this chilly lady, he wondered as, with his purchase pocketed, it remained only to hand over his notes to Sergeant Yarrow.

The station door was locked and bore a well-worn notice that anyone in need of the police should apply across the road. A printed hand helpfully pointed in the direction of the Dewars' cottage.

The door was opened very promptly. Mrs Dewar beamed on him. 'Do come in, sir.'

As he followed her into the kitchen, she said: 'Sandy isn't here at the moment, but I have a visitor I'm sure you'd like to meet.'

Seeing Imogen Crowe seated at the table, Faro hesitated. 'I don't wish to disturb you.'

'Not at all, not at all. Miss Crowe came for a recipe and we're just having a cup of tea. Perhaps you'll join us.'

Despite their recent encounter, amiable as it was, Miss Crowe was the last person Faro wished to see at that moment, and in this setting. He felt his dismay was shared by Miss Crowe, since the glint in Mrs Dewar's eye, as she looked from one to the other with considerable sly satisfaction, unmistakably proclaimed the matchmaker at work.

Faro remained standing, while he and Miss Crowe eyed each other warily. Yes, they said, they had met before. A bow from him, a sharp nod from her.

'Sandy went up the road in the pony cart. Sergeant Yarrow's still abed.' Mrs Dewar raised her eyes in the direction of the ceiling. 'He was late in last night. It's his morning off and I always take his breakfast up and put it outside his door,' she added reverently. 'A gentleman like him needs a bit of spoiling.

'If you take a walk up the road to the hillfort you'll meet Sandy on the way back. Perhaps you'd like to come to supper –' she darted a look at Miss Crowe's glum face, 'both of you – on Sunday evening. I do a nice beef roast, too big for us now that our lads are away.'

Miss Crowe frowned, shook her head, glancing at Faro. He smiled and said: 'You are very kind, but my stepson is arriving this afternoon and I shall be leaving Elrigg.'

'You are leaving us – so soon.' Mrs Dewar darted an anxious look at Miss Crowe. 'That is such a pity. We are just getting to know you, isn't that so, miss?'

Her beaming smile in that lady's direction was rewarded by a polite but chilly inclination of the head enough to convince anyone less determined than Mrs Dewar that her romantic intentions were doomed to dismal failure.

'I'm sorry you must go, sir. I am sure you and this young lady would find much in common...'

Faro avoided Miss Crowe's eyes as he took his departure with more haste than good manners dictated, Mrs Dewar's well-meaning compliments soaring after him.

He had been through this ritual so many times, with so many mothers with daughters.

As he walked briskly up the road, he was a little astonished that a man past forty should still be a potential victim of the matchmaker's art. Would it never end, he thought? Would they never give up and accept him for what he was, a widower with growing daughters?

Having decided to put his notes into Yarrow's hands personally, he planned to enjoy the end of his stay in Elrigg with a pleasant stroll on a warm sunny morning. As he walked happily up the road whistling under his breath he mentally shed 'Mr Faro: Insurance Investigator' and returned to his own identity.

He decided this would be a good opportunity to take another look at the hillfort on the excuse that Vince would want to know all about it. He had another stronger reason: to meet Hector Elrigg once more.

As he reached the pastureland, with the hillfort in sight, his nightmare returned and he approached with extreme caution.

No wild bulls roared down on him, the cattle were grazing nearer to the road than on his last visit, but still safely enclosed behind a sturdy-looking fence.

There was no sign of Hector Elrigg at the excavations and having come this far Faro decided to try his cottage. There was no response but, finding the door partially open, he gazed inside. A fire glowed, the table was set for a perfunctory meal. The atmosphere was elegant, with chairs and tables that would have been equally at home in the Castle; furnishings more opulent than he would have expected from a bachelor archaeologist's estate cottage.

He closed the door, thinking that Hector's good taste would not have gone amiss in Elrigg.

Hurrying back across the pastureland he was sure that the cattle had moved still nearer.

Although they appeared to be peacefully grazing, he also observed that once again all faces had turned in his direction. They were watching him with unnerving stillness and intensity. Quickening his footsteps and resisting the almost unconquerable urge to run, he was thankful to bypass the hillfort and reach the safety of the road.

From beyond the fence, he looked at them in wonder. So little was left of early man's presence, but these beasts, who should rightly have been extinct long ago, continued to thrive, their survival dictated by some secret knowledge of the universe and obedience to the natural laws obliterated by layer upon layer of man's sophistication down the ages.

On the hilltop with the sun behind them, the standing stones looked more than ever like five headless women. What was their secret older than recorded time, what long-forgotten rituals linked them with the hillfort and the wild cattle?

Intrigued by that insoluble mystery and having come this far on a fruitless errand, Faro decided to inspect them more carefully than the advent of the tiresome Miss Crowe had made possible the last time.

Clambering along the margins of the farmer's field with its newly sown crops, he reached the summit of the circle, once more captivated by the views from this vantage point across two countries.

Taking a seat on a large stone, he looked down towards the now distant road. The outlines of the prehistoric fort were more clearly visible from this height, the sunlight casting shadows on the contours which had once sheltered the earliest inhabitants of Elrigg, the nomads who had settled here and given this place its first history.

There was a newer race of nomads now. And he saw a line of brightly coloured caravans trotting down the road; the sound of the horses, the tinkling of the pots and pans, dogs barking and children shouting, echoed through the air. A cheerful sound of bustling humanity, though he doubted whether the gypsies' return would be any more welcome here than it was on the meadows around Edinburgh.

They made careful circuit of the forbidden and dangerous pastureland and headed towards the riverbank where they would make temporary camp.

Far beyond the road twisting away below him, smoke rose into the still air indicating the village of Elrigg, an oasis nestling peacefully among undulating hills, lost in a fold of this wild barbaric land with its blood-soaked history. Beyond the parkland the Castle's towers rose through the trees which hid the drive and the lodge gates.

Shading his eyes, he caught a glimpse of Miss Halliday's cottage and wondered if the twenty-year-old Walter Scott had also been intrigued by the riddle of Elrigg as he walked these roads and touched these stones. It pleased Faro to think that, with his famous novels still in the future, perhaps young Scott had conceived his love of the Borders which was to inspire *Marmion* and *The Bride of Lammermoor* in the Hallidays' farmhouse.

From the distant church he heard the sound of bells. Eleven o'clock, and reluctantly he made his way back downhill and, heading in the direction of the inn, he indulged in the pleasant fancy that on this very spot, echoing his own footsteps, his hero had found inspiration or, in the years of his fame, wrestled with some particularly difficult passage of prose...

'Hey – mister...'

His reverie was interrupted by two young lads who erupted from the field and ran towards him waving their fishing rods.

'Mister, mister. Come quick!'

'Old Duffy's lying with his face in the burn...'

20

Faro sprang over the fence and followed the two lads down the slope to swift-flowing water.

Half hidden by the overgrowing banks, Duffy lay motionless.

'He looks bad, doesn't he, mister?'

He did. Turning Duffy over, Faro said to the younger of the two who had the look of brothers: 'Go and keep a sharp look out for Constable Dewar. He's on the road somewhere. Send him over.' And to the other: 'Run and get Sergeant Yarrow. Fast as you can.'

'Will he be all right, mister?'

'I don't know.'

'Shall I get me father, sir? He's the vicar.'

'Yes, tell him. But get the Sergeant first.'

Obviously the Cairncross lad recognised the signs of death. And, left alone, Faro knew Duffy was dead. Drowned.

The signs were unmistakable, as was the smell of whisky about him.

Faro knelt by the body. Only another unfortunate accident, to be dismissed as one more coincidence, he told himself. And no connection with any information that, according to Bowden, Duffy had been anxious to impart (or sell) to the 'insurance mannie'.

Of course it was an accident, Yarrow and Dewar would say reassuringly. They knew Duffy well, the kind of man he was. Everyone had been expecting something like this. He drank too much, one day he'd keel over, fall into the river.

As Faro looked down at him, he noticed that from one clenched hand a thread hung. As he tugged, what at first glance was a silver coin rolled on the ground.

Faro picked it up, turned it over. If this meant what he thought it did, then Duffy's death was no accident. He had been murdered.

He was still thinking about the implications of his discovery when a horse and rider came into view. It was Yarrow, shortly followed by Dewar, the vicar, his sons and a couple of estate workers.

Reverend Cairncross knelt by the body, took the cold hands in his and murmured a prayer.

Almost roughly, Yarrow pushed him aside and also bent over the body. 'You can smell the drink on him.'

Faro leaned over and sniffed. 'You can that, Sergeant.'

'As if it had been poured over him,' sighed the vicar.

Yarrow gave him a sharp look, asked: 'Has he been moved?'

Faro indicated the Cairncross brothers. 'They found him. While they went for help, naturally I examined him to see if there were any signs of life.'

'Naturally,' echoed Yarrow sourly and turned to Dewar who was ready with the stretcher carried in the pony cart for emergencies, its use seldom required apart from farming accidents.

Reverend Cairncross said: 'I can do nothing here.'

'Has he any family?' Faro asked.

Yarrow answered, 'Not in these parts. There's a woman looks after his cottage.' And to Dewar, 'Best take him there till we make the proper arrangements. I'll walk back with Mr Faro.'

It wasn't a great distance, but Yarrow was slow on his feet and insisted on leading his horse. Faro's silence (related to whether this was an opportune moment to hand over the notes in his pocket) was presumed by Yarrow to be the layman's first sight of a drowned man or a corpse.

'You get used to it in time,' he said sympathetically.

Faro could think of no suitable reply and Yarrow continued: 'Are you to be staying long in Elrigg?'

'Not much longer. My investigations are complete and my stepson is arriving today. We will probably take a few days' holiday before returning to Edinburgh.'

'That is awkward.'

Faro was conscious of Yarrow's intense gaze. 'Indeed?'

Yarrow cleared his throat apologetically. 'I might have to call on you to give evidence as you were the first on the scene, the first to touch the body. A passer-by, of course, nothing to worry about,' he added hastily as if Faro's silence was an indication of guilt.

'I hope it won't take too long.'

Yarrow shook his head. 'Just routine, Mr Faro. Paperwork, that's all.' In a voice elaborately casual, he added, 'When did you last see Duffy alive, by the way?'

'A couple of days ago.'

'Oh! I thought you had a meeting arranged with him last night. At the inn. Heard Bowden discussing it with you.'

'True. But he failed to appear. As you know,' he reminded him gently.

Yarrow considered that for a moment, nodded. 'Have you any idea what it was he wanted to talk to you about?'

'None at all.'

'You've talked to him before? Privately, I mean.'

'Never. Bowden suggested that he probably wanted to borrow money.'

There was a slight pause. 'Can you think of any reason why he should imagine that a stranger to the district would be willing to give him money?'

'I haven't the least idea, Sergeant.'

Yarrow stared ahead, frowning. 'May I ask your whereabouts yesterday evening?'

'Certainly. I was at the inn. As you know.' Faro's laugh held a note of exasperation. What was Yarrow getting at?

Yarrow did not share his amusement. He continued to eye him sternly. 'You were seen in the vicinity near where Duffy was found.'

'I might well have been. I had an evening stroll.' And Faro turned to him, his laughter now disbelieving. He was being cross-examined. Detective Inspector Faro was a suspect.

His mirth faded at Yarrow's expression.

'It was the earlier part of the evening I was considering – before we met.'

'Oh, I have an alibi for that too, if that's what you're asking, I was visiting Miss Halliday. She will vouch for me. We had tea together and she was most informative on the history of the village – and her clever pupils. We talked about Sir Walter Scott and I admired some of her paintings. She's very good.'

Yarrow nodded. 'So I've heard. Could have made a name for herself.'

Relieved at this change of subject and return to normal

conversation, Faro said: 'That I can believe. There was one portrait – of a young lad, one of her pupils, a brilliant lad by all accounts – killed in a shooting accident. He looked ready to speak – it was remarkably lifelike...'

Yarrow frowned. 'That would be one of the beaters. They still talk about him. Before my time, but memories are long in places like this.' As they approached the inn, he added: 'Thank you for your help, Mr Faro. Perhaps you'll let me know when you're leaving in case I need to talk to you again.'

Faro watched him go. Yarrow obviously suspected that Duffy's death might not have been an accident. Having overheard the poacher asking for Faro at the inn was enough to alert any policeman worthy of the name of detective when a man is subsequently found dead.

Faro was not quite as amused as he might have been to find himself in the classic situation of the stranger, the newcomer to the district, immediately under suspicion and the first to be questioned.

As he awaited Vince's arrival, he thought about the tiny piece of evidence resting in his pocket beside his notes on the two deaths at Elrigg. As he wrestled with his conscience he decided that Duffy's death could not have come at a worse time. Another twenty-four hours and he would have been clear of Elrigg.

Clear of suspicion!

21

'You could tell Yarrow who you are, of course,' said Vince as he unpacked and hung an array of shirts and cravats in the capacious wardrobe. He sounded irritable and with good reason.

Within their first few moments of conversation on his arrival at the inn, he had seen fast disappearing all hopes of that splendid walking holiday he was looking forward to. His stepfather had got himself hopelessly involved in yet another crime.

'You're impossible, Stepfather, too conscientious by far. These murders, if murders they are, have nothing to do with you. This isn't your province. You know that perfectly well. The Northumberland Constabulary will tell you sharp enough that you are out of order, Inspector Faro.'

He shrugged. 'And as for this latest happening, it isn't unknown for a poacher who's fond of drink to accidentally drown while under the influence.'

'Perhaps you're right, Vince,' said Faro weakly, almost eager to be persuaded.

'Of course I am.' Vince closed the wardrobe door, thrust his valise under the bed and said: 'Let's join the others.' He led the way downstairs to where Owen and Olivia were already enjoying afternoon tea in front of the large fire.

'Two more places, Mr Bowden, if you please,' said Faro.

Approaching the Gilchrists, he saw that an adjoining side table was solely occupied by Imogen Crowe, awaiting her order.

She looked up and smiled a friendly greeting.

Faro, somewhat taken aback, suspected that the recipient of this transformed Miss Crowe was his handsome stepson. Vince, with his fair curls, his deceptively angelic countenance, had that effect upon young women.

'Two places, did you say, sir?' said Bowden.

Olivia looked at Faro, smiled encouragingly and said quite loudly, 'Why don't you ask your friend to join us, sir?'

'Heavens, no.' whispered Faro, assiduously turning his back on Miss Crowe.

Olivia considered that lady for a moment and gave him a reproachful look. 'A pity to have her sitting on her own, is it not?' she murmured.

'Yes, indeed,' responded her brother with an admiring glance at Miss Crowe. 'The more the merrier, I always say.'

Vince turned, joined in his friend's enthusiasm, bowed in her direction and was rewarded by even more smiling Irish eyes, a pretty inclination of dark red curls.

Turning sharply to Faro he said enthusiastically, 'Yes, Stepfather, why not?'

'No,' said Faro firmly, almost too loudly for politeness. While he studied his empty plate with tightly closed lips, the others looked across at Miss Crowe, were pleased by what they saw and stared back at Faro reproachfully.

Their expressions made him angry. Mrs Dewar's weakness it seemed was shared not only by most womankind, but had spread to his own family and friends.

Matchmaking. He grimaced, he was sick and tired of it. He had thought Olivia Gilchrist might have more sense.

But as the tea was poured and the scones eaten at a leisurely pace, Miss Crowe was forgotten. Out of the corner of his eye Faro thankfully watched her depart. Grateful that the jarring incident created by her presence was over, he joined in the laughter as the two young men reminisced about college days, meanwhile keeping a sharp eye on Olivia's reaction to his stepson.

He would have been shocked indeed had someone told him that he was indulging in exactly the same behaviour as poor Mrs Dewar and that this pairing off was endemic in the human race.

The young couple seemed so fond of each other, laughing, teasing. Almost like brother and sister. He groaned. That was what he feared, that they had been dear friends too long for romance to blossom.

'Delightful place, this, sir,' said Owen. 'You were lucky to find it. Full of atmosphere.'

'It wasn't difficult to find,' Faro laughed. 'It's the only place.'

'My bedroom floor squeaks abominably,' said Vince.

'Quite right,' said Olivia solemnly. 'That will keep you from straying.' Then to Faro: 'Great-Aunt is so sorry she couldn't accommodate Vince too. Her cottage is just too tiny. Have you told your stepfather the arrangements, Vince?'

'I haven't. We've had other matters to discuss.'

'Nothing as important as the party.' And leaning over, she said: 'You mean he hasn't told you that we have been invited to the Castle here for Great-Aunt's birthday celebration?'

When Faro shook his head, she looked at Vince.

'Dash it all, Olivia. I've been keeping it a secret – a surprise, as you told me,' was the reproachful response.

'Honestly – men!' Olivia gave a despairing sigh and turned to her brother. 'You tell him, Owen. This is so exciting – you being here already, sir,' she added to Faro.

'Hold on, Livvy,' said Owen. 'We've just heard ourselves, when we called in to see Great-Aunt. She was governess to Mark Elrigg long ago. They have always been very close. When Mark's mother died, he didn't even as a child get on very well with his stepfather –' He looked at Vince and Faro. 'Not like some I could name. Anyway, he turned to Great-Aunt for love and comfort. He's never forgotten her kindness and he's kept in touch with her by letter and frequent visits to Branxton.'

'The really exciting part is that we've been asked to stay the night at the Castle after the party. I'm so looking forward to that,' Olivia put in. 'Apparently Mark wouldn't hear of his dear Miss Gilchrist travelling all that way back home.'

'Great-Aunt says he has a very special surprise for her...'

Anything concerning the Elriggs was of great interest and this indeed might prove a rewarding turn of events, thought Faro. As Vince's glum expression betrayed a certain lack of enthusiasm, he realised that any change of plans, or possible new evidence of mayhem at the Castle, upset his own wish to get Faro away from Elrigg as speedily as possible.

At the moment, however, Faro's chief concern was how he could escape the embarrassing situation whereby his real identity would have to be revealed and explained to Mark and Lady Elrigg.

Suddenly he became aware of a figure hovering behind him. 'Excuse me, sir.'

It was Dewar. 'Could I have a word, sir?'

As the constable strode purposefully in the direction of the bar, Faro followed him with a sinking sense of disaster. Long ago he had realised the truth of the maxim that murders, like troubles, seldom come singly.

He was not to be disappointed.

'Miss Halliday's cottage has been broken into, sir. She's been badly hurt. Sergeant Yarrow found her lying at the bottom of the staircase when he went to collect his quarantine papers for the authorities. He reckons she probably disturbed the burglar.'

'Have you any idea who...?'

Dewar shrugged. 'Sergeant reckons it might have been Duffy.'

'Duffy? But how could –'

'Well, Dr Brand says it might have happened late last night, before the accident.' Dewar shook his head. 'I don't agree, sir. Duffy was ready to lift anything that ain't nailed down, but I've never known him resort to breaking and entering.'

'Was there a motive?'

'What kind of motive would that be, sir?'

'Did she have anything of value?' Faro said impatiently, remembering a few nice pieces of furniture, antiques but hardly things with an immediate resale value for a poacher. 'And how did he get in?'

Dewar looked astonished at this remark. 'Bless you, sir, no one round here ever locks their doors. We don't live in that kind of society. We all trust one another.'

In Miss Halliday's case badly misplaced, thought Faro, as Dewar's naivety confirmed his original assessment that the constable's reaction to real crime would be shocked disbelief. Such things were unthinkable in Elrigg.

'Where is Miss Halliday now?'

'Dr Brand says she's concussed, got a nasty shock, that's for sure. The minister's wife will look after her till she's better. We're a caring society, here, sir,' he added defensively in case Faro should be in any danger of thinking otherwise.

He had indeed read Faro's thoughts. Very caring indeed, especially when some person hit her on the head and left her for dead.

'Did she have any difficult pupils?' he asked.

Dewar's eyes widened in horror at such implication.

'I get your drift, sir. But you're wrong. The children are all obedient and law abiding, sir. Things might be different in big cities like where you come from,' he added stiffly. 'But here the bairns are brought up from their earliest days to be God-fearing and to respect their parents and other people. Besides, Miss Halliday's loved by everyone; she's taught several decades their three Rs. Now if you'll excuse me, sir.'

With an air of silent reprimand, Dewar saluted him gravely and marched out of the inn.

At the table he had just left, the twins were preparing to return to Branxton. Waving them off, the air heavy with instructions for the following day's festivities, Vince smiled: 'Well, that's that. What shall we do now?'

'A walk, perhaps.'

'A good idea. What did your local constable want?'

Faro told him about Miss Halliday and the break-in.

Vince, adept at reading his stepfather's mind, sighed deeply. 'So that's where we are going?'

Faro nodded eagerly. 'Bearing in mind that doors are never locked in this law-abiding community, I thought we might avail ourselves of a little private investigation.'

Vince's sigh was despairing this time. 'You never give up, do you, Stepfather?'

'She was very kind to me. I owe her that much. And I'm very curious. I'd like you to see her paintings too. They're very impressive.'

'How far is it?' Vince demanded, in a voice notable for a lack of enthusiasm, Faro having temporarily overlooked the fact that his stepson felt the same way about amateur painters as he did about amateur thespians.

'We'll do it in about forty minutes, there and back,' he said encouragingly.

Vince thought about it and yawned. 'Forgive me, Stepfather, if I don't come with you. Truth is, I'm devilish tired. Out till the wee sma' hours delivering a baby.'

Faro smiled sympathetically. 'I've noticed that they always seem to choose times when it's least convenient for your social life.'

Vince nodded, stretching his arms above his head. 'Must be on form for the long day tomorrow. I think, if you'll excuse me, I'll take a bath. Bowden assures me hip baths are readily available. He even has a special room put aside for such ablutions. See you at dinner, eh?'

Setting off for Miss Halliday's cottage alone, Faro felt a little lonely, his spirits cast down. When he got too close to a case and became enmeshed and thoroughly baffled, it was almost always Vince who could be relied upon to stand back and view it coolly from a different and often enlightened angle.

If only Vince had been free of other obligations this time. He shouldn't really feel like this, he told himself sternly, he had guessed that his stepson would not be a great deal of use on this occasion, involved with the Gilchrists and their great-aunt's birthday celebrations.

He sighed. The sooner he got used to the new regime, the better for everyone. It was what he had always wanted for Vince, to see him happy with a girl like Olivia. What he was experiencing, this sudden bitter shaft of loneliness, was no more than the normal pattern of parenthood, a glimpse into the future when he would no longer enjoy the comradeship they had shared since Vince's boyhood.

Opening the door of Miss Halliday's cottage cautiously, he noted that it was remarkably tidy inside. In the kitchen, a few papers lay scattered on the floor, a broken ornament, a shattered cup, but there was a gold watch on the sideboard and a purse full of sovereigns.

Money had not been the burglar's object.

Turning back again to the kitchen table, he noticed that it was set for two people, one each side of the table; one cup was almost full, the other empty.

He stood back and regarded the scene carefully. The clues were all there.

Miss Halliday had been attacked by someone she knew well enough to take out her best china. He looked at the mantelpiece and visualised the scene indicated by two broken ornaments and a framed photograph on the floor, swept off by her arm no doubt as she fought off her attacker.

Picking them up and returning them to their rightful places with the complete recall that was one of his remarkable assets, he saw that Sir Walter Scott's letter was missing. Walking round the table again, he stood beside the cup of tea that had been abandoned. Opposite it, the painting of the boy Eric was missing.

As he closed the door, he had no longer the least doubt that the killer of Sir Archie and the poacher Duffy had also attacked Miss Halliday. His experience indicated that the three people were linked in a murderous chain of events.

Or could it be that the presence of Detective Inspector Faro upset someone with a guilty conscience?

Going over his conversation with Miss Halliday, he decided to cross the road to the Castle lodge and call upon Miss Imogen Crowe.

There was no response and, trying the door, he found it unlocked. He was not as surprised as he should have been to see Scott's letter lying on her kitchen table.

He picked it up. His fascinated re-reading of it was interrupted by Miss Crowe's arrival.

Then she saw what he held and pointed an accusing finger.

'No!' He forestalled her accusation with one of his own. 'This is, I believe, the property of Miss Halliday.'

'It is. She lent it to me. To make a copy.'

Faro laughed. 'Oh, did she indeed? And do you know where she is at the moment?'

Miss Crowe shrugged. 'Across the road in her house, I expect.'

Faro leaned on the table. 'Then you expect wrong, miss. Someone broke into her house last night. She was attacked –'

There was a shocked exclamation as Miss Crowe asked: 'Is she all right?'

'She is unconscious.'

'Where is she? I'll look after her –'

'No need to trouble yourself, the minister's wife is more than capable.'

Miss Crowe clenched her hands. 'Will she recover?'

'Who knows?'

'But how did it happen – I mean –'

'We gather she intercepted a burglar.'

'A burglar?' whispered Imogen Crowe.

'That is so, miss.' And, laying down the letter, he tapped its frame. 'I suppose you know you could go to gaol for that.'

He had the dubious satisfaction of seeing her face turn deathly pale, white as the cloth on the kitchen table, as he turned on his heel and left her.

22

At the inn, Faro found Vince looking forward to supper. Refreshed and bathed, in a good humour, he was eager to listen to his stepfather's latest experiences.

'You had better get it all off your chest,' he said, 'then you can consider the case finally closed and we can begin to enjoy ourselves.'

'First of all, there's this visit to the Castle. They don't know I'm a detective and it's bound to come out.'

'Ah, I'm well ahead of you there. I've explained to the twins and Miss Gilchrist that you are on a secret mission of national importance. They were very impressed and you can rely on them not to give the game away. Now, what have you found out?'

As Faro went through the details, item by item, Vince listened carefully: 'One thing is obvious, those missing paintings are tucked safely away somewhere in the attics of the Castle. To be brought out and discreetly restored to their original places, once Her Majesty has forgotten all about then. I think it will be safe enough for I doubt whether Bertie will make any more incognito visits to Elrigg, don't you agree?'

'Indeed. Two unfortunate fatal accidents should be enough to cool even his ardour,' said Faro.

'And you can certainly remove from your mind that he had any part in the bull's horn business. That is hardly his style. I understand he is not even passable with a rifle.' Vince paused to take a second helping of game pie. 'I'd hazard a guess that Philip Gray's death was an accident. As for the laird's – that comes into the dubious area of "might-have-been-murder". Trouble was you arrived far too late to be of any use proving anything to the contrary.'

'True enough, even if they had wanted my help,' said Faro. 'With the blessing of Sergeant Yarrow and the Northumberland Constabulary, the trail was cold.'

'Worse than that, Stepfather. As far as I can see there isn't a shred of real evidence against anyone. As for your suspects.

Well, I'd be prepared to bet a great deal of money that it wasn't Lady Elrigg in the classic role of husband-murderer. I'm sure she had enough experience of the wicked world not to get rid of the goose that was laying the golden eggs for her.

'As for Mark. I'll tell you more when I meet him, but I'd be surprised because it doesn't sound likely, from what I've heard of him through the Gilchrists. And from what you've told me, there is no real evidence of guilty lovers.'

Vince gestured with his fork. 'I wonder why there are no children to the Elrigg marriage. As a doctor, that intrigues me most. Not only the first marriage to Mark's mother, which proves she could bear children, but what about the second to this nubile young woman? Could it be, do you think, that Sir Archie was impotent? That he knew it and that's why he was prepared, even eager, to make his stepson, who had a dash of the genuine Elrigg blood, his heir?'

'You could be right, Vince lad. That possibility had never occurred to me, and it's certainly an interesting one. Explains a lot of things.'

'Who else have we?' Vince looked down at Faro's notes lying beside his plate. 'You do this uncommonly well, Stepfather. You are to be congratulated on a masterpiece of clarity. Sergeant Yarrow will be grateful, I'm sure. Let's see...

'Hector Elrigg, the disgruntled archaeologist who believes that he was cheated out of his inheritance by a reprobate father. He would be my best bet, he has the most impressive motive, a wound festering over the years. I realise you haven't much in the way of evidence, but still – there may be something important we've missed.'

As Vince flicked back through the notes, Faro shook his head. 'You may be right, yet I have a feeling – no more than that – just a feeling that we're dealing with the dedicated historian who is keener on getting on with his work of digging the hillfort and the standing stones, than being laird of Elrigg.'

'Meanwhile, of course,' said Vince, 'we may have a number of dissatisfied tenants whose activities as well as their names are unknown to you, since there has been neither time nor opportunity to conduct a thorough investigation. I appreciate that distances to be travelled single-handed are somewhat daunting.'

And rubbing his chin thoughtfully, 'What about the good Dr Brand whose daughter drowned in the ornamental lake? If she was seduced by the laird, he would have good reason for killing him off.'

'But since you've suggested the impotence factor, the pregnancy fits in with the lover who was sent away in disgrace.'

'True,' said Vince. 'Then who are we left with? The unfortunate poacher, Duffy.'

'No, but I do think he knew something, or had seen something.'

'Perhaps he gossiped and was overheard?'

Faro agreed. 'Not a man of discreet habits, I gather from Bowden. Blackmail would be a profitable business for him.'

Vince consulted the list again. 'I think we can safely cross off the Reverend Cairncross in spite of his daughter's odd reaction to the Elriggs. And, as a victim, Miss Halliday.'

'I can't see any reason why she would want to murder Sir Archie,' said Faro.

'But there's always Miss Imogen Crowe and your latest foray into a different sort of crime. What was her motive for stealing the portrait?'

'It wasn't the portrait, Vince. It was Sir Walter Scott's letter.' Faro frowned. 'I keep going over that scene in Miss Halliday's kitchen. There's something there, if only I could remember. Something I saw.'

'It'll come, I'm sure,' said Vince soothingly. 'The only link I can see is that she is Irish and so was Philip Gray – But that's a bit tenuous.'

Vince was aware that he no longer had his stepfather's attention. 'What's wrong?'

Faro shook his head. 'Just an idea I've had.'

He was silent so long that Vince laid aside the papers and said: 'By the way, the carriage is coming for us in the morning. There's to be a Maytime pageant at Branxton, with a celebration of Miss Gilchrist's birthday among other things. There'll be floats, so I'm told, with the children performing scenes from history, a monologue written about the Battle of Flodden. What do you think, Stepfather?'

'Think?' Faro came back to him with a start. 'I don't know,' he said lamely. 'What was it you were saying?'

Patiently Vince repeated the programme of the day's activities and Faro shook his head very firmly. 'No, Vince lad. Absolutely not. I'll save my energies for the festivities at the Castle. I just might have to have my wits about me then.'

Vince considered him. 'Anything you'd like to share, Stepfather? Some new observations?'

Faro smiled. 'Only when I can give them substance and that may take some time.'

Next morning, having seen Vince off, Faro was deciding how he could most profitably spend his day when Sergeant Yarrow arrived at the inn. After a perfunctory greeting he saluted Faro gravely and said: 'Sir, I owe you an apology.'

Faro smiled vaguely. 'Ah, you have decided to remove me from your list of suspects?'

Yarrow looked contrite. 'Dewar has just told me who you are, sir. I cannot tell you –'

'Think nothing of it, Sergeant. It's the sort of mistake any policeman worth his salt might make. You are to be commended for that.'

Yarrow smiled wryly. 'It's the lesson we all learn, isn't it? First on the scene most often is the prime suspect.'

'And a stranger in the neighbourhood, too,' said Faro.

Yarrow held out his hand. 'May I take this opportunity of welcoming your assistance, sir? Anything at all you may have observed during your time here might be of considerable help to us.'

When Faro didn't reply immediately, Yarrow continued to regard him quizzically. 'You think Sir Archie was murdered? Political, maybe. Equerry to the Prince of Wales and that sort of thing?'

Faro remained silent, and Yarrow shrugged. 'Come now, sir, that is obviously the real reason why you are here. We do know something of your background –'

'Not in this instance, Sergeant. Such matters – crimes or political investigations, if you wish – in Elrigg are entirely the province of the Northumberland Constabulary or the Metropolitan Police, you know that. And Edinburgh City Police would have no right to interfere.'

Yarrow's eyebrows raised mockingly. 'I can hardly believe that a man as important as yourself would have been sent down here to investigate some missing paintings.'

'You must take my word for that. Let us say I was here on behalf of a very important client. That is all I can tell you, I'm afraid.'

Sergeant Yarrow looked thoughtful. 'I wonder if you have any ideas about Miss Halliday's attacker.'

'None at all. Living here you must know a great deal more than any stranger about likely suspects.'

'True. There aren't many, I can assure you. Take the man Duffy, he's the nearest we get to criminal activities, he's well known as a petty thief, but we never have been able to pin anything big on him, he was too wily for that.'

Faro remembered Dewar's words. 'You think he might have attacked Miss Halliday first – before his accident?'

Yarrow nodded eagerly. 'I'm positive that's the way of it. Miss Halliday's homemade wine was famous. He couldn't resist drink of any kind. Might have sampled a bottle with dire effects. She caught him at it – and we know the rest.'

Faro looked at him. There had been no evidence of empty bottles or glasses in that disturbed room. 'You are seriously considering this theory?'

'Except that we have no record of Duffy ever being violent, or of breaking and entering a private residence. A genial rogue rather than a genuine criminal.'

'What about the gypsies? Have you considered that there might be less genial rogues among them and that their arrival coincided with Miss Halliday's attack and Duffy's death?'

Yarrow shook his head. 'Assault and battery isn't their style at all. Like Duffy, it's more clothes off lines and a hen or two.' After a long pause, he added: 'There is, however, one matter which is perturbing me greatly at the moment. A matter that is well out of our province, but perhaps with your greater experience you could advise me.'

'If I can.'

Again Yarrow hesitated before continuing: 'It concerns the woman Imogen Crowe. Did you know, by any chance, that she has a police record?'

Faro shook his head. This was a surprise – or was it?

'What did she do?'

'Went to gaol for harbouring Fenian terrorists. I've been keeping an eye on Miss Crowe's activities. I don't suppose you remember the case in Scotland. There was a Brendan Crowe – her uncle and guardian, so she claimed – who took a shot at the Queen riding in St James's Park.'

Faro sighed. 'I vaguely remember the case. There have been similar incidents. About twelve years ago, wasn't it?'

Yarrow regarded him admiringly. 'Correct first time, sir. Year after the Prince Consort died and Her Majesty had gained a great deal of public support and sympathy, her being a widow and so forth. Crowe was shot and wounded by us – we cornered him but he managed to escape to his lodgings. Topped himself before he could be arrested –'

'And his niece – Miss Crowe?'

'She was in the house with him, fought the arresting officers tooth and nail. Protested that she knew nothing about his political activities. We didn't believe a word of it, naturally, so she was sentenced as accessory. Lucky for her that he never stood trial or she might have been hanged.'

'She must have been very young at the time,' said Faro.

'Not all that young, sir, eighteen. Old enough to know right from wrong, I'd say.'

It was a situation Faro knew well and one that he deplored. A public outcry means that the police are expected to produce a scapegoat, someone the mob could vent their anger on. An eighteen-year-old girl, terrified and confused, horrified by her guardian's death, would do excellently.

'She was very probably speaking the truth,' he said.

'Once a terrorist, always a terrorist.' Yarrow gave him a hard look. Clearly, he did not share Faro's sentiments. 'An eye for an eye, a tooth for a tooth,' he added grimly. 'The Bible got it right, you know.'

When Faro said nothing, Yarrow added: 'We put her behind bars for a couple of years.'

'What is she doing in Elrigg then?' asked Faro, already knowing the answer.

'She writes books.'

'Romances?'

Yarrow laughed. 'Hardly, sir. About Women's Rights, the

sort of thing females who have been in prison write if they are literate, encouraging other women to believe that they've been ill-treated – all that sort of nonsense. Shouldn't be allowed.'

Faro felt a fleeting compassion for Imogen Crowe, knowing only too well the notorious conditions of women's prisons in London: verminous, ill-treated prisoners, starved and beaten. Unthinkable that she might have been innocent, as she claimed.

Yarrow was regarding him shrewdly. 'When Dewar told me about you, my first thought was: is he here in connection with Imogen Crowe? And your very important client has confirmed that for me. You can rely on my discretion, of course, sir, and you don't need to say whether I'm right or wrong. I'll understand perfectly.'

When Faro smiled, he continued: 'I'd hazard a guess that the authorities believe, with the Prince of Wales being a frequent visitor to the Castle, that there might be a Fenian plot and that she's here to spy for them.'

As he waited for a reply, he scanned Faro's face carefully. 'You think she might be involved in something?'

This was a new aspect of the case which had never occurred to Faro. Could Yarrow be right? There had been no mention of Fenian activities. Surely the Prime Minister would have known and the Edinburgh City Police would have been alerted in the interests of national security even though it was outside their province.

He shook his head. 'It doesn't sound like a Fenian plot to me.'

Yarrow looked disappointed. 'That actor fellow. The one who was gored by one of the wild cattle. He was Irish too, been on the boards in Dublin. Food for thought, eh, sir?' he said.

'It is indeed.'

'I'm about to look in and see how Miss Halliday is. I don't suppose...'

'Yes, of course, I'll come with you.'

As they walked towards the Manse, in the light of Yarrow's information regarding Imogen Crowe, Faro decided to err on the side of caution and keep his observations – and his notes – to himself for the time being.

23

Mrs Cairncross's relieved expression as she greeted them at the Manse said that their worst fears had not been realised.

'Yes, she's awake, the poor dear. Dr Brand's with her now.'

At that moment the doctor descended the stairs, smiling and shaking his head when he saw Yarrow. 'You won't be needed after all, Sergeant. No need to put cuffs on anyone this time. Simple explanation. Rattling window woke her up, she came down and tripped on the stairs in the dark. Tried to save herself, grabbed at the mantelpiece and hit her head a mighty crack on the hearth as she fell. Good job she's got a thick skull –'

'There was no burglar?' Yarrow sounded shocked.

'That's what she says,' said the doctor cheerfully, fastening his bag and turning to Mrs Cairncross. 'Told me to say, yes, please, ma'am, she would like her breakfast now.'

'Can we see her?' demanded Yarrow.

'Later. We must keep her quiet for a while.' And to the minister's wife, 'Keep her in bed for a day or two, if you can manage.'

'I'll do my best, Doctor, but she's a very determined lady.'

Dr Brand frowned, looking at the two men. 'I think I'd best be honest with you. I don't think our dear Miss Halliday is speaking the truth.'

'I knew it,' said Yarrow triumphantly. 'She's protecting someone, that's for sure.'

The doctor smiled. 'Only herself, Sergeant.'

'I don't understand.'

'You might if you were her age. She should have retired long ago but she's determined to keep on teaching until she drops – which, candidly, she will do quite soon if she doesn't give up. You see, the fall she took I believe was due to a mild heart attack.'

'A heart attack, oh, the poor dear,' said Mrs Cairncross. 'How on earth will she continue at the school?'

'I suspect the very same thought is troubling her, so she makes light of it, says it was only a bad fall. I've examined her and found no damage, no paralysis of arms and legs or facial muscles, so we can deduce that this was just a warning. A warning that she must take seriously. Like some of my other patients,' he added, darting a significant look at Yarrow. 'You haven't been to see me lately.'

'I'm much too busy to fuss about aches and pains. They've been with me for a long time,' said Yarrow brusquely, leaving Faro to wonder if the greyness of his complexion was natural or due to some more serious cause, as Imogen Crowe had hinted.

'What about the school, Doctor?' asked Mrs Cairncross, remembering her brood of children and their future.

'She must get help, a younger woman, to take some of the burden –'

He was interrupted by Miss Halliday, calling from upstairs: 'Hell – o – Mrs Cairncross, are you there?'

Mrs Cairncross picked up the tray. 'She's out of bed. I knew it. Once my back is turned. Coming, my dear.'

'I'll be back when she's had her breakfast,' said Yarrow.

Dr Brand nodded. 'You come with me, Sergeant.'

When Yarrow protested with a helpless look at Faro, the doctor seized his arm firmly. 'I've got some of my splendid pills waiting for you.'

Faro lingered, waiting for Mrs Cairncross to return. 'Do you think I might have a few words with Miss Halliday? I'm to leave Elrigg shortly. This might be my last chance.'

Mrs Cairncross looked doubtful. 'If you think it will be all right, sir. You won't tire her, will you?'

Miss Halliday was sitting up in bed, her face badly bruised, but otherwise she was remarkably cheerful. When Faro exclaimed sympathetically, she smiled painfully. 'I'm perfectly all right, no bones broken. A silly accident, but I'll be back with my children on Monday. It's good of you to come and say goodbye –'

'There is something else, Miss Halliday. I realise this is an inappropriate time – Sir Walter's letter. I was absolutely fascinated –'

'And you would like a copy. I don't have it, I'm afraid.'

She laughed at his solemn expression. 'Ask Miss Crowe. She looked in after you yesterday and I lent it to her for that very reason.'

And Faro had the grace to feel ashamed.

Miss Molly Gilchrist's visit to Elrigg Castle was to be memorable for its surprises, none of which could have been anticipated by the guests.

The sunny warm weather held and the gardens, with their budding trees laden with birdsong, made a pretty and nostalgic background for the old lady, whose face was a map of her life, of its joys and sorrows. Her eyes, still bright, constantly searched for her beloved pupil, Mark.

'Where is he?' she whispered, as she perambulated the gardens on Faro's arm. 'Dear, dear, I did expect he would be here to greet his guests,' she added anxiously. 'And he did promise me a nice surprise. We share the same birthday, you know. He is twenty-five today,' she added proudly.

'A double celebration,' said Owen. 'No doubt that is what is keeping him.'

And Faro remembered that this day was the day Mark came of age, when all of Elrigg would be his.

'These gardens must be full of memories for you,' said Olivia. 'Is it exciting to come back?'

'It is indeed.' And Miss Gilchrist proceeded to regale them with stories of Mark's childhood. As is so often the case of rich children whose parents had little time for them, motherless Mark had been treated by her more as son than pupil. He had returned her devotion and had kept in touch with her over the years, by letter and by frequent visits.

Suddenly two figures emerged from the topiary surrounding the rose garden. Lady Elrigg walked swiftly towards them, apologising for Mark's absence. This was greeted by an audible sigh of relief from Miss Gilchrist and, as introductions were made, Faro observed that Lady Elrigg's companion Miss Kent stepped back, as if eager for the shadows of the great cypress hedge. She curtsied to the group and then, in an almost imperceptible gesture, touched her mistress's arm.

Still smiling, Lady Elrigg turned to her immediately and together they moved a little distance away. Apparently the talk was brief but urgent, for with a quick glance towards the assembled guests, Miss Kent hurried of in the direction of the Castle.

'Some urgent domestic niceties I seem to have overlooked for this evening,' they were informed. 'Fortunately Miss Kent remembered.'

But Faro wasn't all sure she was speaking the truth. Her colour had heightened slightly and he felt certain her sharp, uncertain glance had concerned the guests and something more important than was warranted by a housekeeping consultation.

'I trust your rooms are quite comfortable?' At the murmurs of 'Very' and 'Delightful', Lady Elrigg smiled. 'And now, if you will excuse me. We will meet again in the drawing-room at five o'clock.'

'Will Mark be there?' Miss Gilchrist asked in a bewildered voice.

Lady Elrigg took her hands. 'Of course, my dear, of course, he will. Now do enjoy the last of the sunshine while you can.'

When they returned to the house, Mark rushed out to greet them. Exchanging hugs and kisses with a relieved and tearful Miss Gilchrist, he said: 'I so wanted you to be here, I have a very special surprise for you.'

It was a surprise for everyone. In the drawing-room Poppy Elrigg now wore a gown of violet lace and the Elrigg diamonds. Even in humbler attire she would have overshadowed every other female present.

Hector Elrigg arrived with Dr Brand and both greeted the Elriggs with a geniality that raised Faro's eyebrows a little considering how vehemently they had both railed against Sir Archie. Presumably their angry feelings did not extend to his pretty widow and his stepson.

Faro made a mental note that Hector in particular had taken great pains with his appearance. His suit, although a little out of fashion, was considerably smarter than the rough countryman's attire he normally appeared in. Dr Brand too was wearing what Faro suspected was his Sunday best.

The latecomer was Imogen Crowe.

This was indeed a surprise and not a particularly pleasant one for Faro. He suspected he would be seated next to her at dinner. But much was to happen before that.

'Right,' said Mark. 'Now that everyone is here, will you please follow me.' He gave his ex-governess his arm and the group made their way back down the staircase out and across the courtyard to the private chapel which had served the Elriggs of several past generations.

With his hand on the open door, Mark put his arm about Miss Gilchrist. 'This dear lady, as you all know, has been my mother in every way but the accident of birth. She is the dearest in all the world to me – except for one person,' he smiled, 'and it is appropriate that she should stand by me on my wedding day.'

'Your wedding day!'

There was a very audible gasp from the group at this unexpected announcement. He said: 'Yes, dear friends, I am to be married.' And throwing open the door, he said, 'There is my bride.'

Standing before Reverend Cairncross at the altar were his wife and, now radiant in her bridal gown, their once-weeping daughter Harriet, whom Faro had met briefly in the churchyard.

Turning to Molly Gilchrist, Mark said: 'I shall want your blessing.'

'That you have always had, my dearest boy. I am so happy for you.'

And so they were wed. Poppy Elrigg was obviously delighted and had relished helping Mark plan the event with such great secrecy. As for Faro, he was glad to have been in grave error regarding the affection of two young people drawn together in a trying household.

Reverend Cairncross and his wife were doubtless gratified by this conclusion to their own problem for, without wishing to be indelicate, or stare too heavily, it was obvious that Harriet was pregnant.

The wedding party returned jubilantly indoors to dine in the elegant room with its eighteenth-century damask wall-hangings, faded but still intact. The faces of ghostly bygone

Elriggs stared down from the walls at the diners in a setting that was everything an old family servant like Miss Gilchrist could have wished for.

It was also an occasion to provide Faro with some interesting observations and conclusions.

'Miss Kent has asked to be excused,' said Poppy Elrigg. 'She suffers from wretched headaches and this one refuses to disappear.'

Vince offered pills, Aunt Molly offered reliable home remedies seconded very firmly by Imogen, while Olivia and her brother offered sympathy.

'I was hoping to see her again,' murmured Olivia to Vince and when he said 'Really', she put a hand to her lips, glancing at Faro, who had overheard.

'Shh – tell you later.'

As Faro had suspected, Imogen Crowe was seated next to him at the table with Hector on her other side. However, with much good food and wine, particularly the latter, he found himself oddly forgiving and forgetful of her disagreeable qualities. They talked about books and Faro found her also knowledgeable about his own particular favourites, Shakespeare and Mr Dickens.

Quite remarkably so, he thought, and found himself looking at her and remembering what Yarrow had told him about her past. Miss Crowe having survived a gaol sentence and writing books about it would never have been tolerated at most Edinburgh dinner tables. In the society he knew there, she would be shunned, a social outcast.

There was one more event to be celebrated as Reverend Cairncross invited them to raise their glasses in birthday greetings to 'Mark who now inherits the estates of Elrigg and to Sir Hector who now inherits the title,'

In return Mark held up his glass to Hector. 'And you, my dear cousin, have my blessing to excavate the hillfort, the standing stones and any piece of Elrigg that takes your fancy.'

Hector was delighted, and another toast was drunk to his success.

Faro was naturally suspicious of happy endings, but tonight he listened, mellowed by good wine and content with the conversations circling about him.

Across the table, Dr Brand deplored the gypsies' annual presence while Imogen Crowe defended them.

'They're not to be trusted, miss, there's always the danger that they leave our pasture gates open – they are not too fussy about bars and latches, I can tell you.'

'They aren't used to gates, Doctor. It is not part of their way of life...'

Faro only half listened to the argument.

'Don't you agree with me, Mr Faro?'

Not quite sure what he was expected to agree with, Miss Crowe speedily enlightened him.

'They make their annual pilgrimage to the crowning of their king at Kirk Yetholm every year.'

'Another king,' said Faro. 'Does this entail a mortal combat like your wild cattle?'

Imogen Crowe eyed him coldly. 'Not at all – the gypsy king –'

But her explanation was cut short as Hector interrupted: 'Mr Faro is fascinated by the cattle, Mark.'

'Are you indeed?' asked Poppy since Mark and his bride had their heads close together, lost in some magic world of the newlyweds. 'Do show him, Hector. The wooden box on the desk.'

Hector brought out the yellowed parchment and laid it before Faro. 'Perhaps you'd like me to read it to you: this is their earliest recorded mention – when the Scots troops occupied us in January – see, 1645:

> 'What with the Soldiers and this continuing Storme, if it lye but one Month more, there will bee neither Beast nor Sheepe left in the country. Your Honour's Deere and wild Cattle I fear will all dye, do what we can: The like of this Storme hath not been known by any living in the Country. The Lord look upon us in mercy, if it be his blessed Will.'

'Fascinating,' said Faro.

'There is another account,' said Hector, warming to his subject. 'Our neighbour, the Earl of Tankerville, celebrated his son's birthday in 1756 by ordering a great number of the cattle to be slaughtered, which, with a proportionate quantity of bread, were distributed among upwards of six hundred poor people.

'It's certainly a wonder the animals did survive.'

'They had no predators, Hector,' said the minister.

'Only man,' put in Dr Brand. 'The worst predator of all.'

But Faro shivered, as the ghost of his recurring nightmare glared down at him from the wall opposite. The head and horns of an enraged bull.

24

When Faro and Vince left the Castle some hours later, dawn was breaking and the ladies had long since retired. Only Imogen Crowe remained, in earnest and, Faro admitted disgustedly, argumentative conversation.

Although she represented the new breed of womankind of whom he was a little contemptuous and a little in awe, gallantry remained. However, his offer to see her safely down the drive was scornfully rejected.

'Good heavens, no. I wouldn't dream of it.'

Alarmed in case she had misinterpreted his offer, he said hastily, 'Vince and I will be leaving in the carriage shortly.'

'Carriage, indeed. It's no distance at all and the walk will do me good. I need the exercise and you gentlemen need your port. Yes, you too, Hector,' she said firmly.

Hector looked so put out that Faro, regarding him sharply, wondered if he was in love with Miss Crowe. A situation he found personally unimaginable, although on closer acquaintance she was pretty enough and intelligent too. But he cared little for opinionated young females with their militant views regarding women's position in society.

'If they ever get the vote, heaven help us,' he said to Hector, who still looked annoyed at Imogen's rejection of his company as he shared their carriage, silently wrapped in his own thoughts.

As they prepared to retire for what remained of the night, Vince yawned: 'What a day, Stepfather. And what a curious wedding. At least Mark is one suspect you can cross off your list.'

Faro didn't care to disillusion Vince by suggesting that the possible intrigue of the pretty widow and her stepson had been neatly explained, simply to give rise to another more sinister reason for Sir Archie's demise: the obstacle to Mark's marriage had been conveniently removed.

Faro would have given much to know the exact location of Mark Elrigg, expert archer, when his stepfather died. Murders had been committed for much less than Mark's and Harriet's urgency.

Perturbed by his stepfather's silence, Vince asked: 'What do you make of Miss Crowe?'

'Not a great deal,' said Faro shortly.

'She's quite a stunner,' was the encouraging reply.

'Indeed. I hadn't noticed,' said Faro, removing his cravat. 'And what about Olivia?'

'Livvy. What about her?'

'Aren't you being, well, a little unfaithful?'

'Who said I had to be faithful to Olivia?' Vince demanded sharply.

'I presumed –'

'You presumed wrongly, Stepfather. I have no intentions but those of the friendliest towards Olivia.' He looked out of the window at the sun rising behind the standing stones. 'At present.'

Faro was thankful for those two words when Vince went on: 'Besides it wasn't for myself I was putting forward Miss Crowe as a marriageable proposition. She is a little old for me, past thirty, I should think. I had her in mind for you.'

You – thought –' Faro was at a loss for words.

'Indeed I did. You were getting along famously and I noticed, and I'm sure everyone else did, what a handsome pair you made.'

'Then you and everyone else are quite wrong.'

'Come, Stepfather, you really should have a wife,' Vince sounded suddenly sober. 'You aren't all that old – in your prime, most men would say, and Rose and Emily won't always have Grandma, they would take a young stepmother to their heart.'

'Indeed? As you took a stepfather to your heart at their age,' said Faro in bitter tones that reminded Vince of how deeply he had resented his mother marrying a policeman.

'It was only until I got to know you,' Vince said meekly.

'And may I remind you that I worked very hard at that. You were an obnoxious child.' Faro grinned suddenly. 'Amazing that you turned out so well under my guidance.'

Vince shared the laughter and then Faro said sadly: 'I'll never find another woman like your mother again. If I could, I swear I'd marry her. What I don't want is a clever opinionated wife, I want someone nice, kind, loving and homely – like my Lizzie.'

Vince smiled. 'There is someone who fits that description exactly, you know, Stepfather. And she is right under your nose every day.'

Faro frowned. 'Who could that be?'

'Our housekeeper – Mrs Brook, of course.'

Faro opened his mouth, closed it again. In a voice heavy with indignation, he said, 'I have never even considered such a thing. The whole idea is quite intolerable, Vince. I trust you are joking,' he added coldly.

'Come now, Stepfather, give it a little thought. She has all the qualifications my mother had. Homely, kind, a good cook – a damned good cook, come to that. And she is the right age for you,' he added triumphantly.

'The right age, is she?' Faro demanded. 'Nearer fifty-five than forty. Really, Vince. I'm appalled. Quite appalled. I do need a little intellectual stimulus beyond the kitchen stove and the household accounts, you know.'

'You didn't get it from mamma, did you? But it didn't stop you loving her and producing two daughters.'

Faro was speechless as Vince went on: 'Don't you see what I'm getting at? You've come a long way since you met my Ma. Granted she was right for you then but, alas, she wouldn't be right for you now. You've gone up in the world, she would never have kept up with you. You'd have left her in the kitchen long ago,' he said sadly. 'You need a wife who could enjoy the world at your pace, share your love of books and music, your vast and ever-growing knowledge.'

'The kind of relationship you have with Olivia,' said Faro, determined to have the last word on marriages.

'Perhaps. Time will tell.' Vince's expression gave nothing away, but because he was equally determined, 'Like Mark and Harriet, we hope. They seem well suited. Miss Gilchrist says they have loved each other since childhood, but the vicar's daughter was not a suitable match for Sir Archie's heir. He wanted an alliance with this rich plain girl, coal owner's only daughter. But Mark and Harriet wanted each other. As you saw, true love won the day.'

Faro, listening silently, hoped it hadn't been helped by murder.

Mysteries were by no means ended and next morning yet another was thrown into the equation. Invited to accompany Owen and Olivia back to Branxton, Miss Gilchrist was extremely keen that they should see the old battlefield of Flodden and the pretty villages of Ford and Etal.

As they met in the Castle grounds, Olivia said, 'I don't know how I will ever manage to eat luncheon. Such a breakfast. I was hoping to see Miss Kent again when we said goodbye to Lady Elrigg. I'm very curious about her.'

Asked to explain, she continued, 'I am almost certain she is the same Beatrice Kent who was at boarding school in Edinburgh at the same time I was. Of course I didn't know her very well, she was a few years ahead of me. And it was all hushed up.'

'What was all hushed up, Livvy?' asked Vice patiently, knowing her weakness for going off on a tangent.

'Protecting the younger girls from scandal, of course.'

'What sort of scandal?'

Olivia regarded the two men, biting her lip. 'You know, I don't even care to discuss it.'

'Oh, come along, now that you've told us this much, we're intrigued. Don't be mean, Olivia,' said Vince as she glanced uncomfortably in Faro's direction.

'Well – I don't know.'

'Oh, don't be a goose, you can tell Stepfather anything. I do.' Vince chided her gently.

'Yes, but you're different. You're a man.'

'So I've heard,' Vince laughed. 'So is Stepfather. And he has seen and heard of most of the frailties of human nature, haven't you?

'I'm afraid so.'

'Well, what was it? Don't tell me she cheated at exams?' said Vince.

Olivia shuddered. 'Oh no, that was quite common.'

'Games, then?'

'We all cheated at games. No. It was much worse than that.'

'I know,' said Vince triumphantly. 'She flirted with the gardener's boy and was seen kissing him behind the garden shed.'

Olivia pushed him, laughing, then, suddenly serious, 'If only it was just that.'

'Surely you can't get anything more serious in a girls' boarding school than an illicit kiss with the gardener's boy –'

'Vince, listen to me, please. It was nothing like this. I mean, normal.' She stopped and then went on rapidly. 'She was expelled and the music teacher dismissed.'

'That bad,' Vince whistled. 'Pupils do fall in love with their teachers, especially in girls' schools.'

'You still don't understand. We didn't have men teachers at St Grace's.'

'Oh?'

'This was a woman teacher.' Olivia gulped and blushed. 'They were caught – together – in bed,' she whispered.

Faro, listening to the conversation in mild amusement, did not take in the immediate significance. Girls in schools frequently slept in the same bed and his first thought was that it was the fact of a schoolgirl sleeping next to one of the teachers.

But the emphasis 'together' and Olivia's accompanying blushing discomfort removed all doubts. Although he had encountered the homosexual's forbidden world during his years with the Edinburgh City Police, he found it difficult to understand – as did many of his fellow men, Vince included – that women were capable of a deep physical relationship.

Indeed, although there was a criminal law against male homosexuals, there existed no such law against lesbians, simply because Her Majesty, outraged at such a suggestion, refused to believe her sex capable of such depravity.

Faro sighed. Olivia's revelations gave an added motive for murder. Two women who loved passionately and between them the unwanted husband.

'It is also one possibility,' said Vince later, 'why there were no children. Sir Archie was known as a collector of beautiful objects. Presumably he regarded his lovely wife in the same light. I wonder if he knew about Miss Kent when he married her.'

'I doubt whether he would have considered it of any significance, since most rich women have companions,' said Faro.

'Perhaps he was impotent. That would account for no children by his first marriage and the adoption of his stepson as the future heir of Elrigg,' said Vince.

How ironic, thought Faro. A castle with splendid estates, a life, to the outside world, that had every material blessing and yet Sir Archie had every reason to envy the poorest tenants on his estate their quivers of children, many unwanted but undoubted evidence of their boundless unrestrained fertility, while his legendary sexual prowess was a lie.

'I'd like to know a great deal more about Mark's relationship with Sir Archie. From hints dropped by Aunt Molly to Olivia, which she has now confided in me, I suspect that he may well have been ill-used by him. She didn't call it that, of course, and I doubt whether he ever spelled it out even to her. But there was certainly a curious relationship between them.'

If that was so, it was indeed a motive for murder, Faro decided gloomily.

25

Vince was to leave for Branxton with the twins and Miss Gilchrist. The latter, enchanted to learn that Miss Crowe was an authoress, had included her in the party.

Two extra passengers plus the luggage that had accompanied the twins from Edinburgh created a difficulty for the carriage, which comfortably accommodated only four people.

Heads were shaken but the problem was not insurmountable. Vince, who was required to drive the carriage, should take the twins and Miss Gilchrist. Lady Elrigg would be delighted to put the governess cart at Mr Faro's disposal if he would be good enough to take Miss Crowe with him.

Faro concealed his emotions carefully. But his sharp look in Vince's direction asked clearly as any words: if this is yet another plot to throw us together then they are in for a disappointment. He had already decided that Hector was enamoured with Miss Crowe and she had shown no evidence that she resented his attentions. In fact, through dinner at the castle, she appeared to be encouraging him.

Faro was happy to keep such observations to himself and wished the pair good fortune since it would seem to be a very suitable match – if any man were found brave enough to take on the formidable Miss Crowe.

And so the two set off for Branxton with Faro determined to be agreeable and cautious in his conversation, risking nothing that would ignite the temper that seemed to match the lady's flaming hair.

The weather was in their favour, sunny and pleasantly warm, a day to loiter in the grandeur of hill and dale. Just clear of Elrigg village, they had to pull into the side of the road to allow a troupe of gypsy caravans passage.

'On their way to Kirk Yetholm,' said Imogen, who seemed pleased at the sight of them and greeted the leading caravan in their own language.

Faro was surprised at that and she laughed. 'The Irish tongue has its uses. Besides I was brought up among their kind in Kerry. My grandmother was one of them.'

The caravans had stopped while she was speaking. A withered old woman, her hair in long white braids, leaned across so that she was level with Imogen. Toothless, she smiled, obviously demanding her hand.

Imogen gave it to her reluctantly and Faro watched that dark hand holding the white long-fingered one. The gypsy said some words and Imogen gave an anxious cry and tried to withdraw her hand.

When she succeeded, the old woman shrugged and, turning eyes milky pale in that dark heavily seamed face upon Faro, she held out her hand in a demanding way.

Misreading the gesture he took out a coin from his pocket and gave it to her. With an indignant cry, angrily she hurled it to the ground.

'What on earth –'

'You have insulted her,' said Imogen Crowe quietly. 'She wanted to tell you something important – something written in your hand.'

'My apologies, please give her my apologies...'

'Oh, she understands English quite well, they just don't care to speak it if Romany will do.'

Faro turned to the old woman. 'I am sorry, I did not mean to insult you.' And, although he also didn't believe in such nonsense as fortune-telling, he gallantly held out his hand and smiled at her.

The smile won the old woman. She shrugged and took his hand, stroking it, her eyes closed, her palms surprisingly soft and warm for one so old, he thought. The soothing hands of a healer.

But he knew when she looked up at him that healing was not what she saw. Her eyes were sad, full of tears. And he knew without any explanation or translation from Imogen that the cold feeling filling his bones was the presence of death.

His own. The silence and the stillness of that moment seemed to last for an eternity.

'No,' said Imogen sharply, as the old woman murmured. 'No,' she repeated. Then, realising that Faro did not understand the words, she spoke to the gypsy in her own language, very gently, pleadingly.

It was enough. The cloud that had been hiding the sun

vanished, the road was again filled with the noise of rattling carts, of jingling pots and pans, the smell of horses, dogs barking and children's laughter. The shadow of death had passed by and he and Imogen Crowe continued on their way as if their journey had never been interrupted.

But Faro was conscious of Imogen Crowe watching him intently, speculatively. Catching her eye, he turned away sharply.

'What was the old woman babbling on about?' he asked lightly. 'What did she want to tell me?'

'Nothing.'

'It didn't sound like nothing. Tell me what she said, I want to know, Imogen.'

She looked startled. It was the first time he had used her given name. She shook her head.

'She said I was going to die, didn't she?'

'No. No. Just that you were in terrible danger. But I could have told you that,' she added.

Faro laughed. 'Could you indeed?'

She shrugged. 'I have the sight.'

'Have you now?' Faro asked with a lightness he was far from feeling. 'Then let me tell you, young lady, there is nothing in the least remarkable about such an observation. I am a policeman and I've been in some kind of danger practically every working day of my life and I will continue to be so until death puts an end to it.'

She looked at him sadly. 'This time it is different. This danger is from within – from where you least expect it. Oh – look, over there.' She pointed to a handsome castle on the hillside.

'That's Ford.' And obviously glad to change the subject, 'King James the Fourth spent the night before Flodden there.'

'Not, I suspect, as it looks now.'

'Well, the old tower still remains, they tell me. His room with its secret staircase leading down into Lady Heron's. They were enemies; her husband and their sons were prisoners of James. Rumour has it that she was more than hospitable to the King. She wanted to get on his good side, so she used woman's only weapon. She seduced him with her charm and he was so captivated by her that, before they made love, he removed the chain of penitence that he had sworn to wear about his body until his death. True or not, it was a fatal decision.

'We don't know what happened afterwards. Perhaps he fell in love with her and she rejected him. But when he left there was ill-will between them, a sense of betrayal – so much so that he gave orders to set her castle to the torch, a poor thanks for all her kindness. Fortunately it wasn't destroyed.'

She was silent, watching the road ahead. 'But enemies they were.' And turning to him, 'You can't really ever love your enemy, despite the Sermon on the Mount, can you?'

'Why are you telling me all this? Was this part of your gypsy woman's warning?' he asked.

She smiled. 'No, I am telling you a story, that is all.'

Suddenly he remembered her book with its revealing flyleaf and that he must return it to her. He did not feel like mentioning it at that moment and he urged on the horse. She spoke no more until they climbed down the steep hill to where Miss Gilchrist's house looked down on the village of Branxton with its smoking chimneys.

To their right lay the battlefield of Flodden. Its closeness made Faro uneasy, as if the carnage of that September day lingered still, never to be obliterated by even the rains of three hundred years. Nor could the blood spilt and the weeping be healed by a million larks and their rapturous song of hope and joy.

He looked down and thought that the screaming ghosts of dead and dying must forever haunt the rafters where the first swallows swooped, filling the air with their gentle excited cries. And that the pale wild flowers opening in the hedgerows must be forever crimson, blood-tainted.

As they approached the house, there were voices in the garden. Miss Gilchrist, the twins and Vince were seated under a shady tree. There was the rattle of teacups, sounds of laughter.

Imogen Crowe looked at Faro, frowning. She understood. Neither were ready to exchange this sombre past for the jollity and the light-hearted banter of the present occupants of that sunny garden.

'Come with me.' Faro led the way down the hill towards the site of the battle. 'Here ten thousand men – fathers, sons, brothers – entire families – the flower of Scottish nobility – fell, wiped out in a few hours.'

At his side she said: 'Can you take it so calmly, you a Scot?'

Faro smiled. 'I'm no more Scottish that you are. I've told you that. I'm Orcadian by birth.'

She looked at him sharply. 'Of course, that's why you're so different from the rest.'

'Am I? In what way?'

She jabbed a finger at him. 'You are Viking – pure Viking. I thought that the very first day I saw you. Put a horned helmet on him, I said, and every woman within miles would run screaming –'

'I didn't realise I was such a monster as all that,' Faro interrupted in wounded tones.

'You didn't let me finish – I hadn't said in which direction they were running,' she ended impishly with a mocking coquettish glance that left him feeling not only contrite but highly vulnerable.

26

Their arrival in the garden was greeted warmly and their long absence commented on, but as the maid brought out refreshments the weather was changing, grey skies, like an army of vengeful ghosts, creeping over the battlefield.

Miss Gilchrist shivered and said they had better go indoors.

The house was welcoming, alive with flowers, the smells of ancient wood well waxed and polished. Everything gleamed with a lifetime's devotion to crystal, pictures and furniture.

But as Faro sat in that cosy atmosphere, his eyes strayed constantly to the window overlooking the battlefield, astonished that such peace and tranquillity could exist alongside such memories of bloody carnage. A few hours that with the death of King James and his nobles altered the course of Scotland's history for ever.

After luncheon, they played at cards and, losing as he invariably did, Faro retired somewhat aggrieved to examine the well-filled bookshelves. Laughter and teasing comments echoed from the card table and he looked at the old lady so sensitive and charming, marvelling that she had lived here alone all her life. That for her each day and night would pass untroubled by the scenes the very stones on her doorstep had witnessed and remembered.

'Lucky at cards, my dear,' she said consolingly, as she also retired from the fray. 'You know what they say.'

'I don't seem to be lucky in either,' said Faro.

But Miss Gilchrist didn't hear, her eyes on Imogen Crowe who frowned intently over her hand and then, with a whoop of triumph, threw them down, fanned wide and called: 'Game – to me!'

'Imagine Miss Crowe being an authoress,' said Miss Gilchrist admiringly.

'Depends on what – or who – she writes about,' Faro said drily. Writers made him nervous. He did not want to find himself pilloried in her next romance. A Viking indeed.

'I am sure she will be very kind to her friends. And discreet too. Perhaps she'll marry Hector.'

'You think so?'

'Yes, of course. Everyone notices that he is quite captivated by her. And she seems to encourage him. He is a fine young man and he deserves a good wife. Mark and Poppy would be pleased too. Sir Archie treated him badly.' Pausing, she studied Imogen critically. 'And she seems such a lady – for an Irishwoman.'

That made Faro laugh out loud. It was so totally out of character with his hostess. 'Are there no Irish ladies then?'

Miss Gilchrist frowned. 'There must be, I'm sure – a few. But most of the ones I've met have been gypsies or vagrants. Not very clean. And there were occasional Irish servants at the Castle in my time. Not very clean or very honest either. Twice I had coins stolen and a brooch I was fond of.'

'Perhaps poor immigrants faced with the necessity of survival cannot afford high principles,' Faro said gently. 'Famine recognises only the fight for survival.'

When he first came to Edinburgh as a policeman in 1849, the potato famine was it its height and every boat to Glasgow and Leith was packed with Irishmen and women and their vast families, ragged, desperate, starving. A terrible sight, his mother used to weep for them and although the Faros had little, she gave them money and food – and clothes too when they came to her door.

'God bless you – and yours,' they'd say.

That was enough for Mrs Faro. For her, money and goods had nothing to do with it. There were only good people and bad people and the good ones were welcome to her last crust.

Other than Sergeant Danny McQuinn, the only Irishmen Faro had encountered as a policeman had bombs in their pockets and were a constant threat to Her Majesty and a menace to Edinburgh's law and order. But he felt obliged, as one who also belonged to a vanquished race, to say a word or two in defence of another nation similarly and more cruelly affected.

'There have been noble Irish ladies,' he said, 'Like Deirdre of the Sorrows.'

'Yes, indeed. Such a sad story. And so depressing, like all their legends. Never a happy ending anywhere. Indeed, when they are honest they are so mournful.'

Faro was not to be defeated. He pressed on. 'There were saints among them too. Patrick and Columba who brought Christianity from Ireland when the rest of Britain were all heathens.'

Miss Gilchrist stiffened. She was not convinced. 'But our St George was a knight,' she said proudly. 'And he slew dragons.'

They went down to the little church at Evensong. For his own reasons Faro would have preferred to remain where he was but politeness demanded that he accompany them.

The vicar, recognising Miss Gilchrist had brought strangers who swelled out his tiny congregation, was eager to give a good report of his church. Proudly he welcomed the visitors from the pulpit: 'These walls sheltered the dead of both warring nations after Flodden. There are no enemies once death has ruled the line. Then men are all equal, all differences forgiven in the blood of Christ.'

When they trooped out afterwards, Faro, always a practical man, considered that frenzied burial, with a nightmare vision of what ten thousand corpses heaped together looked like to the men whose task it was to bury them.

Half hoping there might be some forgotten memorial among the scattered tombstones, he wandered around reading inscriptions, deciphering weathered stones with their skulls and crossbones, their intimations of mortality.

There were names famous on both sides of the border: Elliott, Armstrong, Scott – so many young people. Thirty to forty was the average age. And there were sad reminders. A 'relict' aged nineteen, 'beloved wife aged twenty-three' with an infant one week old.

Like his Lizzie, many had died in childbirth. Children too. Died in infancy. 'Died in an accident – Elrigg – aged eleven.'

He was still staring at the stone, aware suddenly of Vince looking over his shoulder. He whistled softly and pointed to the stone. 'I think you have found your murderer, Stepfather.'

But Faro was still unconvinced.

Miss Gilchrist's party having been invited to dinner with the local doctor, the twins were returning to Edinburgh next day and they had persuaded their great-aunt, much against her will, to allow Vince to sleep that night on the very comfortable sofa in the parlour.

The arrangement pleased him. 'I like to be informal and I love this house.'

Imogen Crowe declined his somewhat reluctant invitation to share the governess cart back to Elrigg. Her excuse that Hector was coming for her later was a relief for Faro, who pleaded a necessary return to the inn before setting out on holiday with Vince.

As Faro paid his bill at the Elrigg Arms, Bowden said: 'By the way, a lad came a while ago with a message from Mr Hector Elrigg. You're to meet him at the hillfort. He said it was urgent.'

The fickle weather had changed once again and it would be dark soon. A dull evening, heavy with mist, and Faro was suddenly reluctant to leave the warm fire.

Vince would say: 'Let well alone, leave it. The case is closed.'

But Faro was tempted. This might be the last link in the evidence. He told himself of course it wasn't necessary, but to ferret out the truth was the habit of a lifetime. He had to know the murderer's identity for his own satisfaction, otherwise he would always be plagued by a case unfinished, a question forever posed.

He realised that the mist was thicker than ever on the road. The ground underfoot was wet with visibility limited to a few yards, a few ghostly hedgerows. He shivered as the atmosphere gripped him like a clammy shroud. Peering into the gloom, he realised that the standing stones had also vanished, hidden behind that dense grey curtain.

At the boundary fence he hesitated, caring little for the idea of crossing the open pastureland to the hillfort. The mist now clung heavily to his eyelashes, blinding him. He blinked, feeling sick with apprehension, searching the mist for shadows and finding them. He remembered being told that the cattle come down from the hill in bad weather, nearer the road, seeking shelter. Now he fancied he could hear them, the grass rustling. And smell them too.

Something rose I front of him, large and white...

He stood still, heart-thumping, prepared for flight as a solitary sheep rushed off bleating at his approach.

He breathed again. Then the sound of hoofs, heavy this time.

A stray horse, riderless, swerved from his path, whinnied and disappeared.

Another shadow.

A man. The outline of head and shoulders, a soft-moving, gliding shadow.

'Hector! Hector?' he called. 'Over here.'

The air behind him was cut by a whirring sound. Instinctively, swiftly, he ducked and the arrow that was to have killed him struck his shoulder. He felt the searing agony as he staggered and tried to reach the shaft of the arrow, to drag it out, aware that he was the target for an excellent archer, one who could take his time killing him.

Through his own folly, he was going to die.

He should have listened to Vince, heeded more carefully the clues that had come his way, that pointed undeniably to the killer...

He heard the next arrow's flight and dropped to the ground. Through the pain, he began coughing. He felt the warm blood flowing and as the blackness of merciful unconsciousness enveloped him he fainted away.

The blackness was invaded by light, sound and smell.

He opened his eyes. At least he wasn't dead, pain told him that he was still alive. He lifted his head. It was an animal noise that had stirred him, the pounding of hoofs reverberating on the ground near him.

And then he saw it. Running towards him, the heavy head, the shining horns. For one second only, he thought he dreamed again, that this was yet another return to childhood's nightmare. But this was no shaggy red Highland beast. The animal that bore down on him with its acrid stench was the terrible reality of a white king bull.

He could not rise, in the grip of that same paralysis of nightmare. He was transfixed by fear, fear greater than the searing agony in his shoulder.

If only he could leap up... run... run...

And then clearly across the years he heard the voice of his aunt from that Deeside croft.

'Never run, lad. Never do that. The only way you can save yourself is to lie as still as you can. Play dead. Don't even breathe. He'll sniff at you and, if you don't move, he'll give up and go away.'

Nightmare had blocked that memory, had turned it into a screaming horror. Now in the face of death again, the words had returned razor sharp, undimmed by the passing years. Knowing this was his only hope of survival, he almost lost consciousness again in those heart-stopping moments when the beast's hoofs trampled the ground inches away from his face.

He felt its hot, stinking breath on his neck, drips of saliva on his hair. Its nose touched the arrow shaft, questing, and he bit his lip hard against the scream of agony.

The smell of blood. Was that what it sought before lowering its horns into his back, lifting him bodily from the ground...

Every second seemed like an eternity as he waited for that terrible death.

O God – God help me...

And like a miracle, his prayer was answered. By a single gunshot. A second...

The animal grunted, lifted its nose from its quest over his body. Then he heard the hoofs beating on the ground. Growing distant.

Then no more.

No more.

27

When he opened his eyes, it was to pain. He screamed against it but was glad even to feel pain. He was still alive.

Turning his head cautiously, he looked into the face of Imogen Crowe who held the arrow she had dragged out of his shoulder.

'I didn't know you could handle a gun.'

'Oh yes,' she smiled sarcastically. 'I use one all the time. We're never without them where I come from in Ireland. But surely you as a policeman know that.'

She lifted her head. 'Here they are. Hector's brought Dr Brand. He'll soon have you mended.' She pointed towards the fence. 'I don't know about Sergeant Yarrow. He's lying over there. In a bad way, I'm afraid.'

The two men were supported into Hector's cottage and much later, after a lot of blood and bandages, the doctor smiled at Faro.

'You're a brave man and you'll live. That shoulder will be sore for a while, but the arrow just skimmed the muscle, went sideways. You were lucky.' He looked towards the bedroom. 'Luckier than poor Yarrow.'

'Is he – '

Dr Brad shook his head. 'Not yet. But it won't be long. Took a haemorrhage from the lungs. Wouldn't listen to advice. Are you able to stand?'

'Of course.' Faro tried to swing his legs off the sofa, failed and decided against another attempt.

Dr Brand smiled. 'I couldn't help noticing as I was patching you up that you have many scars, you must have lived a very dangerous life for an insurance assessor.'

'It has its problems.'

Dr Brand nodded towards the bedroom. 'Sergeant Yarrow would like to see you.'

Faro nodded. 'Where's Miss Crowe?'

'She's in the garden. With Hector.'

'I owe her my life, you know. She scared that damned bull away.'

'You're wrong on two accounts, lad. It was Hector fired the gun. And it wasn't the king bull or you wouldn't be telling the tale. It was a cow. Maybe a young heifer.'

'A cow?'

'Yes, but her horns are just as sharp, and she can be just as dangerous. Fortunately, like all females, she suffers from curiosity. Her mate might not have wasted so much time sniffing around you.'

Faro shuddered. 'I must thank Hector.'

Dr Brad shook his head. 'Not now. See the Sergeant first. There may not be much time before Dewar gets here.'

Faro went into the bedroom quietly. At first he thought he was too late, that Yarrow was dead.

There was so little life in the face, so little difference from the colour of the pillow on which he lay, that Faro was almost taken by surprise when his lips moved: 'I should have killed you.'

'Another murder? Harder to explain away than Sir Archie.'

'How did you know?'

'I didn't. Not until I saw Eric's portrait. He was the image of you. Your eyes looked out at me. And then there was his grave in Branxton kirkyard. But most of all were your own words, first on the scene of the crime...'

Yarrow laughed soundlessly. 'You begin with what is certain, what you are sure of, then you build on to it.'

'The first lesson in detection, I see you still remember that,' said Faro. 'My only certainty was that the killer had to be first on the scene. And after I'd ruled out the Prince of Wales, I was left with only one man it could be – yourself.'

Faro turned round painfully and touched the sleeve of Yarrow's uniform jacket hanging over a chair. 'See, there's a button missing.'

'I know. I must have lost it.'

'And I found it. Clutched in Duffy's hand when I pulled him out of the water. The final piece of evidence, of course, was your name on the gravestone in Branxton.'

'And enough to hang me,' said Yarrow slowly.

Faro looked at him. 'Was it revenge? A eye for an eye, a tooth for a tooth?'

'Not only for my lad's death, shot by that drunken devil, but for my wife and the end of my marriage. Eric's death killed her as surely as if the bullet had struck her heart.'

He sighed, staring out of the window. 'She was never strong after he was born and he was her whole life. After he died I watched her creep steadily away from me month by month, then week by week, then each day, each hour.'

Breathless again, he paused. 'I wanted to die too when I was shot up in the Covent Garden massacre. I was pretty smashed up and they didn't expect me to survive. I was a long time in limbo, at the gates of death and to be honest I was very disappointed when they told me I would live.

'But I knew my career, my glorious future they had talked about, was over. I'd never be fast on my feet again. I hated London after that and when I got the chance to come to Elrigg, it seemed that fate had taken a hand. I'm not a superstitious man, I don't believe in ghosts, but Eric started to haunt me. I dreamed of him constantly – I was obsessed, convinced that he wanted me to avenge him.

'As for Sir Archie, I was sure he'd see it on my face whenever we met – arrogant bastard that he was and me so servile: yes, sir, no, sir! But there were never any opportunities of getting him alone. I've waited years, sometimes I was with him alone but, without using my bare fists, I couldn't kill him.

'The first real opportunity came when we were riding escort to the Prince of Wales. We saw them disappear towards the copse and then the Prince left alone. You know the rest, Dewar set off for the village and I went to – help – Elrigg. He was unconscious and I knew I'd never get such a change again. But what to use for a weapon? And then I remembered that the day before I'd found Bowden's horns in a ditch and shoved them in my saddle bag. Evidence to nail Duffy, I thought.'

He smiled wanly. 'Now it seemed like fate, for I held in my hands a weapon to avenge my lad and make it look like an accident. I broke one of the horns off, didn't even check to see that he was still breathing in case he opened his eyes – just thrust it – hard – with both hands – into his back. It went in easily, like a stiletto. I don't know where I found the strength but he had a soft fatty body,' he added in a tone of disgust.

'I thought he groaned, but even if he wasn't dead then he had never seen my face. I hid the horn in the stone wall – '

'Where I found it.'

Yarrow smiled wearily. 'I might have guessed. And that it wouldn't take long for you to guess the rest. I hadn't bargained on Duffy either. He'd been lurking around and knew there was never a bull in sight.'

'Blackmail.'

'Yes. I paid him a few pounds but it wasn't enough and then he said he'd tell you – the insurance mannie – what he knew. I overheard him asking you, leaving messages with Bowden and knew I had to do something about it – quick. So I arranged to meet him, promising him more money for his silence. Had a bottle with me – whisky this time. As we talked he was already drunk – and very abusive when he realised I didn't have a hundred pounds on me.

'He hit me. We both fell and struggled on the ground. I pushed his face down into the water – held him till he was dead. Then I poured the rest of the whisky over him.'

'What about Miss Halliday?'

Feebly he held up his hands. 'Not guilty. I never attacked her. I liked the woman, respected her. I'd called to collect the quarantine papers. I'd never been inside her house before. She gave me some tea, and as I sat there I saw Eric's face smiling at me.'

And Faro remembered that the abandoned cup of tea and Eric's likeness to Yarrow had helped him guess the killer's identity.

'That painting, dear God, like he was trying to speak to me. Such a likeness, tears came into my eyes. I had to have it. So I went back late that night intending to steal it. I was clumsy in my eagerness, knocked an ornament down in the dark. It smashed, she heard the noise, came downstairs, tripped and fell headlong. She never moved. I thought she was dead, took Eric's picture and ran.'

He shook his head, pale and exhausted, his voice growing fainter. 'I wasn't sure how much you knew or guessed – I didn't want to kill you – I don't suppose I'm the first.'

'By no means, Sergeant. But they were usually criminals, not honest policemen.'

'Honest,' Yarrow repeated mockingly. 'I was tired of being honest. It had got me nowhere and now I was a goner anyway. Dr Brand told me my time was up, that I could go any day. It would have been something, some small compensation to have written on my tombstone: "Here lies the man who murdered Inspector Faro of the Edinburgh City Police." Quite an epitaph. After all those famous criminals, he'd been bested by a lowly sergeant in a country police station.'

He shook his head. 'At least there won't be enough of me to hang,' he added, indicating the silver button.

Faro handed it to him. 'Get Mrs Dewar to sew it on again.'

Yarrow looked at him in wonder. 'You mean – '

'I mean that I am going to assist a miscarriage of justice. Life has dealt you enough blows, Yarrow, blows that you are paying for dearly. You had a splendid career, an unsullied reputation. And that's how it will be remembered as far as I'm concerned.'

There was a message from Vince at the Inn. 'Returning to Edinburgh immediately. Had a telegraph that Balfour is in hospital. Sorry about the holiday. In haste.'

Yarrow died that night, mourned by all who knew him, especially by the Dewars who spread the word that while practising for the archery contest he had mistaken a moving shadow for one of the wild cattle looming out of the mist towards him. The arrow misfired and hit Faro a glancing blow. A sick man, the effort of pulling back the bow had caused a fatal haemorrhage.

Only Imogen Crowe and Hector Elrigg knew the truth and if Dr Brand had his suspicions then he kept them to himself.

As for Faro, it seemed an unlikely explanation that might have satisfied Dewar but would have opened up an immediate inquiry for any detective inspector. The insurance mannie was a different matter.

Dr Brand signed the death certificate and the Sergeant was laid to rest. The Metropolitan Police he had served so gallantly in London most of his life as a police officer sent a representative to the funeral at Elrigg kirkyard.

No connection was ever hinted at concerning Eric Yarrow's grave in Branxton. At least, Faro thought, father and son lay only a few miles apart, to rest for all eternity under the same windswept skies, the same bird-haunted hills.

Imogen Crowe did not attend Yarrow's funeral. When they met, Faro expected that she would be announcing her engagement to Hector Elrigg.

She laughed. 'You are quite wrong: for once your deductions have played you false, Inspector Faro.'

'You would be surprised how often you are right about that,' he said bitterly.

'Just be glad you are alive – that we were in the vicinity when you fell into Yarrow's trap, his lure to get you there. You want to know why I was there that night. Hector has been courting me each time I have come to Elrigg. Perhaps this past weekend I was tempted for a while and then... well,' she looked at him and quickly looked away again as their eyes met.

'I intended telling him that I couldn't marry him as we drove back from Branxton. By the time we reached the hillfort the mist had got worse and I went into the cottage with him. One thing led to another, I insisted on leaving – and I wanted to walk – alone.'

She paused, embarrassed. 'Hector said if I insisted on walking back across the pastureland in heavy mist, he'd better get his gun. He carried it as a matter of course in heavy mist, when the cattle come down from the hill. A shot is all they need to scare them off. I waited for him, I heard you calling. The mist lifted for just a moment, like a swirling shroud, and I saw Yarrow, creeping along by the fence. He was heading in your direction, loading a crossbow.'

They were both silent and then Imogen said: 'When are you leaving?'

'Tomorrow, I'm going back to Edinburgh. I wouldn't be much use on a vigorous hill-walking holiday with my arm in a sling. What about you?'

'I'm going to Ford Castle for a little while, to continue my book. I'm leaving this afternoon.'

'So am I. By train. May I offer you a lift this time?'

She smiled, remembering. 'That would be most kind. But I insist on seeing you to the station.' When he began to protest,

'I have to go into Berwick anyway. I need some more writing materials.'

On that journey they spoke little to each other.

'Will you be returning to Elrigg?' he asked.

She shook her head. 'I think not.'

There was another silence. Handing her *The History of Civilisation*, he said gently, 'Your book. Tell me about Philip Gray.'

Turning, she smiled. 'What do you want to know?'

'Was he your lover?'

'You make that sound uncommonly like an accusation, Inspector Faro,' she said mockingly.

'None of my business,' he shrugged, trying to sound casual but sure she lied, as he saw again the words on the flyleaf. 'To my dearest Imo, with my love always, Philip G.'

'As a matter of fact,' she said slowly, 'I did love him. He was my cousin.'

'Your cousin?'

'Yes. His name was Phelan Crowe. Uncle Brendan brought us up. I went to gaol for him,' she said bitterly. 'And friends urged Phelan to change his name because of the association, so when he came to London, he became Philip Gray.'

'Was the fact that he died here what brought you to Elrigg in the first place?'

'Yes. He was more brother than cousin, you know. I had an idea someone had killed him. I was like Yarrow. I wanted vengeance but I had no idea how to go about it.'

She was silent, her face sorrowful 'I'm glad I was wrong but that Royal Family of yours has a lot to answer for.'

They reached the station as Faro's train steamed into the platform.

'Well – goodbye,' he said, taking her hand.

She brightened suddenly. 'Maybe you will have time to see me when I come to Edinburgh again.'

'Of course. Wait – I'll give you my address.'

'You'll miss your train. I can find you. I'm familiar with police stations, you know.'

The carriage door closed. The guard blew his whistle.

And Faro realised he had a great deal more to say.

As she stood on the platform and raised a hand in farewell, the sun gleamed on her hair lighting her with sudden radiance. With a whoop that was part joy of discovery, part despair, he realised he had not even kissed her yet.

He had a sudden desire to throw open the door, leap back down the platform. And take her in his arms.

He saw her smile, her lips formed the words.

'Till Edinburgh!'

THE
MISSING
DUCHESS
1876

For Dick and Elizabeth Warfel
and the magic of Cockleshell Cottage,
East Lothian

I

The discovery of a woman's body in the Wizard's House in the West Bow was a sombre end to what had been an unusually convivial evening for Detective Inspector Jeremy Faro.

The Annual Regimental Dinner in Edinburgh Castle had provided everything to his taste; victuals excellent, drams in constant supply, toasts short and witty. But the highlight of the occasion was his reunion after many years with his cousin Leslie Faro Godwin.

The war correspondent was guest of honour. That in itself was something of a novelty where newspapermen were still regarded by the rich and famous with suspicion. Jackals of society, who earned a contemptible living by scandal-mongering and exposing the shortcomings of their betters for the titillation of their readers.

'Gentlemen sometimes wrote for the press, but newsmen were rarely gentlemen.'

Whoever penned that sneering epithet had never encountered Leslie Faro Godwin, thought Faro proudly as he listened to his cousin's talk. Leslie, who was five years his senior, was the veteran of many campaigns. Brave as any soldier, utterly fearless, he had 'lived in the cannon's mouth', as he described it, for twenty years and made light of his imprisonment and torture by the late Emperor Theodore of Abyssinia during the early years of the war which had ended in 1868. After eight years of dodging Maori spears in New Zealand and Ashanti spears in Africa, he had recently returned from covering military operations in the Malay Peninsula.

The evening's entertainment left scant opportunity for private conversation between the two men. As they dived for shelter from the heavy rain to await their carriages, Godwin shouted: 'Edinburgh weather never changes, that's for sure.'

'It can be relied upon to be totally unreliable,' said Faro as they shook the moisture off their evening capes.

Godwin regarded him with satisfaction. 'Good to see you after all these years, Jeremy. You're quite a celebrity.' He chuckled.

'Hardly surprising really. You had a very enquiring turn of mind, even as a small child.'

'I appreciate your delicacy. Some called it just plain nosey!'

'Perhaps, but it paid off. You certainly fulfilled your early promise.'

'And so did you to all accounts.'

Faro glanced at his cousin approvingly. Experiences calculated to turn most men's hair white overnight, had not even flecked with grey his thick dark hair and splendid military moustache. Difficult, Faro thought, to label him as past forty.

'It has been a very long time,' said Godwin, as if he read his mind. 'All I recall is that I was an unpleasant little beast, such a bully,' he added apologetically.

If that were so, then Faro realised it had not quelled the hero-worship of a lonely four-year-old child for this older cousin. And he still remembered vividly the sad and terrible nightmares that had persisted long after their parting.

Their rare meetings had been memorable occasions in which he first set foot in the awesome splendour of a New Town mansion. There Thora Faro Godwin enjoyed a very different lifestyle to that of her policeman brother Magnus, Jeremy's father.

Thora's progress had been steadily upwards on the social ladder, from the day in Orkney when she met Hammond Godwin, a rising advocate and Member of Parliament. Struck by her beauty, for she had little else to offer, he had married her.

'I remember the last time we met quite clearly,' said Faro sadly. 'It was at my father's funeral.'

'Of course.' Godwin nodded. 'And I felt very grown up and important at being allowed to follow the cortège with the men, for the first time.'

His words brought the scene back vividly. Whatever the circumstances, that last visit to the Godwins had been a farewell gesture. They were never again invited to Charlotte Square. A child did not understand such things, but Jeremy's mother, once a domestic servant herself, recognised and respected, without the least resentment, a social gap too wide to be bridged by anything less that the courtesy of attending a poor relation's funeral.

Mary Faro knew her place. She would not have dreamt of embarrassing her widowed sister-in-law by calling upon her without invitation.

'We must meet again, catch up on the family news,' said Godwin heartily.

'Where are you staying?'

'I've rented a place in the Lawnmarket. What about you? Married? Children?'

'A widower, alas. I have two bairns – girls – staying in Orkney with their grandmother.'

Godwin looked at him. 'Orkney. A long way from Edinburgh, isn't it?'

'Best I could do under the circumstances. A detective's life was bad enough for my poor Lizzie, hardly ever seeing me. Too many hazards for my daughters.'

'Surely there are admirable governesses in Edinburgh?'

Faro laughed. 'Maybe so, but not affordable on my salary. Besides, they have a better life in Orkney. Are you married?'

Godwin smiled sadly. 'I was once – a long time ago.' He sighed, staring ahead as if seeing it bleakly. 'But successful marriage and parenthood require the presence of a reliable husband and father and I could never guarantee either role. So – it ended.' He paused and sighed again. 'Even my parents have long gone. You are alone, too?'

'Fortunately, no. My stepson Vince Laurie is a doctor and we share a house on the south side of the town. An agreeable arrangement – for the present – until he decides to take a wife.'

As they studied each other, Faro was unaware of a common bond, a sense of identification running through both their lives. His desire to hear more of Leslie Godwin's early life was frustrated by the arrival of the carriages.

'Share mine,' he said. 'We'll set you down at your lodging.'

As they stepped forward another guest emerged from shelter. Staggering wildly towards the carriage, waving his arms frantically, it was obvious that he was heavily intoxicated.

'Shall we...?' Godwin whispered. Faro nodded and the man gratefully accepted their offer of a lift.

As they bundled him inside, he hiccupped his name at them three times without leaving them any the wiser, while his rendering of a sentimental ballad threatened any attempts at conversation.

'Thank heaven the rain's stopped,' said Godwin, opening the window in an effort to disperse the whisky fumes from their now inert companion.

'That's much better.' Faro smiled.

'It is indeed. We must meet again soon, cousin.'

'Of course. Here's my card.'

Godwin pocketed it and sighed. 'I don't have one, I'm afraid. I'm never long enough in one place to indulge in the niceties of polite society.'

'Where is your permanent home?'

Godwin looked at him and laughed. 'My dear fellow, I haven't enjoyed the luxury of a permanent residence for more years than I care to remember. A poste-restante address, the most comfortable hotel, friends... such have been my homes.'

An idea was taking shape in Faro's head as he asked: 'How long are you to be in Edinburgh, then?'

Godwin shook his head. 'Haven't the least idea. All depends on what assignments come up. Meanwhile, I am working on my war memoirs.'

Faro looked suitably impressed and Godwin smiled. 'I have been trying to compile them for a very patient publisher for more than ten years now. I thought that coming back to Edinburgh might offer opportunity and inspiration... What the devil – '

Their carriage lurched to a halt precipitating the drunken man across their knees.

They stared out of the window. They were in the West Bow, the main thoroughfare whose zigzag steep descent from Castle Hill to Grassmarket marked one of the most ancient and characteristic streets in the Old Town. Hazardous for vehicles in almost any weather, their progress was halted by a small crowd that had gathered in the middle of the road, where they harangued a harassed-looking policeman who was holding a young lad in a firm grip.

Faro leaned out of the carriage door and the constable, recognising him, saluted smartly. 'Good evening, sir. Constable Reid, sir.'

'What's the trouble?'

'Laddie here taking shelter from the storm found a woman's body in the Wizard's House.'

'The Wizard's House.' Godwin nudged Faro. 'How appropriate for a sinister discovery.'

'I've sent for the police doctor. Glad you're here, sir,' he added gratefully. 'Perhaps you would care – '

'Very well, Constable,' said Faro. 'Don't wait,' he added to Godwin. 'This may take some time.'

Faro stepped out of the carriage reluctantly. He had his own personal reasons for hating the West Bow. It was just yards away, where the West Bow joined the High Street, that his policemen father had been killed by a runaway carriage forty years ago.

Now stumbling into the unlit house on the heels of the Constable and the lad, whose name was Sandy, Faro's scalp prickled with that primeval sense of unease, of being in the presence of death.

The Wizard's House, as Weir's Land was commonly known, had a bad reputation. Empty for years, the passage of two centuries had failed to dispel the aura of evil left by its one-time owner Major Weir, warlock extraordinary, burnt at the stake in 1670.

Inside the house, along a narrow passage, a high-windowed room provided enough light to reveal what looked like a bundle of rags but was in fact a woman lying as if asleep on the floor.

'Let's have some light,' Faro said irritably. 'Turn up the lantern. Are there no candles?' he added desperately.

Constable Reid smiled wryly as he held the lantern higher.

'Doesn't seem to make much difference, sir. And we can't get candles to stay alight.'

'What do you mean?'

'They keep blowing out, Inspector, that's what.' He looked round anxiously. 'As if someone was standing right behind them,' he added, managing, at Faro's stern glance, to turn an uneasy laugh into a cough of embarrassment.

'You shouldn't believe everything you read, Constable.'

'It's a gey uncanny place though, Inspector. And I'm not given to being fanciful.'

Faro could believe that. Constable Reid was a new recruit from Glasgow, nineteen and tough as old boots.

He bent over the body. A beggar-woman in a sour ragged gown. He wasn't very good at guessing women's ages, but she looked youngish, not much past thirty. At least there was no blood, no signs of violence.

'Any means of identification?'

'Nothing obvious, sir. Except that life is extinct. I know that is all I have to establish – before the doctor comes – '

'Quite right, quite right, Constable,' said Faro.

He found himself wishing that Vince had been with him, that he didn't have to touch the corpse himself. He pushed aside a quantity of soft fair hair and laid his hand on the cold flesh of her neck. There was no pulse.

'Some poor unfortunate by the look of her. May I join you?'

Turning, Faro found Godwin looking over his shoulder. His surprise at the request must have shown, for his cousin sighed.

'You never get used to it, do you?'

Faro shook his head, grateful for his understanding. If there was one thing more distasteful than the discovery of a corpse it was one without any means of identification. In his book, that always spelt trouble.

'Wait until you've seen as many as I have, Jeremy, and not neat and tidy as this one.' Leslie paused and added apologetically: 'I hope I'm not intruding.'

'Of course not.'

Godwin nodded. 'This is not just morbid curiosity, I assure you. First lesson for any newsman worth his salt is never to miss any opportunity. A corpse and a wizard's house, well, there's sure to be a story in it somewhere, at least a couple of paragraphs,' he added cheerfully.

As they regarded the body, which Faro realised had probably been dead for several hours, he could see that the lad Sandy was becoming restive. Hopes of the reward his chums had urged might be in the offing if he informed the dreaded 'polis' were fast fading. The appearance of Inspector Faro and the other gentry on the scene in their evening finery, replaced such heady prospects with less pleasant possibilities. They might ask him questions, lock him up in a cell.

Shifting from one foot to the other, he announced with determined regularity that he wanted home. 'I only found her, your worships. I never done nothing.'

Constable Reid drew Faro aside. 'Shall we let him go?'

'I think that would be in order. Get his name and address, though.'

Gratefully, Sandy stammered out the information and bolted

from the scene, his hand tightly grasping the shilling that the gentlemen had given him plus an extra penny and instructions to summon a carriage. His tornado-like exit almost swept Dr Cranley, portly and majestic as a ship in full-sail, off balance.

The Police Surgeon's examination was brief: 'Natural causes. Massive heart attack, I'd say. Vagrant, taking shelter, no doubt; although she looks uncommon well-fed,' he added.

As he straightened up, regarding the fetid dark room of death with disgust, the stark contract of men in evening dress surrounding the corpse struck Faro anew.

'What makes you think she was a vagrant?'

Cranley regarded him irritably. He knew Inspector Faro's reputation but he was already late for a supper engagement and intended to be out of this vile hole as speedily as possible. Death he was used to, but he feared for his elegant clothes where every movement produced an acrid cloud of dust.

'Look at her rags. Filthy. Nothing underneath either,' he added primly, hastily adjusting the ragged skirt he had lifted to reveal a bare thigh. 'Fallen on bad times, I expect, usual story. We'll do a complete post-mortem when we get her to the mortuary. Ah, here they are, at last. You've taken your time,' he added impatiently as two constables bearing a stretcher stumbled along the narrow passage.

Reproached for their tardiness, they explained that they had been delayed at Leith by an 'incident'.

Followed in solemn procession by the living, the dead woman was carried out to the police carriage. Under the flickering lamplight Faro tucked one of her limp hands beneath the rough blanket.

His quick glance confirmed Cranley's diagnosis that she had indeed fallen on bad times. And very recently too. The last resort of starving women who possessed such splendid hair was to sell it to the wig-makers. But like her hair, her fingernails were not only clean but well-grown and neatly manicured, her palms uncalloused.

These were hands that had not seen anything resembling hard work in a very long time. If ever.

Undoubtedly a lady's hands.

2

At 9 Sheridan Place – the home Faro shared with his stepson – Dr Vincent Laurie, newly elected treasurer of the local golf club, was wrestling with his predecessor's accounts. He was therefore only mildly interested in his stepfather's encounter with a long-lost cousin, especially since he knew nothing of Godwin's family connection and had nothing but contempt for their neglect of widowed Mary Faro and her young son.

Vince prided himself on being a man of the people and the Godwins belonged to the social system that had branded him illegitimate after his mother, a fifteen-year-old servant, had been seduced and abandoned by a noble guest in the big house where she worked. Even though she had eventually regained respectability through marriage to Jeremy Faro, such scars were burned indelibly into Vince's soul.

'The family's behaviour wasn't Leslie's fault, Vince. He was just a child at the time.'

'Then why has it taken him so long to track you down, Stepfather? Answer me that.'

'He's been abroad for years,' said Faro defensively, with an added reason for wishing Vince to think well of his cousin.

'I'm not convinced.'

'You will be when you know him better. I'm sure of that. If you'd been with us last night –'

As he went on to describe the scene in the Wizard's House, Vince paid careful attention. Eyeing his stepfather shrewdly, he said: 'I take it you disagree with Dr Cranley's verdict that death was from natural causes.'

Faro shrugged. 'I'm not sure. But let's just say, this was no beggar-woman.'

'No doubt your "missing persons" will provide a satisfactory explanation.'

On the list Faro consulted in the Central Office the following morning, there was no one who fitted the description of the dead woman in the mortuary.

Dr Cranley stared at him resentfully over the top of his

spectacles. Detective Inspector Faro's appearance signalled that the routine the police surgeon endeavoured to keep as smooth and untroubled as was humanly possible could be in imminent danger of severe disruption.

Faro regarded the sheeted figure. 'Any marks of violence?'

'Only a bruised and swollen wrist. She had fallen quite heavily. My findings have confirmed that she died of a massive heart attack.'

'Surely that's unusual in a woman so young,' said Faro. In death, there remained an indefinable look of refinement about that waxen face.

Cranley shrugged. 'Heart failure can happen at any age, Faro. And I would speculate, it is not all that unusual in the case of a protected and pampered middle-class woman who is suddenly subjected to direst poverty.'

Faro sighed, his attention again drawn to clean hair, to delicate hands with long tapering fingers and neatly manicured nails. They worried him.

'What makes you so sure she was middle class?'

Cranley sighed, drew back the sheet. 'Observe the narrowness of her waist, the distorted line of bosom and hips. I would say that she was richly corseted for most of her adult life. You don't get that shape among the poorer classes, Inspector.'

'So what would make this one become a beggar?'

The doctor eyed him pityingly. 'Many things, Inspector. Family scandal, for a start. Bankruptcy. A faithless lover – or a straying husband – '

'I suspect this lady, whatever her station in life, was unmarried.'

'Indeed?'

'Observe the third finger of her left hand. Married women tend to bear marks of a thick wedding ring, the skin it covers is paler due to lack of exposure.'

'Of course, you are probably right.' Cranley smiled thinly. It was a matter of constant irritation to him that Inspector Faro usually was right. 'We will no doubt find that out when her identity is established. Incidentally, she is not virgo intacta, but she has never borne a child. That we do know.'

In the days that followed, Faro went about his routine work at the Central Office praying that there would be no major crisis while Superintendent McIntosh was away attending a family funeral in Caithness. Sergeant Danny McQuinn, who Faro had learned to rely on, was also absent, seconded to Aberdeen on a murder enquiry.

Rifling through the new reports each day, he noted with relief that the Queen was safely tucked away in Balmoral Castle, absorbed by visitors for the last of the autumn shoot.

There had been a flurry of anxiety when unconfirmed rumour hinted that she might be contemplating a brief private visit to the Palace of Holyroodhouse. Even such unpublicised royal one-day visits were calculated to give Edinburgh City Police nightmares. Tight security measures and extra police duties were only a small part of the expenses involved in the protection of a monarch whose popularity had steadily declined during her long widowhood.

Faro sighed. He hoped Her Majesty would change her mind. She frequently did.

As for the newspapers, they had been having a field day. With no sensational crimes for some time, they were quite overjoyed at any item to raise their sales.

'Body found in Wizard's House. A Third Tragedy. Is Major Weir's ancient curse still active? Does his evil spirit still malevolently guard his ancient abode of magic, seeking to avert the threat which hangs over the future of the historic West Bow?'

For some time, the Edinburgh Improvement Commission had been urging that the West Bow be demolished to make room for more salubrious modern dwellings.

'Especially,' they argued, 'as the evil reputation of Major Weir's house has caused it to remain empty for the most part of two hundred years, and has made even the poorest families shrink from sheltering under its roof.'

However, even when fears of witchcraft and black magic began to disperse in the more benevolent wake of the Age of Reason, and Major Weir's house was regarded with less terror by neighbours, all attempts at finding a tenant with strong enough nerves to inhabit it failed miserably.

Some fifty years earlier, in the 1820s, William Patullo, an old soldier of reprobate and drunken habits, moved in with his wife. They moved out again the next day after a terrifying ordeal in which it seemed that all the powers of hell had been loosed upon them. As they spread the story of their discomfort far and wide, the shades of superstitious terror closed in once more.

In more recent years, the house had served as a gunsmith's shop. The business had failed for not even a shopkeeper could stay for long.

Undeniably, two deaths and an accident had followed the Improvement Commission's decision, but they could hardly be classed as tragedies. The first death could not have come as a surprise. The demolition contractor was a man in his eighties, who breathed his last in his own bed, surrounded by his devoted and weeping family.

Even Detective Inspector Faro would have been hard-pressed to find anything remotely suspicious in such a peaceful end. Especially after a talk with the family physician, a golfing friend of Vince's who had expected his long-ailing patient to expire several years earlier. The funeral over, the eldest son, who had inherited the business, fell on the turnpike stair and broke his leg.

An unfortunate accident but hardly classifiable as 'a second tragedy'. Another death, however – the unidentified corpse of a beggar-woman – breathed new life into the old terrors and superstitions.

The press, hungry for sensational news items, were not unhappy at this resurrection. ('What fearful sight had stopped her heart and brought about this untimely end?') As they dusted down and reprinted once again details of Major Weir's infamous life, Edinburgh citizens shuddered and took to the other side of the road to avoid the menacing shadow cast by the newspaper-designated 'house of death'.

When Faro was handed the Procurator-fiscal's report with the Police Surgeon's usual request for an 'unidentified and unclaimed' corpse, his questions were once again greeted with a certain lack of enthusiasm.

'I can find no evidence of anything other than heart failure,' Dr Cranley told him.

'You are quite satisfied with the post-mortem?'

'If I wasn't, Inspector, then I would hardly be making this request. I regret having to disappoint you,' Dr Cranley added heavily.

'I think "disappoint" is an inappropriate word, doctor.'

Dr Cranley sniffed. 'Come now, Inspector. I realise with few murders on hand at the moment you must regard it as your duty to be on the look-out for anything remotely suspicious –'

'Let me assure you, sir,' Faro interrupted, 'murders are a commodity I could well do without. I don't invent them for my own amusement.'

Cranley smilingly dismissed Faro's protest and indicated the document on his desk. 'Then perhaps you would be so good as to sign the paper, Inspector, so that no more time might be lost.'

As Faro hesitated, Dr Cranley continued, 'I must urge you to be brisk about it. You surely realise more than most the value of this still-fresh corpse for my students. It is rare indeed that we get the chance of such an excellent unmarked specimen. One, in fact, with all the organs in prime condition –'

'Spare me the details, if you please.' Faro shuddered. 'I'll take your word for it,' he added, stretching out his hand for the paper.

The doctor, relieved, nodded happily. 'Then I may take it that you are quite satisfied with our findings?'

Faro wasn't, but he could not think of one reason to justify his unease.

He tried to explain his feelings to Vince over supper that evening. Their meetings at meals were rarer than ever, since Vince held his surgery and consulting hours in the downstairs rooms. Fast acquiring a thriving practice, his leisure hours were increasingly devoted to reducing his handicap on the golf course.

'There are lots of reasons why an unmarried woman – thirtyish, you said – might have run away from a respectable middle-class life, Stepfather.'

'Tell me some of them.'

'An unhappy love affair – maybe hopes of marriage with a suitor over several years that had failed to materialise. Perhaps he married someone else and being jilted affected her mentally.'

Faro was disappointed, having hoped that his stepson would be able to come up with a more original selection of ideas than Dr Cranley had offered.

'A *Bride of Lammermoor* – is that what you have in mind?' Faro shook his head. 'Such situations belong in Sir Walter Scott's novels, Vince. Surely no sane woman –'

'No sane woman, Stepfather – ah, there's the rub,' said Vince triumphantly. 'For whatever the post-mortem revealed about her physical condition, it can tell us nothing of the state of her mind at the time of death.'

'Are you suggesting that what she died of was that condition known to ladies addicted to romantic novelettes as a broken heart?'

'Something like that.' Vince nodded eagerly. 'It can happen, you know. And the reason she was not on the missing persons file is easy. In all probability her wish to escape from the past brought her to Edinburgh from some other town or village.'

'It doesn't explain why a woman gently bred should feel obliged to change into a filthy beggar's gown. And what happened to her middle-class dress and middle-class undergarments?'

'The answer is really simple, Stepfather. No doubt she had to sell them for food and lodging. Hunger can do incredible things to even the most fastidious.'

'This woman wasn't half-starved. I have Dr Cranley's word for that and the evidence of my own eyes.'

Vince shrugged. 'Perhaps she wished to shed her identity with the clothes.'

Faro looked at him. 'You are suggesting the utter destruction of self, of the woman she had been.'

'Something like that. There is another possibility. That whoever found her decided that it was a shame to waste good clothes when they could be sold.'

Faro thought of Sandy. 'I don't think the lad would have that much ingenuity. He seemed quite terrified to go near the body.'

Vince sighed. 'I should stop worrying about it, if I were you, Stepfather. Vagrants are ten a penny and every month some unfortunate falls to the students' dissecting knives. After all, we have to be practical about it. And once dead, the fresher the bodies the better for our purposes.'

'You make it sound like a flesher's shop,' Faro said accusingly.

'And so it is.' Vince eyed him candidly. 'All in the interests of medical science. Remember that one dead body dissected may lead to a hundred – perhaps a thousand – live ones being saved from the ravages of disease.'

Then, almost eager to change the subject, for he know only too well what his stepfather was like once he got a bee in his bonnet, namely, an unidentified corpse in the police mortuary, Vince continued: 'But you wanted to ask me something about this new-found cousin.'

'I have invited him to dinner on Sunday. You will have your chance then to form your own impressions.'

3

At their first meeting, when Faro had set down Leslie Godwin at the somewhat bleak lodging in the Lawnmarket, he had found himself thinking of his own comfortable house in Sheridan Place, run so smoothly by their housekeeper Mrs Brook, that model of efficiency. Guiltily, he had remembered the empty rooms upstairs and almost involuntarily this space had been filled with a satisfying picture of his cousin in temporary residence.

As the days had passed the idea grew in his mind. Faro had few relatives and Leslie was quite a find. A second successful meeting when he came to dinner and was very impressed by his surroundings confirmed that the two men had much in common.

Both had been subjected to danger from an early age, Leslie to wars, Faro to violent crime. Both knew how to deal with the unexpected, the art of survival perhaps an inheritance down the generations from that distant Viking ancestor.

Faro noticed with delight when Leslie dined with them that Sunday how Vince's air of reserve fast dissolved as the evening progressed and the talk veered from Leslie's recent progress as guest in the homes of Scottish nobility to his more exciting tales from the battlefield. Of how, confessing to the sketchiest of medical knowledge, acquired out of necessity, Godwin had used his own ingenuity and common sense to keep a seriously wounded prisoner alive until help arrived.

Faro, listening to the two men swapping medical experiences, decided that perhaps Godwin, who talked so cynically about taking enemy lives, was being excessively modest about those he had also saved.

The fact that Vince too was impressed by this relative reinforced the proposal Faro had in mind. He now felt certain that his stepson would approve of Godwin sharing their house during his short stay in Edinburgh.

Vince's reaction was exactly what he had hoped for.

'A capital idea, Stepfather. Let's ask him tomorrow night.'

Godwin, returning to his lodging the following evening, was clearly puzzled but pleasantly surprised to find the two of them waiting for him.

Faro had to put their proposal to him then and there, guessing by his cousin's nervous glances towards the window of his apartment as they talked that he was too embarrassed to invite them inside.

'My dear fellows. I'm grateful – touched even – by your kindness.' He shook his head. 'But I must decline. I am somewhat set in my ways, I've lived alone and lived rough, too long. It's no use trying to civilise me. I come and go and sleep and wake all hours of the day and night. I couldn't put you and your excellent Mrs Brook to all that inconvenience. I'm much better off with my Sergeant Batey, he's served me faithfully for umpteen years and he's used to my ways.'

'He could come too. We have plenty of room in the attics.'

Godwin chuckled. 'You haven't met him yet. I guarantee he's as eccentric as his master, which suits us both well. He'd drive Mrs Brook – and you – mad. No – no – I couldn't think of inflicting us both on you.'

'We might persuade him yet,' said Vince as they walked home. 'Incidentally, we're invited to Aberlethie for the weekend. Terence and Sara are having a few guests.'

The weekend house party was popular among Edinburgh's rich and fashionable merchant class – those with mansions grand enough and gardens magnificent enough to allow gratifying illusions of rubbing shoulders with the aristocracy. And this was the society, Faro thought cynically, that Vince, self-declared man of the people, now moved in.

Sir Terence Lethie was one of his stepson's new golfing friends, and the proximity of a course to the castle suggested to Faro that he might have to make his own amusement.

Faro had a solid lack of interest in golf; he was immune to its fever, declaring that he spent enough time on his feet without regarding the pursuit of a golf ball across a green full of holes and aggravating hazards as an agreeable way of spending his leisure hours.

When he protested that he would be out of place in such an assembly, Vince smiled.

'Some of Lethie's Masonic friends have been invited. And Terence wants you to come specially, a guest of honour.' He coughed apologetically. 'He wants you to tell them about some of your cases.'

'So I'm to sing for my supper, is that it?'

Seeing his stepfather's expression, Vince said: 'I thought you wouldn't mind. And since you are so interested in local history you'll have a chance to meet Stuart Millar. He's a near neighbour.'

The local historian came of a famous family of travellers, one of whom had accompanied Sir James Bruce of Kinnaird on his travels in Abyssinia in the last century.

He was also a Grand Master in the Freemasons. Most of Vince's new acquaintances belonged to the order and Vince was being urged to join as an 'apprentice', the first rung on the ladder.

This was an invitation Faro had resisted personally for many years, despite Superintendent McIntosh's hints that 'it could do great things' for him. Although he refrained from saying so to his superior officer, Faro was happy to have reached his own particular niche in the Edinburgh City Police by his own merits, rather than by joining what he regarded as an archaic secret society for ambitious men.

He was also content to remain Chief Detective Inspector, since the next step up that ladder would involve sitting behind a desk issuing orders and signing documents, work which he would find extremely dull after twenty years of chasing criminals and solving crimes by his own often unorthodox methods of observation and deduction.

'The Lethies are having some quite illustrious visitors,' Vince assured him. 'None other than the Grand Duchess of Luxoria, the Queen's god-daughter.'

Faro had read about Luxoria, one of the bewildering number of European principalities set adrift by the breakup of the Holy Roman Empire, its borders forever under threat of annexation by other powerful states. But the tiny independent kingdom tucked away in central Europe had managed to survive centuries of warring and predatory neighbours.

He knew little of its complex politics since European history was not one of his interests, but he had been vaguely interested to read a legend connected with the Scottish Knights Templars, who had taken refuge there from persecution, rewarding the Luxorians with some holy relic brought from Jerusalem.

Luxoria might have remained in obscurity and never achieved even a small paragraph in the local newspaper but for the Scottish connection. The Grand Duchess Amelie claimed descent not only from Mary, Queen of Scots, but was related to both Her Majesty the Queen and the late Prince Consort.

'Didn't they have a revolution – oh, fifteen years ago? I seem to remember reading about it,' said Faro.

'Full marks, Stepfather. I had it all from Terence. The Grand Duchess inherited after her father's death. She was opposed by her wicked cousin, who had been set up, not against his will, as President and puppet ruler. She was then forced to marry him in what is to all accounts still a wretchedly feudal system of government.' Vince continued: 'A political marriage which would guarantee the succession and save further bloodshed. The Luxorians love their Royal Family, it seems, in spite of it all.'

At the thought of their own Royal Family, Faro smiled wryly. There were many disillusioned citizens in Scotland who applauded Ireland's demand for Home Rule. There were many others too in Britain generally who would have considered it a 'good thing' to bring down the Throne. The Queen was far from popular, spending most of her time in Balmoral Castle guarded by the fiercely protective John Brown, with only token appearances at the seat of government in London, to the dismay of her statesmen.

The French Revolution remained heavily in the forefront of men's minds. Less than a century old, others than the Luxorian Royal Family were feeling echoes of a drama that could still make princelings shake in their shoes. The secret files of the Edinburgh City Police held information concerning a tide of aristocratic refugees seeking sanctuary at the Palace of Holyroodhouse as privileged guests of Her Majesty.

On the eve of their departure for Aberlethie, Faro was summoned to Edinburgh Castle to investigate an attempted burglary. As he walked up the High Street from the Central Office along the West Bow, the bright moonlight and a sky wreathed in stars seemed to emphasise the sinister menace of the darkly shuttered Wizard's House.

Again Faro relived the child he had been, four years old, holding tightly to his weeping mother's hand as she took him on a pilgrimage past the spot where his father had died. Or had been murdered, as she maintained and as he was to prove beyond a shadow of a doubt many years later.

At the Castle, Colonel Wrightson, who had entertained him so regally at the regimental dinner, was surprised to see him again.

'Good of you to come, Faro. I appreciate your personal interest.' He smiled. 'Surely this is rather low-key for you?'

'Not at all. Anything that happens on the outside of the Castle walls is for the police. Once inside, then it's yours.'

There was little to see beyond a broken window and a displaced iron bar, but all suggested that the would-be intruder was a man of considerable strength as well as the possessor of a remarkable head for heights. It also hinted to Faro that this might be a situation worth keeping his eye on, a prelude to something even more dangerous.

When he said so, Wrightson smiled. 'I see from the newspapers' report that you had quite an interesting epilogue to your last evening with us. Another crime for you to solve.'

'Not this time, Colonel. Death was from natural causes. Some poor woman with a heart condition taking shelter.'

'I'm relieved to hear that. All these ridiculous stories about ghosts and ancient curses.' He sighed. 'They should spend a night here. That would set their imaginations going. Ghastly deeds in the Wizard's House indeed, they're nothing compared with the violence this castle has seen over the centuries.

'As for the Palace.' He sighed indicating Holyroodhouse, where he had been Captain of the Household Guard some ten years ago. 'It has an even worse reputation if that's possible. Rizzio's murder and God knows what other evil-doing. Yet I've spent many a night alone when the Queen wasn't in residence and I've never seen a single spectre. Lot of rubbish, if you ask me.'

Despite these reassurances, Faro was glad of the carriage the Colonel insisted on providing for him. As it made the tortuous steep descent of the West Bow, the horses' hooves striking sparks off the cobbles, the cloudless sky had vanished and a moon now trembled between clouds breathing life into the mullioned windows of the West Bow's ancient houses.

At one stage, the sergeant-driver reined in cursing, narrowly avoiding a closed carriage racing past at high speed. As they swayed dangerously, he heard the soldier shout:

'Not so much as a damned lantern. And black horses, too.'

Faro watched the carriage disappear, the sweating horses, their breath still on the night, the only evidence that this was no phantom coach.

A black carriage and black horses –

From the depths of memory loomed an almost remembered childhood nightmare that had engulfed his father and his beloved cousin Leslie.

The next instant he was faced with the unpleasant reality of the present. As the driver set their carriage to rights, there was an almighty crack as one wheel hit the high stone kerb.

Faro clambered out and shouted: 'What is it?'

The man was surveying the damage, swearing volubly.

''Fraid you'll need to wait till I fix this, sir.' And shaking his fist at the Wizard's House, towering above them, a vast black shadow: 'Aye, curse you too! Might have known it would happen here. Be a good thing when that damned place is pulled down.'

'I wouldn't have taken you for a superstitious man, Sergeant.'

'Not me. But my second cousin tried to live there once. You've probably read the story, it was in the newspapers. Ghosts and hobgoblins –' He looked up. 'An' he's not fanciful. Fought in the Crimea, he did –' The driver paused to kick the buckled wheel viciously. 'This is going to take some while, sir. You'll like enough pick up a hire at the stance down the High Street.'

Faro walked quickly away. Another accident in the making or just one more coincidence.

He looked back at the tall land and resolved that tomorrow, with daylight on his side, he'd have a careful look round, carry out his own investigation and prove to Edinburgh's nervous citizens, and to himself, that Weir's Land was only wood and stone. As such it had no earthly powers to harm anyone except those who were gullible by nature and predisposed to place every misfortune at the door of superstition.

Tomorrow morning, however, was still several hours away.

In Sheridan Place, Vince was impatiently awaiting his return with a story of his own unpleasant encounter.

4

Faro had failed to locate another carriage after the accident. Hardly surprising since it was past eleven o'clock, a time at which all respectable Edinburgh citizens were presumed to be in bed and asleep, especially by coachmen in foul weather. And the storm that had been threatening all evening now turned the full force of its attention upon the sleeping town.

Wind and rain fairly hurled Faro down the High Street and through the Pleasance to Newington, where he unlocked his front door, very wet and in no very good mood, to find Vince far from sympathetic. Mrs Brook's excellent steak pie and treacle sponge pudding, Vince's particular favourites, had been ruined by his late arrival, to that good lady's distress and his own annoyance.

Following Faro to the kitchen, Vince watched as he peeled off his outer garments and spread them out to dry, Mrs Brook having retired some time earlier.

'You'll never credit this, Stepfather. I was called into Solomon's Tower to attend a visitor. Yes, you do well to look surprised, our Mad Bart had company.' And pausing dramatically, he pursed his lips. 'A lady.'

Sir Hedley Marsh, or the Mad Bart as he was better known in the locality, lived in a crumbling sixteenth-century tower at the base of Arthur's Seat. A recluse, a woman-hater, this novel occurrence was of sufficient interest to take Faro's mind off his discomfort.

'Youngish and quite comely. Walking along where Samson's Ribs joins the road to Duddingston. And there was a landslide.'

'Not again, surely.' The exposed rockface known as Samson's Ribs could be dangerous, especially in bad weather when rocks and loose earth were dislodged with nothing to stop them falling on the road far below.

'We had complaints of a landslide quite recently. I thought they'd done something about it,' he added.

'You know what these authorities are like, Stepfather. No doubt they're waiting for a fatality, and then the Improvement Commission will take action.'

'Tell me about this young lady. Was she badly hurt?'

'Nothing serious. Knocked off her feet, a few bruises. Not nearly as bad as it could have been, but she was very shocked, quite inarticulate. Kept weeping all the time.'

Vince shook his head. 'You know how the Mad Bart mumbles, but I got the gist of it. He had opened his front door and found her there sobbing and crying. Thought it was one of his cats in trouble. He didn't know what to do but wrap her in a blanket and go for help. And then, of course, just as he was leaving: "There you were, young fellow, golf clubs and all,"' Vince mimicked with a grimace of distaste. 'Really, Stepfather, that dreadful old man –'

Faro, having dealt with wet clothes, now packed newspapers into his soaked boots to speed up the drying process. He only half-listened, with amused tolerance, to Vince's tirade. His stepson hated few people, but Sir Hedley Marsh was one of them.

From their earliest days at Sheridan Place it seemed that Vince had found particular favour in the Mad Bart's eyes and Solomon's Tower was hard to avoid if they walked to Newington by the short cut through the Pleasance and Gibbet Lane.

As the Tower was adjacent to the more cheerful surroundings of the modern golf course, it had now become increasingly difficult for Vince to evade encounters with the aristocratic recluse.

'I would swear he sits by that window all day, though how he manages to see anything through the grime is a mystery. I now have to sidle past like a criminal, for if he sees me he rushes out, invites me in for a dram. A dram, in that squalor, surrounded by his infernal cats everywhere –'

Faro tried not to smile, for Vince, who could sit for hours reading quite contentedly with Mrs Brook's ginger cat Rusty purring like a kettle on his knee, entertained no such sentimental feelings about Sir Hedley's 'feline army', the innumerable stray cats he had given home to over the years.

'It's disgusting –'

'Come now, Vince, I consider that rather an admirable and endearing trait,' said Faro. 'Can't you see it as a pathetic gesture, an appeal for companionship from a lonely old man?'

'I can't see it, but I assure you, I can smell it. When he opens the door – really, Stepfather, the place should be condemned as a hazard to health. I could hardly breathe. That poor woman, too. I just hoped she wouldn't succumb to asphyxia before I did.'

Faro, who had been unfortunate enough to cross the threshold on several occasions, could only agree. Still, he did find Vince's animosity trying. He went on and on about it. Why on earth should he hate this tiresome but well-meaning old man? Such venom was quite out of character with Vince's normal serenity, his generous spirit.

'What happened to your patient?'

Vince shrugged. 'I left her there. Offered to see her safely home, of course. But she said no, she would prefer to rest a while. She did seem in rather a state,' he added, frowning. 'In the normal way, I would have insisted, but I just had to get out of that house. I had to breathe fresh air. He said he'd go out and get a carriage and I wasn't to worry. So I didn't,' he ended, closing his mouth defiantly.

Faro had been too preoccupied with getting dried and heating water to make himself a hot toddy to feel sympathetic towards Vince's encounter with the Mad Bart.

Now when he mentioned his own unpleasant near-accident with a runaway carriage that hurtled out of the darkness, he was somewhat hurt by Vince's merriment as any possibly sinister implications were mockingly dismissed.

'Really, Stepfather, it happens all the time. After all, the West Bow's a threat to everyone, the sooner it's pulled down the better.'

Glancing at Faro's solemn face, he smiled. 'Come now, you know as well as I do that carriages are positively uncontrollable there if the cobblestones are wet or icy. You are lucky there was no more damage than a buckled wheel –'

'And a long walk home on a very wet night,' Faro put in acidly, seized by an uncontrollable fit of sneezing.

Vince was unrepentant. He stretched out his hand firmly. 'And I'll take some of that hot toddy too, if you please. I could do with it, I can tell you. After my experiences.'

Faro said no more. Bidding his stepson goodnight, he went grumpily up to bed where he fell asleep to be haunted by bad dreams. Closed carriages drawn by wild black horses swept towards him and ghostly lights appeared at the windows of

Major Weir's house, to a grisly accompaniment of maniacal laughter.

As always, Vince's good temper was restored by a night's sleep. The prospect of a weekend house party at Lethie Castle with some decent golf pleased him to no end.

The impending visit to Aberlethie had also caused a flurry of extra activity in Mrs Brook's kitchen, where the warm smell of baking battled with the aroma of hot irons and boot polish.

As the two men cautiously entered her domain, she beamed on then proudly. She did like her gentlemen being well cared for. A task she sometimes found extremely difficult since Inspector Faro cared not the slightest what he wore as long as it was clean, moderately tidy and comfortable, appropriately warm or cool according to the prevailing state of the weather.

Now to his disgust Faro was called upon to pay particular attention to sartorial matters, the choice of shirts and trousers, collars and cravats. At last the hour of departure dawned, the Lethie carriage arrived and they set off in some style with a proud Mrs Brook waving goodbye.

'And enough luggage behind us,' said Faro, 'to accommodate an entire family of grown-ups and children on a seaside holiday for a month.'

Aberlethie lay some twelve miles east of Edinburgh on the shore of the River Forth. It was a journey that, given the right weather, no traveller could fail to enjoy.

Faro, unused to such luxury, relaxed happily against the well-upholstered seats which smelt pleasantly of expensive cigars. The horses trotted briskly down twisting tree-lined roads and lanes, all with a splendid view across the estuary to the hills of Fife, following a coastline which had seen a fair share of Scotland's turbulent history.

Through Prestonpans, where Prince Charles Edward Stuart, victorious after battle, glimpsed through the mirage of destiny himself crowned king in Edinburgh. A mirage as false, alas, as the gold shimmer of the sandhills twisting through the bent grass by the shore. To their left the long white rollers moved in majestically to break in a gentle thunder upon the sandy beach. Above their heads the plaintive calls of seabirds, of curlew and sandpiper; while on the rocks seals raised their heads to stare lazily at the passers-by.

Behind them a fast-retreating prospect of Arthur's Seat, a crouching lion rampant over Edinburgh Castle on its rock. Ahead of them, the skyline was now occupied by the glacial leftovers of the Bass Rock and North Berwick Law. Their more immediate horizons were obliterated by groves of sea buckthorns, those eldritch trees forever leaning against the wind in attitudes of intense desolation which even the sunniest day refused to dispel.

This scene of melancholy was at last interrupted by the high gates and drive to a pleasing Georgian mansion which had replaced the original Lethie Castle.

Faro nodded approvingly. He found its clear and stately lines pleasing, preferring both his architecture and his lifestyle to be kept as simple and uncluttered as possible.

At his side, Vince smiled. He had long ago decided that his stepfather's everyday existence, dealing with the tortured minds of criminals, had influenced his aversion to the modern taste for Gothic architecture.

Climbing to the front steps, they were met at the door by the butler and ushered up a grand oak staircase to their rooms.

While servants brought in his luggage, Faro stared into the rose garden below his window. One of the best views in the house, he decided, with its tranquil outlook over the once magnificent Cistercian priory, now reduced to a solitary ivy-clad wall.

Vince appeared at his shoulder and whistled appreciatively.

'You did better than me, Stepfather. I only overlook the front drive.'

Warm water and soft fleecy towels had been provided for their ablutions, and when Vince returned a little later, his stepfather was adjusting his cravat in the long mirror. Vince watched approvingly. For one who cared not a jot for how he looked or what he wore, Jeremy Faro would, as usual, be the most distinguished presence at the gathering downstairs.

Vince sighed, tugging at his own cravat and wishing he had

chosen a different colour. It didn't seem quite fair that his handsome stepfather should have this inbuilt flair for what was right, without seemingly paying such matters the least attention.

'Shall we?' he said.

As they descended the stairs, the murmur of voices indicated the drawing-room where the Lethies already mingled with their guests.

Sir Terence and his wife Sara were an attractive, lively couple in their late thirties. Sara was known to be bookish and a supporter of good works. A necessity, Faro suspected, since her husband spent a considerable time in London and when he was at Aberlethie was to be found mainly on the golf course.

They greeted Vince warmly and, Faro duly introduced, they were whisked in the direction of a group of men chatting near the window. There were no familiar faces for Faro. Most were his stepson's golfing acquaintances, and after the briefest and most perfunctory of greetings, Vince was speedily involved in the mysteries of handicaps and birdies, the tragedy of the rough and the language of the golf course.

Faro had no part in this, and neither apparently had the golfers' female partners, who had long since withdrawn to the opposite side of the room and taken over two sofas where they chatted amiably on more domestic and social topics.

As Faro devoted himself to a study of the book-lined walls, he was addressed by a cheerful: 'Detective Inspector Faro, is it not?'

'It is.'

The tall white-haired man smiled, and the rather anxious self-conscious look he darted towards the book Faro held served as introduction.

'Mr Stuart Millar, I presume? I'm delighted to meet you.'

As they shook hands, Millar frowned. 'Have we met before, sir?'

Faro shook his head. 'I think not, sir.'

'Then how –?'

As Millar, frowning, looked round the assembled guests, Faro said: 'Let me explain. You are the only gentleman present who is not absorbed by golfing matters. You are also, if I may say so, a little older. Your face and hands are deeply tanned, not with the transient Scottish summer tan which quickly fades, but with the accumulation of many years of foreign travel. Also – may I –'

He took Millar's right hand. 'Your index finger is calloused, just here at the top joint, a frequent indication that a man spends much time with a pen in his hand. And last of all, I could not fail to notice that you recognised the book I'm holding as one of your own. Your latest, in fact, which I look forward to reading.'

Millar laughed. 'Well done, sir. And I guarantee it will appeal to you, for it is a kind of detective story. I have been looking for the clues that my grandfather hinted at when he accompanied James Bruce of Kinnaird on one of his expeditions to the source of the Nile in 1770.

'Bruce belonged to the minor Stirlingshire aristocracy and inherited enough wealth to indulge a passion for foreign travel. He was something of an enigma, an eccentric we would call him, absorbed by the theory that the Jews in Abyssinia were descendents of King Solomon's misalliance with the Queen of Sheba which had resulted in a son, Prince Menelik.

'His research was meticulous, but my grandfather suspected there was a great deal more in his letters than scholarly research, which Mr Bruce for his own reasons did not wish to have published.'

Faro's interest in the goings-on of Old Testament worthies was somewhat limited and he could only smile politely as Millar went on: 'My grandfather's letters hint that Mr Bruce might have been on the track of a greater treasure.'

Pausing, he regarded Faro quizzically. 'In fact, you might find the Luck o' Lethie particularly interesting –'

Before he could say more, they were interrupted by the arrival of an attractive, vivacious woman with black curls and sparkling eyes. Petite, pretty and breathless, she took Millar's arm.

'Stuart, dear, aren't you going to introduce me?'

'Of course, my dear. My sister –'

Elspeth Stuart Millar, who Faro guessed was nearer his own age than her brother's, took his hand eagerly. 'You are a celebrity, Inspector Faro, and my brother is very naughty to monopolise you.'

Looking at Bruce's book which Millar held, she said: 'Do leave all your boring old theories at home, dear. I'm sure Mr Faro didn't come here to linger in the dust of past times.'

Transferring her hold to Faro's arm, she looked up into his face. A ravishing smile completed the picture of elegance and charm. 'Dear Stuart has a bee in his bonnet about our grandfather. I assure you, he was a most tiresome old man. And desperately mean too –'

Millar gave a good-natured shrug as Faro, with an apologetic glance over his shoulder, allowed himself to be led away to a sofa by the window where Elspeth spread her skirts, and fan in hand, settled herself comfortably.

'There are so many things I'm just dying to ask you, Inspector. I know you won't probably be allowed to tell all. One has to be discreet –' She leaned forward confidentially. 'Do tell me, do you ever meet the dear Queen when she's at Holyrood?'

This was one of the questions most frequently addressed to Faro across dinner tables. His answer was a smile and a vague nod and a refusal to be drawn into further discussion on the subject. He was well acquainted with Her Majesty and the Prime Minister. The people who questioned him would have been very impressed by such information.

But Elspeth Stuart Millar was quite right in her assumption. Such information was classed as 'highly confidential', for several times during his years with the City Police he had been instrumental in averting disaster and royal murders which would have changed for ever the path of British history.

Some day, in a distant future when all the main characters including Faro himself were part of history, no doubt those stories would be told.

'What is she really like, I mean? And er, is there any truth in those shocking stories about her behaviour with John Brown?'

Faro was saved further comment as, turning, he saw Vince rushing towards them, his manner considerably agitated.

'Excuse me, madam.' And leading Faro away, he pointed. 'Over there, Stepfather. By the door –'

5

Following Vince's anguished stare, Faro saw Sir Hedley Marsh standing in the doorway, blinking owlishly at the assembled guests.

As if still unable to believe his eyes, Vince murmured: 'The Mad Bart, Stepfather. What on earth is he doing here? Surely the Lethies never invited him!'

Faro shared his stepson's surprise. It was unknown for the aristocratic hermit to be lured out of Solomon's Tower to a social gathering.

'Dear God,' groaned Vince. 'If I'd seen the guest list, I'd have refused –'

But wonders weren't over by any means. As the Lethies went forward to greet him, from the shadows of the hall a young lady emerged.

At first Faro wondered if he was witnessing a manifestation of the family ghost in a dress of a bygone age.

'That's the woman I told you about,' Vince murmured. 'I didn't know this was to be fancy dress –'

Even though Faro's experience of female apparel was slight, he could see that the full skirt and *décolleté* neckline were reminiscent of the paintings of the young Queen Victoria on the walls of Holyroodhouse. The white silk of the gown had acquired the yellowish hue of age while the silk roses swirling across its skirts were faded blooms indeed.

As for the wearer, her face was as pale as the gown she wore. She was having considerable difficulties with the revealing neckline and a waistline that flowed rather than fitted. In fact the picture presented was of a garment whose original owner had been of shorter and more robust proportions.

As for the guests, they were too well-bred, too well-clad and in full control of any expressions of astonishment as their host and hostess led a shambling but reasonably clean and tidy Sir Hedley and his lady into the room.

'What on earth can Terence be thinking of? – Oh Lord, he's seen us.'

There was no chance of escape as Sir Hedley rushed forward and, ignoring Faro, eagerly seized Vince's hands.

'My dear young fellow. What a pleasant surprise. If I had known you were to be here we could have shared a carriage. You remember – er – this young lady.'

As Vince bowed over his erstwhile patient's hand, a sudden smile banished her anxious and bewildered expression. 'Of course I remember you – the doctor. You were so kind.'

'And this is Dr Laurie's stepfather, Detective Inspector Faro. My – er – niece – Miss Marsh.'

At that extraordinary introduction, 'Miss Marsh' suddenly crumpled, clinging to Sir Hedley for support. She looked ready to faint and Vince sprang forward.

'May I sit for a moment, please?' she whispered.

Sara Lethie, aware that all was not well, came swiftly over and from her reticule produced the smelling salts which she wafted briskly under Miss Marsh's nose.

Eyelids fluttered open, regarded the faces staring down at her. 'Where am I? What has happened?'

'You are with friends, my dear,' said Sara. 'And this is Dr Laurie – And here is your uncle –'

'Uncle?' Miss Marsh stared up at Sir Hedley, who cleared his throat and murmured: 'Well, my dear, what a to-do.'

At that she closed her eyes hastily and leaned back against the sofa.

By this time the polite guests were stricken in poses of mild curiosity, heads craned in the direction of this interesting tableau.

Sara was mistress of the occasion. She was used to dealing with the vapours of her female friends. 'I think it would be best if Miss Marsh rested upstairs for a while. Come, my dear.'

'Allow me to assist you, Sara dear.' Elspeth Stuart Millar sprang forward and with Vince bringing up the rear, Sir Hedley's thoroughly improbable niece was escorted out of the room.

Faro watched them go, followed by the curious glances and whispered speculations of the guests. The young woman was undeniably comely. Tall and willowy, with honey-blonde hair, Miss Marsh fitted admirably into that category Vince, so susceptible to female charms, in happier circumstances would have described as 'a stunner'.

At his side, Sir Hedley, aware of Faro's disbelieving expression, shuffled his feet and looked uncomfortable. 'Not really my niece, y'know. Can't remember her name. Lost her memory. Dare say it'll come back –'

Faro was saved further comment by the sonorous pounding of the dinner gong as the guests took their seats at the table set for fourteen. Only thirteen places were taken, but this fateful number passed without comment as the butler discreetly removed the extra place setting.

If any of the diners noticed the absence of Sir Hedley's niece, they politely ignored it as Elspeth Stuart Millar returned and reinstated her claim upon Inspector Faro. In reply to his question about the young lady's condition, he was told she was recovering nicely. Then Elspeth turned to more important maters, relentlessly pursuing possible scandals in the Royal Family on which Faro, even if he knew they were true, was unable to comment.

Across the table he watched Vince return and, with a nod in his direction, scramble in an undignified manner for a seat as far as possible from the Mad Bart.

The dinner party proceeded without further incident. All excellent courses were consumed, all excellent wines demolished. At last it was time for Detective Inspector Faro to give his talk – so eagerly awaited, according to Terence Lethie's introduction.

His audience knew little of police matters, and in deference to the ladies present, he considered that burglaries were a more appropriate topic for an after-dinner speech than the more bloody and gruesome murders he had solved.

He kept his speech short, aware of the soporific effects that good wining and dining were having on the assembly. Ten minutes later, he sat down to a wave of applause.

'Brave, bravo,' cried Elspeth at his side. And when the applause had subsided, she said wistfully, 'Perhaps you would care to talk to some of my poor unfortunates – the Society for Impoverished Gentlewomen. I know how greatly they would appreciate –'

Faro was saved an answer as Sara invited the ladies to withdraw and leave the gentlemen to their port and cigars. He was looking forward to that part of the evening, a pleasant relaxation. But it was not to be his.

The butler appeared at Vince's side. A whispered word and he was escorted from the room.

Faro watched them leave, followed by Sir Hedley. Guessing that his stepson had been called to attend the young woman upstairs, he was not kept long in doubt as the butler approached.

'Dr Laurie wishes a word with you, sir,'

Excusing himself and leaving Elspeth mid-sentence, he was escorted into an upstairs bedroom where the Lethies, Vince and Sir Hedley hovered anxiously over Miss Marsh.

Reclining on a sofa, she had been removed from her gown and was now enveloped in a lacy peignoir, presumably the property of her hostess.

Her eyes flickered open. 'It all comes back –' she whispered, and looking around the room, she struggled to sit up.

'Good thing too,' said Sir Hedley, eyeing the ancient ballgown that had been discarded on the bed. 'Mamma's gown from the Queen's Coronation – all I could find. Family heirloom and all that.'

'So this was the unfortunate lady caught in a landslide at Samson's Ribs,' said Faro.

'She was hit by a flying stone, knocked unconscious. Recovered, y'know, staggered along the road. Saw my door –'

'Your mistress,' demanded Terence anxiously. 'When is Her Highness arriving?'

Her Highness?

Faro looked across at Vince, remembering his stepson's fury at being called in to the home of his old enemy. And now it seemed that the injured woman had some connection with the Grand Duchess of Luxoria.

'Your mistress,' Terence repeated patiently. 'Where is she?'

Miss Marsh cried out and looked ready to swoon again.

Sir Hedley stared down at her. 'What are you on about, Lethie?' he said angrily. 'Scared the young miss out of her wits. Don't understand –'

Terence held up his hand. 'Listen to me. This young woman is the Grand Duchess's lady-in-waiting.'

'And her name is Miss Roma Fortescue, Sir Hedley,' said Sara, eyeing him reproachfully.

Miss Fortescue opened her eyes and struggled into a sitting position. 'I remember it all now,' she said weakly.

'Take your time, my dear, tell us what has happened?' said Sara, gently stroking her hands.

'We are as you know on our way to Holryroodhouse, Her Highness was to meet her godmother there –'

Faro, listening, frowned. Strange that there had been no mention of this impending visit at the Central Office, where the Queen's movements were followed diligently, especially when she happened to be heading towards Edinburgh. Extra security was a nightmare even on private visits and, as far as the records were concerned, Her Majesty was this moment still in Balmoral Castle.

'... It was the night of the storm, I don't know when –'

'More than a week ago,' put in Terence. 'We had a lot of damage, trees down on the estate.'

'Well, we were delayed. We landed down the coast – somewhere – North Berwick, I think –'

'Are you sure?' asked Faro.

'Yes.'

Faro's frown deepened. What on earth was the entourage from Luxoria doing landing at North Berwick when Leith was the obvious port?

'... The coachman took the wrong route and the road was flooded, a bridge – somewhere – collapsed and we were trying to find a road round when we were swept into the river. I don't remember what happened exactly.'

She shook her head. 'I came to myself lying in a haycart. A carter fished me out. He told me what had happened, that he was heading to Edinburgh. I felt very uneasy about his attitude, he was – ' she paused unhappily '– somewhat over-familiar.'

Even in borrowed robes and a tearful, distressed condition, she still managed to look remarkably attractive, enough for Faro not to find the carter's amorous arousal in the least surprising.

'... So I pointed to a house and said that was my destination and the people were expecting me. They would be so glad I was safe –'

Again she paused, biting her lip, reliving that frightening moment. 'It was that village down the road with a church and a loch – we passed on our way here.'

'Duddingston,' prompted Sir Hedley.

She nodded eagerly. 'I was terribly afraid. I waited until the carter was out of sight, then I wandered along the road. I knocked at your door –' She paused and looked at Sir Hedley. 'Then I'm afraid I must have fainted.'

'Quite so, quite so.' Sir Hedley patted her hand and looked up at Vince. 'You know the rest, young fellow. Took her in, saw you passing –'

Faro glanced in Vince's direction. This was not exactly the same story that Vince had told him about a flying stone. Perhaps that had been Miss Fortescue's polite invention to save the embarrassment of that tale of an amorous carter, and Sir Hedley had presumed the rest. He listened intently as she continued: 'Sir Hedley has been so kind to me,' She smiled up at him gratefully. 'He was too much of a gentleman to ask any questions. I thought my memory would never come back – and indeed, until this minute – everyone will be so relieved to know I am unhurt.'

As she spoke, looks were exchanged, looks of growing horror.

Terence bent over her. 'My dear Miss Fortescue, I'm afraid we haven't yet had a sight of Her Highness.'

'You haven't?' She looked round. 'Undoubtedly she will have made her way direct to Holyroodhouse to see Her Majesty.' She smiled for the first time. 'Her Highness is very resourceful. And independent.'

All now looked hopefully towards Faro. He shook his head. 'We have not been informed –'

'But she could be there?' said Miss Fortescue desperately.

'Not without the knowledge of the Edinburgh City Police, miss. You will appreciate that Her Majesty's residences are very carefully guarded –'

'We expected her to arrive at Lethie several days ago,' Terence interrupted. 'When she did not appear, we presumed that she had been delayed. Or that the visit had been cancelled.'

'Tell me, miss, what does your mistress look like?' Faro asked as gently as he could, hoping Miss Forstecue would not realise the sinister implications of such a remark. If she did not, then others did. The reproachful looks in his direction said louder than words that this was a brutal question expressing their own secret and unspoken fears.

Miss Fortescue seemed merely bewildered. She shook her head. 'What does she look like?' she repeated. 'I have a photograph of her. At least – I had one in my luggage. But why –?' Then as the significance dawned, she whispered: 'You surely don't think –'

'No, no, miss' Faro lied. 'But if you can tell us a little more about your mistress it would help –'

He quailed under Miss Fortescue's cold stare.

'What is it you wish to know, sir?'

Faro attempted to smile reassuringly, and tried hard not to sound like a grim detective soullessly pursuing information for a missing persons enquiry. He had no alternative but to plunge ahead.

'Her appearance, miss, what she was wearing and so forth.'

Miss Fortescue continued to stare at him, and he carried on hastily. 'Look, miss, presumably your mistress was badly shaken by the accident, as you were. She might have had a shock, the same reactions as you've suffered.' Even as he spoke he felt the possibility of two lost memories was very thin indeed.

Miss Fortescue was clearly having a struggle with her own memory. At last she said: 'She's about my height, a bit more well-built, fairish hair, blue eyes. Does that help?'

It did. That slight description thoroughly alarmed Faro, fitting so neatly the corpse of the woman in the West Bow who had been found in such mysterious circumstances... ten days ago.

'The coachman,' said Miss Fortescue helpfully. 'He should be able to tell you what happened. Where he took her and so forth.'

The silence that greeted this observation needed further explanation. With admirable self-control she stifled a scream.

'You mean – he never – Oh dear – the poor man. He must have drowned.'

Now the same thought was in everyone's mind. Miss Fortescue had indeed been lucky to survive. The coachman and the carriage, and Her Highness the Grand Duchess of Luxoria had not been so fortunate. At this moment, they were lost without trace, swept out by the tide, out of the estuary and into the deep and secret waters of the wild North Sea. They might be washed up anywhere, even in Norway, if their bodies lasted that long.

Faro shuddered. How was this news to be broken to Her Majesty? And to whom would fall the unlucky duty of harbinger of these ill tidings? At least he had no doubt of that man's identity.

Himself.

Taking Sir Terence aside, he explained that he must return to Edinburgh immediately and set some enquiries in motion. He refrained from adding what was surely uppermost in all their minds. A missing royal duchess who was also the beloved god-daughter of the Queen and the late Prince Consort.

Terence Lethie's heavy sigh indicated that he knew exactly what was at stake. 'Our carriage is at your disposal, sir.'

Faro glanced towards Miss Fortescue. 'A photograph – or a picture – it would help considerably, sir –'

'I'm not sure that we have one.' He nodded towards the anxious group still surrounding Miss Fortescue. 'She will no doubt be able to describe her mistress – a little later, perhaps, when the shock wears off and she is more composed.'

Vince followed him to the door: 'Perhaps I should stay, Stepfather.'

'I think that would be an excellent idea, lad.'

Faro left with some regret. He had been looking forward to a little hard-earned and agreeable relaxation. He would miss tomorrow's tour of the gardens, a chance to see the Crusader's Tomb in the ruined priory and more important, as he was later to discover, the Luck o' Lethie.

As he prepared to depart he had an ominous feeling of disaster, that too much valuable time had already been lost. Twenty-four hours was difficult enough, but ten days...

If only Miss Fortescue's unfortunate amnesia has cleared up a little earlier.

As the carriage drove towards Edinburgh, he had ample opportunity to brood upon what had happened to the coachman and more crucially the present whereabouts of the Grand Duchess of Luxoria.

6

At Sheridan Place, a message from Superintendent McIntosh awaited Faro. He was to proceed to the Central Office immediately. Realising that it must be important for the Superintendent to interrupt his weekend, Faro found him as he expected in no good mood.

'You're wanted at Holyrood, straightaway. The usual Royal-visit security formula.'

Faro knew a moment's joy. 'I take it that the Grand Duchess of Luxoria has arrived.'

'Who?' McIntosh looked at him blankly. 'I know nothing about any Grand Duchess. Only that the PM wants a word.' And Faro went to the door, 'Try not to irritate him, Faro. It doesn't do any of us – particularly yourself – any good, you know.'

Of course he would be patient, Faro decided, clinging to the hope that he had once again allowed his imagination to indulge in morbid fancies. But even his optimism began to fade, faced with the long gallery, its inquisitorial length deliberately chosen to intimidate all but the boldest and most determined. At its far end, Mr Gladstone was pacing the carpet, his already thin-lipped mouth a fast disappearing line across a grimly set countenance.

At Faro's approach, he regarded his watch in some irritation. A stickler for punctuality on all occasions, he grumbled: 'You took your time getting here, Faro.'

'I came from the office immediately, sir.' Faro was damned if he'd apologise.

The watch snapped shut. 'You were summoned yesterday, Inspector.'

Faro was at a loss for an appropriate response. 'Yesterday was Saturday, sir. I was absent from Edinburgh. In fact, I have already had to cut short my weekend with friends.'

He could have said a great deal more on that subject but Gladstone's impatient gesture dismissed such inconvenience as of no importance.

'Friends, indeed?' he snorted. 'Her Majesty's wishes come first, you've been on the job long enough to know that, Faro,' he added severely, his tone indicating that if Faro wasn't fully aware of the fact, then he might soon be seeking other employment.

It had the desired effect. Faro bit back an angry response and said calmly, 'Am I to presume that the arrival of the Grand Duchess of Luxoria is imminent?'

The Prime Minister looked startled. 'So you aware that she is expected?' Suddenly he thumped his fists together. 'She has not yet put in an appearance. Nor has her arrival been signalled. And that is precisely why you have been summoned, Inspector. Her Majesty is about to leave Balmoral to meet her god-daughter – here. So where the devil is she? Answer me that.'

'I would suggest that she is perhaps making a private visit – to friends –'

'Friends, eh?' The Prime Minister nodded sagely. 'From what I have heard of the lady's unfortunate domestic circumstances, there is no doubt a gentlemen involved?' His head inclined to one side, he regarded Faro, extremely pleased with himself for this sharp piece of observation.

'We will, of course, conduct the usual enquiries,' Faro said sternly.

'With the utmost discretion, if you please.'

'Naturally, sir. Now if you will excuse me.'

And giving Mr Gladstone no chance of further questioning, Faro beat a hasty retreat.

Back at the Central Office, Faro thought rapidly. The Superintendent was no fool. He would have to be told and sooner rather than later about the distraught Miss Forstescue.

'It appears that her lady-in-waiting has arrived at Lethie Castle,' he ended the account of his interview with the Prime Minister. 'Her mistress was making a visit there en route to Edinburgh.'

'And so – her present whereabouts?'

'They don't know – precisely. But they expect her arrival imminently,' he ended smoothly, rather proud of this piece of invention, but the Superintendent roared like a wounded lion.

'You realise what this means, Faro. We've mislaid a member of the Royal Family. This could be the end of all our careers. We'll be lucky if we don't see the inside of the Tower. Dear God, what will Her Majesty say to this? You'll have to tell her.' His laugh was without mirth. 'And I don't envy you that.'

'There could be a quite innocent explanation.'

'Could there indeed?'

'The Prime Minister hinted at a secret assignation of a romantic nature.'

'Ah!' McIntosh sighed profoundly. 'Rumour has it that the marriage is fairly unsound. Presumably he has found consolation elsewhere. The PM would of course know about that from information within royal circles.'

Faro wondered why it had not occurred to the Superintendent as in any way unusual for a duchess to travel alone. Surely a major concern in the appointment of a lady-in-waiting would be her ability to ignore royal peccadilloes when necessary.

'... But we should have been informed of any change of plan,' the Superintendent continued. 'That is quite unforgivable. After all, our discretion can be relied upon. Who do these foreigners think they are, anyway, keeping Her Majesty waiting?' he added, ignoring the fact that, as he had pointed out, the Grand Duchess was a relative.

'Here –' Turning to the desk he seized a fistful of papers which he flourished under Faro's nose. 'You'd better find her. That's your job.' And as he was leaving: 'I take it that you have some ideas of where to start?'

Faro had a few but none that he would care to discuss with his superior at that moment.

'I think we should play for time, Faro. Presume that Her Highness is, er, on a clandestine visit... The message sent ahead could have gone astray. What do you think?'

Faro stifled a smile. The Superintendent could occasionally display an endearing romantic turn of mind. He was searching for a suitable reply when McIntosh sighed wearily, indicating the interview was at an end.

'Your responsibility, Faro. Be it on your head.'

And Faro didn't care a great deal for the significance of that parting shot either. A chill wind sharp as an axe blade touched the back of his neck as he crossed the corridor into his office, where he earnestly considered the contents of a highly secret file marked 'Her Majesty the Queen'.

Under Luxoria, there was mention of a proposed visit, but no final date had been decided. It simply said that the Grand Duchess would arrive by ship at the port of Leith. Travelling incognito – as befitted a private visit – under the name of Lady Moy, she would be accompanied by her lady-in-waiting Miss Roma Fortescue. There was no mention of any coachmen or equerry travelling with them.

Faro's dismal thoughts were interrupted by Constable Reid.

'There's a lady come to see you. She's in the waiting-room.'

'Show her in.' Faro's immediate hope was that this was Miss Fortescue bearing a photograph of her mistress, and he was somewhat taken aback to find that the visitor was Lady Lethie.

As they shook hands he said: 'I'm glad to see you here, I was about to come out to Aberlethie. How is Miss Fortescue?'

'Much improved.' She smiled. 'We have persuaded her to accept our hospitality until – until things sort themselves out. She will be more comfortable with us, and now that her memory has returned she does not feel she can impose any further on Sir Hedley. Although, of course, his place is more adjacent to Holyrood.'

Her frown indicated that the decision had been difficult. Faro thought that it was all too obvious to anyone who had ever set foot – or nose – within the walls of Solomon's Tower.

As she spoke she opened her reticule, but instead of the photograph Faro now hoped was the reason for her visit, she took out a dainty lace handkerchief and patted her nose.

'Fortunately, I can provide her with items from my wardrobe, we are of the same size – until her luggage arrives – eventually,' she added, but Faro felt there was little hope in the word or in her expression as she said it.

'Miss Fortescue still has no idea of what might have happened to her mistress?'

'Not the slightest. We do try to keep her spirits up, Inspector, we try to get her to look on the bright side. But it is extremely hard, very hard indeed. She is prone to the most gloomy thoughts.' She paused before adding: 'She could, of course, have gone to Holyrood. I think that was on her mind at one point. But as you see, that would not do at all. She is most anxious that there is no fuss, as she calls it. The Grand Duchess would be most distressed when she, er, arrives.'

'But, surely – look, Lady Lethie, I have it on good authority that the Queen is on her way down from Balmoral. Once she arrives, then Miss Fortescue must go and tell her what has happened.'

'Oh, so Her Majesty is coming,' Sara Lethie smiled. She looked oddly relieved by this information. 'Perhaps you will let us know immediately she arrives. I do hope it will be very soon as we are due to go to France for a family wedding –'

And Sara Lethie stood up and drew on her gloves. Conscious of her air of relief, he decided to spare her the painful details of his interview with the Prime Minister.

'I do hope you will forgive me intruding upon you in this way, Inspector. I'm sure you are a very busy man, but as I was coming to Edinburgh today – one of my committees, you know – I decided I must try and see if there was any further news I could take to Miss Fortescue.' She paused for breath.

'She really is most anxious. In fact, we all are. Everyone is pretending that there will be a perfectly logical reason for the Grand Duchess not arriving, but after the accident –' She shuddered.

'How well did you know Miss Fortescue?'

Sara Lethie looked startled by the question, but only for a moment. She managed a nervous laugh. 'Not at all really. But the Fortescues have been friends of ours for – oh, generations. Roma's father is a court official in Luxoria. They have served the Grand Duchy since the eighteenth century when they followed Prince Charles Edward Stuart's father into exile.'

She looked at him earnestly. 'You will keep us informed, Inspector – when you have any further news.'

'Immediately, Lady Lethie.'

At the door she turned. 'Do you think this could be the work of, well, some foreign conspiracy?'

'That thought had not occurred to me.' So she wasn't aware of the unsound marriage and the possibility of a romantic assignation. 'Are you suggesting that the Grand Duchess might have been kidnapped?'

If only that were true, he thought. That she was still alive, and in one piece.

'Something like that, perhaps.'

'I'm sure you're mistaken, Lady Lethie. However, it would be a great help if you had a photograph of Her Highness – solely for our purposes. You can rely on our discretion.'

Sara Lethie frowned. 'I think there might be one, taken a long time ago. Possibly Miss Fortescue will have one of a more recent date.' She smiled. 'I'm sure she'll be best able to help you. They have been together since childhood. Very close, you know, grew up together. Why don't you talk to her?'

That was precisely what Faro intended. A personal talk with the lady-in-waiting would better suit the purpose of his enquiries than any picture of the missing woman. His growing misgivings weren't helped by Constable Reid handing him a reply to his telegraph to the North Berwick constabulary: 'No wreckage of coach on road or shore reported.'

As he was leaving, the Superintendent caught him at the door. 'Message from Balmoral, Faro. Her Majesty has had a slight chill and is to remain indoors for a day or two on the advice of her physicians. Let's hope her god-daughter deigns to appear before the Queen arrives. If not, heads will roll,' he added grimly.

Faro shuddered as he closed the door.

He had not seen Vince since his return from Lethie Castle when he had been called away on an urgent and difficult confinement.

'All is well,' he said as they met at supper that night. 'Mother and son doing famously.'

'How did you leave your patient at Aberlethie?'

'Miss Fortescue? Seemed to be making a fine recovery. Healthy young woman, despite a tendency to the vapours. Any further developments in the saga of her missing mistress?'

For Vince's benefit, Faro went over the details of his interview with Mr Gladstone and of Lady Lethie's visit.

Vince frowned. 'I think the romantic assignation is a bit thin, Stepfather. Surely Miss Fortescue would know if she and the Duchess are such close companions?' He paused and then added: 'What do you think of the kidnapping idea?'

'We must consider it as a possibility. But bearing in mind the complexity of Luxorian politics and that the Duchess was forced into a loveless marriage, the odious President might have good reason to want rid of her. But, I suspect, on a more permanent basis than mere kidnapping,' he added grimly.

'A closer acquaintance with Miss Fortescue might indeed bring forth some illuminating thoughts on that subject,' said Vince.

Faro smiled. 'Would you care to volunteer?'

'Alas, no. She isn't quite my type, Stepfather. Pretty and all that, but there's – well, something strange about her. Too reserved – and foreign for me, despite all that good solid British education. She wasn't much in evidence over the weekend and the Mad Bart took himself off, grateful, I think, that the Lethies were willing to look after her. We managed a few rounds of golf and a look at the Luck o' Lethie.'

'Stuart Millar told me it was worth seeing.'

Vince shrugged. 'It's just a battered old horn that hangs in a glass case in the old chapel, the only part of the castle they didn't pull down, in fact. Apparently it was brought back from King Solomon's Temple by the crusader David de Lethie – the one whose tomb is in the priory.'

'Why is it called the Luck o' Lethie?'

Vince smiled. 'Legend has it that as long as it survives, so will the Lethie line continue. Considering the swarm of offspring, and the deafening noise they were making, there seems little doubt about it.' He sighed. 'But none of this helps much with our missing Grand Duchess, does it?'

Faro looked at him. 'Vince, I've had a terrible thought.'

'You're too ready to look on the gloomy side, Stepfather. It's one of your failings. You know that. You must try to keep it under control,' he added severely, and at Faro's expression, he continued, 'Look, the fact that she's still missing doesn't necessarily mean that she's been drowned – or kidnapped, Stepfather. It could be something quite innocuous, as has been suggested, a visit to a secret lover. After all, this is no ordinary missing person –'

Vince stopped suddenly. The same thought was in both of their minds. A woman's body, unidentified, that didn't fit any description on the missing persons list at the Central Office.

'Dear God,' Vince whispered. 'You're surely not thinking – there could be some connection between the – West Bow corpse –'

Faro looked at him slowly and Vince jumped to his feet.

'Oh, no – she couldn't be – could she?' he added weakly.

When Faro didn't reply, Vince sat down again sharply. As sickening realisation dawned they regarded each other with mounting horror across the table, neither fully able to complete the dreadful thought.

That, even as they spoke, Dr Cranley's medical students might be deeply absorbed in dissecting what remained of Amelie, Duchess of Luxoria, the well-beloved god-daughter of Her Majesty the Queen.

7

Faro slept little that night.

His thoughts like rats trapped in a cage, he searched in vain for the vital clues that he was certain he had overlooked or whose significance he had failed to recognise when it had been presented to him. Such shortcomings, damnable in his profession, were by no means a novel experience, but left always the dry sensation of defeat in his mouth, the dreaded whisper: was he losing his skill?

He took a deep breath. There was only one solution: before visiting Aberlethie again, and talking to Miss Fortescue, he must return to the discovery of the woman's body in the West Bow and prove to himself – somehow – that his suspicions regarding her identity were false.

After a hasty breakfast without Vince, who had been summoned to attend a sick patient, Faro set off for the Central Office by the short cut through Gibbet Lane, bordering Solomon's Tower.

On an impulse he decided to call upon Sir Hedley. Eight o'clock was striking on the city clocks as he approached the door, but he had no doubt that the old man would be up and about. It was Sir Hedley's proud boast that he rose with the larks and retired with the setting sun.

The tower was gloomy and forbidding in darkness, and much the same even in the daylight of a grey Edinburgh morning, which did little to raise Faro's spirits as he applied his hand to the rusted and ancient bell-pull. The clanging sound reverberated through the surrounding area but failed to bring any response.

Deciding that Sir Hedley must be deaf indeed not to have been roused by the din, he observed with some unease that the front door was very slightly ajar. It yielded instantly to his touch. Was this no more than a nocturnal convenience for the cats, he wondered, as they assailed him from all directions with yowls of protest that he had not arrived carrying saucers of milk? Only the boldest, however, were confident enough to sidle out and insinuate themselves around his ankles.

'Sir Hedley! Sir Hedley!'

There was no reply and Faro decided that he was getting unduly nervous. There was absolutely no reason why Sir Hedley should not be away from home; he might have visited friends and stayed the night. An unduly optimistic thought, Faro decided, knowing the nature of the reclusive occupant's character.

With a growing sense of foreboding, he carefully pushed his way inside, as cats of every colour, shape and age noisily scampered after his ankles, anxious not to let the possible source of sustenance out of their sight.

'Sir Hedley? Sir Hedley?'

Silence greeted him. Opening the door, he stepped carefully into the stone-walled parlour, and averting his eyes to the squalor and his nose to its odours, he tried not to breathe too deeply as he climbed the twisting staircase to the upper floor. Dreading what he might find inside, he opened an ancient studded door. A bedroom, at first glance no better than the apartment he had just left.

His inclination was to close the door again hastily. Instead he approached the bed. Half a dozen privileged cats gave him haughty stares from the comfort of a plumed four-poster. Faro suspected that it dated back to the seventeenth century when necessity dictated that grand beds were built into upper rooms approached by a turnpike stair. Since there was no method of transporting them either up or down afterwards, many thus survived both the attentions of thieving enemies and the changing fashions of time.

Faro approached the bed cautiously. Sir Hedley wasn't lying there with his throat cut as imagination had so readily prompted, but his cats were very much at home, resting on the remains of a once well-made and handsome garment, certainly not the property of Sir Hedley. The delicate lace and embroidered bodice, stained by cats and ripped by their claws, suggested that this was yet another of the Dowager Lady Marsh's elegant cast-offs.

The sight offended Faro, deeply. By no means a frugal man, he deplored such waste. Such a gown, now a bed for cats, would have fetched an excellent price in Edinburgh's luckenbooths, and provided meals in plenty for many a starving family.

Without any further compunction about searching the house for the missing baronet, he went down a few steps and opened an old studded door, where there was another surprise in store.

He was in a stone-walled chapel-like apartment. Instead of the religious symbols its mitred roof suggested, here were the accoutrements of the Ancient Order of Templars. Doubtless Sir Hedley had belonged to the order in his youth, as did so many of the nobility. But what struck Faro as extraordinary was that the room was clean and obviously well-tended and completely out of character with the sordid condition of the rest of the house. Who then was the guardian of this shrine, for Sir Hedley seemed an improbable choice?

The sight of this serene chapel left him with a sense of disquiet, as he pondered other inconsistencies such as Sir Hedley's apparently innocent role as rescuer of Miss Fortescue.

Had he misjudged Sir Hedley, dismissed him as a harmless eccentric? Was Vince's loathing unconsciously justified and did the Mad Bart, in fact, hold a sinister role in the Grand Duchess's disappearance?

By the time Faro had put some distance between himself and Solomon's Tower, the thought of Sir Hedley's complicity became even more unlikely, and as he approached the High Street, his sense of logic reasserted itself.

The truth was undoubtedly that he had been too involved with his own distaste for the West Bow. His eagerness to get the investigation over with as soon as possible had permitted the unforgivable in a detective. He had allowed his preoccupation with bitter personal emotions regarding his long-dead father to blunt his normally acute powers of observation and deduction.

With a dawning sense of horror at a nightmare that had already begun and from which there was no probable awakening, he could no longer delay reliving the scene from that moment Constable Reid summoned him from his carriage to view a beggar-woman's corpse.

This time he would proceed as a diligent detective on the look-out for anything even slightly out of the ordinary that would never be considered except in a possible murder investigation.

He stepped into the Central Office to be hailed by Danny McQuinn, who had newly returned from Aberdeen. Faro was glad to see his young sergeant again and, after a few moments' social conversation, he decided that McQuinn had better become acquainted with the case of the missing Grand Duchess. Once the bane of his life, the passing years had smoothed the rough edges of the Irishman's personality. Trust, respect and even grudging admiration had grown between the two men.

In addition, Faro recognised with gratitude that, on more than one occasion, he owed his life to McQuinn's quick thinking. And this had extended to members of Faro's family.

McQuinn was sharp, none better, and Faro was consoled that he made no immediate connection between the missing Duchess and the dead vagrant in the West Bow. Or at least if he did, then he refrained from comment.

'Drownings in the Forth, sir? Nothing reported. Weather's been good since the storm,' McQuinn added.

'Try further afield, McQuinn. Bodies can be carried right across the estuary to the coast of Fife or down the East Lothian coast.'

'What sort of a corpse are we looking for, sir?'

'A coachman, possibly in some sort of livery.'

'I take it he was driving the lady's carriage.'

'Yes.'

McQuinn thought for a moment. 'As both are missing, could there be some connection? I mean, like kidnapping, holding her to ransom.'

'I've thought of that.'

'The newspaper might have a photograph of her, sir. Dare say Miss Fortescue will oblige with a description of the coachman. Servants usually know one another uncommonly well.'

Faro watched as McQuinn pocketed his notebook, thankful that he could be relied on.

'I'll check with the North Berwick harbour authorities. With luck I might find someone who knew – or saw – this coachman. Shall I go to Aberlethie, talk to Miss Fortescue?'

'No. Leave that to me,' said Faro.

But first, the Wizard's House.

Faro's route to the West Bow took him close by the Grassmarket, a part of Edinburgh which had witnessed many grisly executions in Scotland's history. And here, he thought, he stood on the threshold of what might prove to be yet another sensational case in the annals of that country's crime.

But as his footsteps led him through the Lawnmarket past his cousin's lodging, he was guiltily aware that he was sorely neglecting Leslie Faro Godwin. The temptation to do something normal again, to see a pleasant smiling face, to talk to a man whose only interest in crime was its value as a news item, was overwhelming.

As Faro walked along the narrow wynd, his nostrils were assailed by increasingly unpleasant odours of cooking, cats and human excrement.

Looking up at the bleak lodging, once more his mind flew in vivid contrast to his own comfortable but mainly empty house in Sheridan Place. Doubtless it would be useless to try and persuade his cousin to change his mind. Too much time had been lost, the indication had been that Leslie Faro Godwin intended his stay in Edinburgh to be brief.

Faro smiled wryly. What would his mother make of all this? It was some time since he had written to her in Orkney and his conscience smote him regularly on his neglect of his daughters, Rose and Emily, who were fortunate indeed to receive even a postcard from him on rare occasions.

He could almost hear his mother's reproachful sigh when she heard about Leslie Faro Godwin. A firm believer in 'There's no one like your own flesh and blood', she would have been horrified at his treatment of a close relative, despite any reminders that the Godwins had abandoned her after her husband was killed. 'That was a long time ago,' she would say, 'you've both come a long way since then. Thank God.'

There was no response to his rap at the front door. It was unlocked and he entered a dank dim corridor where doors on either side indicated other apartments. Following a narrow, evil-smelling stair twisting upwards, he found himself outside the first-floor apartment which Leslie had indicated from the street. Here was a more promising door, and Faro tapped on it. As he awaited a response, he heard voices within. His cousin was at home.

The door was opened by a tall, dark and swarthy man of villainous aspect. A pock-marked countenance was not helped by a huge scar which puckered one side of his face. He looked like an old soldier who had seen many campaigns, and even as Faro awaited his reply as to whether his cousin Mr Leslie Faro Godwin was at home, he decided that, used as he was to dealing with violent men, this one belonged in the category he would have avoided encountering on a dark night.

'Someone to see you, master.' Faro recognised the voice as one of the two he had heard.

'Who is it, Batey?'

So this was Sergeant Batey. A man with the cold dead eyes of a killer. No doubt he was loyal to his master. Certainly, Leslie Godwin would be safe wherever he went with this man to look after him.

'Sez he's yer cousin.'

'Jeremy? Do come in –'

Godwin was alone, seated near the window. He rose to greet Faro, book in hand. The window was tiny, and the dim light revealed a room furnished with only the meagre essentials. There were two other doors, which might lead either into more rooms or into cupboards.

Godwin's greeting was cheerful. He cut short Faro's apologies.

'No need for that, Jeremy. I'm always full of good intentions and promises that I never manage to fulfil. With the best will in the world, time just runs away with me.'

He paused, giving Faro a curious look. 'Any developments with your West Bow vagrant?' he asked eagerly.

Faro hesitated then shook his head, anxious that the fewer who knew about the missing woman, the better for all concerned. Particularly himself. So he decided against mentioning Miss Fortescue, realising that however loyal a cousin, the newsman who was also Godwin might find the temptation of pursuing such a story irresistible, thereby making it public property with results that would be nothing short of disastrous.

Leslie had observed his hesitation, for he smiled. 'I scent a story somewhere.'

'I'm afraid we didn't get very far with our enquiries.'

'I've seen that lad who found her a few times, by the way. Sandy, wasn't that his name? Batey caught him with his hand in my pocket the other day. He lives just round the corner in one of the tall lands, Bowheads Wynd, they call it.'

This was an unexpected stroke of luck. 'There are a few questions I'd like to ask him about that night.'

Godwin looked at him. 'D'you know, I had the same feeling. That he knew a lot more than he was telling us. For instance, I shouldn't be at all surprised if he knew what happened to the woman's clothes.'

'Clothes?' Faro was a little taken aback by this astute observation.

Godwin laughed. 'Surely, Jeremy, you saw at once that the dead woman was no vagrant. Such hair and hands never went with a beggar's gown. They belonged with silks and satins, with jewels and fine clothes.'

'So you think they might have been removed?'

Leslie nodded eagerly. 'Undoubtedly the case. And the lad Sandy might have been scared to rob a corpse himself but he would have soon seen the possibilities of making some profit out of those who don't share such a sense of delicacy. It was probably all taken care of, long before he was sent to summon the police.'

'You could be right,' said Faro.

'Of course I'm right.' Leslie continued: 'From my slight acquaintance with the Grassmarket, I see plenty of booths selling clothes for pennies. Mostly rags.'

Pausing, he studied Faro thoughtfully. 'But what we might dismiss as rags might keep a poor family in food for a week.'

Faro smiled wryly. Obviously he wasn't the only member of his family who had inherited the ability to observe and deduce.

'A splendid idea, Leslie. Well worth following. But not what I came for – Shall we have dinner one night? Say, the Café Royal? Saturday evening at seven?'

Accompanying him to the door, Godwin said: 'Look, I'd like to help. Seeing that I was in at the very beginning, there with you, so to speak, when the woman was found. If I see the lad Sandy again, I'll try and buy some information for you. A few pence might work wonders at loosening his tongue. Really – I mean it.'

He put a hand on Faro's arm. 'I want to help you solve your beggar-woman mystery. Not only for the news value either.' He grinned. 'Just because I enjoy a challenge.'

Faro left him and walked down the stone stairs, suddenly happy and confident. Having his cousin's assistance was exactly what he needed to solve this baffling case.

8

Faro's route to the West Bow took him past the entrance to Bowheads Wynd, where he decided to call on young Sandy. A couple of shillings thrust into his hand, with the promise of more to come, should be ample to loosen the lad's tongue about his gruesome discovery and the events which took place before he summoned Constable Reid to the scene.

Faro had to knock on several doors before he received even a scowling oath in response to his enquiry. Whereas his cousin's lodgings were merely shabby and poor, Bowheads Wynd was depressingly lacking in hope as well as cleanliness of any kind.

From each opened door, his nose was overwhelmed by the stench of crowded humanity within. He remembered that these tall 'lands' had once been the pride of Edinburgh, town residences to the nobility, lived in by one family only – along with their many servants. Now each room on all six floors was occupied by perhaps twelve people – a man and a woman, their swarm of children and maybe a couple of elderly relatives or hangers-on.

He had almost given up hope of finding Sandy when at last a woman, with several small children clinging to her skirts, answered to the name of Mrs Dunnock. Her clothes were clean, shabby but neat, and when she spoke she nervously pushed a gold bracelet back from her wrist.

'I'm his ma. What d'ye want wi' him? What's he done this time?' she said wearily, her manner that of a parent used to receiving constant complaints about her unruly offspring.

'Nothing. Just tell him Inspector Faro came by.'

'Inspector Faro?'

Mention of his name panicked her. She stepped backwards, glancing over her shoulder as if someone else might be listening.

'You're a polis!' she said accusingly, as if he had wheedled his way to her door under false pretences.

'I'm a detective, Mrs Dunnock.'

She took a great gulp of air, her hands clutched her wrists and she pointed to his tweed cape and hat. 'Proper policemen wear uniforms.'

'Detectives don't.'

'And that gives you the right to come poking your nose into what don't concern you? We ain't done nothing wrong,' she added in a pathetic whine.

'Neither has Sandy – at least not that we know about,' he said. 'Just tell him there's a couple of shillings for him to put to good use.'

The woman's eyes glittered at the mention of money, almost as if he had given her a glimpse into paradise. Her defensive manner softened so rapidly, he guessed that this was obviously not what she had been fearing as the outcome of his unexpected visit.

She managed a smile. 'He's no' at home, but I'll tell him, mister. Where d'ye bide?'

'He knows that too,' said Faro, and lifted his hat politely as he walked away down the steps.

An adept at shallow breathing, he was glad to fully extend his lungs again, for even the reek of smoking chimneys in the High Street was ambrosia compared to the vile stench in the fetid house he had just left, with its dreadful odour of rotting meat. God only knew what cheap cuts the poor got from the flesher's disease-ridden stocks, and why many more did not succumb to food poisoning. And as always his final thought when faced with direct poverty was: But for the grace of God, there go I. For such he was fully aware might have been the squalid circumstances of his own life, but for an accident of fate that had made him a policeman's son with a widowed mother prepared to make material sacrifices for his education.

Even in broad daylight, with a thin sun turning the Castle into the setting for one of Sir Walter Scott's romances, Faro approached the wizard Major's abode with reluctance. Its chilling atmosphere and sinister emanations had remained untouched by passing years and changing seasons. Facing north-east, its windows were untroubled by sunshine, but it was not aspect alone which added to the feeling of foreboding and melancholy.

Clocks from all over the city were striking eleven o'clock, and it was a bright sunny autumn morning, yet Faro observed how passers by avoided the tall shadow thrown across the narrow cobbled street by the Wizard's House. Men hurried along, heads down, while women, wrapping shawls closer about their heads, drew small children more closely to their sides with a hushed word of warning.

Through the doorway with its ironic inscription, '*Soli deo honor et gloria*, 1604', Faro proceeded along the low vaulted passage which led through the tall land to a narrow court behind. There, solitary and sinister, stood the entrance to Major Weir's house. Legend had it that the wizard had cast a spell on the neighbouring turnpike stair so that anyone climbing up it felt as if they were instead climbing down – to the infernal regions below being no doubt the implication.

Faro shuddered. Only the appalling coincidence of a woman's body and a missing duchess, the nightmare possibility that they might be connected, had driven him back to this hell house.

His last visit had been made in darkness; now every detail of the building, every stone, might conceal a vital clue to the mystery. The discovery of a corpse pronounced as dead from natural causes would involve no search for clues except for the purpose of identification.

The door was slightly ajar. Hanging by one creaking hinge, it was unlocked and Faro doubted whether it had seen a key for that purpose in living memory. With only the vaguest idea of what he was looking for, what might be of significance in this puzzling case, Faro was suddenly hopeful. Long undisturbed dust is of admirable assistance to a man searching for evidence of violence and the Major's house was most obliging in this respect. In the thick coating on the floor were the recent footprints of the policemen intermingled with tiny animal tracks identifiable as rats and mice.

Closer observation revealed a clean but wide trail in the centre of the dirt from the front door into the squalid scene of death, ending at the place where the body had been found. He sat back on his heels. Some of the dust had caked into mud. He crumbled it in his hands. Something, or more likely, someone had been dragged along the floor, someone whose garments were wet. Searching carefully again he discovered threads, a piece of cloth caught on a rusty nail. No ordinary cloth either but a shred of fine lace, which he pocketed carefully.

A little further into the room, near an inside drain, the light from the dim window above touched a thin line of gold. He bent down and dragged out a chain bearing an ornamental cross.

Not a Christian crucifix but an eight-pointed cross pattée.

Faro sat back on his heels, weighing it in his hand. He wished he hadn't found it here, for he had seen the emblem of the Templars very recently. On a backcloth in the chapel in Solomon's Tower.

And a chill – cold and malevolent as the wizard's ghostly hand – stole over him as he remembered that Major Weir had been a Templar as well as a member of the Edinburgh City Guard.

Did this indicate a further sinister twist to the mystery and did the solution to this nineteenth-century disappearance have its roots back in history?

Taking it a step further, was the Mad Bart's Tower a Temple of Solomon and Sir Hedley Marsh the last of its guardians? Could his life as an eccentric and a recluse be a disguise for a secret and never-ending quest?

No. It was too preposterous a theory even for Faro. Besides, it led him far from the missing Grand Duchess, a mystery which must be solved urgently if he was not to find himself facing an irate Prime Minister.

He had a great deal to think about as he sat on the train to Aberlethie. He enjoyed train journeys. Staring out of the window at the passing countryside gave him leisure to get his facts in order and make a few notes.

A halt had been conveniently arranged with the railway company where the line passed over Lethie estate grounds. The walk to the castle through the little hamlet with its cluster of houses was delightful.

He stopped to watch the horses being led across the fields, gathering in the late harvest with the seagulls screaming at their tracks as the uplifted soil revealed fresh delicacies of worms.

Deciding he was in no hurry after all, Faro lit a pipe and leaned on a fence to watch this pastoral and peaceful scene. Around him lay evidence of all those earlier settlements which had held their sway in Scotland's history, then one by one had disappeared. And in the fullness of time, Faro realised, this must be the fate of his own era, too, giving place to a new world waiting in the wings and a destiny as yet unborn. But all would owe their origins to those centuries long gone which had formed the traditions of the Scotland in which he now stood.

When almost reluctantly he at last walked up the stone steps to the castle, he was told that Miss Fortescue was walking with the laird in the gardens.

'They went in the direction of the old priory.'

The neat lawns and geometric flowerbeds surrounding the castle gave way to a wild garden, the domain of ancient trees of huge girth. Through them could be glimpsed a distant sea, glittering on the horizon, and a ruined wall thrusting into the sky.

Here was the twelfth-century Priory of Our Lady which had once dominated the whole area. Its buildings and harbour, once vital links in a flourishing port, had vanished with a retreating coastline that had left an estuary of the River Forth no longer deep enough to allow sailing ships and steamers safe harbour.

For a while, Aberlethie had acquired notoriety and the close attention of the exciseman as a landing place for smugglers and those on dubious errands and journeys, with their own reasons for entering Scotland at secret and safe locations.

As he made his way through the dense shrubbery, Faro heard voices which halted him in his tracks. Although the words were indistinct, what he was overhearing was undoubtedly a fierce argument.

Reluctant to make his presence known, he decided on immediate retreat, but his cautious withdrawal from the scene had not taken into account the laird's dogs, who pricked their ears and, barking fiercely, darted towards this intruder.

With Sir Terence calling them sharply to heel, Faro emerged somewhat sheepishly, endeavouring to look as cheerful as was possible in the circumstances.

Sir Terence and Miss Fortescue were standing by the Crusader's Tomb in its niche in the one remaining wall of the priory. They were not alone. Another figure emerged. Sir Hedley Marsh.

At the sight of him, Faro's relief that he was very much alive was intermingled with a curiosity about what he was doing here, a participant in a conspiratorial conversation.

Miss Fortescue, he noticed, had fully recovered and looked none the worse for her recent ordeal. In fact, she looked decidedly pretty. As she came towards him, hand outstretched in smiling greeting, she appeared to be in perfect command of the situation.

Obviously Lady Lethie had been generous with her extensive wardrobe, he thought approvingly. The two ladies were of similar height and dimensions. Miss Fortescue, carrying a lace parasol and wearing a muslin afternoon gown covered in tiny sprigs of flowers, provided an attractive picture for any man.

'How nice to see you, Inspector,' she said, and he had an odd feeling that she meant it.

As he exchanged greetings with Sir Hedley, Faro decided to avoid any mention of his morning visit to Solomon's Tower.

'Sir Hedley has been giving us a history lesson on our Crusader,' said Sir Terence.

'I'm sure Mr Faro would like to hear it,' Miss Fortescue added with an anxious glance that begged his interest.

But the looks exchanged between the three suggested that this was by no means all that had been under discussion. And Sir Hedley, with much clearing of throat, stared anxiously in the direction of the Crusader's Tomb, his manner suggesting one hard-pressed for immediate inspiration.

He rose to the task gallantly. 'David de Lethie was one of a band of Scottish knights who survived the Crusades in Jerusalem and returned to fight at the side of his king, Robert the Bruce, at Bannockburn. There are some discrepancies about this effigy. His sword arm, for instance.'

Faro looked down at the worn stone of the coffin, which had been broken open centuries ago when whatever remained of the Crusader had been removed. As for the once-proud helmeted face lying eyes open to the sky, the harsh elements of East Lothian wind and weather had all but obliterated his noble features.

'The sword arm,' Sir Hedley repeated. 'Crusaders always had their right arm crossing over on to their sword hilt on the left side – so –' He demonstrated. 'De Lethie, however, did not.'

Faro looked down on the effigy. 'Rather looks as if he was holding something in his sword arm.'

'But what?' Sir Terence nodded. 'That's a mystery we've been trying to solve for centuries past.'

Sir Hedley turned to Faro. 'What was he holding that was more important than a sword, d'you think?'

'Perhaps you can tell us, Faro,' Sir Terence cut in. 'You're the detective, after all.'

Faro smiled. 'My province is recent deaths, not those six hundred years ago.'

'There must be some clues.' There was a note of desperation in Miss Fortescue's voice which made the three men all look at her quickly, and all for different reasons. Curiosity – and perhaps even warning.

Faro turned his attention to the effigy. 'I'd say what he was carrying was a chalice.' He looked again. 'Or a staff of some kind.'

'A staff?' they repeated.

The sun dipped low and the silence that followed this observation seemed to last for several moments.

'Undoubtedly Inspector Faro is right,' Sir Terence sounded as if the words were being forced out of him. 'I wonder why?' he added lightly.

'More important, what happened to it? Interesting to know that,' said Sir Hedley.

'Interesting, indeed,' said Faro. 'The evidence would suggest that you aren't the first to give this matter serious consideration, sir.'

He pointed to the broken coffin on which the effigy rested. 'It must have taken considerable force to open that and remove the body. And whatever treasures it held.'

The word 'treasures' stunned them again into momentary silence.

'We suspect that it happened in the sixteenth century when the priory was sacked during the Reformation, long before the castle was built,' said Sir Terence at last.

'You think – that whatever – they were looking for – might have been buried with him,' said Miss Fortescue.

'That is the general opinion.'

'Grave robbers rarely leave sworn testimonies of how and why. Is there nothing in the family records, sir?'

Lethie shook his head. 'Nothing earlier than the sixteenth century and very sparse afterwards. Only the main events were considered worthy of posterity, like the brief visit Queen Mary and Bothwell made shortly after their marriage. But the family's enthusiasm didn't extend to her descendant Prince Charles Edward Stuart. Or if it did, then they were too discreet to put it on record.' He looked at Faro. 'So all we have on the Crusader is legend.'

'Was he a Templar by any chance?' Faro asked.

'Perhaps.' The reply was vague. 'It is possible.'

It was more than possible, seeing that the Crusader's shield bore upon it the still decipherable cross pattée. Odd that Sir Hedley failed to recognise the significance of something he encountered daily in his own house.

More worrying still was the possible significance of that same cross found on a broken chain in the Wizard's House in the West Bow, a fact Faro felt was linked with the body whose identity he was increasingly and most unhappily aware might prove to be the Grand Duchess of Luxoria.

'It's all very strange, isn't it?' said Miss Fortescue. Shivering, she drew her shawl closer around her shoulders and Sir Terence seized upon the gesture with relief.

'You are cold, m'dear. Let us return to the house. You will come with us, Inspector, take some refreshment.'

As he accompanied them he realised no one had asked him his business there, or why he had suddenly appeared as they were talking by the tomb.

They were much too polite. In fact no one showed the slightest curiosity about his presence. As if a visit from a detective inspector investigating the mysterious non-arrival of the Queen's god-daughter was a commonplace event in their lives.

Surely the first question his appearance should have aroused in that conspiratorial group he had disturbed was: 'What news of Her Highness?'

9

As they walked towards the house, Faro's responses to Sir Terence's remarks about weather, crops and estate management were quite automatic. One of his useful accomplishments was the ability to carry on an agreeable conversation while his mind dealt with more important matters.

The Crusader, David de Lethie, had been a Templar, bearing the cross pattée on his shield. That Sir Hedley Marsh was connected with them, too, was evident from the chapel, so unexpectedly immaculate amid the squalor of Solomon's Tower. And from Vince, Faro knew that Sir Terence was a Templar as well as being a Grand Master in the Freemasons, whose origins and rituals were based on that society. But of perhaps even greater significance, Major Weir, the seventeenth-century owner of the Wizard's House, had also been a Templar. That he had terrified citizens by his identification with the devil and his ability to perform magic tricks, Faro was sure fitted somewhere into a pattern concerning the dead woman's identity and the reason for her death.

Faro sighed, wishing he could interpret, above Lethie's polite remarks, the low-pitched murmurings between Sir Hedley and Miss Fortescue. Was there some conspiratorial connection between these three people, some deadly link with the gold cross on its broken chain in Weir's Land?

He was rapidly discarding his original suspicion that a murder had taken place in the West Bow. All the evidence suggested that she had already been dead when she was carried into the Wizard's House.

As he sat politely through the ritual of afternoon tea, served with great elegance by Lady Lethie, his eye wandered constantly in the direction of Miss Fortescue. She was not only extremely good to look at, he decided, but she also had undeniable presence, the aura of authority that was perhaps the first requirement of a royal lady-in-waiting.

Sir Hedley Marsh sat at her side and monopolised her completely. While she gave smiling, patient answers to some bumbling nonsense about fishing in Dunsapie Loch, Faro considered what measures he must take to direct this pleasant but ineffectual teatime conversation towards the object of his visit: namely, the promised photograph or picture of Duchess Amelie, now so vital to his search.

The clock melodiously chimed four, reminding him that the train from North Berwick to Edinburgh was due at the Aberlethie halt in less than an hour.

'May I help you to a piece of cake?' said Lady Lethie with an encouraging smile, aware of his empty plate and distracted air.

'No, thank you. I wonder – the photograph?' he reminded her gently.

Although the words were spoken quietly, his question succeeded in bringing all conversation to an abrupt end.

Sara Lethie smiled at him vaguely, shaking her head in the apologetic manner of one who had forgotten entirely: 'Of course. Of course, you wanted a photograph, didn't you.' And to her husband. 'Terence – do we have a picture somewhere?'

Sir Terence responded with alacrity. 'No, my dear. Not in the album, I've already had a glance.' And to Faro: 'I did think we had one taken at Holyrood, but I must have been mistaken.'

'Would have been a long time ago. Mere child. Not much use to you now, I'm afraid,' Sir Hedley put in.

Faro turned to Miss Fortescue. 'What about you, miss? Do you happen to possess a recent photograph of your mistress?'

Miss Fortescue shook her head sadly. 'There was one, very recent – a present for Her Majesty, you know. In a silver frame. But I'm afraid it is beneath the waters of the Forth now, with all the rest of our possessions.'

Faro stood up abruptly. So that was that. His journey to Aberlethie had been a waste of time when he could have been pursuing more urgent and productive enquiries in Edinburgh. But not one of these polite, well-bred people thought that an apology was due for his wasted effort.

'If you will forgive me. My train, you know.'

'Of course, Inspector. Of course. Sorry you must leave us,' said Terence with undue heartiness. An angry and frustrated Faro felt that was a lie. They were not in the least sorry to see the back of him.

Then as if his urgent thoughts had communicated themselves to Miss Fortescue, she rose to her feet.

'If Inspector Faro is ready to leave now, I will walk with him to the railway halt.'

The Lethies exchanged worried glances. They sprang to their feet, followed a little creakily by Sir Hedley. For a moment, Faro had an unhappy feeling that they were all coming too. With relief he realised it as just another gesture of politeness. Or was it Miss Fortescue's thinly veiled frown of annoyance that quelled all three?

Miss Fortescue waited while Sara Lethie picked up a shawl and draped it about her shoulders. Their backs were turned to Faro but on that moment of stillness he had a strange feeling that uneasy glances were exchanged. Uneasy and warning, perhaps?

And then it was over and Sir Terence was showing them to the door, cordially shaking hands with Faro. Waving them farewell he anxiously regarded the sky.

'Rain's not far off, you're – um, going to get wet. Shall I fetch an umbrella?'

'I shall be quite all right,' said Miss Fortescue. She sounded rather cross, and her manner was suddenly that of someone who heartily disliked being fussed over. She set off determinedly at Faro's side.

As they walked through the formal gardens, Faro accommodating his loping stride to her more leisurely pace, he discovered that Miss Fortescue was having problems with her light shoes on the gravel. It occurred to him that she was brave to tackle a walk outdoors at all, especially as the one pair of sturdy, sensible shoes even ladies-in-waiting to Grand Duchess might be expected to possess had been lost with her luggage on the night of the accident.

'Shall we keep to the grass, miss? That would be more comfortable for you.'

'It would indeed.' Her smile was grateful.

'What was it you wished to talk to me about?' he asked.

She looked at him wide-eyed. 'How ever did you guess? You are clever.' And as Faro shrugged off the compliment: 'It is such a relief to get you alone. I desperately need to tell you the whole story – as it is coming back to me, quite gradually, of course.'

Her tone warned him not to expect too much. Then halting, she gazed up into his face. 'Quite frankly, Inspector, I am frightened.'

Frightened. He hadn't expected that.

She sighed deeply before continuing. 'I have decided that I must take you into my confidence, Inspector.'

Ah, thought Faro, now we're getting somewhere at last. This could be the break he was waiting for, the thread to lead him through the labyrinth of mystery and misinformation.

' – You see, Amelie wished to keep her journey secret from the President, her husband. She didn't want him to know that she was in fact negotiating with Her Majesty's government to intercede in their problems –'

'May I be permitted to enquire – the nature of these problems?' Faro interrupted.

'I'm not sure...' she began vaguely.

Faro stopped walking. 'Look, miss, if I'm to help you and you have decided to trust me, then it is essential that we go right back to the beginning –'

'The beginning,' she echoed, as if that thought had never occurred to her.

'Yes, miss. I'm told that you have been with the Duchess since you were both children and I expect that means you are very close.' He paused. 'And that you share her secrets?' Silence followed this statement. 'Am I right?' he asked gently.

Miss Fortescue sighed.

'Perhaps you know better than anyone else the reasons for her disappearance. Without being aware of it, you may even hold the key to her present whereabouts.'

It was a bold suggestion, considering the doleful nature of his own suspicions, but he added encouragingly, 'I gather from what I have heard, officially and from private sources, that Her Highness is a lady of spirit and courage.'

Miss Fortescue laughed. 'Indeed she is. Rumour has not lied, Inspector.' She looked up at him earnestly. 'Yes, and I am quite sure she would put her trust in you, as I am doing.'

With a sigh she continued: 'You are right, I probably know her better than anyone else, far better than her husband – that odious man –'

'The beginning, miss, if you please.'

'Of course. Amelie is related to both the Queen and Prince Albert, as you probably are aware. She was born on their wedding day, 10 February 1840, and that made her very special to both of them. Indeed, they regarded her sentimentally as their very first child, rather than a mere god-daughter. Their visits to Luxoria were frequent and she came to Windsor Castle with her parents –'

She paused to sigh sadly. 'She adored Uncle Albert, was distraught when he died, and I do believe she was a great comfort to her Aunt Vicky at that time.' She was silent, staring bleakly at the treetops, as if overcome by the memory.

'And you accompanied her on these visits?'

She looked at him blankly for a moment, still lost in the other sad world. 'Some of them.' She sighed. 'When she was seventeen there was a revolution in Luxoria. Such a thing had never happened in its history before. Her bastard cousin Gustav had himself elected President. He knew that by marrying Amelie he would destroy the final opposition. Amelie scorned the idea. She hated him. But he refused to take no for an answer.'

She was silent, walking faster now at his side, as if to escape that distant sorrow.

'And – ?' said Faro.

'He forced himself upon her.' Her voice rose. 'He got her with child so that she had no other option but to marry him. Three months later, a few weeks after their marriage, she miscarried. There will be no other child now, and Gustav needs an heir.'

He smiled. 'She is young still to give up hope.'

'In years, perhaps. But after fifteen years of marriage it seems highly unlikely. Besides, Gustav has a mistress who has recently presented him with a son.'

She paused to allow the significance of that remark to sink in.

'Are you hinting that your mistress might be in danger?' Faro asked. Here at last was a clue, the one undeniable reason for murder. Royal princes throughout history had resorted to the disposal of barren wives by fair means or foul, when presented with an heir, even an illegitimate one.

'Danger?' Miss Fortescue repeated. 'I don't think that has

ever entered her mind. Amelie refuses to divorce him, for by so doing, she would relinquish any hope of restoring the Royal party to power. Besides, she has learned through all these dreadful years that personal interests must never be allowed to intrude where her main duty lies. To her country and her people.'

She looked at him. 'Perhaps it is difficult for you or anyone not of royal blood to understand such things, Inspector.'

Faro smiled and shook his head. 'Not for me, miss. I understand perfectly. I know all about duty. It is, or should be, a policeman's first rule. To his sovereign and to the people he serves.'

Miss Fortescue laughed and put a hand on his arm. 'Why, Inspector, we seem to have a great deal in common.' And eyeing him shrewdly: 'I was right, I am sure. Amelie would approve. She would trust you.' With a sigh she went on: 'Knowing how powerful Britain is in world politics, she had some thought that Her Majesty might be able to intercede on her behalf. That by selling some of her jewels she might even be able to raise an army, bring the Royal party back into power.'

'Drastic measures, miss.'

She regarded him dolefully. 'I know. I see now what a mad scheme that was. But, as I said, Amelie is a creature of impulse.'

There was nothing Faro could think of as an appropriate response. Worried by his silence, she said: 'You will respect my confidence, please, Inspector – I must beg of you –'

'Of course, you have my word, miss. I was just wondering about these jewels. Any idea where they might be?'

'Under the waters of the River Forth by now. With all our other possessions,' she said bitterly.

'Including the photograph she was taking to Her Majesty, I believe.'

'That too.'

'Is there nothing more you can tell me about your mistress? Anything that distinguishes her in particular?'

Miss Fortescue shook her head. 'It is so difficult, Inspector, when you have been with someone every day, practically all your life, to try and say exactly what they look like. There are lots of photographs in the palace at Luxoria, of course.'

And utterly useless by the time they reached Edinburgh, Faro thought grimly. A germ of an idea had grown out of this conversation though. Was it too fantastic, he wondered?

'This coachman. What did he look like?'

'The coachman?' she repeated, surprised by the question. Shaking her head she laughed lightly. 'You know, I haven't the least idea. He just looked like, well, a coachman.'

Faro tried again. 'Was he young or old?'

'Of middle age, I expect,' was the prompt reply.

'Short or tall. Stout or thin?' Faro persisted.

'Middle height.' She looked at Faro's withdrawn expression and added apologetically. 'Well, you see, I only saw him very fleetingly.'

Obviously Faro was expected to know that coachmen, like soldiers and policemen, all looked alike. How foolish of him to expect otherwise. So much for McQuinn's theory that servants had intimate knowledge of one another.

'Had he served long in your mistress's employ?'

Miss Fortescue frowned. 'Oh, no. He merely met us when we disembarked at North Berwick. As a matter of fact, I hardly saw his face.'

Ah, then perhaps his idea wasn't so fantastic after all.

Thee were now spots of rain, an ominous sky. Faro hoped the approaching storm would contain itself for a little longer.

'I'm truly sorry about the photograph, Inspector. So much was lost that night.' Her sigh made Faro feel just a little ashamed of his concern for what must seem to her of little consequence. There was a slight pause before he asked: 'What was your mistress wearing when the accident happened?'

'Wearing?' Miss Fortescue repeated. 'I think – yes, a woollen travelling cape. Yes, it as violet, her favourite colour, velvet trimmed.'

Progress at last, thought Faro. 'And underneath –?'

But before Miss Fortescue could reply, the storm broke above their heads, a jagged streak of lightning split the sky, followed by a thunder-clap. The spots of rain turned into a steady flow.

'Oh dear. Oh dear, I must leave you, Inspector. I must run –'

Aware that she could never run anywhere in those slippers, Faro in a gallant gesture removed his cape and slipped it around her shoulders.

Her tender, grateful smile was his reward. 'You are so kind, Inspector, so very kind.'

'You had better hurry, miss.'

'But your cape – you will get wet.'

'I'll get it later. Go – quickly –'

He watched her disappear as the deluge broke, and turning, he ran swiftly towards the railway halt, which afforded little shelter beyond an ancient oak tree.

He was greatly relieved to hear the distant sound of a train approaching. By good fortune it was on time, but too late to save him from a drenching.

As the train steamed to a halt, a carriage door was flung open to allow a man to descend to the platform.

The passenger was the historian, Stuart Millar.

10

'Why, Inspector Faro. What are you doing here?' Stuart Millar demanded.

Faro explained that he had been visiting the Lethies.

'But you are soaked through, man. You must come back with me.' He pointed. 'That's my cottage over there.'

The guard blew his whistle. Millar put his hand on Faro's arm. 'I won't take no for an answer. Elspeth will have supper ready, I'll get you some dry clothes and you can get the later train.'

Faro considered his wet clothes and the tempting invitation. Tempting and convenient, too, since it would give him a chance to find out what the historian knew about the Lethies and Major Weir.

Millar put up his umbrella and they raced through the rain.

At the cottage, Elspeth was absent. A note said that his supper was in the oven. Taking Faro's coat to the kitchen to be dried, Millar returned with a smoking jacket: 'Put this on. My apologies, Inspector. This is my sister's guild evening. Dear, dear. And I'm playing cards with friends – but never mind. We have an hour or so –'

Faro did not mind in the least. In fact he was grateful for this unique opportunity that the storm had brought his way. It was no difficult task to lead the conversation towards the slums of Edinburgh and the proposed demolition of the West Bow.

'Major Weir? We don't know much about the Major's early life except that he was born near Carluke and was an officer in the Puritan army in 1641. He served with Montrose during his Covenanting campaign and after the execution of Charles I he retired and settled in Edinburgh and became Captain of the City Guard.'

Millar paused and smiled at him. 'I expect all this is well-known to you. And that the City Guard was not as blameless or efficient as our present-day police force. According to legend, however, it was based on an ancient secret society whose original members were present at the sack of Jerusalem. In the confusion afterwards these respectable Edinburgh citizens ransacked King Solomon's Temple and carried off the portrait of Solomon. There were rumours, however, of more important thefts.'

'Such as?'

'King Solomon's Rod, the staff Moses carried when he received the Ten Commandments and which he used subsequently to divide the waters of the Red Sea to see his people safely over to the land of Egypt. But I digress –'

'You were telling me about this remarkable Major.'

'When he retired form the City Guard he became absorbed by spiritual matters. The West Bow was very respectable in his day, occupied by a hard-working and fanatically religious group of tinsmiths, known as the Bowhead Saints. The Major lived there with his sister and became known as Angelical Thomas for his powers of oratory. And according to the records he was never to be seen "in any holy duty without his rod in his hand".

'He had an imposing personality and presence, as well as the gift of the gab. Very tall and saturnine, he always wore a long black cloak. Possessed an astonishing memory too. Could quote reams from the Scriptures and had a genius for leading public prayer, quite irresistible to those who heard him, from all accounts. The staff, he said, was his gift from God, his Holy Rod. It had some strange power, could turn itself into a snake or a serpent, and he was able to work some minor miracles and produce magical effects from rags and powders thrown into the fire.'

'Gunpowder, of course,' said Faro, 'and very impressive for the superstitious. All you are telling me about the Major describes an alchemist who could convince ignorant folk that he was in fact some kind of a minor prophet.'

'Exactly,' said Millar. 'If he had kept it that way, all might have been well. But there was a dark side too. He had one weakness. Ladies could not resist him and he couldn't resist such earthly temptations. Eventually, in his seventies, he took ill, and knowing that his life was near its end, he made an amazing confession of depravity and blasphemy which included a statement that he and his sister had sold their souls to the devil on the road to Musselburgh. This so shocked the authorities that the Lord Provost of Edinburgh summoned the City Guard and thrust them both into the tolbooth for safe-keeping.

'In prison, however, the sister lost her nerve, perhaps knowing all to well the dreadful fate that awaited witches and warlocks, and she implored the bailies to secure the Major's staff. He was, she assured them, powerless without it. But if he were allowed to grasp it then he could drive them all out of doors, regardless of any resistance they might make. She further explained that the devil had given the staff to her brother that momentous day in 1648 when, in exchange for their souls, they were transported to Musselburgh and back again in a coach pulled by six black horses which seemed to be made of fire.

'The Major was burnt at the stake at Greenside in April 1670 – I expect you know it, a village between Leith and Edinburgh. A few days later his sister met the same fate in the Grassmarket. To the end, she was more concerned about her brother's staff than their terrible sentence. When she was told it had been burnt with him, mad with rage, she tore off all her clothes to die stark-naked.'

While Faro listened, a picture was taking shape in his mind. The road to Musselburgh passed through Aberlethie. Destroyed by the Reformation, the priory was in ruins and the Crusader lay on his ravaged tomb.

'The bailie in charge of burning the Major's rod described it as looking like a serpent, hissing like a snake, as it perished. The Major's money was entrusted to his care. He took it home with him and locked it in his study. None of his family slept that night. There were dreadful noises issuing from the locked room, as if the house was going to fall down on them –'

'This bailie,' Faro interrupted. 'Do we know his name?'

Millar smiled. 'Yes. Bailie James Lethie.'

'Lethie!' Faro exclaimed, and Millar nodded.

'In all probability a relation of the present-day family.'

'The original castle – when was it built?'

'Begun in September 1670, completed two years later.'

Surely it was no coincidence that it had been built by the same bailie soon after he had both the magic staff, which he had been entrusted to burn, and the Major's money, too.

No great feat of detection was needed to unravel this two-hundred-year-old mystery. Major Weir's secret was certainly in the staff he carried, and he issued warnings about its supernatural powers in order to keep it safe. Everyone who came into contact with him would be too terrified to steal it.

Intriguing as this information was, Faro decided that it contributed little to the more urgent matter of solving the mystery of the missing Grand Duchess. He did not greatly relish the prospect of facing an irate Prime Minister and having to give an account of his failure to the Queen herself.

When Faro took his leave of Millar, he decided to walk over to the priory before catching the next train.

The storm had cleared and left in its wake the legacy of a mellow autumn evening with the rich smell of damp earth and a sky, azure and cloudless, echoing with birdsong.

As he looked down at the Crusader's Tomb for the second time that day, his experience was quite different from his earlier visit. Gone was the electric atmosphere which he had interrupted between Miss Fortescue and the two men. Now he felt there was nothing left in this heap of mouldering stone, nothing in this effigy that could help solve his more immediate problem.

The truth or fiction behind the history so colourfully interwoven with legend that had once marked this spot had been lost for ever under the dust and ashes of centuries past.

Often, when Faro stood on a spot where history had been created, he would have given much to be transported back in time for just one brief glimpse of that magic occasion. He could never walk towards the new university on Chambers Street without seeing Kirk o' Field on its site and wishing with all his heart that he could have been there and solved one of Scotland's most tantalising mysteries.

What had really happened that February night? And was the Queen of Scots implicated in the destruction of her odious husband, Lord Darnley? Now there was only hearsay, dry as dust. But if one could have been there to pick up the clues and prove Mary innocent, then her desperate plight might have changed the whole course of Scotland's history.

Such is the stuff dreams – or nightmares – are made of. And now, in like manner, Faro wished for a time machine that could carry him back to the scene of David de Lethie returning triumphant from the Crusades, bearing with him a strange trophy.

But tonight he was not the only pilgrim.

Miss Fortescue walked cautiously through the shrubbery. A manservant who had the unfortunate look of a gaoler hovered at a discreet distance, trying to look as if he hadn't been instructed to keep an eye on her.

It was an interesting idea, one which would bear further investigation, Faro thought as he stepped out of the shadow of the priory wall.

As for Miss Fortescue, she was not at all put out by his sudden appearance. She smiled. 'Why, Inspector Faro, I am so glad to see you. I have your cape. It is thoroughly dry now – if you would care to accompany me – ' She motioned towards the castle.

'Of course.'

Opening her reticule she handed him a paper. 'I was to have this posted to you, Inspector. It is a list of the contents of the jewel box –'

After a quick glance Faro thrust it into his pocket, as Miss Fortescue continued: 'I hope it helps. It's the best I can do, until Her Highness can confirm the contents.'

Faro found this even more surprising. 'When do you think she is likely to arrive?' he asked politely.

'Oh, I've been thinking it over and I haven't the least doubt that she'll just walk in. Or send us a message from Balmoral. Her Highness is like that. She's very resourceful and impulsive.' She paused to let that sink in. 'But I am most concerned about that poor coachman.'

'Isn't it possible that he may be with her?'

She shook her head. 'I'm afraid that he may have been sent with a message and something has happened to him.' Her eyes filled with tears and she put a hand on his arm, gazing up into his face appealingly. She looked bewildered, overwhelmed by frightening circumstances entirely new in her hitherto sheltered life.

'What do you think we should do meanwhile, Inspector?'

'My colleagues and I are doing all we can to find out what happened. How much do you remember, miss?'

Again she shook her head. 'Only the fierce storm, the carriage swaying. A tree fell. And then – oblivion.'

'What was your last sight of Her Highness?'

'We were clinging to each other.' Her voice broke for an instant. 'The coachman yelled a warning. The bridge is down. I remember falling free of the carriage, rolling down the hill and hitting the water. I thought that was the end as I sank. Then I came to myself, my clothes dripping wet. I was lying on a load of hay. Being carried along a dark road. You know the rest, Inspector.'

He looked at her. 'What are you going to do now? Until such time as your mistress returns for you,' he added hastily.

She shrugged. 'Wait for instructions of some kind. I have no reason to return to Luxoria – if – if –' And in her eyes he read the words neither dared to say, in case by so doing they gave them the breath of life and a monstrous reality.

'What about your family and friends?' he asked gently.

'I have no commitment of any kind. As you probably realise, I am not a national.'

'You are British?'

'As Scottish as you are, Inspector,' she said proudly.

Faro bowed, not feeling this was the time or place to explain that Orcadians consider themselves from a country apart.

'The Queen is, as you know,' Miss Fortescue continued, 'much in favour of Scottish governesses and maids. There are such intimate connections between Her Majesty and most of our royal houses.'

She fell silent and Faro, anxious to return to the more urgent topic in hand, prompted her: 'When the storm interrupted us you were telling me what your mistress was wearing when the accident happened. A violet travelling cape with velvet trimming, was it not?'

'Yes.'

'And underneath?'

Miss Fortescue frowned. 'A blue merino dress, with long sleeves, an embroidered yoke and a quantity of lace around the neck.'

Faro would have given much at that moment to produce the piece of lace he had found in the West Bow. But the time was not yet ripe. He needed to know a great deal more about the part Miss Fortescue had played before producing such evidence.

'What jewellery was she wearing?'

Miss Fortescue thought. 'A sapphire and diamond ring, gold bracelets.' She rubbed her wrist nervously. 'In the shape of a snake with ruby eyes. No earrings. And a pendant.' And touching her throat, 'Yes, she always wore a pendant. Just a simple gold cross.'

Faro sighed. In that statement, Miss Fortescue was confirming his worst fears.

'And underneath the dress?'

Miss Fortescue was taken aback by the question. She blushed. 'The usual garments ladies wear, Inspector. Petticoats and so forth.'

She sounded offended but Faro persisted. 'Can you be a little more precise, miss?'

'No, I'm afraid I can't,' she said coldly.

Faro gave her a hard look. 'I presume that as lady-in-waiting and sole travelling companion, you were also in charge of her wardrobe and of dressing her each day.'

'I just can't remember, exactly.' She shook her head and pursed her lips firmly, indicating that particular subject was closed.

Faro waited a moment. 'Did she by any chance wear corsets?' he prompted her gently.

'Of course, all ladies wear corsets, Inspector.'

Faro frowned. 'If you are finding this too painful and embarrassing, miss, perhaps you'd be good enough to write it down, as you kindly wrote the jewel-box list. And a drawing would be most helpful if you could manage that.'

'A drawing. I couldn't possibly draw Her Highness,' she said indignantly.

'I meant a drawing of her clothes.'

Miss Fortescue sighed. 'Oh, very well. If I can.'

'If you can, it would be most helpful,' he repeated.

They emerged from the formal garden in silence and both were relieved to find that the castle was in view.

Miss Fortescue's pace quickened and Faro was aware of the servant keeping then within range. He was desperately searching for some safe conversation when she suddenly said: 'When last we met you were rushing for a train. I presume you missed it.'

'I met Mr Stuart Millar, the historian. He lives on the edge of the estate and I allowed him to persuade me to return to his cottage. He was kind enough to give me supper and a most interesting account of the Crusader and the Luck o' Lethie.'

'Oh, indeed,' she said vaguely. 'You would see it when you were staying at the castle, Sir Terence is very proud of it.'

'I had to leave early.' He consulted his watch. 'But perhaps, if I have time – I'm quite curious –'

Miss Fortescue pushed open the front door. 'There is Sir Terence now.'

Sir Terence, thought Faro, was looking mightily relieved to see her. He had the look of an anxious father repressing reproaches to a wayward and obstinate child.

'Inspector Faro would like to see the Luck o' Lethie,' she called, and leaving them to it, she ran lightly upstairs.

Sir Terence smiled. 'Our family mascot – come this way.'

Faro followed him into the library.

'This is the oldest part of the house, you will observe the original stone walls.'

He pointed to a niche above the ancient fireplace where a glass case, its velvet backing long devoid of colour, had resting on it a golden horn anchored by metal clips. It was not like any horn Faro had ever seen, resembling a fiery dragon's head, with the mouthpiece at the back of the neck. Its eyes glittered with the blue of sapphires and its scales were embossed with green and red stones which Faro did not doubt were emeralds and rubies.

At his admiring murmur, Sir Terence said: 'Brought back by our Crusader from Jerusalem. According to legend, one of the treasures the Templars stole from King Solomon's Temple after the city fell.' He paused. 'Or so Mr Stuart Millar tells us.'

Faro didn't doubt there was something in the legend. The horn looked exceedingly old and not a little battered, but if this was the head of Solomon's Rod, then it predated Christianity by a thousand years.

'Could do with a bit of a clean-up,' said Sir Terence apologetically. 'Has hardly left this room since the castle was built in 1670.'

'So it has been carefully preserved by your family for two hundred years. Remarkable.'

'Yes, indeed. We're very superstitious about preserving the Luck o' Lethie.' Sir Terence surveyed it proudly. 'As long as it survives, so will our line continue. It is supposedly a cure for barren women and the only time it has ever been removed from its case was when there were, er, problems.'

His brooding gaze rested suddenly on a painting of himself and the first five of their eight children. 'Not one of ours, I need hardly add,' he added heartily. 'Our women are never barren.'

Faro, aware of someone behind him, turned to see Miss Fortescue framed in the doorway, his cape over her arm. Her gaze was watchful and she betrayed an air of listening very intently to their conversation.

Thanking them both, Faro announced that he must hurry or he would miss his train.

'Train, Inspector. By no means. You shall have the carriage.' He cut short Faro's protests. 'It is sitting in the coach-house idle, and you have already suffered enough inconvenience for one day. See, it's raining again.'

As they stood together on the front steps, smiling, to wave him goodbye, Faro was not at all displeased to sink into the luxury of the Lethie carriage and be transported home to Newington, where he was greatly looking forward to mulling over the day's events with Vince.

His stepson could be relied upon to be helpful. Vince's suggestions and encouragement were both urgently needed.

Although Faro had, without difficulty but with considerable reliance on his intuition, found a plausible explanation to the two-hundred-year-old mystery of Major Weir's staff and the building of Lethie Castle, a ten-day-old mystery was at present beyond his powers.

II

Vince was not at home. Much in need of his stepson's buoyant presence to banish his anguished thoughts, Faro had to wait until breakfast next morning to relate Stuart Millar's story of King Solomon's Rod.

Vince was intrigued, knowing something of the Templars from his Freemason friends. 'I'm told that the oldest Scottish lodge at Kilwinning was founded by Robert the Bruce for the reception of those Knights Templars who had fled from persecution in Europe. A Templars contingent fought at the king's side, you know, on the field at Bannockburn.'

'After inflicting such a crushing victory over King Edward II, one would presume that their future was guaranteed,' said Faro.

'True. But there was more to it than that. Edward's army was considered invincible and some said that his was no normal defeat of a powerful army. Rumour had it that witchcraft and magic were involved –'

Faro laughed. 'Not unknown sentiments for losers to indulge in. They have to have a better excuse than telling their people they just weren't good enough to beat the enemy.'

'I agree. But rumour also claimed that the Templars had some holy relic, which they carried before their king. Certainly it was extraordinary that, even in the heat of battle and some fairly bloody hand-to-hand fighting, neither the Bruce nor any of their number suffered a single scratch.'

'Ah!' said Faro.

Vince looked at him quickly. 'You're thinking perhaps it was the Luck o' Lethie. You might be right at that, since the serpent's head goes back to the very origins of the Templars movement. I've often wondered –'

'And what have you wondered?'

'Well, about Solomon's Tower. As you know, it was built on the ruins of a twelfth-century religious house. And that could well have been a Templar chapel. A rich and powerful international brotherhood of religious warriors, Stepfather. Don't let us underestimate them.'

'A secret society so strong that popes aware of their power had tried to suppress it,' said Faro. 'A society important enough to be taken under the King of Scotland's protection. Gives one food for thought, doesn't it?'

Vince nodded. 'Especially when you now tell me there's a shrine-like upper room in the Mad Bart's cat-ridden establishment. What blasphemy.'

All Faro's training, combined with an extra sense that had served him well in the past, now compelled him to believe that the disappearance of the Grand Duchess was no coincidence, but the outcome of some international intrigue.

As Vince's first patient of the day was announced by Mrs Brook, Faro considered what he hadn't told his stepson.

Was Sir Hedley involved, his pose as an eccentric recluse a screen for less innocent activities?

But aware of Vince's loathing for Sir Hedley, he decided to keep such speculations, as yet wholly without sufficient evidence to support them, to himself.

'I won't be at home tonight, Stepfather. I'm staying at Owen's place. And I must get in a few rounds of golf,' Vince added, with a speculative sight at a rather threatening sky, 'if I'm to reduce my handicap in time for this Perth tournament.'

Faro smiled. Both he and his stepson seemed doomed to disastrous affairs of the heart. But he felt encouraged that these overnight visits to Cramond, which were becoming more frequent, signalled that Vince might be considering the advocate's pretty sister Olivia as a suitable wife.

At the door, Vince turned. 'Met your cousin Leslie last night. He was at the Spec with some friends and we had a most convivial evening.'

Edinburgh's Speculative Club was famous as a meeting place for graduates where serious matters for discussion were leavened by youthful joviality and high spirits.

'Now that you mention it, you do look as if you might be suffering from a more urgent handicap than the state of your golf,' said Faro.

Vince smiled weakly. 'You miss nothing as usual, Stepfather.'

Faro laughed. 'I also observe that you declined a second helping of Mrs Brook's excellent sausages. Now that is cause for comment. What about Leslie?'

'Tell you about it later. He was Colonel Wrightson's guest.' Vince chuckled enthusiastically. 'What tales he has to tell. Knows everybody who is anybody. Been a guest in practically every noble house the length and breadth of Scotland,' he added in tones of awe. 'Didn't get home till two. Tried to persuade me to go riding with him in the Queen's Park. Rises at six – dear God, what a thought.'

'And what energy,' said Faro.

And as Vince dragged himself off, still yawning, to his surgery, Faro hoped, for their own sakes, that all his patients were reasonably healthy that day.

Shortly afterwards, as Faro was closing his front door, the familiar police carriage rattled round the corner.

A young policeman leapt out and saluted smartly.

'Constable Burns, sir. Glad I caught you, sir. Man out walking his dogs found a man's body in the shrubbery by St Anthony's Chapel. Dr Cranley's there. Wants a word with you before moving the body.'

Faro jumped into the carriage with an ominous feeling of disaster. In reply to his question the constable shook his head.

'No, there wasn't any identification.'

'Any signs of violence?'

'Nothing that a quick look would reveal.' The constable gave a grimace of distaste. 'Been there some time, I'd say.'

Another mysterious corpse. Was this the missing coachman?

'Indeed. Have you seen anything unusual – any reports of disturbance in the area?'

'Nothing, sir. My beat is in that area of the park with Constable Reid. We don't usually patrol Arthur's Seat or Salisbury Crags yard by yard, unless we have special instructions to do so,' he added anxiously, 'I expect the dead man was taken with a heart attack.'

Like the Grand Duchess, Faro thought grimly as they left the carriage and set off on foot up the steep bank which overlooked Holyroodhouse. The Palace's extensive gardens were now grey and empty, the trees stripped bare. A melancholy wind came from the sea beyond Salisbury Crags, hurling before it heavy clouds, towards a skyline dominated by Edinburgh Castle and the High Street's tall houses.

Ahead of them lay the ruins of St Anthony's Chapel. There, according to tradition, a hermit had once tended the chapel altar and kept a light burning in the tower to guide mariners safely up the River Forth. Built in the fifteenth century, a hospice for those afflicted with 'St Anthony's Fire' – epilepsy – the chapel guarded the Holy Well whose pagan origins predated the Abbey of Holy Rood, site of King David I's encounter with a magical stag bearing a cross between its antlers.

Faro paused to look back at the loch gleaming far below. A peaceful scene of swans gliding in majestic serenity untroubled by the follies of men, he thought, staring at the group of tiny figures who bustled back and forth high above.

The corpse was half-hidden by shrubbery. Dr Cranley, Sergeant McQuinn and Constable Reid hovered nearby. And at a safe distance, looking rather green, was the man who had made the discovery.

Introduced as Mr Innes, Faro recognised him as a Newington shopkeeper. Middle-aged, well-to-do, Innes was clearly unused to such dramas threatening the sanctity of his early-morning constitutional. He wore a look of outraged respectability that he should have found himself in the undignified predicament of discovering a body and having to associate with the police.

'It was Daisy found him,' Innes pointed accusingly towards a small bright-eyed Skye terrier. Possessor of the only nose quite unoffended by the stench of decomposition, Daisy looked proud enough to burst. Overcome by a fury of tail-wagging and seizing every opportunity to dash forward, she whined softly, eyeing the body with the proprietary and almost predatory relish of a dog prevented from demolishing a particularly succulent bone.

Mr Innes was much embarrassed by such ill-bred behaviour and Daisy was frequently called to heel, rewarding her master with a gentle-eyed reproach. When she was finally put on her chain she continued to whine in protest, deprived and ill-treated and looking as down in the mouth as a canine could manage.

Mr Innes wasn't looking particularly happy either.

'When will I be allowed to return home?' he asked.

'I requested that he remain here until you arrived,' Dr Cranley called across to Faro, neatly side-stepping the responsibility.

'My wife will be anxious,' Mr Innes consulted his watch. 'I have already missed breakfast and we have a business to run.'

McQuinn came over and said to Faro: 'Constable Burns came for me. I've taken a statement from the gentleman.'

'In that case, sir, we need detain you no longer,' said Faro.

Innes turned to leave, took a few steps and changed his mind. Pointing to the body, he said to Faro, 'However long that – that – has been here, it certainly wasn't there last night.'

'Are you sure?' asked Faro.

'Certain sure. This is our evening walk, regular as clockwork and in most weathers too. It's Daisy's favourite. She's a great ratter and is always in that shrubbery after them, sniffing around. I can vouch for that, if necessary.'

Faro took the card Innes handed him, and thanking him for his help, he watched them depart, the man relieved, the dog dragged reluctantly from her scene of triumph. Her reproachful whimpers indicated that this was what a dog's life was all about.

Dr Cranley, who had been bending over the corpse, strode towards Faro. Removing the handkerchief covering his nose and mouth, he said: 'Thought you'd better have a look before we move him.' He shook his head. 'This was no heart attack. Can't tell until we do the post-mortem but, at a rough guess, I'd say he most likely drowned.'

'Drowned?'

'Yes, drowned.'

'When?' Faro demanded sharply.

'More than a week ago, I'd estimate.'

'Which fits in with what Mr Innes suggested,' said McQuinn. 'That the body wasn't here last night. Probably dumped a few hours ago.'

Dr Cranley nodded. 'I'd say he was right about that.' He jerked his head in the direction of the loch far below. 'Probably down there.'

'So where has he been all this time?' Faro demanded. 'He certainly didn't get up here unaided.'

The doctor shrugged. 'That's your business, Faro. Mine is restricted to the facts regarding the cause of death, not his whereabouts since death occurred.'

Faro hardly listened. He was a very worried man. The significance of the time-lapse was ominous, it slotted almost too neatly into the grim discovery in the West Bow.

The two fatalities, he felt sure, were unlikely to have been coincidental.

'Any identification?'

'None. Pockets empty.'

Faro sighed like a man whose worst fears have come to pass as he followed Cranley, who said: 'You'll need to cover up.'

And as Faro withdrew a handkerchief from his pocket, Dr Cranley continued: 'it's not a pleasant sight. Damn rum business, I'd say, in more ways than meets the eye.'

The doctor was strongly addicted to rum and clichés and Faro would have appreciated a less sensitive nose as well as a fortifying strong drink as he looked down on the remains of a middle-aged man. Of middle height and middle build, no longer with any features of distinction except for thinning ginger hair, his clothes worn but respectable, his description when circulated, Faro decided wearily, might fit one-quarter of the male population of Scotland.

McQuinn had been listening attentively to the conversation between the doctor and Faro. 'If he drowned down there, sir, why carry him all this way uphill to leave him in the shrubbery? It doesn't make sense.'

Faro sighed. 'His body was obviously concealed somewhere.'

'Not in the open air, that's for sure,' said the doctor. 'Animals would have got at him and there would have been maggot infestation by now.'

'There's been a lot of rain and his clothes would have been ruined too,' said Faro, examining the man's hands. Smooth, with no callouses, not the hands of a labouring man. And whatever his occupation, the dead man had not been a professional coachman with palms hardened by daily contact with horses' reins.

Watching Faro, Cranley said: 'He wasn't in the water long. Was that what you're looking for?'

Faro nodded. Within a few hours of being immersed in water the skin on the hands and feet of a dead body takes on a characteristic bleached and wrinkled appearance, commonly known as 'washerwoman's hands'.

'We'll see what the post-mortem reveals. But I can tell you

one thing. I'd be prepared to swear that he's been kept in a closed dry place since he died.'

'Such as?'

Cranley shrugged. 'A trunk, or a closet,' he said grimly. 'Or some airless space, like a cupboard. Well, well, here's another little mystery for you to work on, Faro. If you want my opinion on this one – although I don't suppose we'll find any marks of violence – I won't be surprised if there was foul play involved somewhere.'

When Faro managed a wry smile, 'Not as much use to our students as the last one we had from you,' he added appreciatively, as if Faro was somehow responsible for the personal freshness of the corpses supplied to his medical students.

Faro had an unhappy feeling that they would get no further with the dead man in St Anthony's Chapel than they had with the mystery woman in the West Bow. But he would very much have liked an answer to one vital question.

According to Miss Fortescue's account of the events, the coachman who drove the Duchess from North Berwick had probably drowned when the carriage went into the river. Had the accident been prearranged and the coachman murdered, his body concealed for nearly two weeks to be resurrected and left at St Anthony's Chapel on the slopes of Arthur's Seat?

But why, when there were so many less tortuous ways a corpse could be disposed of? With plenty of water around, the River Forth was an obvious choice. Hopefully the body might drift out with the tide and never be seen again.

What was the purpose behind this sudden resurrection? He asked himself this as he watched the body being bundled on to a stretcher and carried down the hill by the two constables in the wake of Dr Cranley.

McQuinn remained with him, and now that the corpse had been removed, there was further evidence that its sojourn in the shrubbery had been brief. The leaves and grass where the body had lain were flattened but there was none of the yellow discolouration and decay that would have occurred had the vegetation been covered for several days.

'I had a walk round, sir, nothing to be seen out of the ordinary,' McQuinn added.

As Faro poked round the shrubbery with a stick and without

much hope of finding anything significant, he smelt murder as well as decomposition in the air.

McQuinn frowned. 'It's only a thought, sir, but the fact that the man was drowned – well, do you think there could be a link with the missing Duchess?'

'I think there's a very strong possibility that they are connected.'

McQuinn nodded. 'Pity the newspapers couldn't produce a photograph of her. That would have been a great help. One thing I don't understand though, why keep the body – for a week?'

Faro would early have loved the answer to that question. All it indicated to him was that the assassin was getting nervous.

Of the Grand Duchess's entourage, only Miss Fortescue now remained alive.

But for how long?

12

As Faro and McQuinn emerged from the shelter of the ruined chapel and prepared to rejoin the police carriage, they were hailed by a figure toiling up the hill.

It was Leslie Godwin, leading a horse, and on the path below, Sergeant Batey.

'Shall I wait, sir?' said McQuinn.

'No. You head back.'

Leslie approached Faro eagerly. 'I'm out later than usual. Missed my early-morning ride.' He gave his cousin a quizzical glance. 'I expect Vince will have told you. We had a somewhat convivial evening at the Spec.'

Faro smiled. No doubt Leslie's tough and dangerous existence though the years made him impervious to the excesses of high living. Although considerably older than Vince, Faro decided that his cousin was also in better shape than either of them.

As they watched the forlorn cavalcade descending the hill with their stretcher, Leslie explained: 'Saw your policemen gathered and – ' He grinned. 'You know me – I decided there must be a story. As soon as I spotted you, I knew I was right. So here I am.' He sat down on a nearby rock, anchoring his horse's reins.

'Well, what have you got to tell me?' At Faro's stern expression, he laughed. 'Not another mysterious corpse, I trust.'

When Faro frowned, his cousin's eyes widened. 'That was meant as a joke – not in the best of taste, I realise.'

Faro received this observation in silence and Leslie whistled. 'Some connection between the two, eh? Well now.'

Faro couldn't think of a reply and Leslie continued sternly. 'Come now, Jeremy, don't you think it's time you brought me into this? You know I want to help and, who knows, maybe I can – '

'There isn't anything – ' Faro began hastily.

Leslie held up his hand. 'Please don't try to fob me off, I'm an old hand at the game,' he added in wounded tones. 'Besides,

I know that you are involved in what might turn out to be a scandalous piece of international intrigue.'

Faro felt suddenly chilled. 'And what makes you think that?'

Leslie smiled. 'From hints dropped – confidentially, of course – at the Spec last night,' he added with an impish smile, 'I gathered that none other than the Grand Duchess of Luxoria had gone amissing.'

Damn Vince. Drink loosened his tongue. He had never learned to control that particular student weakness. Damn him, Faro thought angrily as Leslie continued: 'And I suddenly realised that this is where I might be able to help you.'

'In what way?'

'The best possible,' Leslie regarded him triumphantly. 'You see, I've been to Luxoria. A couple of years ago when I was travelling across Europe, I had the honour to be received by members of the Royal family – '

This was an unexpected piece of luck. Faro looked at him gratefully. 'You met the Grand Duchess?'

Leslie shook his head. 'Alas, no, she was absent, if you please, with her husband, the odious President. As nasty a situation as anyone could imagine, a piece of emotional blackmail worthy of any grand opera.'

'How so?'

'I got the general drift, that her family had literally sold her to save their skins, whatever they were pretending. You don't know the story?'

Faro did but he wanted to hear his cousin's version, which confirmed exactly what Miss Fortescue had confided in him. Then he added: 'He'd like to divorce Amelie and marry his mistress – if that wouldn't mean the end of his power.'

It was even worse that Faro had thought. The President had very good reason for disposing of the Grand Duchess, and a professional assassin could easily be bought for the kind of money the ruthless President was prepared to pay.

As they stumbled through the bracken, the short cut to the road far below, Faro turned and asked with sudden hope: 'Did you by any chance see any photographs of her?'

Leslie thought for a moment. 'I was only there very briefly, a few days. Hardly enough to do more than take a passing interest in my surroundings. There were some family paintings on the walls, sentimental reminders of the Royal Family in their heyday. But seventeen-year-old girls can change quite a bit with the passing years – not to mention an unhappy marriage.'

'But there is a possibility you might recognise her again?'

Leslie laughed. 'I don't know what you're getting at, but yes. I've got quite a good memory for faces, and if the setting was right, I suppose.' He paused, then added, 'There's a strong family resemblance to the House of Hanover and the Saxe-Coburgs. Hardly surprising since they're all related. And let's not forget that artists who know when they're on to a good thing tend to err on the side of flattery.'

He looked hard at Faro. 'What are you getting at, Jeremy?' And when his cousin didn't answer, he indicated a large boulder and, sitting down on it, made a place for Faro. Then smiling encouragingly, he said gently: 'Why not start at the beginning? Who was the last person to see the Grand Duchess?'

'Her lady-in-waiting, Miss Fortescue – '

'And where is she now?'

'At Lethie Castle – '

Leslie listened carefully, frowning occasionally as Faro told him the events of the disastrous landing at North Berwick and Miss Fortescue's flight to Solomon's Tower.

At the end, Leslie sighed, his only comment: 'Vanished into thin air. Just like that.'

Before replying, Faro said a silent prayer that his fears were groundless. 'I take it that the corpse in the West Bow that night didn't strike you in any way as familiar?'

'Familiar?' Leslie stared at him. Then as realisation dawned, he whispered: 'You mean – you think – '

'Well, could it?'

'Oh lord, Jeremy. I don't know. I haven't the foggiest. I didn't look at her very closely. You know how it is.' He looked thoughtful. 'Have you considered that another talk with the lad Sandy might be useful? It could well be that he's hiding something.'

And studying Faro, he shrugged. 'I'm no detective, you know, but right from the start the lad's manner struck me as suspicious.'

'That he was plain scared, you mean.' Faro smiled. 'It isn't every day that a twelve-year-old lad stumbles on a corpse. Or finds himself surrounded by the police.'

'I agree. It could be that the scent of the law so near home put him off. Most of these lads live by dubious activities, and as you know Batey grabbed him by the ear, with his hand in my pocket.' He laughed. 'Quite brazen about it, he was too. Yes, I think you would be well-advised to have a talk. And it would help if you had a coin or two in hand. Nothing like the sight of money for lubricating information.'

'I have tried,' said Faro. 'Called at the house when I left you the other day.'

'Well?'

'He wasn't at home, but I left a message with his mother and the promise of two shillings.'

Leslie nodded eagerly. 'That should bring him running to your door.'

They got up and walked in silence for a few moments before Leslie turned and added: 'If in doubt, you could have the corpse exhumed.'

'I'm afraid not. There is no resurrection for this particular corpse. All unknown and unclaimed bodies become the property of Dr Cranley and his students.'

'Dear God. You mean – ' And Leslie made a grisly gesture of using a knife.

'Precisely.'

'How awful.'

And as if in accompaniment to grim realisation, they reached the park pursued by rain sheets that crept steadily over the hill, shrouding Arthur's Seat in thunderheads. The sky rumbled ominously in the grip of an approaching storm, reminding Faro that this swiftly changing weather signalled golden autumn would soon be replaced by dark November. Cold winter days, where early darkness made petty crime more profitable and detection a hundred times more difficult and uncomfortable.

On the road, Sergeant Batey was waiting. He helped his master to mount, looking neither to left nor to right. Faro might not have existed, nor McQuinn standing a few yards away.

Batey's behaviour made Faro uneasy. There was something unhuman about him, an attitude he had only ever met in the most hardened criminals, killers by inclination rather than by the circumstances that make men into soldiers.

He looked at his cousin Leslie, so open-faced and frank, then at the handsome Irish McQuinn, and was struck by the comparison. Batey might be a good servant perhaps, but not one Faro would have cared to keep under his roof.

Leslie waved a cheerful farewell with a promise to meet again soon. Winking broadly at his cousin, he called: 'You've given me plenty to think about. I'll let you know if I come up with any brilliant ideas.'

Faro watched the two men, so completely dissimilar, gallop back towards the Canongate. Then turning, he surveyed the ruined chapel thoughtfully. The sloping foothills of Arthur's Seat were almost deserted, except for one other domestic building, almost as ancient as the chapel itself.

Solomon's Tower. Not very far away, in fact quite conveniently accessible and offering splendid opportunities for hiding a body. With or without the Mad Bart's knowledge or consent, he thought grimly.

Narrowing his eyes, he remembered Miss Fortescue half-alive, staggering into the Tower, her story not quite the same as the one the Mad Bart had produced. And on the off-chance of finding him at home, he decided to call and direct a few searching questions on what had really happened that night.

He was unlucky. There was no human response to the clanging bell which, however, alerted the feline inhabitants. As he opened the door, he was engulfed in a purring tide of cats, all intent on insinuating themselves about his ankles. Faro no longer had any worries that Sir Hedley might be lying dead in his cat-haunted tower. So, restraining them from escaping into the garden, and having endured enough strong and unpleasant odours for one day, he beat a hasty retreat.

Before going out to Aberlethie to see if Miss Fortescue could shed any light on the identity of the corpse in St Anthony's Chapel, Faro had decided to make certain that the dead man was not already on the Edinburgh City Police's missing persons list.

At the Central Office, Sergeant McQuinn had forestalled him. He shook his head. 'No one even resembling him, sir.'

'You're quite sure?'

Faro was surprised, having expected several missing men of similar ordinariness whose descriptions might roughly fit the one he now thought of as the missing coachman.

'I'll make the usual routine enquiries, sir, but it looks as if we might be landed with a Mr Nobody.'

The missing persons lists was not, Faro knew, completely reliable. For every person who disappeared and was urgently sought by relatives for reasons of love or loathing or by creditors for lucre, there were dozens more husbands and wives, sons and daughters who disappeared discreetly and whose relatives for their own reasons kept silent. If enquiries had been made, doubtless the police would have found that these same people were grateful to see the last of their missing relative, saying their prayers each night that they might never again be troubled by the sound of that dreaded footfall crossing their threshold.

'We've had the list of the contents of the Duchess's jewel box distributed, sir. None of the pieces have turned up with any of the legitimate dealers.'

'It's early days for that. How about some of the illicit ones?' Even as he spoke, Faro realised the hopelessness of such a task. Fences would be hanging on to them for a month or two until the scent grew cold, or trying to sell them on the Continent for quick disposal.

More than an hour had passed since Faro and McQuinn had left the scene on the road below St Anthony's Chapel.

On the off-chance that Dr Cranley had made a discovery of some importance, they went together to the mortuary where, having just completed his grisly business, the doctor was washing his hands.

Giving Faro a triumphant look, he said: 'I was right, you know, he was drowned. His lungs had ballooned as a result of distension with water. That's how he died, but he wasn't in the water for long – '

As Dr Cranley proceeded to reiterate what Faro knew already, he listened politely, then took his leave.

Outside, McQuinn said, 'Looks as if we have a murder inquiry on our hands, sir.'

'I'm afraid so.' Faro looked at his watch. 'Take care of the preliminary business, will you, McQuinn. I'm off to Aberlethie – there's a train to North Berwick in half an hour. I want to talk to Miss Fortescue again.'

'You think she may know something?'

'My thoughts are leading steadily in that direction, McQuinn. Something vital to the case, that she doesn't even realise she knows until she's prompted and it surfaces into her memory again.'

McQuinn looked at him frowning. 'You think the dead man might be the missing coachman?'

'I am fairly certain of that, at least.'

As Faro was leaving the Central Office, Constable Reid came up the steps. 'A burglary inside the Castle, sir.'

'Civilian?'

'Yes, sir.'

'You take care of it – '

The constable looked uncomfortable. 'Colonel Wrightson asked to see you specially, sir. Urgent, he said it was.'

'Very well.' Constable Reid's cape gleamed with rain, and as Faro looked with little enthusiasm upon the downpour, the constable said encouragingly, 'I'll get you a carriage, sir.'

Five minutes later, the police carriage was toiling up the High Street and the Esplanade, transformed into twin rivers of brown water and debris from overflowing gutters.

At the Castle, he was escorted to the Colonel's private apartments. Wrightson was waiting from him. He smiled apologetically.

'Nothing serious, Faro. Nothing to worry about. Do sit down. Have a drink.'

Faro did as he was bid and with a whisky in hand tried to suppress his impatience. He had too much on his mind to be in a mood for the trifling details of a break-in at the Castle that any of his constables could have dealt with efficiently.

'... in this room, but nothing was taken, as far as we can see,' the Colonel went on. 'In fact, we wouldn't have known that there had been a break-in except that the man was spotted leaving the room. He wasn't in uniform and when challenged, took to his heels. It was then my man gave the alert. I came immediately – '

Faro was looking round the room. With trophies on every shelf, every inch of wall space occupied by paintings and army group photographs, it would be extremely difficult at first glance to know if anything was missing. His glance wandered to the massive desk, awash with books and documents.

Wrightson followed his gaze and nodded. ' I suspect that the desk was the target.'

At Faro's questioning look, he continued, 'Well, there was one drawer – over here.'

Faro saw that the lock bore marks of a sharp instrument being used on it. 'Is there anything missing?'

Wrightson wriggled uncomfortably. 'That I can't honestly say.'

Faro looked at him. 'Surely you know what the drawer contained, sir?' And when the Colonel looked blank, he prompted: 'Documents, for instance, perhaps of a secret or confidential nature?'

The Colonel laughed. 'No. That's what's so odd. I think he must have broken open the wrong drawer. There are such papers – here – and here – ' He indicated several drawers. 'But this one is where I keep my mementoes and stationery. Everything relating to my years serving Her Majesty at Holyrood, I just thrust in there. Not a bit of use to anyone, that I can assure you.'

'Nothing of value, then? You are certain of that?'

The Colonel smiled. 'Only to me. You see, Faro, I'm a bit of a hoarder, can't bear to throw anything away. I kept all the menus, notes from Her Majesty, memos – ribbons off cakes. Everything and all purely sentimental things.'

'You wouldn't by any chance have a list of the contents?' Even as he asked Faro realised that was a forlorn hope.

At his bleak expression, Wrightson shook his head. 'I'm not a list man. I'm sorry, Faro, I've really wasted your time,' he added apologetically.

'Not at all, sir,' said Faro gallantly, as he considered that was precisely what Wrightson had done. 'Who has access to these rooms, sir?'

'None of my men, if that's what you mean. There's tight security about that. Officers' quarters, strictly out of bounds.'

'So none of them could come in here without your knowledge?'

The Colonel shook his head. 'Or without my batman. He accompanies any soldier – or officer – who has reason to seek an interview. And they wouldn't be left alone by him, not for a minute, if that's what you're hinting at.'

'Have there been any such interviews recently?'

'None at all.'

'When was the last time this room was occupied by anyone other than yourself and your batman, sir?'

Wrightson thought for a moment. 'The other evening, at the dinner party, why, you were here, Faro. Remember, we all had drinks before going in.'

Faro shook his head. 'I missed that part of the proceedings, sir. Unavoidably detained, I arrived late.'

Wrighton gave him an indignant look. 'Wait a moment, Faro. What are you getting at? Not suggesting that one of my guests would go though my desk when my back was turned – I hope.'

'I'm only saying that your friends are the only persons with access to this room apart from your batman.'

'Well!' Wrightson gave a shout of indignation. 'I don't have those kinds of friends, that I can assure you, sir. The very idea.' Suddenly speechless, he continued to regard Faro angrily, his face scarlet, outraged by such a suggestion.

'It's my duty to ask such questions, sir, unpleasant though they may be for you,' Faro added in what he hoped was a mollifying tone. 'I'm not insulting your friends, merely endeavouring to investigate the burglary you have reported.'

'I see, I see,' said Wrightson impatiently.

'I need to know whether you've had anything of value stolen. The man who was apprehended might well have been a civilian who sneaked in out of curiosity – or bravado – got lost and found himself in this part of the Castle – '

But even as he said it, as he hoped in firm and convincing tones, Faro didn't believe it and neither, he suspected, did Wrightson, although he was prepared to accept this as a possible explanation.

As Faro rose to leave, the Colonel said, 'My apologies for bringing you here on a wild-goose chase.'

'Not at all, sir. If civilians are involved then it is our business to protect you.'

Wrightson thought for a moment. 'I did wonder at first, if this might have something to do with that other attempted break-in – from the outside. Remember, Faro, more than a week ago?'

The same thought had been in Faro's mind. He could see no connection between the two events but the idea was vaguely disturbing.

He left the Castle feeling that he would much rather have had a proper burglary to investigate, with a few silver trophies taken and a few clues to follow, than an apparently motiveless petty crime.

The possibility of a passer-by overcome by curiosity was too remote and yet oddly sinister in its simplicity. Secret and confidential documents for sale to foreign powers seemed the most plausible reason.

Faro sighed. At least with silver trophies and items of value, there existed a list at the Edinburgh City Police of what they called 'the usual suspects', criminals to be rounded up from the notorious warrens of Wormwoodhall in Causewayside. But from their number, few violent men would risk breaking into the well-guarded officers' quarters in the Castle merely to open a drawer in Wrightson's desk full of sentimental royal mementoes. This certainly did not bear the mark of any of the city's well-kent criminal hierarchy, who all left recognisable trademarks.

As the carriage headed towards Wavereley Station through the torrential rain, Arthur's Seat was obliterated by mist. Faro wished the incidents of that morning could as readily be dissolved, but one thought in particular refused to be banished.

Was it significant that Miss Fortescue had suggested that the coachman had drowned? Did she know a great deal more about the events of that night than she was prepared to disclose? If so, in common with those who knew too much about assassins, she might well be in mortal danger.

13

'Not another train till six o'clock, sir,' said the railway guard cheerfully, as Faro, dashing to the barrier, watched the North Berwick train steaming out of the station.

Slowed down by the appalling condition of flooded roads from the Castle, he'd missed it by seconds. And now he made the discovery that his boots were leaking. This damned rain!

Leaving the empty platform, cursing Edinburgh's foul weather, he decided he might as well return to the Central Office and log his interview with Colonel Wrightson about the break-in. He set off at brisk pace towards the High Street, to be caught in yet another downpour.

'Where in damnation is it all coming from?' he demanded of McQuinn, who was leaving in the police carriage, heading for Liberton. The young sergeant took pity on his bedraggled appearance.

'Why don't you get some dry clothes, sir – we'll drop you off at the house.'

Faro was glad to accept, and as they drove in the direction of Newington, in answer to his question, McQuinn said: 'Nothing to report, sir. Thought you were going to Aberlethie?'

'There was an attempted break-in at the Castle –'

As Faro related his meeting with the Colonel, McQuinn listened sympathetically.

'Doesn't sound like one of our lads, sir. Doubt if rounding them up would do any good.'

'Complete waste of time, I'd say,' Faro agreed.

Opening his front door a few minutes later, Faro realised that the house was unusually silent without Mrs Brook's bustling presence. Her niece was getting married in Dundee and she had been persuaded, very much against her will, to take a couple of days off.

Swept off balance by a false step on the hall carpet, he cursed again, sniffing the air. Mrs Brook refused to take seriously his warnings about putting carpets on highly polished floors. Certain that the whole structure of 9 Sheridan Place would collapse in her absence and her two gentlemen die of neglect, she had once again been over-generous with the beeswax.

Changing his boots and taking the damp ones down to the kitchen, Faro looked into the larder. It was filled to overflowing with covered and labelled dishes complete with neatly written menus for each meal.

He stood back, exasperated by such efficiency. He deplored waste, and the prospect of tackling what appeared to be enough provisions for a whole regiment on a month-long siege made him feel guilty.

The room was suddenly lit by a flash of lightning. As thunder rumbled angrily back and forth across the sky, like a dialogue between two ill-tempered giants, Faro gave up any idea of travelling to Aberlethie and back again. He had had quite enough for one day. Tomorrow morning his best boots would be dry, and hopefully the rain which had persisted all day would have worn itself out with its continued efforts.

The decision made, he sat down at the kitchen table with a slice of cold pork pie before him, suddenly charmed at the novelty of having the house to himself. He couldn't remember the last time, if ever, this agreeable experience had occurred.

Discovering that he had an appetite and was hungrier than usual at this hour of the day, he was attacking a second slice of Mrs Brook's excellent fruit cake when the front doorbell clanged through the house.

As it jangled noisily a second time, he decided to ignore it. Doubtless some tradesman was seeking Mrs Brook. Resentful at having his peaceful meal interrupted by this intrusion, he was taking another bite of cake when conscience told him that the caller might be a patient in urgent need of Dr Laurie's attention.

In Vince's absence, such cases were referred to a retired colleague in Minto Street. Now, where was the card?

The doorbell had clanged vigorously a third time when he found it on the mantelpiece, and hoping he wasn't too late, he ran upstairs.

On the doorstep, he was taken aback to find, not a frantic patient, but Miss Fortescue.

'I'm so glad to find you at home, Inspector. I called at the Central Office and they told me you had left –'

She was obviously very agitated, staring back over her shoulder, nervously searching the street in the manner of one who suspects she is being followed. And Faro almost expected to see the Lethie servant hovering at a discreet distance.

'I had to see you, Inspector.'

'Won't you come in?'

Her travelling cape was almost as wet as her umbrella. He wondered if this was a planned departure from Lethie Castle – the word 'escape' came to his mind unheeded, for she carried a straw-lidded travelling basket, the kind favoured by ladies on short summer expeditions.

Releasing her from her cape he said: 'I'll take this down to the kitchen, miss. It'll soon dry out on the stove.'

As Mrs Brook's highly polished floor threatened to claim its second victim, he seized her elbow, apologised and pointed her in the direction of the drawing-room: 'Take a seat if you please, miss. I'll be with you directly.'

He put out his hand for the travelling bag. Shaking her head firmly, she smiled up at him.

'I'm sorry to be a nuisance. I did get rather wet waiting for a carriage at the station. They were all claimed immediately they arrived. I'm afraid I haven't quite the knack of rushing forward and arguing with strong men brandishing stout waking-sticks.'

'It's always like that in bad weather, miss,' said Faro, surprised that she hadn't come in the Lethie carriage.

When he said so, she shook her head. 'No, I came by train. I left them a note. You see, Inspector, I'm quite desperate. I'm not a very patient person. I must take matters into my own hands. And do something,' she emphasised.

It all seemed very courageous, thought Faro, but hardly what he expected. And more important, what precisely did she expect him to do? He had problems enough without a distressed lady-in-waiting on his hands.

'I need hardly tell you, Inspector, I am utterly weary of sitting out there at Lethie listening to Terence and Sara assuring me that everything is going to be all right.'

She looked at him steadily and added slowly, 'When I am absolutely sure now that something has gone terribly wrong.

Otherwise, news of some sort should have reached me by now. Don't you agree?' And without waiting for his answer: 'Of course the Lethies have been so good and kind. They're very patient and conscientious, especially as they are leaving for a family wedding in Paris at the end of the week.'

Pausing, she regarded him helplessly. 'We haven't discussed what will happen to me in their absence, what arrangements they have made.'

What indeed, thought Faro. She could hardly be returned to Solomon's Tower and the hospitality of Sir Hedley Marsh, that was for sure.

'I felt I couldn't just sit in that empty house a moment longer,' she continued, shaking her head vigorously, 'I am used to an active life, you know. Routine, and all that sort of thing. I must confess I am terribly bored by all this enforced idleness – sitting waiting for news is very disagreeable for one's nerves. Each time a servant comes in or a rider appears on the drive, one's hopes are raised and then dashed severely to the ground again. I feel like a prisoner, waiting to be released.'

She sighed, looking at him expectantly.

Faro's murmur of sympathy seemed to encourage her and she went on: 'While they were out visiting this morning, I decided I must try to – well, escape for a while. I was so longing to see something of your lovely city. So I left them a note and caught the train at the halt.' Staring ruefully at the streaming windows, she added: 'I hadn't bargained for the weather, of course. It was dull but still fair when I left this morning.'

As Faro listened, he was grateful for the missed train to North Berwick that had saved him a futile visit to Lethie Castle.

'– I've had a perfectly splendid day,' Miss Fortescue went on. 'Princes Street is a delight, such lovely shops. And I didn't mind getting wet. Rain like this is something of a rarity in Luxoria. And we are never allowed to get wet –'

Faro was wondering how he was expected to respond to this burst of enthusiasm when she sighed deeply, troubled no doubt by thoughts of her royal friend and companion.

'We're all doing as much as we can, miss, to find your mistress,' he reminded her gently.

Straightening her shoulders, she said sternly, 'And that is precisely why I am here, Inspector. I am absolutely certain that she must have reached Her Majesty by now. That was the prime intention of this visit. Lethie was to be an overnight stay only, renewing old acquaintance with – with my family who have served hers so well. Why then has there been no word to them – or to me? She is such a thoughtful person, I assure you. She cares deeply about her friends and those who serve her.'

Again she looked at Faro, who could think of no answer beyond nodding in agreement.

'I keep thinking of her sitting in Balmoral Castle – at this very moment, Inspector, perhaps believing that I was drowned that awful night. Do you think it is possible, as I suggested to you, that she has sent word to Lethie Castle and some misfortune has befallen the messenger? Have you any means of finding out?'

When Faro didn't respond, she put a beseeching hand on his arm. 'I must find her. Please, Inspector – you must take me to her. She will be so relieved to know that I am unharmed.'

Faro stared at her, at a loss for appropriate words. Or any words, in fact. His hesitation was mistaken and she went on hastily: 'Oh, I'm not reproaching you in any way, Inspector, please don't think that. I do regard your efforts most highly. I'm sure you have our best interests at heart. Indeed,' she added with an engagingly shy smile, 'I think of you as a friend almost.'

Faro bowed, and playing for time and some suitable response to Miss Fortescue's proposal, he removed the fire-guard and attempted to light the fire which Mrs Brook had set in readiness. As it smoked dismally, he said: 'I'll just go and see how your cape is drying, miss. If you'll excuse me.'

She smiled. 'I imagine that your wife is used to such weather and dealing with emergencies like drying wet garments.'

'I'm not married, miss.'

'Oh, I'm sorry.' She looked round with a puzzled frown. 'Then you have a very good housekeeper – this room has a woman's touch.'

'That is so. This is her day off. However, I shall endeavour to make you a cup of tea.'

Having put on the kettle, he returned to find her looking out of the window. 'This is such a pretty house, Inspector. I love these small rooms. Such lovely windows and what a delightful view,' she said, pointing across to the commanding mass of Arthur's Seat.

Faro suppressed a smile. The rooms with their high ceilings could only be classed as small by comparison. 'Hardly what you're used to in a palace, miss.'

'I know. But it's all so charming. Palaces are hateful places to live in, I assure you. There is so little comfort, vast rooms with inadequate fires to heat them, miles and miles to walk every time one wants something that isn't there.' She clasped her hands delightedly. 'I would give anything to live in a little house like this.'

'Excuse me, miss – the kettle –'

When he returned, she was sitting close to the dead fire, her arms clasped tightly together.

Faro sighed. 'I'm afraid that's beyond redemption, miss. It is chilly in here.'

Politely she suppressed a shiver. 'Just a little.'

'It's warmer in the kitchen, miss, a good fire down there. Would you care –'

'I would indeed.' And seizing her bag, she followed him downstairs. There her admiration of his home now extended to Mrs Brook's domain. She looked around at shelves and cupboards as if she had never encountered a kitchen before, exclaiming with delight over gleaming brass saucepans and rows of china plates.

'You should see our kitchen in the castle. It's a terrible place, big and gloomy as a dungeon. Oh, do please – allow me –'

And Faro, rather relieved, handed her Mrs Brook's precious tea-caddy. Watching her, he suddenly laughed out loud.

'What is so amusing?' she asked.

'You're better than I am at tea-making. Of course, I should have expected that in a lady-in-waiting. I suppose it's part of your duties.'

She smiled. 'Not really. It's usually brought in all prepared. And as he took out Mrs Brook's cake: 'I'd love a slice of that –'

As she ate, Faro, having reassembled his thoughts, decided he must escort her back to Lethie Castle immediately, a double journey he could well do without. Her impulsive action was a nuisance and a waste of his time, but he could sympathise with the anxiety and boredom that had driven her to escape for the day.

The Lethies, he guessed, would by now have discovered her absence. Perhaps she did not realise in her sheltered life in Luxoria that in respectable society, ladies of gentle birth did not promenade the streets and shops of Edinburgh, even during the day, unescorted or without a maid in attendance. And despite the note she had left, Sir Terence and his wife would be frantic with anxiety when they realised she had gone off alone.

He sighed. Somehow on the way to Aberlethie he must tactfully get her to understand that he had no authority to set out for Balmoral Castle with her and make an impromptu visit to the Royal residence on the assumption that her mistress was already there.

If only he could believe that were true, what a happy man he would be.

He smiled at her, so pretty and gentle. And safe too, when just a few hours ago, while she was promenading along Princes Street, he feared she might have been in grave danger. What an opportunity the hired assassin had missed there, he thought with a shudder.

He looked at the clock. 'There's a train back to Aberlethie in half an hour. We'll take that one.'

She allowed him to help her into her cape somewhat reluctantly. 'Oh, very well. I suppose I must go. But I've so enjoyed talking to you, Inspector, you have been very kind.'

As he picked up her bag she seized it back from him. 'I'll take that, thank you.'

He wondered what it contained that was so precious, deciding that it was remarkably heavy and solid too, for feminine fripperies. But rather admiring her independence, he said: 'You wait here in the hall, miss. I'll get a carriage.'

A few minutes later they were heading towards Waverley Station. Armed with their tickets, Faro led her towards the platform.

At the barrier, the guard shook his head. 'Not tonight, I'm afraid, sir.'

Faro pointed towards the waiting train.

'Aye, sir, and there it stays till morning. There's been a cloud-burst, line is flooded past Musselburgh and there'll be no trains till it subsides.' The porter looked at the grey sky. 'If it stays fine, then you'll get away first thing tomorrow morning.'

Faro regarded Miss Fortescue anxiously as they walked back into the booking office.

'Don't worry, miss, we'll get you back somehow.'

But far from being worried or dismayed, Miss Fortescue laughed, obviously treating this new disaster as a huge joke. 'Here's a pretty pickle. Well, Inspector, how do you solve this one?'

'That's easy, miss. We take a carriage.'

'What an adventure.' She chuckled happily.

It was the kind of adventure Faro could well have done without when he saw that the usual line-up of hiring carriages was absent from outside the station. At last a solitary one appeared and Faro rushed forward.

'Where to, sir?' asked the coachman.

'Aberlethie, if you please.'

'Aberlethie, did ye say?' The man shook his head. 'Not tonight, sir. Just come from Musselburgh, that's as far as we can get. Roads are all under water. You and the missus'll need to wait till morning and take a train like sensible folk.'

And looking at Miss Fortescue's bag, presuming they had come off a train, he said: 'I can take you to a good hotel.'

'A hotel.' Miss Fortescue grasped his arm. 'Oh no, Inspector, I couldn't – I just couldn't,' she whispered.

'Why ever not, miss? There are some very comfortable establishments on Princes Street. Very respectable too.'

'I'm sure there are. It isn't that, I assure you. I'm just – scared.'

'Scared?'

'Yes. You see, I once stayed in a hotel and it took fire. So I can't.' She shook her head firmly. 'Not ever again.'

He wasn't sure he wanted to let her out of his sight, aware that she might have been followed. 'I'll stay there too, if you wish. Take a room close to yours –'

'No – no – you're very kind. But not even if you were in the – the same room – I just – can't.'

'Are you wanting this carriage or not?' the coachman demanded.

If it was possible that she had been followed, then Faro could see dangers in the hotel idea. He now had to consider reluctantly the alternative that remained. And that was to keep her under his own roof where he could be sure she was safe till morning.

And as if she read his thought: 'Perhaps you have a spare room,' she whispered.

14

The carriage set them down in Sheridan Place and as Faro opened his front door, Miss Fortescue sighed.

'I'm greatly obliged to you, Inspector.'

Faro led the way down to the kitchen. And deploring Mrs Brook's absence, he said: 'Take a seat by the fire and I'll see what I can do about a room for you.'

Where would he put her? He seldom set foot in the spare rooms and had no idea whether the housekeeper kept beds made up for unexpected guests. He soon discovered that was not the case. The rooms he entered were cold and desolate, beds stripped down to their mattresses.

So where were the sheets and blankets kept? He wasn't even sure he knew how to make a bed properly.

Then he remembered his daughters' room, and throwing open the door, saw that Mrs Brook's proud boast that it was always kept aired and in readiness for their next visit was evidently correct.

Miss Fortescue followed him upstairs and, setting down her bag by the bed, she looked round delightedly at her surroundings.

'Thank you so much, Inspector. Yes, I'm sure I'll be most comfortable.'

'Let me know if there is anything you require, miss.'

A few minutes later she returned to the kitchen, where he was spreading the table with some of Mrs Brook's abundant provisions.

'Such a pretty room you've given me. Is it your sister's?'

'No, my two daughters occupy it when they come to stay during the school holidays.' He was ashamed at making those sadly infrequent visits sound so regular.

'They are not at school in Edinburgh?'

'No.' He explained to her that he was a widower and it was convenient for his daughters to stay with their grandmother in Orkney.

She was all sympathy. Very sweet, he decided, and a good listener. Splendid appetite, too. She obviously relished Mrs

Brook's cooking and begged to be allowed to take over preparation of the meal. Far from being baffled by cavernous pantries and belligerent stoves, she found one of Mrs Brook's vast aprons and was soon in complete command of the domestic situation.

Faro looked on, laughing approvingly. 'I'm glad you came, miss.'

She shook her head, smiled. 'Not miss, please. Roma.'

'Roma,' he repeated. 'An unusual name.'

'My parents spent their honeymoon in Italy.'

As they enjoyed a pleasant and companionable meal together he found himself telling her not only his life story, but his problems at the Central Office and even details of some of his most baffling cases. He found she had a surprising knowledge of the major governmental issues in Britain, as well as a keener understanding than he had ever aspired to, of the boiling-pot of European politics.

Miss Roma Fortescue, he guessed, belonged to the new breed of independent and enlightened women. And Faro was one man who didn't feel threatened by them. In many of his cases, he had learned to deal with women who were the equal of any man, and infinitely more ruthless. He had his own personal reasons, and carried some indelible scars, for regarding the fair sex not as the weaker, but in many instances, the stronger.

This one, he thought, was far too bright to be wasted in a stultifying existence as a mere lady-in-waiting to an impulsive headstrong royal duchess, with her talents limited to plying an embroidery needle, playing the pianoforte and playing up to her mistress's constant demand for entertainment.

Afterwards, when he tried to do so, he could never clearly remember details of their conversation, only her ready flashes of wit and humour.

As she cleared the table and carried the dishes to the sink, refusing his help, she sighed happily. 'This is my dream come true. I get so little chance to do this sort of thing. I am not even allowed to set foot in the kitchens.' She paused and looked at him solemnly. 'Shall I tell you what my favourite book is?'

'Please do,' he said, expecting some learned philosophical treatise.

'Promise you won't laugh?'

'I promise.'

'Mrs Beeton's *All About Cookery* book.' She looked at him suspiciously. 'You don't find that amusing?'

'On the contrary, I find it very worthy.'

She looked around and smiled. 'A kitchen, warm – and small. A cosy fire and a table full of baking materials. Half a dozen menus to prepare – that is my idea of bliss.'

'And a husband perhaps to appreciate your culinary efforts,' he added teasingly.

Her face darkened. 'Perhaps.' Then the shadow lifted and she regarded him intently, with a look that flattered him. 'Or a kind friend. That would do perfectly.'

Faro wondered why, past thirty, she was still unmarried. He suspected a sad love story, some hidden grief. Pretty, charming, attractive – were Luxorian men daunted by such qualities and by this clever Scotswoman? Scots? No. She wasn't really, he thought, she was quite foreign sometimes, in turns of phrase, a word sought after vainly – in the manner of British subjects who spend most of their lives in other countries and are more at home in another language.

He was delighted to find that Miss Fortescue was extremely well-read. She shared his own passion for Shakespeare's plays, her early years as companion to her English-educated royal mistress had obviously served her well. He was agreeably surprised to hear that she also enjoyed Sir Walter Scott's novels.

'And we had all Mr Dickens' latest books sent out specially to Luxoria.'

Music too, Faro discovered, was something they shared. Mr Mendelssohn and Mr Liszt had been welcome visitors to Luxoria.

In no great hurry to bring the evening to a close, they talked and laughed together. Meanwhile the storm continued to rage outside, but they were oblivious of wind lashing the windows, of doors creaking in the gale.

At one stage, pouring more wine, Faro looked at his companion and saw her for the first time as a woman to be desired. He realised wistfully that this cosy domestic scene, this simple meal in a warm kitchen, was one being repeated in houses all over Edinburgh.

How long had it been since he spent an evening at home with

a woman he loved, he thought wistfully, his hand shaking a little as he picked up his wineglass? It had been so long since Lizzie had died. His skirmishes into love had been transient, wounding, disastrous.

As Miss Fortescue looked at him he felt embarrassed by the pain in his eyes. Was she lonely too? Did this kitchen scene remind her of the years that were gone, of sad days and glad days and lost love?

Faro sighed. The Wagnerian storm outside with its lightning flashes and thunder-claps that shook the walls and guttered the lamps was all the passion this particular house would know tonight.

Midnight was past. Where had the hours gone? He wanted to call them all back again, to relive each minute, suddenly precious, each sentence, each burst of laughter in a perpetual motion of happy hours. Eternity should be such a night as this. Eternal bliss –

And now it was almost over. Miss Fortescue stood up, yawned. He regarded the dregs of his empty wineglass.

'Of course, you must be tired.'

She sighed. 'A little, yes. It has been such a day.'

He poured warm water into a ewer for her washing and took the candle off the table. 'I'll see you to your room.'

He followed her upstairs, opened the door of his daughters' room for Miss Fortescue. Turning, she smiled. 'Such a lovely day. A tremendous adventure.'

'I'll bid you goodnight, miss. Sleep well.'

'You too, Inspector. And thank you once again.'

Here today, gone tomorrow, a bird of passage, with plumage strange and rare. Only a fool would fall in love, Faro thought, closing the door on her.

His dreams were wild and strange, full of erotic images. The Crusader came from his tomb, stalking him across the years and thrusting the Luck o' Lethie into his hands. It turned into a snake becoming part of his own body.

He was awake. It was that strange hour twixt wolf and dog when familiar shapes of furniture become gross and ghostly aliens of nightmare and all the world holds its breath.

Someone was shaking him.

'Wake up – please, wake up.'

It was Miss Fortescue.

'Someone – someone is trying to break into the house,' she whispered. 'In the kitchen –'

Faro leaped out of bed and threw on his dressing-robe. An attempted break-in. There could be only one purpose. He felt sickened and confused by the knowledge that someone had followed Miss Fortescue and knew she was here. The assassin –

'You stay here,' he said, and ran lightly downstairs.

The kitchen was filled with grey uneasy dawn. But the door was still locked, bolted.

'They must have run away,' Miss Fortescue whispered. She was brave, he thought, she had followed him.

'What made you think – ?'

'I heard a noise. I was thirsty, too much wine, I suppose. You didn't leave me a carafe –'

Cutting short his apologies: 'My fault. I didn't ask. I came downstairs. And I saw a shadow – a man – at the window. Look –' She pointed.

Faro went to the window above the sink. A small pane of glass was broken. He opened the back door cautiously, walked the few steps to the window, saw the slivers of glass on the ground.

She watched him relocking the door.

'Well, you must have scared him off,' he said. 'I think you'd better go back to bed.'

'Are you sure he won't come back?' she said, pointing to the window.

'No. No one could climb in through that tiny space. I think we're safe enough now.'

She walked ahead of him up the stairs. She was wearing a light petticoat, prettily frilled with ribboned lace, and he realised that she must have slept in it in the absence of a nightgown.

He opened her bedroom door. 'You'll be quite safe now.'

'But – how –'

He shook his head, gently closed the door on her protests and went back to his own bed.

There he lay awake, his hands behind his head, pondering the night's strange events. In a little while he dozed, and opening his eyes, he thought he dreamed again, for she stood at his bedside.

'I'm so frightened. And I'm so cold. I've never been so cold.'

She held out her hands. He smiled and pulled back the covers, taking her into his arms. She was as passionate as she was clever, as tender as she was sweet.

At last the storm rolled away, and the golden light of early morning sunlight touched the bed where they lay still entwined.

Faro sighed, looking at her sleeping face. Soon it would be all over. The wild sweetness of one stolen night about to be obliterated by another day when dreams are quenched by the solemnity of duty.

She stirred in his arms. He kissed her hair and left her.

When she came down to the kitchen where he was stirring the embers of the fire, she looked towards the broken pane of glass.

'I can't believe it really happened,' she whispered.

'It didn't.'

'You mean – the break-in?'

'Exactly. It didn't happen. There was never a burglar.' He put an arm around her and laughed. 'So much trouble to come into my bed,' he whispered.

She understood. Laughing lightly, standing on tiptoe, she kissed him.

15

Sergeant McQuinn arrived as they were leaving the house together. He managed to conceal well both his surprise and his curiosity at the presence of a young woman in Inspector Faro's hall at eight thirty in the morning.

Saluting smartly, for the lady's benefit, he said: 'Superintendent McIntosh's compliments, sir. He needs to see you urgently.'

'I was about to escort Miss Fortescue back to Aberlethie.'

McQuinn looked at Miss Fortescue. 'Perhaps I can do that for you, sir.' He pointed to the street. 'The carriage is there.'

McQuinn did not miss the lady's frantic look in Faro's direction, nor how completely the Inspector chose to ignore it.

'You will be quite safe with Sergeant McQuinn, miss. Er – I'll call on you later.'

Bowing to her, he felt that he failed completely to convey the emotion concealed within those few words. She darted him a frantic look as McQuinn reached out a hand for her bag. But refusing to be parted from it, she allowed him to hand her into the carriage.

Again Faro wondered what shopping had been so precious or heavy and, more important, where the money had come from. Obviously Lady Lethie had been generous with more than her wardrobe.

Helplessly he watched them go, lifting a hand in farewell, angry at McIntosh's ill-timed command and with a shaft of jealousy for the young Irishman.

Would McQuinn exert all his ready charm on Miss Fortescue, Faro thought, remembering how successful McQuinn was with the ladies? All ages too, even his own young daughter Rose had lost her heart to him.

But in another part of his mind, Faro was secretly relieved that McQuinn's arrival had been so opportune. No words of love had been spoken between Roma Fortescue and himself. They had been two lonely people hungry for comfort. Of greater embarrassment would have been an explanation of why she had felt it necessary to pretend there was a burglar lurking on the premises.

That failed to make any sense at all.

In the Central Office, he found Superintendent McIntosh pacing the floor anxiously.

'Where do you think you've been, Faro? I've been waiting for you here since eight o'clock.'

Faro did not feel up to explaining that his arrival had been delayed by Miss Fortescue's departure on the nine o'clock train for North Berwick. Superintendent McIntosh would doubtless have asked the question he was most anxious to avoid: What was she doing at his house and where had she spent the night?

'There's a couple of lads downstairs. Claim that the man you found in St Anthony's Chapel is their father. They're with Dr Cranley now. He wants you to talk to them.'

The downstairs room was stark and bare with whitewashed brick walls and a disagreeable smell. Used for the questioning of criminals, its intimidating atmosphere offered little by way of consolation in breaking bad news to bereaved relatives.

Constable Reid was in attendance and Dr Cranley indicated a seat at the table. As he sat down opposite the pair, the doctor said: 'This is Inspector Faro.'

Introductions were unnecessary, the Hogan brothers knew him well already. Their paths had crossed many times before, and as far as Faro could see the only thing they had in common with the dead man was ginger hair.

'... They have identified the body as that of their father, Joshua Hogan, aged fifty-five, who went missing from home two weeks ago. I have explained the circumstances of his discovery to them and they have made a statement...'

As Cranley spoke, Faro studied the two men. The elder, Joe, was a petty criminal, a fence for stolen goods, the younger, Willy, a pimp for their sister, a notorious prostitute. All three had at some time been involved in fraud cases.

'Have you any idea what caused your father's death?' Faro asked.

'Bad lungs, he had,' said Joe, who had appointed himself spokesman. 'He was fooling around, drunk as usual. Fell into the horse trough outside the World's End Tavern. Lads he was with were all larking about, didn't realise he was dead, took him home, put him to bed. Will and me wasn't home – we was at the horse sales in Glasgow, so he lay for a week. When we got back, the lads was scared they'd be blamed, and so to cut a long story out, they carted him up to St Anthony's, dumped him there.'

'Have you names and addresses of these lads?'

'They're on the paper there,' Hogan said smoothly. 'Constable wrote them down along with our statement. Gave my word no harm would come to them. Gave my hand on it.'

And I dare say you had a lot of money pressed into it, thought Faro grimly. He looked at Dr Cranley, whose expression said he didn't believe a word of it either.

'And here's Da's birth certificate, if you want it,' said Willy carelessly.

'What next?' Faro asked McIntosh after the pair of highly improbable grieving relatives had left.

'Not a great deal,' the Superintendent replied, glancing through their statements.

'Dammit, the man was murdered.'

'We can't prove it. You know that and so do I.'

'The Hogans are criminals –'

'And so are their friends. They'll all swear blind that the brothers are speaking the truth.'

'I want to look further into it, sir. I'm not prepared to let it go at that.'

'You're wasting your time, Faro.'

'I've done that before and I'm prepared to do it again in the cause of justice.'

'Then try not to bring down a hornet's nest on our heads.'

'If it means bringing a murderer to justice, I'll even do that, sir.'

When McIntosh looked doubtful, Faro asked angrily: 'Look, you don't believe that story, do you, sir?'

'It's just daft enough to be true. The whole family is wild –'

'Extortionists, fraudsters –' Faro began heatedly.

'But always clever enough to evade arrest. There's money behind them.' The Superintendent shook his head. 'We all know that.'

'Stolen goods, smugglers, too. And no lack of alibis –'

'We haven't a hope in hell of finding who's backing them, Faro,' McIntosh interrupted impatiently.

'Why not?'

'He's not in our "Secret and Confidential" files, that's why. He could be a foreigner. Or a stranger – we have Highlanders, Irishmen, God knows all, passing through the warrens of the High Street, every day and lurking in the sewers of Wormwoodhall.'

'Then we should be looking for whoever is behind them, the man who pays them.'

'Indeed we should. He should be the subject of your most scrupulous investigations,' said McIntosh primly.

'And I'm starting right now, sir,' said Faro, picking up the statement that Dr Cranley had given him.

He spent the rest of the morning in the area of the High Street that the Hogans called home, known to the constables on the beat as the Thieves' Kitchen.

Much to his surprise he found the first two men on the list readily enough. They were sitting smoking their clay pipes on their front doorstep. For once they were not in the least troubled by the arrival of a senior detective. They greeted him genially, ready and agreeably available to answer his questions.

Too readily available, even anxious to corroborate in exact detail the statement that the Hogan brothers had made, thought Faro grimly.

'Aye, we kent the auld fella well, a demon for the drink he was, right enough. Ever since he left the sea, two months ago and arrived back in Edinburgh, nothing but trouble –'

Faro left with a warning that they could be charged with criminal activity. Concealing a dead man. They were not easily frightened by this threat of the law and Faro realised that it would be a waste of time talking to the other two youths on the list.

He walked down the street, conscious of their sniggers behind his back, knowing that for a couple of golden guineas they would have sworn that their grandmother was the Archbishop of Canterbury and their grandfather the Pope in Rome.

His way back to the Central Office took him past the head of Bowheads Wynd. He stopped and regarded it thoughtfully.

His cousin's observations had confirmed his own suspicions that the lad Sandy had been withholding vital information. A word with the lad might be all the use he was going to get out of an otherwise wasted morning.

He would take Leslie's sound advice, persuade Sandy Dunnock by gentle means and a lubrication of silver, or if that failed, something more forceful like a threat or two, to disclose in full the events of that fatal night.

It was not to be.

There was a small crowd gathered around the tall land where Sandy lived. With a sense of foreboding, Faro pushed his way through.

Two constables were already there bending over Sandy Dunnock, who lay with his arms outstretched to the sky. Unmarked except for the back of his head, mercifully hidden, and the angle of his neck.

He was dead.

'Capering about on the roof. Lost his footing,' Constable Boyd told Faro, as they prepared to carry Sandy's broken body up to the top floor.

Faro followed them inside, suddenly feeling old and sick. As they climbed the stairs, he asked Constable Boyd what had happened.

'I've already talked to his mother. She was sleeping. Heard nothing. In a bit of a state, as you can imagine. Neighbours are with her.'

Faro stopped, leaned against the cold stone wall.

'What was he doing on the roof?'

'Someone was chasing him. Escaping the police, so the folk down there say.' Listening to Boyd's account, Faro had already substituted 'murderer' for 'police'. He had come too late and someone had effectively silenced for ever any dangerous answers Sandy might have given to his questions.

The accident or murder of Sandy made Faro angrier than he had been so far, and with anger came determination to solve the case. He would no longer tread gently or discreetly, either, for fear of distressing any royalty involved. Death was the same in the end whether you were a duchess or an Edinburgh pickpocket.

Boyd's account ended: 'Folk below saw it all. One of Sandy's cronies said he was running away from a tall man, looked like an old soldier. He had a scarred face. They'd seen him about –'

Even as Faro retuned to the street below, aware that the description fitted Sergeant Batey, Leslie Godwin was hurrying to meet him.

The few of the small crowd who had not discreetly vanished at the sight of the police, shouted curses at the tall sergeant walking at his master's side. A few of the bolder ones threw stones.

And that was all the confirmation Faro needed before Leslie said a word.

'I know why you're here, Jeremy. And I'm desperately sorry about the accident. Should never have happened. I saw the lad Sandy. He recognised me and Batey here. When I called that I wanted a word with him – I just wanted to tell him that you had money to give him, dammit, but I never got a chance. He wouldn't listen, thought we had it in for him because of the pickpocket business. He took to his heels. Batey in pursuit – you know the rest. God, I can't tell you how awful I feel. I blame myself –'

'You weren't to blame for his bad conscience,' said Faro in a poor attempt at consolation.

'Has the lad any family?' his cousin asked.

'A mother and siblings.'

'Right,' said Leslie, taking out a purse from his pocket and weighing it in his hand. 'I shall go and see them. I know it won't replace the lad, but it's the best I can do.'

As they turned towards the house, Faro said to Constable Boyd: 'You'd better accompany Mr Godwin. Might be trouble.'

'Thank you, Jeremy. Oh God, what an infernally sad business. If there's one thing I never get used to it's talking to bereaved relatives.' He sighed. 'You stay here, Batey,' he shouted over his shoulder to the sergeant.

And looking very unhappy indeed, Leslie started up the stone stairs with Constable Boyd.

Faro, left alone with Batey, said: 'Tell me exactly what happened, if you please.'

Batey shrugged. For a moment Faro thought he was going to ignore the question. 'Come on, man, I need to know. You're a witness to a fatal accident.'

'Told the constable. Ask the people who saw it,' Batey said sullenly. 'They'll tell you what you want to know.' And unrepentant, he grinned, turned on his heel and walked away with such an insolent swagger that Faro had a sudden desire for violence.

Staring after him, clenching his fists, he was still shaking with impotent rage, when Constable Boyd reappeared.

'Mr Godwin is with the lad's mother now. She wouldn't let me in, started screaming abuse at the sight of this –' he added, pointing to his uniform.

And Faro knew he could no longer avoid playing his part in this sad drama by visiting Mrs Dunnock, although God only knew what kind of comfort and consolation he could offer for the loss of her eldest bairn, doubtless the breadwinner in the household.

The words he rehearsed as he climbed the stairs sounded like cold sympathy, sentiments that always stuck in his throat.

The door was slightly ajar, and although the dreadful smell he had first encountered had moderated somewhat, the sound of weeping deterred him.

Leslie emerged and shook his head, and taking Faro's arm he led him away. 'Don't advise it, Jeremy. Not just now. Leave it for a while. I've done all I can.'

As they walked down the stairs, Mrs Dunnock appeared on the landing above them, her tear-stained face pale and strained, staring over the iron railing.

'Don't you bring your polis back here. Not ever,' she shouted to Faro. 'We don't want your sort here. Bastards,' she screamed, and shook a fist so violently that the bangle she wore fell off and rolled down the stairs, landing at Leslie's feet.

Snatching it up, he threw it back to her. With a final curse, she ran inside and banged the door shut.

'Poor woman,' said Leslie. 'At least she has a crowd of bairns and relations to help her through it all –'

'That bracelet,' said Faro. 'It looked quite valuable.'

'Quite a contrast to the rest of her.' Leslie nodded. 'I was thinking the very same thing. Doubtless booty from one of young Sandy's forays into crime.' And halting, he asked: 'What am I going to do about Batey?'

'I can't answer that question, Leslie.'

His cousin sighed. 'I don't know what to do, really I don't. You see, he believed he was helping me. When that happens, all other thoughts go to the wind. I suppose you've realised the poor creature is quite devoted to me. And a bit simple.'

Simple wasn't the word Faro had in mind for the unpleasant sergeant. Evil would have fitted his image much better.

'Head wounded. Tortured too. I feel responsible for him. I really do. And he would lay down his life for me. Did once. You can't repay those debts of loyalty.' He paused. 'I gather your enquiries are still in the doldrums.'

'And likely to remain there,' Faro answered shortly. Declining his cousin's sympathy and cheerful suggestion that they sink their sorrows over a dram together, he excused himself.

He didn't feel sociable. He needed to think, and as he walked towards the High Street through the market booths, he found himself again considering the significance of recent events.

All around him stall-holders bawled their wares. Food and rags were the main sales. He hardly glanced at them.

And then he saw it hanging at the front of a rag stall, in the place of honour. A handsome travelling cloak, violet wool with a velvet collar.

Could it be – ?

To his question 'How much?', he was told one guinea.

Such a high price was unusual, pennies were the usual currency on rag stalls, and this price was doubtless the reason why it had remained unsold.

'Have you had it long?'

The stall-keeper, suspecting this well-dressed customer was a gentleman and a prospective buyer, eyed him keenly as he examined the garment. And when Faro repeated the question: 'A wee while, ye ken. Too guid for the folk round here. They're only wantin' rags.'

'Where did you come by such a handsome garment, may I ask?'

The stall-keeper didn't like the question. He avoided Faro's eyes, murmured cautiously, 'Came from somewhere, big house over Glasgow way.' Then afraid that he might be losing his best sale of the day, he added anxiously: 'Your lady wife would look grand in it, so she would –'

A piercing whistle interrupted him. He froze and stared at

Faro, who knew the signal had been given. The booth-holders had recognised the presence of a detective in their midst. That spelt trouble and his identity had been speedily declared.

'I'll take it,' said Faro, and thrusting the money into the man's hand, he grabbed the cloak even as the stall-holder attempted to snatch it back again.

'You're right,' he said. 'My wife will be delighted.'

As he walked away with it over his arm, he wondered how Miss Fortescue would react to seeing what he was certain had been the cloak her mistress was wearing on the night she disappeared.

16

Faro abandoned his first inclination to go straight out to Aberlethie. For one thing, he felt self-conscious about travelling on the North Berwick train with a woman's cloak over his arm. Doubtless there would be some suitable receptacle in Mrs Brook's capacious cupboard.

And thoughts of Mrs Brook reminded him of a more urgent reason for a return to Sheridan Place. In his hurry to leave that morning he had omitted to clear up the broken glass from outside the window.

There was a glazier in the Pleasance and he hoped that the repair could be carried out before the housekeeper returned.

The glazier was reassuring, but when Faro opened his front door he discovered that the conscientious Mrs Brook had been unable to stay away. He found her with Vince outside the kitchen door, staring in consternation at the damaged window.

'I was just saying to Dr Vince here that this sort of thing never happened before when I was in the house,' said Mrs Brook in outraged tones. 'Looks like someone trying to break in, sir –'

'I know about it, Mrs Brook,' Faro interrupted. 'No harm done. It was an accident.'

She regarded him curiously. 'Oh, was it, sir?' she asked, obviously expecting some explanation – but that he wasn't prepared to supply. 'I was just about to clear it up when Dr Vince said you had better see it first.'

'You may clear it up now, Mrs Brook, if you please. The glazier will come later today.'

'Very well, sir. We wouldn't want to attract burglars, would we now?'

Faro smiled. 'I should think the size of the window panes would deter any but a very tiny criminal. You might have more success with your admirable floor polish,' he added pointedly.

Mrs Brook didn't find that amusing. 'First thing I did was get Dr Vince to go through the house with me, make sure all was in order.'

'And was it?'

She exchanged a look with Vince. 'Oh yes, sir.'

Vince had remained silent throughout this conversation. He followed Faro upstairs. Pausing, he looked at the violet cloak on the hallstand.

'That's new, Stepfather,' he said lightly. 'Hardly your colour, is it?' he added.

'I have quite a lot to tell you,' said Faro.

'I thought you might have,' said Vince, and his mocking tone as he led the way into his consulting rooms made Faro distinctly uneasy.

Faro quickly outlined the events of the previous day, the finding of the body at St Anthony's Chapel, and his subsequent interview with the Hogan family, ending with the death of the lad Sandy.

Vince listened carefully. 'So you think this man they claimed to be the Hogan parent could be the missing coachman?'

'The timing of his disappearance certainly fits. He could have been hired on that particular occasion. And provided that the pounds Scots offered were tempting enough, he would refrain from asking too many questions.'

'In his case, that was a pity, since once his job was completed, he was then disposed of.'

'True. And I suspect that all they had in common was the colour of their hair,' said Faro. 'But I expect they were paid handsomely to tell the story about him being their drunken old father, drowned in a horse trough.'

'But why keep the body? Why didn't they dump both of them?'

'Don't you see, lad? One murder could be passed off as a heart attack, but it would have been exceedingly difficult with a drowned man to make it look as if both had died of natural causes after taking shelter in the West Bow. Even the Wizard's House couldn't be guaranteed to rise to those dizzy heights of imagination.'

Vince thought for a moment. 'So someone concealed him – for a price – until the woman's body had been neatly disposed of and there would be no connection between the two deaths.'

'Exactly – But how and, more important, where?' When Vince didn't reply, he added: 'The answer to both queries is –

for a handsome price to make the risk worth while. And if we can find out who paid the Hogans, we will be well on the way to solving both murders.'

'So you think Sandy knew something?'

'I do, indeed. It was a very unfortunate coincidence that his guilty conscience regarding petty thefts made him run away from Batey –'

Vince shivered. 'I'd have done the same, even without a bad conscience, if that face had been pursuing me –'

Faro sighed, 'I'm afraid this is one mystery I'm never going to solve, Vince. There are too many threads, weaving in and out and leading nowhere. And the worst isn't over yet, I'm convinced of that. If my suspicions are correct, the Queen will have to be told. God knows how she will take it – or Superintendent McIntosh when he knows the truth. I'll probably be out of a job, and Dr Cranley, too. What a scandal. We'll be lucky if we don't spend the rest of our lives locked up.'

'Come now, Stepfather. It isn't like you to give in so easily. You're a fighter, remember?' And with a shrewd glance, he added softly: 'Your emotions are too involved with this one.'

Emotions. Yes, Vince was right.

'You had something more you were going to tell me, I believe,' said Vince gently.

'Had I?'

'I think so. Such as who was sleeping in your daughters' bed last night.'

Damn, thought Faro. Why hadn't he made up her bed or, more to the point, why hadn't he checked it to make sure? Another blunder like leaving the broken glass outside.

He sighed. 'I gave a benighted traveller shelter. You saw what the weather was like.'

Vince ignored that. 'And –' he prompted.

'What do you mean – and?' Faro tried to sound outraged, hoping his tone would discourage any further discussion.

'I want to know more about this stranger. Was this benighted traveller tying to escape? Was there a fight? Is that why the window was broken?'

'Of course not. It could have been anything, a flying roof-tile during the storm, I expect.' Faro had already decided on this as a promising explanation.

'Come now, Stepfather. You and I both know better than that. This window was broken from the inside, otherwise the glass would have been on the sill, not in the garden. What was going on?'

At his Stepfather's expressionless face, he asked gently, 'Who are you trying to protect?'

When Faro looked away, Vince murmured: 'A lady's honour, perhaps.' And when he didn't answer. 'I suspect there is a lady involved. I'm as gallant as the next man, so you'd better tell all. I might even be able to help.'

Faro remembered ominously that the last person who had suggested he might be able to help had been his cousin Leslie and that had ended in Sandy's death. Faro felt he would never quite cease to blame himself in some measure for the lad's tragic end.

'Miss Fortescue stayed here last night –'

And Faro told him the whole story, omitting that after coming to his bed to report a suspected burglar, she had stayed there too.

'What extraordinary behaviour,' said Vince. 'Why on earth should she do such a thing? Unless –' He paused.

'Unless what – ?'

'It is possible that the lady wanted some attention from you and by pretending – of course, it is a ridiculous suggestion.'

That wounded Faro into saying: 'I don't find it in the least ridiculous.' Too late, he saw that he had fallen neatly into the trap.

Vince's smile was triumphant. 'Ah!'

'Oh, very well. She was scared, so she said. She spent the rest of the night with me.'

Vince nodded, he wasn't taken aback as Faro thought he might be. 'So what happens next?'

'How the devil do I know!'

'Stepfather – don't explode – I'm trying to help, remember. All I want to know, for your own good, is – are you in love with Miss Fortescue?'

'I haven't had time to think about it,' said Faro shortly.

'Then I suggest you take time to do just that.' When Faro looked hard at him, Vince continued: 'Sounds rather as if she might be a suitable wife for you, if she could be persuaded to leave the warmer climate of Luxoria –'

Faro laughed. 'This is incredible. For once, the situation is reversed and I find myself having to listen to the sort of advice I am usually giving to you.'

'Don't change the subject, if you please,' said Vince sternly. 'Are you contemplating asking her to be your wife?'

'No,' said Faro shortly.

'And why not? In the circumstances it would seem appropriate. Making an honest woman – and so forth –'

'According to convention, Vince, but then I have never been a slave to convention and I'm too old to start now.'

'You could try.'

Faro shook his head. 'I'm not in the least sure that Roma – Miss Fortescue – is bound by convention either. She seems as impulsive as her royal mistress. And talking of that, do you honestly see an ex-royal lady-in-waiting settling down in Sheridan Place and running a policeman's household?'

'You're not a policeman, you're a very senior detective, and not at all bad-looking, come to that. Yes, Stepfather.' Vince considered him thoughtfully. 'Even a quite conventional woman might just leap at the prospect.'

'Rubbish. How could I support her in the luxury she has been used to in the household of Luxorian royalty?'

'Oh, do stop being such a snob, Stepfather. Greater social leaps have been taken – and are being taken – every day. And I am assured by those who know that love is a bridge.'

'Love.' Faro shook his head sadly. 'I'm afraid I haven't got to that yet, Vince. I'm still bewildered by the whole thing, by a situation over which I seemed to have no control. All I can say is that I'm just damned sorry that it happened –'

'Then why didn't you send her packing before it began?'

Faro shivered. 'Because there was something wrong –'

'Wrong? How?'

'The whole night was odd, out of time, somehow – enchanted. Oh, I can't explain –'

'Can't you? Well, I can. It's happened to me many times,' said Vince. 'It's called infatuation, Stepfather. And I am very experienced in that particular field – as well as you know,' he added bitterly.

'I've also fancied myself in love, Vince, but truly, I have never felt – well, taken over. I've always turned my face against magic, don't believe in it.'

Ignoring his stepson's cynical expression of disbelief, Faro continued: 'And yet last night, it was as if there was some other force here in this house. I even dreamed of the Luck o' Lethie –'

'The famous fertility symbol.' Vince frowned. 'I hope not. What if she has a child –'

'Oh, don't be so damned ridiculous, Vince. I dreamed of the Crusader alive, leaving his tomb. It was all so vivid.'

Vince's expression said that he was unimpressed and Faro went on hastily, 'Look, I neither want, nor do I expect does she want, any lasting relationship. Not even a transient one, for that matter. There are too many mysteries surrounding that lady and her mistress.'

'Dangerous waters, I'd say,' Vince agreed. 'Best steer clear of them.'

Faro sighed. 'And talking of dangerous waters and the advisability of discretion, Cousin Leslie brought up the subject of our missing Duchess.' He stopped, reluctant to accuse Vince of betraying his trust.

But Vince merely smiled. 'Did he indeed?' What was he on about? 'I didn't realise you had confided in him?' He sounded surprised.

'I hadn't. But apparently you had,' Faro said angrily.

Vince's mouth dropped open and Faro cut short his protests.

'I gather you had rather a lot to drink and, well – in absolute confidence with a relative, of course – you let slip the whole damned business of the Royal disappearance.'

'I did WHAT?' Vince shook his head. 'I swear to you, Stepfather, I never mentioned it. I wouldn't, would I, for heaven's sake.'

'Not in the normal scheme of things, lad, but you know as well as I do what you're like when you have taken a drink. Throw all your cares away and all discretion to the winds. You've never overcome your student recklessness –'

'Wait a minute. My own secrets, I grant you. I can't be guaranteed to keep them. But not confidences relating to your criminals – or my patients. Such are sacrosanct.'

'Well, someone told him –'

'Honestly, Stepfather. I didn't. You must believe me. I never said a word –'

'Not that you remember, anyway,' said Faro coldly.

And Vince's further protests were cut short as the front doorbell rang and Mrs Brook admitted the doctor's first patient of the day.

17

Hurt and angry at Vince's lack of discretion, Faro gathered his notes on the case which he would read on the train to Aberlethie.

As he glanced through them, there was something at the back of his mind, a significant fact or comment that had failed to register when he had heard it. Of the utmost importance, he felt this was the vital clue that still eluded him and held the solution of the mystery.

He sat down. The morning train to North Berwick was forgotten as in his precise neat handwriting he added to his notes an account of the death of Sandy Dunnock and his purchase of the violet cloak –

As he wrote, the scene came vividly before him –

The jewellery Miss Fortescue had told him that her mistress was wearing on that fatal night. He drew out the list, checked the items again.

'A gold chain with its eight-sided cross –' The same chain which he suspected was the one he had recovered from the Wizard's House lay in the open drawer beside him.

'A gold bracelet with a snake's head and ruby eyes –'

He threw down the pen with an exclamation of triumph. For he knew where he had seen the bracelet. On Mrs Dunnock's wrist as she leaned over the stairhead in Bowhead's Wynd, brandishing a fist at Leslie and himself, screaming abuse –

He saw it again slipping from her arm, falling at their feet. Saw Leslie throw it back to her –

The violet cloak, the visit to Aberlethie could wait. They were suddenly of minor importance compared to a visit to Bowhead's Wynd and a confrontation with Sandy's mother.

It was not an interview Faro looked forward to as he climbed the odorous stairs. The door was opened a couple of inches and one of the Dunnock children peered out.

From inside, a shout: 'Who is it?'

'A man – I dinna ken him.'

'Tell him yer ma's no weel.'

Faro pushed his way in. 'I must talk to her.'

The room was crowded with mourners and Faro hated intruding on the woman's grief. Sandy had been coffined. He lay on a trestle-table at one end of the room, his countenance pale and angelic in the face of death.

As Faro removed his hat and stared down at the lad, had he been able to lay hands on Batey at that moment, he would have dragged him here, forced him to look at this pathetic sight. Surely even his cold heart would have felt remorse for this sad waste of a young life.

Pushing his way through the neighbours, he observed that there was food and drink in plenty at this wake. Those he encountered knew who he was. They stepped aside hastily, averting their heads as if to avoid recognition or the touch of his shadow. He was unpleasantly aware of murmurs and hostile stares, of fists shaken after him.

Mrs Dunnock regarded him dully. 'What do ye want wi' us now? Have ye no' done enough?'

'I'm sorry, Mrs Dunnock. I bitterly regret what happened, but my men weren't responsible for your lad's death. You ken that fine well. The man chasing your lad had naught to do with us.'

Watching her closely he opened the bag, took out the violet cloak. He had the satisfaction of seeing recognition – and fear – as he asked:

'Is this yours?'

'Mine? Chance would be a grand thing.' She laughed harshly. 'I didn't steal it either if that's what you're getting at. I had nothing to do with that.'

That was all Faro needed to know. She had confirmed his suspicions of some connection between Sandy's family and their cronies regarding the disposal of the dead woman's garments. They had guessed their resale value and without too many scruples had removed them and substituted a beggar's ragged gown.

He guessed that whatever had happened, her clothes had not suffered from immersion in the water as had Roma Fortescue's. It fitted into the pattern that, terrified, she had died of a heart attack.

He held up the cape again to let Mrs Dunnock have a good look. 'Did Sandy find it, then?' he asked gently.

In answer she turned her face away. 'I dinna ken – I dinna ken anything about it.'

Faro nodded. 'Thanks for your help. I am grateful.' As she gave him a look of surprise, he leaned forward and took her wrist as if to shake her by the hand. A quick look confirmed that the bracelet with its snake's head was no longer there.

'That bonny bangle you were wearing,' he said lightly, 'have you lost it?'

The fleeting panic in her eyes was swiftly replaced by mockery. 'Oh, is this what you mean?' And from her apron pocket she took a large brass curtain ring, the kind gypsies in the Lawnmarket sold for ten a penny.

Faro shook his head. 'No. The one with a snake's head.'

Avoiding his eyes, she said calmly. 'This is the only bangle I've ever had. The only kind the likes of me could afford.'

So she knew the value of the other one, Faro thought, as she continued: 'Your eyes must be going bad, mister, with staring into other folk's business.'

'Is this man bothering you, Meg?' The Hogan brothers came over. 'Get going, Inspector, there's nothing for you here. Leave the poor soul to mourn her lad.'

Faro left with the dubious satisfaction of knowing that Mrs Dunnock had lied. She had recognised the cloak and had been told to get rid of the bracelet.

The Hogans were certainly involved. They would have helped with the sale of the bracelet and the proceeds would have bought the abundant food and drink littering the table. Whoever was behind that sale, Faro thought grimly, was responsible for both deaths – of the woman in the West Bow and the drowned man in St Anthony's Chapel.

Thee seemed little point in making a special journey with the cloak for Miss Fortescue's further identification. That could wait, he decided as he returned to the Central Office.

McQuinn was walking up the front steps.

'Trains all back to normal, sir. Delivered the young lady right to the Castle door. She suggested I leave her at the Aberlethie halt to make her own way across the grounds, but I insisted on escorting her.'

His glance was enigmatic, then he grinned. 'Much against her will, I fear. That's a strong and independent lady – benighted in Edinburgh – all on her own too,' he added, shaking his head.

'Don't I know it. I had to give her a night's lodging.' Faro hoped he made it sound casual and unconcerned enough to convince his sergeant. 'How did Sir Terence and his lady react to her reappearance?'

McQuinn shrugged. 'They're very good at concealing their feelings, that class of people. Give nothing away, but Lady Lethie seemed uncommon relieved to see her. Quite pink she went. However, his lordship had more pressing problems than Miss Fortescue's return.'

'What kind of problems?'

'Well, as I was walking the young lady towards the house, one of the servants came rushing out followed by Mrs Hall, the housekeeper. She was very excited and agitated. She'd seen us coming down the drive from the kitchen window, "You got here fast, officer," says she. She'd recognised the uniform and thought I was there about the burglary.'

'Burglary? What burglary?' Faro demanded.

'Seems that one of the family treasures had been stolen.' He took out his notebook and read. 'The Luck o' Lethie, they call it. Very old and very valuable. According to Mrs Hall, it was in its usual place a couple of nights ago when she checked that the windows were secure before going to bed. But the next morning, when she went in to see if the fires had been laid for the Laird's return, the cabinet containing the Luck was empty.

'Naturally she gave the alarm and told the local constable – I've talked to him, sir, he confirms all this. Mrs Hall was in a proper panic, wondering what his lordship would say when he got back this morning. Wringing her hands, she was, usual story. They'd hold her responsible for what happened in their absence. Like as not lose her situation, be packed off without a reference.'

Faro's thoughtful expression indicated that he was well ahead, reconstructing the scene with quite a different explanation.

It was so simple, he should have known immediately. 'How did Miss Fortescue take all this? Was she scared?' he asked.

'Not a bit of it. Didn't seem to find it particularly interesting. Just dashed into the house and left us.'

'Ah,' sighed Faro happily, as McQuinn continued:

'I took the usual statements from the staff, sir. This had to be an inside job, there was no sign of forced entrance, doors and windows securely locked. I was assuring Mrs Hall that no one could blame her in such circumstances when his lordship appeared in a great hurry. Said it was all a mistake, that the Luck hadn't been stolen at all.'

'Indeed!'

'Rum business, sir, if you ask me. His lordship then went on to say it was back in its usual place, would I care to look? Right enough, it was there in the cabinet. His lordship then explained that he had had it removed for cleaning, and had completely forgotten to tell Mrs Hall. He was most apologetic for wasting our time.'

McQuinn stopped, frowned. 'You know, sir, I didn't believe a word of it.' He paused. 'He was protecting someone – I just got that feeling. Do I proceed with this one, sir?'

'No need. We'll take his lordship's word for it.'

Faro didn't need to go to Lethie Castle to find the answer to the Luck o' Lethie's miraculous reappearance. He knew where it had been and who had taken it. All he needed to know was why.

A lot of light was suddenly being shed on the mystery. The only complication was that one particular facet which now concerned him personally was becoming darker and more sinister than ever.

As he was making some notes in his office, the door opened to admit Superintendent McIntosh.

'Where do you think you've been, Faro? I've been waiting for you for hours.' He flourished a paper, effectively cutting short any of Faro's explanations.

'Never mind about that. You have a special assignment here, Faro. Direct from the PM. You're to take Miss Roma Fortescue, at present residing at Lethie Castle, to an assignation in Perth – to be presented to the Queen –' Pausing, he read, 'At Errol Towers, home of Her Majesty's equerry, Sir Piers Strathaird –'

'Why Perth?' Faro interrupted. 'Why can't she come to Holyrood?'

McIntosh stared at him angrily. 'I wasn't aware that we had

any rights in deciding Her Majesty's movements about the country. It's one of her favourite jaunts, a decent distance from Balmoral, less than a day's ride.'

'I was thinking of security, sir,' said Faro.

'Oh, she knows what she's doing. Besides, what happens in Perth isn't the business of the Edinburgh City Police, Faro. I expect they have it all tied up nicely. Can't teach them their business, can we?'

McIntosh's grin suggested relief, a complete absence of the anxiety that generally added ten years to his age and decreased his life expectancy by a similar amount each time his sovereign set foot in Edinburgh.

'Seems the Grand Duchess of Luxoria is at present with Her Majesty at Balmoral.' He stared at the paper again.

'Naturally wants her lady-in-waiting –'

Faro stared at the Superintendent. 'The Grand Duchess is with the Queen? At Balmoral?'

McIntosh nodded. 'That's what it says. Here, read it for yourself.'

Faro stared at the letter written on the familiar personal notepaper of the Prime Minister. He had seen it many times and while it usually spelt trouble for him, the signature was undoubtedly Mr Gladstone's.

'The Grand Duchess wishes to be reunited with her lady-in-waiting Miss Roma Fortescue at the earliest.'

'How did the Grand Duchess got to Balmoral, sir?'

McIntosh shrugged. 'How the deuce do I know?'

'Well, aren't you curious, sir? She was reported as missing,' Faro reminded him. 'The last we heard of her was in an overturned carriage on the road from North Berwick from which she apparently vanished without trace.'

'Presumably someone assisted her.'

'They did indeed,' said Faro grimly. 'But who?'

'Don't ask me. She has a tongue in her head.' He gave Faro an arch look and shook his head sadly. 'I'm surprised at you not being sharper on to this one, Faro,' he said in the manner of one wise after the event. Tapping the side of his nose, he winked broadly. 'A secret assignation. Get the drift? One she was so canny about, she wasn't even taking her lady-in-waiting into her confidence.'

Pausing, he regarded Faro triumphantly. 'A man, Faro,' he said heavily. 'There's undoubtedly a man in this somewhere. I decided that right at the beginning,' he added carelessly. 'Knowing the circumstances of her unhappy marriage – and various rumours – it's quite obvious that the whole disappearance was a ruse, prearranged very carefully to get her and this man together.'

Faro sat back in his chair. Not for the first time, he wondered what kind of literature the Superintendent read in his leisure time. Here he was talking like a lady's novel and providing a rather superficial and improbable, but highly romantic, solution for a sinister disappearance.

Bewilderment was followed by relief. Although Faro couldn't yet believe that he had been wrong all the way along the line and that the man in St Anthony's Chapel and the beggar-woman in the West Bow were purely coincidental and unrelated deaths.

The Grand Duchess, whom he thought had died in mysterious and inexplicable circumstances, her body disposed of by medical students, was not only alive and well, but sitting happily with her royal godmother in Balmoral Castle.

And Faro was suddenly angry. 'They might have kept us informed, sir. We've been wasting time searching for a missing duchess, thinking the worst –'

McIntosh cut short this tide of justifiable resentment. 'Ours not to reason why, Inspector,' he said smoothly. 'The ways of royalty are not for us to question. Ours but to obey their command, however unreasonable it seems –'

'What about the woman in the West Bow – ?' Faro began.

McIntosh held up his hand, regarding him as if he had taken leave of his senses. 'A beggar-woman, Faro,' he emphasised. 'Are you seriously suggesting – ? Good Lord, what absolute nonsense.' And with a barking laugh of derision. 'How could you ever have entertained such a notion for one moment?'

McIntosh wagged a finger in Faro's face. He smiled, a happy man from whose shoulders all responsibility had been removed.

'After all, Her Majesty hasn't been in the best of health. Perthshire seems a suitable halfway meeting place. She and the late Prince Consort enjoyed many happy days at Errol Towers, you will doubtless recall. It no doubt has sentimental connections for their god-daughter too, more pleasantly informal than Holyrood. And takes far less heating.'

Pausing, he regarded Faro's sober expression. 'Come along, man. You should be glad, too, far less work involved for you.' And producing a map, he unrolled it carefully. 'Here, see. And as the railway goes right across a corner of the estate, there is a halt.'

This arrangement had become popular as well as desirable since the increase in train travel had opened up the length and breadth of Scotland. Now landowners were eager and most agreeable to allow this arrangement of a special halt, in return for permission to take the railway line directly across their estates, thus saving the cost of many extra miles of new track. A new era had begun, hitherto undreamed of, offering travel from their very back doors, so to speak, instead of the slow, tortuous travel by carriage over often unmade roads with attendant inconvenience and discomfort.

'I don't need to tell you that you are to go alone, make this look as informal as possible. Travel by train as a couple can be done very discreetly. Besides, it is safer that way than by carriage.'

Faro looked at him quickly. 'You are suggesting by "safer" that some attempt might be made to stop Miss Fortescue joining her mistress?'

'Not at all,' was the smooth response. 'Merely in accordance with the desire of Her Majesty and the Grand Duchess for complete informality.'

McIntosh considered Faro's sombre expression. 'Come along, you are showing too much imagination.'

But it seemed that the Superintendent's laugh had a hollow sound and Faro could not shake off a sense of looming disaster.

The word 'safer' continued to haunt him and he left an urgent message for McQuinn on his way out of the office before returning briefly to Sheridan Place to thrust toilet articles, nightshirt and change of linen into a travelling bag.

As he closed his front door, he would have been happier with a more plausible explanation than the romantic supposition provided by Superintendent McIntosh of how the Grand

Duchess of Luxoria had escaped presumably quite unhurt from an overturned carriage approaching Edinburgh one stormy night on the North Berwick road.

And, more important, what kind of woman was this, who would disappear with her lover without a second thought to the fate of a coachman as well as her closest friend and companion?

If McIntosh were wrong, and Faro was certain that there was no lover involved, it was even more baffling. The Duchess had to have an accomplice, otherwise how had she got herself, a lone woman from a foreign country, with no experience of travel in Scotland, to the remote Royal residence of Balmoral Castle, two hundred miles away in Aberdeenshire? To complete such a journey, to arrive safely and thereupon to have access, unchallenged, to the royal drawing-room, would have presented a daunting prospect for any British national. For a foreign duchess who was used to having all arrangements planned in elaborate detail, to make such a journey unaided was beyond belief.

Beyond belief. Faro sighed, for that summed it up exactly. And instead of becoming clearer, the whole bizarre situation aroused every instinct for caution. In his vast experience of intrigue and crime, the pointers indicated a great deal of misinformation still to be unravelled. The signs also suggested that he was running out of time. He had better discover the truth quickly.

If he wished to stay healthy – and alive.

18

Faro met Vince on the doorstep.

'Good! I left a note for you. I haven't much time, lad. A train to catch –' And drawing Vince inside he told him of the Queen's letter and his growing suspicions. This time he omitted nothing.

'But this is incredible. It can't be –' Vince protested.

'It is, I assure you. At the same time and with so much at stake, I'd give anything in the world to be proved wrong,' he added sadly.

Vince looked at him. 'You're going to need some help. And I'm committed to our damned Perth golf tournament.'

'You can't let down the team, lad.'

Faro listened carefully as Vince outlined his arrangements.

'At least we'll be heading in the same direction.'

'Damn the golf, Stepfather. Lives are at stake. Actually, it will fit in very well if I appear to be going there – I'll think of some last-minute excuse. In fact, I have a plan –'

Faro listened and shook his head. 'I don't want you involved in this,' he protested. 'I only want you to be in full possession of the facts – you know where to find them in my study – in case,' he added grimly, 'anything goes wrong –'

As he left the train at Aberlethie halt and walked through the grounds to Lethie Castle, Faro reflected on the fleeting interview with Vince, when he had had little time to do more than confide his suspicions. What if they were wrong and he had set in motion a tide of what was merely superstition?

He was shown into the drawing-room, where the Lethies appeared to be expecting him. Miss Fortescue was nowhere to be seen. He was glad of her absence so that he could test carefully the reactions of Sir Terence to the Prime Minister's summons.

When he produced the letter the Lethies could not conceal their relief. No one could blame them for being glad that someone was going to take the responsibility of their visitor off their hands. No matter how welcoming they had been, her presence would be an embarrassment as they prepared to depart for France.

As Lady Lethie rang the bell and a maid was sent for Miss Fortescue, Faro said: 'I understand your housekeeper had quite a scare. Thought there had been a burglary.'

'Burglary?' Sir Terence, still preoccupied with the contents of the letter Faro had produced, looked at him blankly. Then as realisation dawned, he laughed. 'Oh, the Luck o' Lethie, you mean. All a mistake, as your sergeant has no doubt told you. Come with me.'

Sir Terence led the way across the hall to the library, eager to show Faro that all was well. There on the wall in its glass cabinet was the Luck o' Lethie. 'See for yourself. No harm done, that should put your mind at rest.'

'You mean it was never stolen?'

'No. Mislaid.' And Sir Terence closed his lips firmly in the manner of one prepared to say no more on that particular subject.

Faro examined the cabinet and, turning, regarded him sternly. 'I understand that this is a very valuable object of great historical importance. May I suggest that in future you keep it under lock and key as a deterrent to thieves?'

That idea had clearly never occurred to its owner. 'My dear Inspector,' Sir Terence pointed to the ancient case. 'It has hung there for, well, hundreds of years, and it has never been in any danger from thieves –'

'Times have changed, Sir Terence. As you are probably aware, crime is on the increase and we have travelled a long way from the days when lairds were regarded by their clansmen as sacrosanct and only a little lower than God.'

This particular laird clearly did not like such a reminder. 'I have to tell you, Inspector, that my tenants are one hundred per cent reliable – to the last man,' he snapped.

'Nevertheless, this suspected burglary has now been recorded in my office. Such matters are regarded as very serious offences –'

'As I told your sergeant,' Sir Terence interrupted impatiently, 'it was all a mistake. The Luck had been removed for – for cleaning – it has since been replaced.'

'Replaced?'

'Indeed so.' Sir Terence frowned. 'I'm not quite sure how to begin.'

Faro was aware of a movement behind him. Roma Fortescue had entered the room. She was looking flushed and extremely pretty.

'Perhaps I should tell him, Terence.' And turning, she smiled at Faro. 'I took it –'

Sir Terence began to protest.

She held up her hand. 'Please – please let me explain.'

'If you would be so good, miss.'

'It's rather a long story. You see, we have a Horn of Plenty in the Palace, identical to your Luck o' Lethie and reputedly brought back by a band of Knights Templars who sought sanctuary with us from persecution in the thirteenth century. It was always understood, although there was no written evidence, of course, that it was part of the booty taken from King Solomon's Temple in Jerusalem and that they bequeathed it to those early rulers of Luxoria in gratitude for their hospitality.

'Our Royal Family have known poverty and hardships in the last few years, but despite pressure from the President, they have resisted any suggestions that it should be sold.'

She smiled. 'A superstitious man, knowing its reputation, he would be afraid to take it by force. What he is unaware of, however – as it is a closely guarded family secret – is that two hundred years ago the Horn of Plenty disappeared, and some time later miraculously reappeared. Whatever happened to it in the interval, whether it was stolen or sold, we have no idea –'

As she spoke, Faro remembered that two hundred years ago Major Weir, the wizard of the West Bow, appeared in Edinburgh, accompanied by a magic staff with a snake's head and amazing powers. Could they be one and the same?

'– This was an additional reason for this visit by Amelie,' Miss Fortescue continued, 'to find out if what we had was, in truth, the original Horn of Plenty. I'm afraid she considered that, regardless of its supposed powers, we could no longer be sentimental and that the time was now ripe for us to sell it.'

'Had you a buyer in mind?' Faro interrupted sharply.

She smiled. 'Indeed, yes. An American multi-millionaire with a young wife who is childless, and who knew of its legends, was very keen to possess it.'

'These supposed magic qualities,' said Faro, 'would they be altered by selling it? Surely that is the traditional belief – that such powers cannot be sold.'

Three faces turned towards him, frowning.

Miss Fortescue shrugged. 'The family and Amelie herself believed most fervently in its fertility properties, it was an assurance of the continuation of the Royal dynasty. But they can no longer afford to be sentimental, they are in dire need of financial help. And without an heir they have no security; the President's power is limitless and he wields it, since they are still popular with the people, by keeping them alive but under what is in effect permanent house arrest.'

At Lady Lethie's sharp exclamation, Miss Fortescue turned and regarded her sadly. 'Yes, they are virtually prisoners, without hope of escape unless they can buy their freedom. The President is not popular. Money might also be put to a better purpose – to raise an army and overthrow him.

She paused. 'I have no wish to sound disloyal, but it is well-known that your Queen is not only a very sentimental old lady, she is not averse to money – and to the power money brings,' she added candidly. 'The feeling was that she might even be persuaded to intervene – politically – in our present situation.'

Miss Fortescue regarded the listeners' faces anxiously, to see if the implications of what she was hinting at were clear to them. Then with a sigh, she continued: 'I have given the matter great thought. In Amelie's continued absence and on an impulse – which I assure you she would have approved of whole-heartedly – while you were away I decided to take the Luck o' Lethie to the jeweller in Edinburgh myself. You will have heard of him –'

The family name she mentioned was of international renown and they had been court jewellers for many generations.

'He studied the jewels in their setting and assured me they were undoubtedly genuine. "This piece," he told me, "is priceless."'

And, as if in echo of Faro's warning, she looked at Sir Terence.

'He asked me how it was kept, and when I told him in a glass cabinet, he threw up his hands in horror. He said it should be kept behind bars under lock and key.'

Sir Terence darted an uncomfortable glance in Faro's direction as she continued sadly: 'I knew then what I had rather expected to find out. That what we have treasured all these years in Luxoria is a worthless imitation.'

Pausing, she looked anxiously at the Lethies. 'I do hope you understand that I was not in the least influenced by this news and that I never entertained the slightest intention of stealing the Luck o' Lethie.'

Conscious of their guarded expressions, she shrugged. 'It was all very embarrassing. You would never have known of its very temporary absence if I had not been delayed by the storm and forced to take refuge –' Her glance slid off Faro – 'in Edinburgh overnight.'

Lady Lethie ran to her side and put a reassuring arm about her shoulders. 'Why didn't you tell us, Roma dear? We would have understood, wouldn't we, Terence? You should have confided in us, dear. We could have helped you.'

'I had a very good reason for silence,' said Miss Fortescue. 'Don't you see, if yours had been the imitation, then I certainly would never have told you. I would not have distressed you by destroying your family's belief in the Luck o' Lethie.'

She looked at Faro, her smile odd and faintly mocking. 'Luck is so often in the mind. What we make of circumstances, don't you agree, Inspector?'

Without waiting for his reply, she turned again to the Lethies: 'At least we know now that your faith is justified and that you can go on believing in its magic.'

'We will, indeed. And we're grateful to you, aren't we, Terence?' said Lady Lethie.

Sir Terence nodded, his polite smile in Faro's direction signalling dismissal. The case was closed.

Faro stood up and said: 'I didn't come about the burglary, sir.' And to Roma Fortescue he handed the Prime Minister's letter. 'This is the reason for my visit.'

He never took his eyes off her face as she read it once, and then with a bewildered expression, read it again.

'May we know –' Sir Terence began.

'Is it something serious, my dear?' asked Lady Lethie.

Although Miss Fortescue smiled and shook her head, Faro noticed that her hands trembled ever so slightly as she read out the letter to them. Nor did she miss the anxious looks that were exchanged between the Lethies before Sir Terence cleared his throat and muttered: 'Splendid to know that your mistress is in Balmoral. And safe, too.'

Safe. There was that word again, thought Faro grimly.

'But what a journey for her to make alone,' Sir Terence continued, with a man's concern for practicalities. 'I wonder how on earth she managed it, Faro?'

'She must be a lady of great resource and courage, considering her sheltered background,' Faro replied drily.

'Oh, she is, I assure you,' said Miss Fortescue. 'She is indeed.' And to Faro: 'I presume we are leaving immediately.'

'If you please, miss, the sooner the better.'

'This time tomorrow and all will be revealed, m'dear. You will know the truth behind this little mystery,' said Terence heartily. 'No doubt, a very simple explanation.'

It was never that simple. Faro knew of old and to his cost that dealings with royal persons could be extremely devious – and dangerous. By careful circumnavigation of the facts, they could be overly economical with the truth.

And what they called truth often turned out to be only the very tip of the iceberg.

'This time tomorrow –'

His growing suspicions confirmed by Roma Fortescue's reaction to the letter, Sir Terence's words echoed in his mind. This time tomorrow, he might indeed know that whole story. If he and Miss Fortescue were still alive to hear it.

19

Faro accepted Sir Terence's offer of a bed for the night. Arrangements made for an early start by carriage to Waverley Station next morning, Miss Fortescue and Lady Lethie departed to discuss wearing apparel. The estate factor appeared and needed his lordship's presence. Sir Terence apologised and Faro, left to his own devices, walked in the direction of Mr Stuart Millar's cottage.

There was no one at home. The cottage which had seemed warmly welcoming only days ago was deserted. The fading light of an autumn afternoon lent a touch of melancholy. Overhead rooks screeched homeward and a sudden breeze sent a flurry of dead leaves rattling down the roof.

Faro walked away thoughtfully, considering again the historian's part in this tangled web of intrigue, where no one, it seemed, spoke absolute truth about anything.

On his way back through the grounds, he stopped by the Crusader's Tomb. Regarding that face almost obliterated by wind and weather, he laid his hand on the faint outline of the cross pattée.

'If only you could talk, my friend.'

Above his head, the trees were silent now. The first faint star glittered in that vast uncharted universe beyond the planet earth, far remote from the cares of mankind.

Roma Fortescue's words regarding the Luck o' Lethie came back to him. Luck is often in the mind. What we make of the circumstances.

Faro thought: If I were a superstitious man, I'd believe in its magic too. If its legendary powers were true, it had given unlimited power to Major Weir of the West Bow and to Bailie Lethie, who rescued it from the wizard's burning and with its help built the first Lethie Castle, ensuring prosperity for himself and his heirs. And Faro had his own reasons for acknowledging that brief magic: the strange dreams and the enchantment of those timeless sweet hours when both the Luck o' Lethie and Miss Roma Fortescue were sheltering under his roof.

He returned to the castle and slept well in a very handsome modern bedroom, untroubled by the Luck o' Lethie and the ghosts that had haunted generations of its owners.

Lady Lethie, who had last-minute shopping to do in Edinburgh before their departure to France, accompanied them in the carriage. Her maid sat silently at her side, giving little opportunity for any conversation other than polite trivialities.

But Faro, glancing across at Roma Fortescue, felt that she was not engrossed by urgent pleas for advice on ribbons and lace and satin gowns. He fancied that her replies were short and distracted. Her constant frowns suggested anxious preoccupation, similar to his own, with the rail journey ahead.

At the station, leaving the two women exchanging farewells and promises of letters to be written, Faro headed in the direction of the ticket office.

The queue was surprisingly long and, just ahead of him, he recognised Stuart Millar and his sister Elspeth, with a porter carrying their golf clubs.

They greeted him warmly. 'You are going to Perth too, Inspector?' said Elspeth.

'Jut as far as Errol.'

They hovered politely while he purchased his tickets, and Faro wasn't at all sure that he really wanted their company at that precise moment.

'I looked in at your house last night,' he said by way of conversation.

Millar smiled. 'We have been away for a few days to the Borders.'

'Staying with friends,' his sister put in eagerly. 'Trying to get in a little practice, you know.'

'I didn't realise you were golfers,' said Faro, waving to Miss Fortescue, who hurried towards them.

Millar laughed. 'Oh, yes, indeed. It is quite a vice of ours.'

Greeting Miss Fortescue, Elspeth's smile was also a question. She would have liked to know a lot more about why these two were going on this particular train, and with luggage. But before she could find the right words, she and her brother were hailed by a foursome, who announced they were keeping seats.

Faro watched them depart, and taking his companion's arm, he walked down the platform in search of an empty carriage. Many with the same idea had been there before them and they had to share a compartment, fortunate to get the two remaining seats.

'The train is unusually full,' said Faro to the four other occupants.

'The golf tournament, I expect. It's always very popular.'

Faro leaned out of the window. Among those hurrying along the platform were Vince and Leslie Godwin, with Batey in tow.

'Didn't know you were to be on this train, Stepfather. We have seats booked further along.'

Leslie hovered, smiling, waiting to be introduced to Miss Fortescue. Faro, observing his cousin's admiring expression, did not miss his arch glance as he said: 'Never expected to find myself on a golfing expedition. Vince persuaded me to come along. All very mysterious, said there might be a story in it somewhere.' He grinned. 'A duel to the death on the greensward, or something of the sort, perhaps.'

As the trio prepared to move on, an elderly man puffed his way along the platform.

Sir Hedley Marsh. He did not look particularly surprised to see Miss Fortescue. Embarrassed perhaps, but not surprised.

'Are you going to the golf too, sir?' Faro asked, guessing that was highly improbable.

'Nothing like that. Off to see one of my relatives. Family crisis and all that sort of thing.'

At the advent of Sir Hedley, Vince had seized Leslie's arm and with a despairing heavenward glance retreated down the train, with the Mad Bart in hot pursuit, much to Faro's amusement.

As the journey began, Faro stared out of the window. He had a great deal to think about and he found his companion had little to contribute. Immediately the train moved out of the station, she took out a book and held it firmly on her knee. However, each time Faro glanced in her direction, she was in fact staring bleakly out of the window. And when their eyes met, she deliberately turned a page with a frown of deep concentration.

Faro had long since decided that the book was merely a protective device against any attempt at conversation – or more important, explanations.

He was relieved when the train drew into Errol halt.

If only he could communicate with Vince. Then Faro's prayers were answered. A window opened further down the train and Vince leaned out and shouted a greeting.

The words Faro was mouthing in reply were cut short when Leslie also leaned out and waved to them, and Vince, making room for him, ducked back into the carriage.

Faro picked up Miss Fortescue's bag and regarded the departing train with considerable misgivings. He now had sufficient evidence to believe he was walking into a trap, but there was no other way of bringing the assassin into the open.

'No train times?'

Miss Fortescue found the absence of this information less disturbing than he did. 'Don't concern yourself about that. I expect other arrangements will be made for your return to Edinburgh. Amelie and the Royal party will have arrived by carriage from Balmoral –'

It was a short walk across the grounds to Errol Towers, a handsome Georgian mansion worthy of the name of castle. Sir Piers Strathaird was famous as a racing enthusiast, and grazing in a field bordering the drive, several splendid horses from his stables trotted over to inspect these strangers and give them a friendly welcome.

Roma Fortescue stopped to stroke the boldest. 'Aren't they simply beautiful?'

But Faro's attention was drawn to the battlements. The flagpole was empty. Odd that this normal indication of the laird in residence was lacking. More significant was the lack of carriages arriving and servants darting to and fro, that characteristic atmosphere of suppressed excitement and activity one would have expected of an imminent visit from Her Majesty.

Even more curious and disquieting, on closer examination, the lower windows were shuttered from the inside and the house looked deserted. He was relieved, however, to find the door promptly opened by the housekeeper, Mrs Ashley.

Inviting them to step into the hall, she announced that Sir Piers was at present with Her Majesty at Balmoral.

'The house itself,' she said, glancing over her shoulder towards open doors revealing shrouded shapes of furniture, 'is closed. The rest of the family are abroad. But the dower house across the gardens has been prepared for your visit. If you would care to follow me –'

Across rambling gardens and twisting paths, the dower house was invisible from the main house. A Scottish castle in miniature, complete with turrets, ivy-covered walls and a rustic porch. It was also very small. Faro decided uneasily that Her Majesty was keeping strictly to her word of secrecy and informality as Mrs Ashley's tour of the premises revealed only four small bedrooms.

Leaving his still-silent companion in one of them, he asked the housekeeper when the visitors from Balmoral were expected.

Mrs Ashley gave him an odd look. 'I'm not quite sure what you mean, sir. I had a telegraph telling me to have the dower house in readiness for visitors from Edinburgh – Mr Faro and a lady,' she added pointedly, unable to conceal her curiosity. And when Faro did not respond, she said quickly: 'You will be well looked after, sir. There are always an adequate number of servants –'

Faro went downstairs. The tiny house had been conscientiously prepared for their comfort. The panelled parlour was attractive with its cheerful fire, the walls adorned by antlers and sporting prints, and every available space held by stuffed animals and gamebirds in glass cases. He sniffed the air. The familiar smell of Mrs Brook's favourite beeswax was greatly in evidence, and on the highly polished floorboards, a large and ferocious-looking polar bearskin rug was further proof of Sir Piers's marksmanship.

From the direction of the kitchen, a young and nervous maid appeared to spread the table for their luncheon.

Cock-a-leekie soup, salmon en croûte, dessert and an excellent wine.

It was a meal worthy of Lethie Castle and Faro discovered that he was extremely hungry. He noticed that Miss Fortescue was imbibing rather freely. Her former sombre mood had vanished, to be replaced by light-hearted banter with a tendency to giggle and to remark with increasing frequency that meeting with her mistress was 'a great adventure'.

'We have so much to talk about,' she added with a happy sigh.

Faro did not doubt that and thought privately that he, for one, would need a great many very plausible explanations for those missing weeks. Even though he was now aware that the Grand Duchess Amelie was alive and well, such knowledge, instead of bringing reassurance, merely made the situation more sinister and bizarre.

Roma Fortescue twirled the wine glass in her fingers as she talked eagerly about Luxoria. Her attitude reminded Faro of travellers returning home who are suddenly overwhelmed with nostalgia for dear faces and familiar places. She was even expansive about Amelie's early days before the revolution.

Faro let her talk.

Occasionally she paused and looked across at him, inviting exclamation or comment. These he readily supplied, his mind busy elsewhere. He did not doubt that they were in the deadliest of danger as he made careful assessment of the vulnerability of their surroundings.

The windows were small panes of glass between wooden astragals. No one could break in that way without using an axe, nor could the windows be opened from the inside. What bothered him most, however, was that in this replica of a castle, the architect had not considered a back door necessary for the dowager lady's servants, or that the elaborate front door required more than a latch for her security. Perhaps the lack of a bolt or any means of locking the door from the inside had been considered a wise precaution for any old lady who might be infirm.

The front door led directly into the sitting-room, an oak staircase giving access to the bedrooms above. The only entrance was also the only exit, he realised grimly.

The maid could not have left the house without them seeing her. She should surely have appeared to clear the table. Faro had rung the bell-pull twice without success before the chiming clock interrupted his companion's soliloquy.

'Surely they should have arrived by now?' she said anxiously.

With no wish to alarm her, and on the excuse that the fire needed replenishing, he said: 'I'll get the maid to see if there's any message up at the house.'

As he hurried towards the kitchen he knew now that there was unlikely to be any message from anyone. At least not one he and Miss Fortescue would wish to hear.

He found the maid with her head resting on her arms, slumped over the kitchen table. He called to her, touched her and, for one dread moment, he thought she was dead.

No, he mustn't let his imagination run away with him. Shaking her proved effective. Telling her: 'Go – at once. No, leave the dishes', he ushered her through the house, opened the front door carefully, and making sure the way ahead was safe for her and that she understood the message, he returned wearily to the sitting-room to find Miss Fortescue fast asleep.

Could it have been the wine? Surely not – then he remembered that, trained as he was to avoid alcohol during work hours, he had only taken a few sips from his glass.

'Roma,' he said to her. And then, 'Miss Fortescue.'

Still she didn't move. He spoke to her again. This time her response was immediate. Sitting bolt upright in the chair, she opened her eyes wide, yawned.

'I don't know when I've felt so sleepy at this hour of the day.' Yawning again, she said, 'Oh, do excuse me – I think I'll retire for a while. I was up and about very early this morning, you know.'

The words seemed to be dragged out of her, and stifling another yawn, her eyes closed wearily and slumped back into her chair.

Seizing the carafe on the table, Faro poured out a full glass of water, then shook her by the shoulder. 'Drink this.'

She gave the glass a dazed look. 'I don't want any more to drink, thank you.'

Lifting her hand, he thrust the glass into it, raised it to her lips. 'It's only water. You mustn't fall asleep just now.'

'Oh, very well.' She took a few sips.

'All of it,' he commanded.

Giving him a puzzled look, she drained the glass which he seized and promptly refilled.

'And again,' he said.

She looked at him in horrified amazement. 'No –'

'You must believe me – you must.'

'But why? – Oh, very well.'

Watching her drain the glass, Faro sat down opposite her.

'We haven't a great deal of time. It would help if you were to tell me the truth.'

'What are you talking about? I really would like to close my eyes for a few moments, if you don't mind. You may wake me when they arrive.'

'No one is gong to arrive. At least no one we would welcome,' he added grimly. 'Go on. Keep drinking –'

As she did so, obediently this time, she said: 'What did you call me – I mean, when you woke me up?' When he didn't reply she protested weakly: 'I don't understand –'

'Oh, I think you understand very well – Your Highness.'

20

Faro discovered that the truth was far more effective than glasses of water at throwing off the effects of the wine.

'You called me – Your Highness,' she whispered.

'I did.'

'But I'm –' she began, and then: 'How did you know?' she demanded indignantly.

'You gave the game away. You didn't respond to either Roma or Miss Fortescue, but when I called you Amelie, you woke up immediately.'

'I'm sorry –' she began, and he cut her short.

'I had guessed already.'

'But how?'

'Some day, if ever we have the time, I'll tell you. But now, Your Highness, the truth, if you please. And all of it. Rest assured our lives may depend on it.'

She said sulkily, 'What else can I tell you, since you seem to know most of it? As Aunt Vicky's favourite god-daughter, I have a particularly privileged place. Anything I need, any help, she wrote to me, I had only to ask. I realise that the President – my husband –' She stopped and drew breath as if the word choked her. 'As he is trying to get rid of me, flight seemed the only way I could stay alive.'

'Had you some evidence of the President's intentions?'

'He tried to poison me,' she said, and went on hurriedly. 'Aunt Vicky could use her influence, I thought. As I told you, anything that relates to poor Uncle Albert – and we were third cousins.

'My absence – or escape – had to be done secretly. I didn't want my family, who have suffered enough, to be held responsible. And as the President only visits me every four weeks or so, I felt I had enough time to make the visit and return without his knowledge.'

'Where did the Luck o' Lethie come into all this?' Faro asked, hastily banishing a suddenly vivid picture of 'Miss Fortescue' lying in his arms.

'I had some naïve idea that it might restore our good fortune.' She sighed. 'All that I told you about its history is true. And had it been the original, then I would have been prepared to sell it to the American millionaire. I realise I behaved foolishly –'

'Impulsively – and in character,' Faro suggested, smiling.

'We had one person we could trust to make the arrangements. Roma's father, Miles Fortescue. He alerted the Lethies to the purpose of our journey –'

'So they knew who you were.'

She shook her head. 'Not at first. Had to tell them. A nuisance. That day you came on us at the Crusader's Tomb. I was trying to persuade them not to make matters more complicated.' Pausing, she smiled at him. 'They suspected everyone – including you.

'Roma's father will be so relieved to know that she is safe. I have been terrified that something dreadful had happened to her. She was not at all well on the voyage, but she was determined to accompany me. Despite her doctor's orders.'

'She was ill?'

'Not exactly ill, but delicate. She suffered from a heart condition – brought about by a childhood attack of rheumatic fever. Despite her frail health, she must have made that incredible journey to Balmoral Castle, alone. And, on my behalf, arranged this meeting. I'll be grateful to her for the rest of my life.'

Without suggesting that the rest of her life might not be long, Faro had now before him the melancholy business of breaking the news that the real Miss Fortescue, far from being in Balmoral, had died of a heart attack on the night of the carriage accident. Sparing her the details, he said that with no knowledge of her identity, she had been buried in Edinburgh.

Amelie was deeply distressed. 'She was so afraid that I might be kidnapped or that somehow the President might have learned of our plan. She insisted we change clothes – and jewellery – everything by which I could be identified, on the ship. When I told her she was being ridiculous and overdramatising the situation, she just smiled and said: "Oh, they'll soon let me go when they find they've got the wrong one."'

She paused and then sobbed. 'And she's the one who is dead. Oh dear God, I can't bear it.'

Rather awkwardly, Faro put an arm about her shoulders. It was one thing comforting a lady-in-waiting, quite another offering comfort which might be misunderstood by a Grand Duchess.

'In an unknown grave. Oh no –' She wept at that. 'My poor Roma. When we get back, we must arrange a proper funeral –'

'Of course, of course we will.'

She dried her tears at last and raising her head, gave him a startled look. 'But then who – who is with the Queen?'

'No one, I'm afraid,' he said.

'What do you mean – no one?'

'The letter was a ruse to get you out of Edinburgh.'

'The Prime Minister –'

'A forgery. There isn't time to tell you, but I beg you, have no illusions, you were brought to this destination with me – for one purpose only. I think you know what that purpose is,' he added grimly. 'You're a brave woman, Your Highness.'

'If you've known – what was intended, then why did you come with me?' she asked softly.

'All part of my line of duty to protect a royal personage.'

'Is that all?' she asked softly, and in her eyes he saw reflected gratitude and something more than gratitude. Leaning over, he kissed her very gently. For a moment, she clung to him –'

'Hush!'

There was a sound outside.

A wisp of smoke curled under the door.

The nightmare had begun.

Faro knew that by opening the door he presented a ready target. But from the small windows it was impossible to see who might be waiting in the porch. The smell of smoke, however, painted a grim picture of their assailant's intentions.

Amelie grabbed his arm. 'Fire – they are setting fire to the house. Don't you understand? Do something, please – for God's sake.'

He heard the panic in her voice, remembered her story of a fire in a hotel which, perhaps, had been true after all.

She watched wide-eyed as Faro took a gun from his valise and opened the door an inch. Clouds of choking smoke billowed in.

Closing it hastily, he had seen enough to realise his worst fears. Their attacker had set fire to the rustic porch, which would soon spread to their door.

'Get water,' he said. Amelie fled to the kitchen, returning at last with a bucket.

'All I could find,' she gasped. 'Hidden away behind a rail of maids' uniforms. We're lucky to have running water.' And with rising panic in her voice: 'There is no back door. Did you know that?'

Faro didn't doubt that whoever waited outside also knew. Telling her to stay out of range, he opened the door and flung the water over blazing wood.

As the flames subsided, smoke gushed through and set them coughing. But there was worse than smoke now to contend with. Faro heard a sharp crack as a bullet hit the stone lintel of the door, narrowly missing him.

He fired at the moving shadow on the edge of the grass. The shadow jerked like a puppet. He heard an exclamation and realised he had hit his target.

Amelie peered over his shoulder. 'Well done. You managed it. We're safe.'

'Oh no, we're not. He wasn't alone. Listen.'

'Father – father –' The voice was Vince's. 'Come quickly.' A scream – and silence.

Amelie stared at him. 'That was Vince. You must go to him. He's been hurt. I'll be all right.'

Faro turned, handed her the gun. 'Can you use this?'

She smiled mockingly. 'I've been through a revolution. Of course I can use a gun – and anything else it takes to stay alive,' she added. 'Now go –'

Opening the door a fraction, he turned and said: 'Shoot to kill. Remember it's you they want, not me.'

'What about you – you're unarmed?'

'I can still use my fists. Don't worry about me.'

As he ran lightly across the grass, his main concern was for his stepson. It hadn't been Vince calling, of that he was sure. Although it sounded like his voice, the lad never called him anything but 'Stepfather'.

In the shrubbery he almost fell across a body. He thought at first it was Vince. It was Batey, shot in the shoulder and leaning against a tree. Realising he had hit his target but not fatally, Faro snatched up his gun and, followed by Batey's curses, ran swiftly back towards the house.

The sudden dimness of the interior blinded him. With relief he saw Vince stagger forward apparently unharmed. But Vince was not alone. From the shadows behind him, a voice –

'You have a choice, Jeremy. Your stepson or Her Highness.'

The smiling face was that of his cousin, Leslie Faro Godwin.

But where was Amelie?

21

Although all the evidence had indicated the assassin's identity, Faro's heart had resolutely refused to accept what his head knew to be true. To the bitter end, he hoped that some miracle would prove his growing suspicions regarding his cousin to be false.

He watched in a daze of unbelief, Vince struggling. 'Damn you, Godwin. Damn you.'

But Leslie held him in an iron grip. 'Throw down your gun, Jeremy. You won't be needing that.' As Faro put the gun on the table, Leslie pointed to a chair. 'And do sit down, if you please. On your feet, you make me feel nervous –'

Faro did as he was told and playing for time he asked: 'Why? Just tell me why?'

Leslie laughed. 'Can't you guess? Money, my dear fellow, always money. Lost heavily in the casino in Luxoria, thrown into jail. Then the President's highly efficient intelligence service hinted that all would be forgiven if I obliged them – in a certain manner. There's no need to look like that. It isn't the first time.' He paused, then added slowly: 'You should know that by now.'

Allowing that information to sink in, he continued: 'If you want to believe in my reputation, then accept that it is only a very small step from killing a man you don't know or hate on a battlefield, risking your life for nothing but glory, to killing a man – or a woman –' he emphasised grimly, 'who is someone else's deadly foe. And being handsomely paid for your trouble.

'While I was at the planning stage, I was housed here as a guest at one of Sir Piers's shooting parties. I saw the unique and admirable possibilities the dower house presented with the family abroad.

'Incidentally, Amelie was followed all the way from Luxoria and Batey rode out to meet them when they landed at North Berwick. He managed to arrange the accident despite that cursed storm. Amelie died (or so we believed) most obligingly, of fright. Not a hand laid on her.

'And all the time while I was at the regimental dinner being reunited with my cousin Inspector Faro, Batey – with the help

of the Hogans and Sandy Dunnock – arranged for the body of
Her Highness, with nothing to identify her, to be found in the
Wizard's House. So that there could be no connection, the
drowned coachman was to be hidden in Mrs Dunnock's closet
– for a day or two. Mrs Dunnock got upset after that,
complained that the smell was upsetting them.

'But where was Miss Fortescue? That worried me, but Batey
assured me he'd seen her roll down into the water. Anyway, I
was overcome with curiosity. I had to be certain my mission
was successful before claiming my bounty. But when I followed
you into the Wizard's House, I realised we had got the wrong
woman. Same colouring, age and so forth. Batey's fault, but
understandable in the dark with a storm raging. However, as far
as we were concerned they were all dead, with two of the three
bodies accounted for.'

He stopped and, smiling, pointed at Faro. 'And then you,
Jeremy, most obligingly, told me Miss Fortescue was at Lethie
Castle. I knew I had to work fast after that. Damned nuisance.'
The smile was replaced by a scowl.

'So Batey broke into Wrightson's study and stole the headed
notepaper from Holyrood –'

Leslie grinned, his charming self once more. 'He did.
Wrightson had bragged about his drawer of royal mementoes,
that evening before you arrived. Another of Batey's modest
accomplishments, which alas has put him behind bars in the
past, is being a damned good forger. I hope he doesn't die out
there. You'll be to blame. I had to leave him, the urgent need for
more important quarry.'

As if remembering, he held the gun at Vince's head. 'And
what have you done with Her Highness? I shall count to three
and if she doesn't appear, then you can say goodbye to Vince.
One – two –'

'Put down your gun.' A bespectacled uniformed maid in
large white cap and apron stood in the doorway leading from
the kitchen, holding Faro's gun. The voice with its unmistakable
note of authority was Amelie's.

Unperturbed, Leslie laughed. 'Ah, I'm slipping. A terrified
maid busy at the kitchen sink, wrestling with steaming pans.
Who ever would have suspected that Her Highness would stoop
so low –'

'I said, put down your gun.'

Leslie shook his head. Shielded by Vince's body, he knew he had won. 'Too late, madam. Hand it to me – or Vince will die.'

Amelie looked hard at Faro and held out the gun at an angle so that Leslie had to turn slightly towards her. The momentary diversion of his attention was enough. Leslie's feet were on the bearskin rug. Knowing what was at stake if he failed, in one swift movement, Faro slid the chair along the polished floor. Swooping down, he grabbed the rug – and tugged.

'What the devil –'

Leslie, holding Vince as shield, was thrown off balance. Vince fell hard against him and twisting round, tried to seize the gun. As they struggled, it slithered across the floor and they both cannoned into Amelie, who was also knocked off her feet, her gun spinning towards Faro.

Seizing it, his finger on the trigger he levelled it at Leslie. But he knew that whatever the cost, he could not kill his cousin like this, at close range.

And Leslie read his mind. Smiling, he bowed slightly. 'I am unarmed, as you see.' Turning, he leaped through the open door. Faro followed him shouting: 'Come on, Vince –'

Vince started forward, then with an exclamation of pain: 'I can't, Stepfather. I twisted my ankle out there –'

'Look after Amelie –' Faro could move quickly but his cousin was even quicker. Pursuing him through the thick vegetation of trees and shrubbery, at last he emerged on the drive.

As he looked round, one of Sir Piers's racehorses jumped over the railings and galloped towards the gates, Leslie riding bareback.

Faro watched him go, cursing. An indifferent horseman at the best of times, he knew that pursuit was useless. Winded, breathless, he headed back to the dower house, to be overtaken by a troop of mounted policemen from Perth.

'Get after him.' But he knew it was already too late.

In the kitchen, Mrs Ashley sat at the table opposite the Perth detective, overlooked by Vince and Amelie.

'... and when my Davey, he's the local constable, came in for his supper, I told him about this Mr and Mrs Faro. Mollie thought there was something very sinister about the pair of them too.'

All heads turned in the direction of the maid who had served lunch at the dower house. This was her moment of glory.

'Aye, there was that – especially *him*.'

Inspector Macrae of the Perth Constabulary sprang to his feet as Faro entered. He didn't know how much he had overheard but had the grace to look embarrassed knowing Faro's reputation with the Edinburgh City Police.

'We were never alerted about any royal arrival,' he told him. 'I'm glad we got here in time to avert a tragedy. Dr Laurie was telling me –'

Faro smiled wryly. They had been too late. The drama was over and they had already lost their man. But Vince was still alive and so was Amelie.

'There's a wounded man out there,' he said, and Vince limped towards the clearing. But Batey, like his master, had disappeared without trace.

Perth Constabulary provided an escort to accompany Amelie, Grand Duchess of Luxoria, on her journey to Balmoral.

For Faro, seeing her into the carriage, this was a formal farewell. As they clasped hands briefly and he solemnly wished her godspeed, there was for an instant reflected in their eyes, the sad certainty that they were unlikely ever to meet again.

Worse than any parting with the woman he would always think of as Roma Fortescue was Faro's disillusion regarding Leslie Faro Godwin. Vince, whose first instinct about Godwin had proved to be the right one, realised how deeply his stepfather was shocked by the discovery that his cousin was a hired assassin.

Over and over, Faro asked himself – and Vince – where lay the difference between them? Was his own role as a detective merely one other facet of the same violence that erupted in Leslie Faro Godwin, making one man fight on the side of law and order and the other, of his own blood, into a hired killer?

And painfully he came to realise that the margin was very narrow indeed, as he remembered how uncovering the riddle of his father's death, he had learned that the highest and noblest in the land were far from incorruptible.

The surprises, however, weren't over.

While Faro wondered how he could spare his mother the awful revelation about her nephew, a letter came from Orkney in reply to his glowing account of their first meeting after many years.

'I don't know what you're on about,' he read. 'Whoever this man is who calls himself Leslie Faro Godwin, he certainly isn't a relative of ours. Your cousin Leslie took scarlet fever and died just weeks after your dear father's funeral. We were just back in Orkney. You loved Leslie and we tried to tell you but you just wouldn't – or couldn't – take it in. You were only four and suffering bad dreams over your poor father –'

And Faro paused, remembering that childish nightmare of his hero cousin and his father carried away from him by a carriage with black horses.

'– You never spoke his name again. Neither did I, God forgive me –'

Faro put down the letter.

'Grandma wouldn't know about a war correspondent, would she?' said Vince. 'Then who on earth was this Leslie Faro Godwin?'

'I don't know, lad, but I intend to find out.'

His enquiries revealed that there was indeed a war correspondent called Leslie Godwin. All his exploits were quite correct. Alive and well, he lived mostly in America with his wife and children. At the time of his impostor's sojourn in Scotland, he was at the White House, receiving an award from the President of the United States.

Faro found the audacity of his counterfeit cousin deeply disturbing. It suggested an association of assassins readily available and funded by an international society which Faro had long suspected lay at the root of many unexplained and unsolved murders. A secret society with origins older and deadlier than the respectable Freemasons to which so many merchants and upper-class citizens were proud to belong.

The case of the missing Duchess had still one more card to play.

Winter came, the year turned, spring bloomed and summer blossomed, and found Faro once again involved in his daily business of solving another series of crimes.

One day, a small paragraph in *The Scotsman* drew his immediate attention:

Heir for Luxoria: After many years of marriage to President Gustav, Her Highness the Grand Duchess Amelie has given birth to an heir. Born prematurely, despite fears for his survival, the prince shows every sign of being a strong, healthy infant.

A week later, Faro received a letter with a Luxorian stamp. In it a copy of the announcement. Underneath, in ink, the words: '*We* have a son. Gratefully, RF.'

THE
FINAL
ENEMY

1889

For Campbell, Suzy,
Benjamin and Grandpa Pierre

I

'ATTEMPTED ASSASSINATION AT KAISER'S HUNTING-LODGE,' ran the headline.

In smaller print: 'Her Majesty the Queen, who is the Kaiser Wilhelm's grandmother, is deeply distressed by the news...'

In the garden of 9 Sheridan Place, the newspaper lay unread on the grass. It did not merit a second glance from Jeremy Faro, recently retired as Chief Inspector of Edinburgh City Police.

The 1880s had been notable for attempts on royal personages. Scandals and assassinations were fashionable, as were highly lucrative pursuits of international villains who found times of political unrest greatly to their advantage.

The Russian Emperor had been blown to pieces by nihilists, and across the Atlantic President Garfield had fallen victim to an assassin's bullet.

Earlier that year, in January 1889, the courts of Europe had been shocked by news that the Crown Prince of Austria-Hungary, only son and heir of Emperor Franz Joseph, had committed suicide after shooting his eighteen-year-old mistress in the hunting-lodge at Mayerling.

'I have your queen. I have killed her!'

A shrill voice at his side and Faro shuddered. The past decade had also been notable for several attempts, all carefully hushed-up, on Her Majesty's life, frustrated by the speedy intervention of Inspector Jeremy Faro.

Had he been tempted by the newspaper fluttering in the gentle breeze, it would have been to sigh with relief that such matters were no longer any of his business or responsibility. His greatest concern at the present moment was averting a more imminent domestic disaster.

Another shrill cry. 'Look, I have killed your queen, Grandpa.'

Faro sighed and glanced at the chessboard. To his cost he had been teaching five-year-old Jamie to play. An apt pupil, though with a regrettable tendency to cheat. This was currently demonstrated by driving his black knight straight across the board regardless of any rules, ruthlessly belting the white queen such a mortal blow that she toppled on to the grass and came to rest in very unseemly royal fashion beside the unread newspaper.

Again Faro sighed. 'Pick her up if you please, Jamie. And the correct term is "checkmate" not "kill".'

Jamie grinned, an endearing mass of yellow curls and guileless blue eyes. 'But I won, didn't I, Grandpa? I polished her off,' he said triumphantly. 'And that is what counts.'

Leaping from his seat, he put his arms around his step-grandfather's neck and hugged him. 'That is one crime you needn't bother to solve, is it not?'

'Indeed it is not. Thank you for that, Jamie,' said Faro drily.

In truth he had no more crimes to solve ever and that pleased him exceedingly. Death and disaster on such a day as this seemed mere flights of fancy, a far cry from his peaceful garden watched over by the long-extinct volcano famous as Arthur's Seat.

He sighed happily, from this oasis of joy with a beloved family, content in the knowledge that there would be many other days just as good. Peaceful days that would stretch into his sunset years...

Again he sighed. At the certainty of a blissful, uneventful life stretching into a future, infinitely preferable to putting up with, and putting his life at risk from, the criminal fraternity.

Replacing the chessmen on the board for the umpteenth time, he smiled. 'We'll try again, shall we, Jamie?'

The only threat to that warm late October day had been a white queen at risk from Jamie's passionate disregard for the rules of the game. The only cloud on his day was a talk to be given on Founder's Day at Glenatholl College. The future had approached with alarming rapidity, to become 'tomorrow'.

It hampered his spirit like an undigested meal, regarded with considerably more anxiety than facing any villain.

This tranquil scene in the garden was overlooked by Jamie's father, Dr Vince Laurie, writing at his open study window. With feelings relaxed and paternal, he observed his pretty young wife Olivia taking off the heads of the last summer roses.

Under shady trees the latest addition to the family, their brand-new daughter, lay in her perambulator and Vince hoped that she would remain inert for a while longer and that peace would continue to reign over the household.

He shook his head in wonderment. In all his years of handling new-born infants he had never heard such a monstrous loud voice issuing forth from a mere six pounds of humanity. It was, he firmly believed, quite capable of shattering crystal and he winced at Jamie's shrill cry, certain it would wake that small volcano of sound.

His son hated to lose, loved this new game, the feeling of infinite power of moving kings, queens, bishops and knights across a chessboard. Laying aside his medical books, Vince went down the stairs and into the garden.

With an arm around Jamie, he said to Faro, 'This one is going to be a politician, I fear, Stepfather. And that will break his dear mother's heart. She has already pinned her hopes on a doctor or an artist.'

He had spoken loud enough for Olivia to overhear. Laying aside the secateurs, she tiptoed over to the sleeping babe and, ignoring Vince's remarks, said sternly 'You mustn't cheat, Jamie – that's very naughty. Gentlemen don't cheat.'

'Are you including doctors and artists in that category, my dear?' teased Vince; and to Faro, 'He has picked up chess amazingly – better than I did when you tried to teach me as a wee lad.'

Faro smiled at the memory, albeit a little painfully since he had been singularly unsuccessful in that respect with the sullen resentful stepson who had been eight-year-old Vince.

Now joining the trio gazing fondly upon the new arrival, he was relieved that Olivia's pregnancy was safely over, remembering all too well the hazards that had taken Vince's mother, his own beloved Lizzie. Two girls, Rose and Emily, then a stillborn son had cost her her life and brought Vince and Faro with less than twenty years between them as close as brothers in their shared grief.

Such were the thoughts in Faro's mind surrounded by that scene of happy family life. Ruffling Jamie's curls, so like his father's in boyhood, he said: 'Aye, I reckon you'll be like all little

lads, won't you? First you'll be a lamplighter and go through all
the stages to Lord Advocate. Then perhaps you'll please your
mamma by settling for a respectable Edinburgh profession.'

'And Baby must be an opera singer with a voice like that,'
said Vince.

Their laughter was accompanied by a blackbird's bitter-sweet
requiem to a dying year, although on that radiant afternoon,
cruel winter and such melancholy intimations were not even
visible as a tiny dark cloud to mar an azure sky.

The kitchen door opened and there was Mrs Brook, bringing
out a tea tray. Vince leapt up to assist her. Jamie followed suit,
rushing forward to be restrained from seizing a piece of her
excellent sponge cake.

As he wailed that he loved Mrs Brook's cakes, she smiled
indulgently on these dear people she had served as housekeeper
for many years and come to regard not as employers, but as her
family.

Dr Laurie now occupied the whole house, his surgery shared
with a medical partner. Two rooms were set aside for guests and
his father's fleeting visits, on the first floor were the family
apartments, and above were attics, the domain of a nanny and
a maid. Mrs Brook had been reluctantly persuaded by increasing
age and a certain stiffness in her joints, which she refused to
admit, plus the doctor's increasing family, that she could no
longer take care of the whole house single-handed.

Sipping his tea, Faro sat back in his chair. So this was
retirement. He sighed blissfully, happy and at peace with the
world.

Vince took the seat opposite and had stretched out his hand
for the still-folded newspaper with its sensational headline,
when a noise like a foghorn, or a ship in distress on the distant
River Forth, signalled that Baby, as she was presently known,
was awake.

The fond father leaped to his feet and rushed over to the
perambulator. 'Baby – hello – a smile for your Pappa.'

Baby indeed, thought Faro, she had not yet a name and would
continue her anonymous existence until her parents made the
difficult choice. A decision which threatened to wreck that
otherwise happy marriage. Vince wanted Mary or Elizabeth

(Lizzie after his mother) while Olivia wanted Amelia after her own grandmother. Daily the argument continued back and forth and as the time of registration loomed, unheeded, it seemed that Miss Laurie would be doomed to be known as Baby for the rest of her life.

Faro, asked to mediate, said tactfully he thought Mary more appropriate. Without the merest flicker of presentiment he had his own uncomfortable reasons for not wanting a granddaughter called Amelia.

Some thirteen years ago he had known an Amelie, the foreign version of Amelia. She rarely entered his thoughts any more and he had little desire to have a constant daily reminder of that thoroughly unsettling incident – a strange mystery and the brief emotional turmoil which had marked his encounter with the Grand Duchess of Luxoria.

Such matters were past history, voluntary retirement had settled dangerous royal rescues for ever. Here was peace at last, he told himself very frequently – the time he had waited for, scarred by thirty years of dealing with the threat of death.

Here was the Indian summer of a man's life. Content, he lolled in a garden chair, with a pile of unread books at his side and an unwritten lecture for Glenatholl College the only serpent in his Eden.

When that was over, he could indulge again his newly found love of travel. The excitement of new places in Europe had been denied him during his long service, which included serving Her Majesty incognito as personal detective within limits set by the borders of England and Scotland. Now the popularity of rail travel, of frequent trains at home and on the Continent, opened up new opportunities for fast and comfortable travel.

At his side, Vince, setting down his teacup, picked up the newspaper and about to open it, folded it once again in an irritable gesture as the sudden breeze threatened to wrest it from his grasp. Seeing Olivia carrying Baby into the house for her afternoon feed, he said, 'Can't read outside – think I'll go in. Come along, Jamie. Grandpa has work to do.'

Faro smiled. 'Let him stay.'

'If he promises to be good. How's the talk for Glenatholl coming along?'

'Where's Glen-ath-oll? Can I come?' demanded Jamie.

'Not this time, but some day when you are older, you will be going there as a pupil. You'll like that,' said Vince.

'Is it far? And will Baby be going too?'

'It isn't very far, and no, Baby won't be going. It's a boys' public school.'

Famous too. And costly since most of the crowned heads of Europe and Asia, and the world's wealthiest and mightiest, sent their sons there to be educated. Without barrier of colour or creed, Glenatholl prided itself on liberalism, or more candidly, the production of a reliable bank account by parent or guardian.

Faro remembered how he had paid for Vince's education after Lizzie died, saving and scrimping on a policeman's salary to send him to university. To be a doctor. Now, unless Vince achieved his ambition of becoming Queen's Physician, his long-dreamed-of ambition, he was unlikely to be able to afford his son's fees at Glenatholl.

Though Vince was delighted when his stepfather had been chosen to give the Founder's Day lecture, Faro, alas, did not share his enthusiasm. Regarding the event with growing dread, he would have liked to find a suitable excuse to refuse, but was unable to do so without sounding churlish, as well as wounding Vince's hopes for Jamie.

In truth his talk was at present only a few notes on the back of an envelope. He felt totally unable to put his thoughts down on paper and read them aloud and, more importantly, was unsure whether his choice of lecture subject would be compelling to the boys. 'Crime', yes, but 'In Our Society'? How could he hope to stimulate the interest or arouse the sympathy of such pupils for the appalling conditions of Edinburgh's poor and the crimes it nurtured? It would be a foreign field indeed for these sons of the rich and noble in their cushioned existence. However, he would tell them interesting anecdotes and hope that no one fell asleep, or had to be excused feeling sick.

'You'll have Arles Castle to look forward to after your talk, Stepfather. Perth should be looking marvellous if this weather holds and it must be – how many years since you last saw Sir Julian? Before he remarried, wasn't it? And there's now a son and heir. What a relief that must be for him after all those childless years.'

Sir Julian's first wife, to whom he had been devoted, had long been an invalid. Faro had been at her funeral four years ago.

'The break will do you a power of good,' Vince continued in his best doctor–patient voice, following Olivia and Baby into the house and clutching under his arm that instrument of his stepfather's nemesis, the daily newspaper.

2

Idly watching his stepfather from the kitchen window while Olivia, having given Nanny the day off, prepared Miss Laurie for her afternoon feed, Vince considered the man and the small boy, their heads bent over the chessboard in a garden tinged with the reds, golds and purple of a perfect autumn day.

The still-handsome man, the Viking from Orkney, the tarnished fair hair becomingly streaked with silver. The strange long eyes, deep blue and piercing, slightly hooded like a bird of prey. The delicately hooked straight nose and full mouth.

Olivia came to his side and interpreted his thoughts as she often did. 'He doesn't look past fifty, does he?'

'Indeed he does not,' and Vince ruefully touched his own thinning hair, once a mass of thick curls like Jamie's.

'Put a helmet with horns on him and he'd still look as if he'd stepped off a Viking ship,' said Olivia.

'And strike terror into the hearts of all the womenfolk,' said her husband.

'Oh I don't know about that, dearest,' was the smooth response, 'there should be worse fates than being carried off by such an attractive man.'

Vince chuckled. 'My darling, you read too many romances.'

Olivia sighed. 'I wish he'd read more romances.'

Her husband looked at her quickly. 'Marry again, is that what you have in mind? Perhaps this visit to Sir Julian will put him in the right frame of mind. After all, he's older than Stepfather.'

'Not marry again in general, I don't mean that. Just marry Imogen. She's so right for him, Vince.'

'It isn't for lack of trying on his part; reading between the lines I think it is what he most wants. Not that Imogen would make the perfect wife. She isn't a county type, like Lady Arles. And I can't see Imogen settling down to an Edinburgh social life of luncheons and dinners and calling cards. Now, can you? Admit it!'

Olivia sighed again and shook her head. 'Not even remotely, dear. Still one of the wild Irish, I suppose.'

'And no bad thing,' said Vince loyally. 'Anyway, Stepfather and Imogen are happy as they are. What's wrong with that?'

'It's so – unconventional. I don't know how to introduce her – '

'Luckily there aren't too many occasions,' said Vince drily, refraining from adding what Olivia clearly knew only too well from her 'wild Irish' remark – that Imogen was still in danger under British law, classed as a wanted Fenian terrorist. Although it had never been proved, she was wise to travel incognito.

She showed wisdom in not wishing to become Faro's wife in the eyes of the law and, knowing Imogen, Vince decided that she remained his companion only – whatever happened when the bedroom door was closed – in Faro's own interests and for his good reputation's sake. Imogen Crowe might have reformed but Vince did not doubt that there were many who would have seized any opportunity to throw her into prison.

'You're quite right, dear, of course,' said Olivia. 'There are many problems they have to face. But relationships like theirs are a little, well – untidy, you must admit.'

Considering that the highest in the land, namely the Prince of Wales himself, had set a fashion in mistresses, Vince did not feel that his stepfather's reputation would sustain any lasting damage.

And as Olivia carried Baby up to the nursery to feed her, followed by Mrs Brook with the week's meals to discuss, his eyes drifted once more to that scene in the garden below. A moment he wished he could capture for eternity, one to take out and regard in wonder over the coming years.

He shivered, his normally practical soul disturbed by a strange feeling that it was vital to halt time's relentless progress. To preserve in amber this scene of a man and a boy, heads bent over a chessboard.

Olivia was a talented amateur painter and hearing her talking to Mrs Brook, he thought this was what she should be doing instead of concerning herself with dreary matters of no importance whatever, such as whether it should be roast beef or lamb on the menu.

He shook his head, unfolded the newspaper and turned to the back page in search of the most important item – the results of the golfing championship at St Andrews' famous 'Royal and Ancient' course.

Meanwhile, unaware that his relationship with Imogen Crowe had been the subject of such speculation, Faro stretched out his hand to the pile of books beside him and selected one more challenge he had set himself – a foreign language to be speedily learned, or so *German in Six Easy Lessons* implied. It would be a useful and necessary addition for his travels in Europe at the side of the Irish writer, his devoted friend and companion, as he described her.

He would very much have liked to change all that and make her his wife, but Imogen would have none of it. She had been free too long and, in her early forties, she considered herself too old to have children even if she had wanted them.

Imogen had a suffragette's attitude to marriage, to any threats to women's freedom for which she had fought so long. And Faro loved her independence, her wit and humour, her passionate dedication to the world's lost causes, although he failed entirely to convince her that he might be eligible for inclusion as a failed suitor. And most of all there was Ireland, her dedication to Home Rule, for which she had sacrificed much in the past, including members of her family murdered for their patriotism.

So Faro followed her to France, to Italy, Austria and Germany, where he found himself for the first time at a considerable disadvantage. Unable to understand a word being said around him, he lurked in the background, a polite observer with a fixed smile, until Imogen, a natural linguist, became aware of his discomfort and embarrassment and patiently translated for him. This was a situation to be deplored, it annoyed him intensely and he made a stern resolve to put his retirement to good use.

Having been constantly shamed and outraged by the British abroad, who believed that if they shouted loud enough in English their wishes could be understood and instantly obeyed, he determined that, as a prospective traveller in foreign parts, he would courteously learn to communicate with his hosts.

At a recent dinner party in Sheridan Place, he mentioned the problem of learning German to a golfing friend of Vince's who was also Professor of Languages at the University. Immediately interested, since everyone who was anyone, he said, knew of Faro's fame as Scotland's most senior detective, the Professor assured him that if he liked solving mysteries then language was a particularly daunting one.

'You have to have a natural ear, a natural aptitude. But perhaps I can help you with some short cuts. I have a couple of hours free on a Wednesday afternoon. Perhaps, if I may offer you the benefits of my experience – '

Faro had been delighted. At this precise moment while he sat in his Edinburgh garden enjoying the autumn sunshine, Imogen would be in Munich, heading for Heidelberg University where she was to meet other Irish exiles, writers and artists, who had introduced her to a new passion – Wagnerian opera.

She enthused in recent letters about Lisa, a new German friend and a diva. 'A wonderful Isolde with a life almost as tragic. You must meet her.' That pleasant thought spurred on his determination to learn *hoch Deutsch* – high German, the accepted tongue for the circles Imogen travelled in.

Faro loved to surprise Imogen, wanting her to be impressed by his perseverance and efficiency, confident that by their next meeting he would have solved his most baffling mystery at present – the basics of German grammar. Once he had cracked that code, he felt, he would be well on the way to success, and he had to admit that this new challenge of mastering language was very exhilarating.

The pronunciation texts at their weekly meetings required considerable concentration from Faro, but the Professor was pleasantly surprised by his new pupil's dexterity.

'Languages,' he had firmly maintained and warned Faro at that first meeting, 'are best learned when one is young.'

He had had to change his ideas, however, for although it was still early days to expect Faro's abilities to stretch to philosophical conversation, his accent and understanding were outstanding. 'Here is a man in his fifties,' he told his friends, 'a better and more apt pupil than many of my young and eager students.'

German in Six Easy Lessons. Chapter Four.

Suddenly the blackbird's eulogy was interrupted by Jamie's triumphant shout.

'I've killed your queen. Again, Grandpa. Bang – she's dead.'

Faro's concentration had been distracted while he closed his eyes and tried to memorise a particularly tricky nominative clause.

Now Jamie, with a cavalier disregard for rules, was lolloping his black bishop across the board.

'Checkmate, Jamie,' Faro repeated patiently. 'Checkmate, remember. That's what we call it. Not kill!'

He turned back to Chapter Four. The blackbird had flown away and all was silent. He was at peace with his world.

But not for very much longer.

That tiny unseen black cloud on the horizon was growing steadily larger and threatening to destroy everything. In the shape of Vince it was hurtling across the garden towards him. The bright day was over and life itself would never be the same again.

'Stepfather!' Vince was in front of him, flourishing the newspaper. 'Stepfather, have you seen this?'

Bewildered, Faro shook his head and Vince said: 'I've just read it. This assassination business in Mosheim. Listen, "An attempt has been made on the life of the Grand Duchess of Luxoria, the Kaiser's guest at his autumn shooting-party. Her equerry took the first bullet trying to save his mistress and died instantly. One of the Kaiser's guards was also fatally wounded."'

Vince took a deep breath. 'There's a bit more, "Her Majesty the Queen is gravely concerned about the condition of the Grand Duchess, who is her god-daughter, as well as any danger threatening her favourite grandson, Kaiser Wilhelm."'

Faro had gone suddenly cold, vaguely remembering seeing the headline as it had lain idly within reach while he and Jamie played chess. If it had aroused any feelings at all, they would have been of congratulating himself that this was one royal murder plot that was no concern of his.

But Amelie... Amelie.

Memory rewarded him with a vision of her sleeping head on the pillow beside him while a storm raged beyond the bedroom window. His bedroom window, visible here from the garden.

He took the newspaper from Vince, hardly daring to read. The words swam before his eyes and Vince noticed that emotion made Faro's hand tremble.

He had tried to abolish Amelie from his thoughts over the years, but the possibility of the new baby in Sheridan Place being given the same name had touched a core of unease.

He had told himself long ago that his brief role in her life was over. By mutual consent the line had been drawn under it. Now old feelings awakened. How would he feel if she were already dead?

His mind sped back over the years. Back thirteen years to the brief wild passion and the official announcement of the royal prince's birth. 'After many years of marriage to President Gustav, Her Highness the Grand Duchess Amelie has given birth to an heir. Born prematurely, despite fears for his survival, the prince shows every sign of being a strong, healthy infant.'

A week later, Faro had received a letter with a Luxorian stamp. It contained a copy of the announcement and underneath in ink, the cryptic words, '*We* have a son.'

No further information arrived, no further communication across the years. Nor did he want any more than that. The child had saved her life from the President who had already attempted to kill her for having failed to produce an heir, determined to usurp the throne and have his mistress and his natural son installed. A child was vital to save the kingdom and Amelie's life.

Faro could count as well as the next man but he had never told anyone of his suspicions concerning the child's conception, although he often thought that Vince knew and was troubled by the possible consequences of that brief interlude.

For years now it had only remained for Faro to convince himself he had misunderstood Amelie's cryptic message, sent only to reassure him that she was still alive, safe and well.

As time passed he began to believe it.

He had never told Imogen.

3

Monday afternoon and had Faro any reason for gratitude, it was to the work on his lecture, which had needed all his powers of concentration. Fortunately it had also kept his mind from dwelling on the bombshell Vince and the newspaper had dropped on his life that Sunday afternoon.

Now, as the train steamed across the Perthshire countryside carrying him in the direction of Glenatholl College, he was again haunted by nightmare and indecision, remembering another train journey, across Europe with Imogen.

They had been close to the Luxorian border and Faro had shown a firm reluctance to visit a writer of Imogen's acquaintance who was living in the capital. Accompanying her never failed to reveal an unlimited swarm of exiled Irish writers and displaced artists, a world-wide fraternity of which Imogen, it seemed, knew every one.

How would she react to the outcome of a romantic encounter, too brief to be dignified as a love affair, he wondered anxiously. Would she even care, used as she was in her dealings with the suffrage of women to the less conventional aspects of a Bohemian life? Would she be sympathetic to a child whom he could never acknowledge as his own?

There was no action he could take. He was helpless to do more than watch and wait for the official newspaper reports, no easy task for a man used to swift decisive action all his life. If only he could travel to the Odenwald, find out for himself – there was always the excuse of Imogen as far as Vince and Olivia were concerned.

Had it been Luxoria he would have been tempted to leave on the next available train, throw caution to the winds. But that was hardly sensible. His German wasn't up to it yet, regardless of Amelie's insistence that Luxoria was very Anglophile, a common factor shared by many minority European states with close kinship to Queen Victoria and Prince Albert. According to Amelie, almost everyone – by that he had guessed she was referring to the upper classes and court circles – spoke fluent English.

Faro was not convinced. His long association with the Edinburgh City Police had developed in him instinctive faculties of caution and tact in dealing with difficult and dangerous situations, particularly regarding impulsive action where personal emotions were involved.

Besides, his hands were effectively tied until after Glenatholl and his visit to Arles Castle. He regarded the latter in a hopeful light, not merely as an opportunity to renew an old acquaintance. Since Sir Julian had been an ambassador in various European courts, perhaps it would yield significant information about Luxoria.

'Perth!' shouted the guard.

Faro strolled along the platform with his overnight valise. He had declined the offer of being met by the Glenatholl carriage at the railway station. There were always hiring cabs at railway stations, he had assured them. At least, such was the case in Edinburgh. Or was he being strictly honest? Was he merely delaying the moment of arrival at the college, of stepping down into a vast array of masters and pupils eagerly awaiting a famous man's arrival?

He did not want that. More than ever he needed time to himself, to think over his talk and plan his next move. All his life, in times of crisis he had learned the value of his own society, of retreating into his own thoughts. Although he sometimes found it difficult to convince his family, and his two daughters in particular, that being solitary was not the same as being alone.

Yes, it had been a good idea to keep his train's arrival time to himself, he decided, sitting back to enjoy the glory of a perfect autumn day and surprising the cab driver with his request to be put down at the college gates.

'It's a fair step, mister, a mile or more,' the driver said, looking his 'fare' over with the gimlet eye of long experience. 'Another sixpence will see you to the very door.'

Although in appearance every indication of a gentleman, smartly dressed and carrying hand luggage, in the driver's experience, well-to-do travellers were the most ready to niggle over a few extra coppers.

He looked slightly confused when he realised from Faro's shrewd expression that his thoughts had been rightly interpreted.

'I like to walk, cabbie. And it's a fine afternoon for it.'

'As you wish, mister.'

The entrance to Glenatholl was marked by a handsome lodge and a winding drive of rhododendrons. A riot of colour in summer, no doubt, but now flowerless, the unmoving mass of dark impenetrable green appeared gloomy and somewhat forbidding.

Faro consulted his watch. Still almost an hour before he was due to give his talk. Time for a little exercise, time to breathe and stretch his long legs. Time, also, for that last invaluable glance at his notes, to commit as much as possible to memory.

He hated the idea of standing at a lectern reading his almost illegible writing and he hated wearing the eyeglasses he needed for such tasks these days. It wasn't so much pride, the threat of increasing age and its devastation on such faculties, he could deal with that, but he had a natural abhorrence of relying on anything, however trifling, that threatened his independence. And eyeglasses he regarded as such, a crutch for use *in extremis*, a weakness not yet for public exhibition.

As he walked, the heavy green bushes opened into a vista of archery course and playing fields where boys were playing out-of-season cricket, doubtless using the time for valuable practice.

Beyond the fields arose the turrets and roof of the college. Across an expanse of turf near at hand was a walled garden. Hoping to find a seat for his meditations, Faro found the gate open and was soon making his way down a terrace flanked by stern-visaged toga-clad Roman senators.

Excellent! The right company for one making a speech, he decided, walking between the two lines of statues to a gazebo in keeping with the style of ancient Rome overlooking an artificial lake. The swans on the lake, although the same ghostly white as the senators, were at least living and watched his approach with curiosity. Bathed in sunshine, the gazebo's stone benches would provide a tolerably warm place with enough light to read his notes.

His profession of catching criminals unawares had taught him to walk noiselessly. ('Like a prowling cat,' was Vince's verdict.) He had not lost that ability and suddenly discovered that he was not alone. From the other side of the stone benches, which were high and placed back to back, a small figure emerged with a startled exclamation.

A boy, aged about twelve he thought, with a book in hand. He had not heard Faro's approach and now, blushing scarlet, he bowed. The miniature frock coat, striped trousers, winged collar and college tie indicated a pupil.

'My apologies, sir. I – I am just leaving.'

Faro smiled. 'Not at all. I believe you were here first.'

The boy came fully into the light, still clutching his book and Faro was amused to see, in large gold letters, *The Complete Works of William Shakespeare*.

Faro warmed to the young reader, for he had a similar edition at home, the last birthday gift from his beloved Lizzie. He never tired of the plays and sonnets and it was the companion of many of his travels. After so many years, travel-worn with loose pages here and there and generally dog-eared, its decrepit appearance managed to offend Imogen's sense of tidiness. She was constantly threatening to buy him an up-to-date edition and he was equally as constantly saying he didn't want one. This was an old friend, its companionship older than her own and that was that!

The boy, aware of his gaze, clutched the volume self-consciously. 'I have to learn Mark Antony's speech for tonight. We are to entertain a very important guest.'

Faro smiled. 'Indeed.' He decided it would be very unfair to add to the boy's embarrassment by saying, 'I am he.' Instead he asked, 'Do you like Shakespeare?'

'Oh, very much indeed, sir. I should like to be an actor.' A shake of the head. 'Although I don't care for learning speeches.'

'Neither do I,' was the sympathetic reply.

A good-looking boy with fair hair tending to curl, deep blue eyes, good features, tall and slim. Faro had seen someone who this boy reminded him of, something in his manner, but the devil of it was that he couldn't think where. He certainly had presence and looks enough to suggest he would make an actor.

'I have often thought I would like to run away and go on the stage. It would have been easy had I lived in Shakespeare's day, sir, boys played all the female roles. Though I should not care greatly for that,' he added hastily. 'I'd rather be Julius Caesar than Lady Macbeth.'

Faro laughed. 'Is there any reason why you should not be an actor when you leave college?'

The boy coloured slightly. 'My mother – she would never permit it – I have other ob- ob- obligations, you see.'

That sounded like a set piece. 'But I do like Shakespeare very much. He is my favourite since I came to Bri- to Glenatholl.'

'You are not British?'

'No, sir. I – I – ' He looked round suddenly confused. 'I must go. I am to practice cricket now. I am in the house eleven.'

Faro smiled. 'It was good to meet you, young sir. Good luck with your speech – and your prospects.'

The boy bowed. 'Thank you, sir.' And with an endearing shy smile, 'I hope our famous speaker is as nice as you.' After that little speech and another bow, he leapt down the steps and was away, hurrying down the avenue between the Roman senators.

Faro watched him go, remembering that the school rules undoubtedly held a clause indicating that boys were forbidden to talk to strangers in the grounds and, further, that it was not good form, quite impolite really, ever to talk about themselves or refer to their elevated position in society.

The college prided itself (according to Vince) on firmly abiding to the principle that 'A man's a man for a' that', although Faro guessed they would have singularly failed to put Robert Burns at his ease or his maxim to the test.

The sun had disappeared below the horizon and Faro felt a shaft of chill and disappointment. Suddenly the grounds seemed empty and the gazebo cold without the schoolboy's welcome. A boy whom he would never meet again but who had shared with him, quite unknowingly, the bond of William Shakespeare.

The Bard does unite unlikely people from many different backgrounds and walks of life, Faro decided proudly, making his way – or so he believed – back through the midst of the senators now throwing long dark and suddenly forbidding shadows across his path as he valiantly tried to memorise 'Crime In Our Society'.

Now full of misgivings – why on earth had he chosen such a pompous title? he thought in despair – he tried to inject much-needed humour into his opening remarks, mentioning the pupil who had made him welcome at Glenatholl.

Expecting to emerge on to the drive, he found himself in dense undergrowth. Where was the gate from the walled garden? Head down, thinking about that accursed speech – Dammit – somewhere he had taken the wrong turning.

Taking out his watch, he groaned aloud. Forty minutes and he would be standing on the platform in the dining-hall with over a hundred eager faces turned towards him, hanging on every word.

'Dammit,' he said again with not the least idea where he was. The grounds could cover a vast estate. Hadn't Vince told him there was also a golf course to prepare the pupils for Scotland's national heritage?

Was it too much to expect signposts? There were, quite naturally, none. Suddenly he panicked.

Then at last he heard horses, the rumble of a carriage near at hand. He must be near the drive. And so it was that the driver was startled out of his wits by a figure emerging from the rhododendron bushes frantically waving his arms.

'Can you direct me to the school?'

'I can, sir. I am going there myself. Jump in.'

'I am most grateful to you.' The man looked at him, observing the papers he was clutching. 'Inspector Faro, is it not?' When Faro bowed he said. 'Glad to meet you. You are tonight's speaker.'

The man introduced himself as one of the governors, but his name, amid the creaking of the carriage on the uneven drive, slipped by Faro who felt it would be impolite to ask him to repeat it.

'I am so looking forward to your talk. There are many questions about your career which have long intrigued me.'

Faro nodded, but hardly listened, acutely conscious that time was short. Then, at last, a distant prospect of the school arose. Richly turreted, it was yet one more imitation Balmoral Castle, not a style of architecture that Faro admired, preferring the classical Georgian style.

There were boys still on the cricket pitch and, walking down the middle of the drive, two uniformed pupils carrying bats. Faro had little difficulty in recognising the two men close at their heels as discreet bodyguards.

The two boys, one fair, one dark, their faces partially concealed by the deepening shadows, turned towards the carriage. At that instant the two men also stopped, hands shot out on to the boys' shoulders, instinctively protective. One of the pair, by the way his right hand moved fast in the direction of his greatcoat pocket, was obviously armed.

Such things were no doubt passed over unnoticed by the ordinary guests or visitors but many years of experience

equipped Faro to observe matters irrelevant to the casual eye.
And Vince had reminded him that the college was chosen for
the education of many sons of royal houses. Doubtless they had
bodyguards, thinly disguised as servants.

As the carriage flashed by, Faro had a glimpse of his
companion from the gazebo, the boy he had so briefly met with
Master Shakespeare tucked under his arm.

A rumble across a gravelled forecourt and the carriage had
reached the steps of the college. There waiting to greet him was
the Headmaster and a group of teachers in a flutter of black
gowns.

'Such an honour to have you, sir. Especially on Founder's
Day, the great occasion of the year for us.'

Introduced briefly to the group, shaking hands and with
Headmaster Banes in the lead, Faro was brought into the vast
panelled hall. Up the grand staircase with its stained glass
window proudly sporting the Glenatholl coat of arms, his
progress was marked by the gaze of portraits, benign,
forbidding or merely superior, of former headmasters.

'We have put you in the Gladstone Room, sir. Mr Gladstone
usually honours us with his presence on Founder's Day,' the
Headmaster added in reverent tones: 'He gives a splendid
talk, but alas, we were unable to have him this year. Quite
unfortunate.'

And since they didn't get him, Faro realised, he had been
second choice, though he was sure that had not been
intentionally implied. Banes showed him into the room, and
consulting his watch anxiously, hoped tactfully that half an
hour would be adequate preparation.

'We will have the chance of a nightcap together with members
of the staff in my study when the evening's activities are over,' he
added soothingly. 'And a little extra entertainment provided by
our very talented young pupils.' Faro had little difficulty in
guessing that scenes from Shakespeare would be included as a
special treat for their visitor.

Preparing to leave him, the Headmaster looked sternly around
the room, letting his gaze rest on immaculate bedcovers,
smoothly draped curtains and a bedside carafe of drinking water.
'I trust you will find everything necessary for your comfort, sir.
We will send someone to tell you when we are ready for you.'

Faro was delighted to find that Mr Gladstone's room was equipped with the modern innovations of adjoining bathroom and water closet. There were towels and ewers of warm water. He shaved and at five minutes to five, earlier than he expected, there was a tap on the door.

He glanced in the mirror, picked up his notes and, taking a deep breath, opened the door. But instead of standing aside for him to leave, the man, a servant he presumed, darted into the room.

'I must speak to you, sir. I know you are Inspector Faro. I have heard about you. An important matter I must discuss with you – a matter of life or death,' he added dramatically.

His stilted English was to be expected in this college with so many pupils from far-off lands, and Faro sighed inwardly. He was becoming accustomed to this kind of thing, for despite having laid aside crime investigation, his reputation continued to follow him. Prepared to be patient and tolerant, since his retirement, he had often been accosted by someone who thought they had witnessed a crime or had certain knowledge of a crime that was about to happen. Or, most often, they required his help to track down a fraud case, a misplaced last will by which they should have been sole beneficiary.

He looked again at the man. Now bare-headed, was he one of the bodyguards he had briefly glimpsed on the drive with the two schoolboys? But as recognition dawned there was another tap on the door.

'Enter,' Faro called.

It was one of the masters. He bowed. 'We are ready for you now, sir. If you will accompany me – ' His frowning glance in the direction of Faro's visitor clearly indicated that he wondered what he had interrupted, and that the man had no business in this region of the house.

Faro looked at the bodyguard, smiled and said, 'Come and speak to me later. I must go now, I'm sorry – you can see – '

The man gave him a despairing look, a bow and departed.

As Faro seized his notes, he felt a shaft of fear. One of his strange intuitions of danger.

Danger to himself? Perhaps – 'a matter of life or death'?

4

The Founder's Day talk went well despite Faro's misgivings. Questions were invited but they were few in number and from the masters who seemed to particularly relish the sound of their own voices. In one notable case, Faro felt he was in danger of listening to yet another lecture, on the moral obligations of a policeman, which was a novelty to the speaker and, judging by a restive audience, a bore to the pupils.

Faro's talk was applauded politely, the boys perhaps a little in awe of the great detective, although he had tried to be friendly and put them at ease by humanising his talk with amusing anecdotes against himself.

He noticed that the boy from the gazebo and his companion were seated in the second row. Behind them their bodyguards, one he recognised as the man who had come to his room just before the lecture to talk to him on a matter of great urgency.

The elder boy was dark, with high Tartar cheekbones, a complete contrast to the one he had already encountered who had almost classical good looks and who later that evening acquitted himself well in his Mark Antony speech.

There was no programme for the entertainment and the boy had been thanked by the Headmaster merely as 'George'. Presumably his identity was well-known to everyone but Faro. In the interests of the college's much-vaunted liberalism, all the performers were referred to by Christian names only.

George's companion was the star of the evening, a convincing Prince Arthur in King John pleading tearfully for his life. He received well-deserved applause.

'Well done, Anton,' said the Headmaster. 'Well done, boys.'

As the young actors returned to their seats, George continued to remind Faro of someone he knew. The devil of it was that he could not think who, or where they might have met before. However, since George was a common British name, Faro decided that the boy was most probably related to the swarm of minor European royals invited to Balmoral each year by the Queen. As most were of the same blood-line, there was often a striking resemblance to the house of Hanover.

Released at last from what had seemed like an interminable procession of scenes from Shakespeare, well-meant, well-played but an addition to the evening which he could have well done without, Faro was looking forward to the 'nightcap' in the Headmaster's study.

Politely sipping a glass of sherry, his hopes immediately shattered for something stronger like a dram of good whisky, he chatted politely to the very important invited guests, the governors, masters and their wives.

It was soon obvious that his lecturing was not quite at an end as he was called upon by various individuals to answer a number of rather naive questions about criminal activities. These mostly concerned the apprehension of jewel thieves, a pressing anxiety and obsession of the wealthy.

As he answered as best he could he realised how sheltered were their lives. How sadly unaware they were of the dreadful measure of city violence amongst those poor humans, that lost stream of society they would shudder away from as their inferiors.

Released at last, he retired to Gladstone's heavily panelled room and sent a picture postcard of the school, from the stationery in the writing desk, to Imogen.

Around him impressive became oppressive, since every available space on mantelpiece and wall was occupied by almost as many pictures of the Royal Family as he had in Sheridan Place. Signed and presented to him, unwillingly displayed and discreetly removed, his wishes for an uncluttered desk were ignored as all were reverentially restored by Mrs Brook, Olivia and even Vince, when his back was turned.

Yawning, he lit a pipe and decided it had been a somewhat longer day than he was used to. But having promised to talk to the bodyguard who had appeared earlier that evening and at such an inappropriate moment, he felt obliged to wait a while before preparing for bed.

Certain that he would never sleep in that monumental bed, he nevertheless drifted away in the armchair by a dying fire to be awakened by the sound of rapid footsteps and raised voices in the corridor outside.

Was it a fire alarm? he wondered anxiously.

Opening the door, he looked out. A master, dressing-gowned and very flustered said, 'A slight disturbance, sir. One of the boys sleepwalking I expect. It does happen.' His smile was strained, even lamplight could not conceal his anxiety.

'Sorry you've been disturbed, sir. Nothing for you to worry about. Our apologies – these things do happen,' he repeated and with a quick bow he was off, speeding down the corridor and out of sight.

At last silence reigned. The clock on the college tower struck midnight. He had slept longer than he thought and as there was no possibility of his visitor arriving now, he prepared for bed. Perhaps the bodyguard had second thoughts, perhaps it was not so much a matter of life and death but an imperfect way of explaining something in English.

No doubt if the matter was serious, the man would seize some opportunity of communicating with him in the morning. Yawning again, he climbed into bed, and despite his misgivings, fell asleep.

He was awakened at dawn by pleasing country sounds, cows mooing, a cock crowing, horses trotting and a flock of quarrelsome sparrows airing their grievances on the roof above his head.

A maid appeared with a breakfast tray. He could not avoid seeing that she was upset. She looked scared and her hands trembled.

'Something wrong, my dear?' he asked, thinking as he did so that he was probably letting himself in for a tale of woe concerning a sad love affair, or a disagreement with matron.

But this was distress of a different kind.

'One of the servants, sir. He fell out of a dormitory window last night. He was trying to close it, leaned out too far. Slipped and fell – right down on to the flagstones. He's dead', she ended on a shrill note.

While sympathising with her distress, Faro considered the folly of boys' windows being open on what had been a very chilly night.

Doubtless, he thought, one of the spartan conditions of life in a public school. He realised that this unfortunate accident had been the disturbance, dismissed as a sleepwalking pupil, that was not supposed to trouble him. 'These things do happen.'

Faro wanted to know more. His blood was up, here was a mystery in the making, in the most unlikely setting of Glenatholl College. He was at it again, as Vince would say, aware that he must steel himself against a regrettable tendency even in retirement to treat every accident as a potential investigation.

Breakfasted, with still no sign of his urgent visitor of last night, who had perhaps thought better of that 'matter of life and death' after a good night's sleep, Faro was ready to leave the sanctuary dedicated to Prime Minister Gladstone. In the cold light of day he was now regretting the impulse to spend a few hours with his old friend at Arles Castle, consumed with anxiety for any official news regarding Amelie.

He picked up his valise and glanced briefly in the mirror. Startled by what he saw, he looked a second time. But before he could sort out some very weird thoughts, there was a tap on the door. Ah, the bodyguard – at last. He did choose inopportune moments.

Faro opened the door to a prefect who said that the Headmaster was waiting to bid him farewell. At the foot of the staircase, Banes asked if he had slept well and thanked him again for his magnificent and interesting lecture.

'Very unfortunate,' he said, in reply to Faro's question about the accident last night. 'A loose catch on the window. One of the, er, servants – a foreigner, alas – didn't know about such things.'

'Indeed. Who was this foreign gentleman?'

The Headmaster looked uncomfortable. 'No one you would know, Inspector. Pray do not concern yourself about our domestic affairs. They are trying, very trying indeed, and inconvenient. But such things happen.'

Again that phrase, now curiously doom-laden, and observing Faro's expression, the Headmaster added gently, 'I can see it in your face, sir. How readily the mind of a great detective turns to crime. But, let me assure you, if this was a case for concern then we have a very adequate and, if I may say so, very efficient police force.'

And that, Faro thought, put him nicely in his place.

However, as the Arles carriage arrived at the front door, it was closely followed by one Faro, from long acquaintance, recognised immediately as a police carriage, dark and discreet, with curtained windows. As a man emerged, there was nothing for it. The Headmaster had to make an introduction.

'Inspector Crane.'

The Inspector was a young man and Chief Inspector Faro's name had been a legend for a very long time. Such a long time, in fact, that as the Headmaster explained about the Founder's Day lecture, Crane was obviously taken aback to find Chief Inspector Faro was not only still active but still alive.

'Very pleased to meet you, sir,' he said in awed tones.

'An excellent lecture on crime in our society, Inspector. It would have interested you. Nothing to do with the unfortunate accident that brings you here,' the Headmaster added flippantly.

'Indeed no, sir. I'm sure such wicked deeds never occurred to your boys,' said Crane and Faro noted a touch, the merest flicker, of sarcasm in his tone. 'Anyway, we mustn't delay you, sir, this is a purely routine matter.'

Indeed, 'Did it happen often?' was Faro's unspoken question as he contemplated the prospect of more than a hundred normal specimens of boyhood, of mixed temperaments and nationalities, all bored with respectability and hell-bent on mischief.

'We must let you get on with your retirement, sir,' Crane added heartily. 'No need to worry. We're pretty smart here in Perth Police, we know what we're about.'

And Faro had to leave. In a mood of sudden exasperation, he acknowledged that there was no way he could follow Inspector Crane and sit in on the inquiry. It might have ended there had he not witnessed a scene as the carriage halted at a corner of the drive.

George was running ahead, with Anton trying to console him, for he was clearly upset. Behind them, panting in the rear, one of the bodyguards. Only one.

As the carriage swept past, Faro heard the bodyguard shout, and even with his inadequate German Faro knew what 'verboten' meant.

And where was the other bodyguard? The one who was in such distress but had failed to visit him after the lecture?

Suddenly he knew the answer. The foreign bodyguard who had wanted to talk to him so urgently was not an admirer of the reported exploits of Inspector Faro, not someone with a domestic problem, or there to request the autograph of a famous policeman. It *had* been, as the man said, a matter of life or – in his case – death.

And Faro knew he would never forgive himself for not delaying, and being five minutes late in taking his place before the college audience. What had happened in this instance to his much-vaunted intuition, his awareness of danger?

Tragic future events were to confirm his regrets.

If only he had listened, danger might have been averted, an assassin apprehended. His target a boy, a pupil at Glenatholl and a foreign royal, was in the deadliest of danger, his mother shot – perhaps fatally – and his kingdom in peril.

And Faro himself would not be spared.

5

Arles Castle was considerably older than Balmoral, somewhat worn and down-at-heel, its arrow-slitted exterior walls scarred by the bullets of Scotland's turbulent history. The turrets were no nineteenth-century architect's fairy-tale fantasy but had been built long ago with the practical purposes of defence in mind, including such niceties as pouring boiling oil on troublesome enemies.

Faro followed a footman to the upper apartments, pleasantly surprised that the occupants were untroubled by modernisation and the present craze for ornate ceilings and cornices. Instead the untreated stone was covered here and there by ancient tapestries and ragged old battle flags hung from the rafters. No handsome swirling oak staircase either, just a winding spiral stair, narrow for defence.

Sir Julian was waiting to make him warmly welcome with a hearty dram of excellent whisky pressed into his hand. As they talked, Faro considered his host. Approaching sixty, he retained the virile air of the distinguished diplomat.

An attractive, well-set-up fellow with handsome features, a head of thick white hair and a military moustache, the eligible and wealthy widower had disappointed many eager county ladies by marrying, three years ago, the pretty young woman who had nursed his first wife in her last illness. To his delight and the crowning glory of their domestic bliss, Molly had promptly presented him with a son and heir.

Julian's study was small, and warmly heated by a large fireplace. Beyond it was the Arles tartan-carpeted dining-room with massive refectory table, tall Jacobean chairs and tartan-covered footstools to elevate guests' feet above inhospitable icy draughts seeping under ancient ill-fitting oak doors.

After some polite interest in Faro's family – both daughters married, Rose in America and Emily in Orkney, Vince a flourishing Edinburgh doctor – Arles shook his head and said, 'Bad business about Luxoria.'

'Indeed,' said Faro, for this was the very topic he wished to discuss. 'Any news about the Grand Duchess?'

Julian paused to refresh the drams. 'There was never any mention of the extent of her injuries in the spray of bullets that killed the two servants. I gather the assassins had been lurking in wait for the shooting-party to return to the Kaiser's hunting-lodge. The ladies were riding in a carriage so it would seem that the Grand Duchess was their target.' He shrugged. 'Since there is no further bulletin, one can safely presume, I hope, that she has survived – so far. From my slight acquaintance with the lady, I fear she will be terribly distressed about those two servants who died.'

This was even better than Faro had hoped for. 'Your diplomatic career took in Luxoria?'

'Indeed it did. I was there fifteen years ago when the President was turning it into a military dictatorship, run by the generals under his command.'

'What was he like?'

Julian frowned. 'He was not a pleasant man. God knows how Amelie put up with him. She has held Luxoria together for twenty years since her father died, a fearful responsibility for a girl hardly out of her teens. Even then it had long been a melting pot for potential disaster, situated as it is on three frontiers. President Gustav, like some latter-day Hannibal or Attila the Hun, seized power by a military coup and forced a political marriage on Amelie. She had no choice but to marry him. It was either that or exile.'

He sighed. 'Then the marriage proved, at first, to be childless. If Amelie hadn't produced an heir, Luxoria would have gone to the dogs and her death warrant would have certainly been signed.'

'Was she aware of that?' asked Faro.

'Indeed she was, very aware,' said Julian grimly.

A maid appeared at the door. 'Yes, Simms. Lunch in half an hour. That suit you, Faro? Where was I? Oh yes, Luxoria.'

And he went on to tell Faro what he already knew from Amelie herself.

'The situation between them was made worse – if that were possible – when it became widely known that the President had a son by his mistress. And President Gustav was so eager to replace Amelie, any excuse would do. Lord knows how she's survived so far in her own country, he must be quite desperate to get rid of her to risk an assassination attempt in Mosheim. What if the Kaiser had been in the carriage with her?'

He shuddered. 'An international incident that doesn't bear thinking about. The consequences could have been a war in Europe. Any excuse would do for countries who are watching Germany's policy of annexing smaller states.'

Julian regarded him thoughtfully. 'This is top secret, Faro – quite unofficial, of course – but rumour has it that the Kaiser has indicated he would be more than happy to gather Luxoria under his own imperial umbrella, offer Amelie and her loyal countrymen his official protection. Certainly, Her Majesty would approve.' He laughed. 'Indeed yes, she would even add a grandmother's blessing. I had that piece of information from Her Majesty's own lips. Very pro-German as you would guess and she loves to relate how her beloved Albert often theorised with the Kaiser's grandfather that he wished to see a liberated united Germany under the leadership of an enlightened Prussia.'

Julian sighed. 'I was glad to get out of Luxoria, and in one piece, I can tell you. Gustav's ambition was boundless. I fancy a case of "After Luxoria, the rest of Europe",' he added wryly. 'A madman, but I imagine if Kaiser Wilhelm gets his way, he will sort him out. And despite his imperial ambitions, it will be no bad thing for Amelie. He's been her friend and supporter ever since they met, you know.'

Pausing, he smiled. 'It was at Balmoral in '78. I was an equerry then so I had a ringside seat, you might say. They were both favoured visitors, adored by Her Majesty and meeting for the first time. Despite the difference in their ages, or maybe because of it, there was an instant rapport between them. Amelie, gentle, sympathetic and quite beautiful, was every man's ideal of a princess and I could see Willy, as everyone called him, was very taken with this lonely woman, unhappily married, with a young baby, who seemed to understand all his particular problems that no one else wanted to know about. And that did not include the physical infirmity of a withered arm, for God knows, the lad had gallantly overcome it through the years.

'He was nineteen years old and everyone at Balmoral knew he wanted to marry Princess Eliza Radizwill but, essentially Prussian in outlook, he had accepted the impossibility of alliance with a non-sovereign princely family. But he pined for his lost love. He carried her photograph with him. I understand he and Amelie wrote long letters to each other until their next meeting, six years ago, again at Balmoral, at one of those innumerable royal weddings.

'Willy had done his duty, made the best possible marriage for Prussia, but not the happiest for himself, with Princess Augusta Victoria, generally known as Dona, of the House of Augustenburg. Once again the bond between two unhappy people was renewed. Once again both were seeking sanctuary and I'm fairly certain that was when Willy, an inveterate traveller, offered Amelie the refuge of his hunting-lodge.

'It's at Mosheim, near Heidelberg. Wooded country, on a hill-top, overlooking a river, picturesque and with stunning views. Twenty years ago while on a tour in the Odenwald, his parents discovered high above the town, in a forest noted for its wild boar, a picturesque but almost derelict medieval castle. Restored and modernised, they realised this would be the perfect setting for their shooting-parties.'

Julian shook his head. 'Amelie has been a regular guest, popular with even Kaiserin Dona, who doesn't regard the older woman as a potential rival although she's lost nothing of her charm for Willy. Poor Amelie, she's had such rotten luck. What's more, for many years she's gone in daily terror of her life.

'Her husband, she knows, has been behind several unsuccessful attempts to have her poisoned, and once the wheel of her carriage was tampered with and it went off the road down a ravine. The coachman died, but miraculously she and the young prince were thrown clear. That was just a couple of years ago.

'About this latest attempt, it must be obvious that Luxoria cannot survive the present turmoil in Europe and Amelie can no longer hold the reins single-handed. Seeing the results of the President's disastrous military rule, I suspect she has needed little persuasion that the people of Luxoria would be better off under the canopy of Imperial Germany.'

For Faro, listening, many things were becoming clear and he was thankful indeed that he had accepted his old friend's invitation. Julian's connection with Balmoral was well known to him, but his link with Luxoria was an unexpected bonus.

'You think that was the reason behind the hunting-lodge incident?'

'Oh indeed yes. I can see President Gustav's hand very clearly directing the assassin's gun. Another thing, I suspect that it was on Willy's advice that Amelie decided to send the boy over here to school last year. An only child, she adored him, would do anything – ' he shrugged, 'even I suspect, turn Luxoria over to Germany in return for the Kaiser's protection. Doubtless it's a bargain package and he has promised to restore the boy to the throne when he reaches his majority.'

'A puppet government, you mean.'

'Exactly, but better for Luxoria than the ruthless man who has driven the country to the brink of anarchy and financial ruin by his excesses.'

'Surely Gustav has a good case for ruling in his son's minority?'

'You mean, God forbid, should the worst happen?' Julian shook his head, smiled wryly. 'If the lad is his own son, that is.'

Faro's heart beat louder than usual as he said, 'Indeed? The birth was heralded as the child of their reconciliation.'

Julian laughed out loud. 'I have always had my doubts about that. The premature baby, the oldest trick in the world. Remember the carriage accident Gustav arranged. He wasn't afraid that the child would die. In fact, that was probably his intention. Kill two royal birds with one stone – or a broken wheel.'

He shook his head firmly. 'No, I shouldn't be in the least surprised if Gustav knows or suspects the truth.'

'What truth?' Even to his own ears, Faro's questions sounded sharper than was necessary.

Sir Julian's eyes narrowed. 'Let me take you back to that first meeting between Willy and Amelie in '78. She brought the wee lad along with her, she was even then seeking a refuge from her husband. There was something I overheard – '

His eager look vanished. 'No matter, no matter. One must be discreet about such things.'

Faro was very eager to know what exactly he had overheard, but to his questioning glance Julian again gave that shake of the head. 'Whatever was the truth, I think Her Majesty knew what was what. She and Amelie were often closeted together. Once or twice I saw them walking in the gardens, heads down, Amelie clearly distressed, bravely trying to conceal tears. I know enough about women to believe that confidences of a very personal and, I may add, highly dangerous nature were being poured into the royal ears, and that Amelie was over in Scotland precisely to take advice from her fond godmother.'

A thought flew unbidden into Faro's mind. Did Amelie come again to Scotland only to seek refuge in Balmoral with her son? Or was it a subterfuge, a yearning to meet him, let him see the child?

'Eliminate the mother first, then the son would be no problem,' Julian went on. 'If Amelie dies as a result of this murderous attack, then I wouldn't give much for the lad's chances of surviving to adulthood. Mark my words, he will be next,' he added grimly.

It was a terrible thought.

'You say he's at school over here?'

Julian grinned. 'Yes. Just a few miles from where you are sitting right now. He's at Glenatholl, no less. You might even have met him last night. Now, what's his name?' He frowned. 'John – no, George. Yes, George – a splendidly Hanoverian name for a Luxorian prince, don't you think?'

And Faro knew what had been tormenting him, why the boy had looked so familiar. He had unknowingly solved that particular mystery when he caught a fleeting glimpse of his own reflection in the mirror at Glenatholl that morning.

There were voices in the hall.

6

The arrival of Lady Arles, proudly bearing son and heir Augustus to meet Julian's old friend, could not have been timed for a less opportune moment. However, this interval of domesticity and the admiring of the new infant, who regarded him with deepest suspicion, was a blessing for Faro, a cover for his confused thoughts.

There were a thousand questions he wanted to ask, revelations that with a little gentle probing and a few more drams consumed by his host might bring forth a great deal more in the way of speculation than Julian was prepared to admit.

How infuriating – Lady Arles was to join them for luncheon. He groaned inwardly. Such a unique opportunity lost, a chance that might never come again.

Later he remembered little of the polite conversation that ensued, beyond Julian's nostalgic comments on days at Balmoral, accompanied by some excellent wine. Rather too much, in fact, Faro thought idly, watching one bottle empty and another appear. He realised he was allowing his glass to be refilled with alarming regularity.

By the time Lady Arles prepared to depart, having wisely refrained from the wine since she had an afternoon engagement (referred to by her husband as 'Another of your good works, my dear'), Faro had accepted their pressing invitation to extend his visit to include dinner, stay overnight and return to Edinburgh the following day. Behind this decision was the fervent hope of more confidences and revelations of royal indiscretions at Balmoral and elsewhere. But he knew this was not Inspector Jeremy Faro at his best. He desperately needed to think and think clearly, no easy task after the reckless depletion of the Arles' excellent wine cellar.

Most of all he wanted to talk about George, the boy in the gazebo at Glenatholl, whose face, a fleeting image, had been familiar. Dear God!

But confidences from Julian were to be further denied him. The estate factor, Lawson, looked in with some papers for signature and Julian, by now somewhat hectic in countenance, decided that fresh air would be a good thing. He wanted to show his guest the stables, the new horses, the old chapel. Faro trotted at his heels inventing ploys to lead his host back to agreeable reminiscences of Grand Duchess Amelie. But far off days in Luxoria were no longer on the agenda.

Julian excused himself. Estate trees to be felled and sold for timber. Lawson needed to show him the woods in question. So Faro went back to the Castle and, in the room they had prepared for him, fell gratefully on to the bed and – thanks to the effects of the wine – slept soundly until the dinner gong alerted him.

Awakening in strange surroundings, his first thought was that it had all been a dreadful nightmare and he had dreamed that the boy he had met at Glenatholl was his son.

He sat up with a groan and a hangover of mammoth proportions told him it was no dream but reality. Worse was to come when he shaved in preparation for going downstairs and encountered in the mirror that fleeting likeness to the boy he had been in far-off Orkney days. The face than now lived again in Glenatholl College...

Sounds of merriment issuing from the drawing-room dashed any further hopes he had entertained of extracting information from Julian. There were other guests for dinner that evening; nice, pleasant country gentry with whom he had not one thing in common and who asked the same questions put to him after his Glenatholl lecture, about burglaries mostly and how they could be prevented. And how thieves who were apprehended might be discouraged from further wrongdoing by a hanging!

Faro was not a sympathetic or patient listener to the problems of the wealthy for whom a few pieces of stolen silver, that did not pivot their world or throw it out of joint, were nevertheless regarded as a catastrophe of fearful proportions. The conversation, or the wine, or both, left him with a giddy feeling that instead of being within a decade of a new century, time had moved backwards and deposited the present company in the age of Hanging Judge Jeffries.

Faro made a valiant but useless effort to convince any of them that much of Edinburgh's petty crime was brought about by the necessity of survival. 'By men who would have qualities as honest as any around this table,' he explained, regarding his companions' shocked countenances, 'if they had work to do, and money to buy bread for their starving families.'

Julian's applause and 'Well done, Jeremy' averted a dangerous situation as did his call for more wine and change of subject to the price of flour. As for problems with the tenants – 'Impossible to cope with them,' put in another guest, with a final outraged glance in Faro's direction, 'Getting quite above themselves these days.'

Somehow Faro got through it all, retired most gratefully to his waiting bed once more, slept well and, after an excellent breakfast, was sped off for the late morning train.

Watching the carriage disappear down the drive, Julian realised that his wife's entrance yesterday had saved him from a major indiscretion. A scene he had witnessed in the gardens at Balmoral eleven years ago. A scene that he had discreetly kept to himself and, indeed, had tried to put out of his mind.

Walking alongside a tall yew hedge in the gardens, he had paused to light a pipe when he heard voices from a concealed arbour on the other side. Her Majesty and one he recognised as the Grand Duchess Amelie. She was crying. 'But he is so near at hand, could I not see him, just once? Just once, when the train stops in Edinburgh? I long for him to see his son.'

'Never. Never!' said Her Majesty. 'My dearest girl, you must never admit that even to yourself. You must put him from your mind instantly. To try to see him again, even to think of it, would be a disaster not only for yourself. Dear God, if you would be so indiscreet, at least think of the child's future.'

'But I do love him – still, to distraction,' was the agitated reply. 'I cannot bear it, that we are never to meet again.'

'Dearest girl, I sympathise. I know only too well what you are suffering. I have spent most of my life pining for my lost love, my dearest husband whom I will never see again on this earth. But you are young still and you must be practical and think of the scandal, I implore you. Think of what it could do.'

There was a slight pause followed by a warning. 'And if Gustav ever had an inkling, the faintest idea, that the child is not his, then you would have thrown away your kingdom. Please, my dear, dismiss this madness from your mind.'

Julian had crept away silently and he had never told a living soul. He was often haunted by the poignant scene and a mystery which had intrigued him over the years.

Indeed, he had been very tempted to tell Faro. He was the very man. The detective had lots of secret information concerning members of the royal family, for in his time Faro had had many dealings with Her Majesty. Yes, indeed, he could well be the man to know the identity of the father of Amelie's child.

It could not be Kaiser Wilhelm of course, Julian decided. But it might have been one of the royals Amelie had met during a visit to Edinburgh the year before George was born.

Whoever he was, good luck to him, for the outcome of that love affair had been a child who had saved Amelie's life and given a future to Luxoria.

Faro was still feeling very out of sorts as the Arles carriage trotted briskly through the mists of Perthshire, the dramatic autumn colours having faded with alarming suddenness into the more normal gloom of monotone Highland drizzle. He realised he was paying dearly for allowing himself to be so recklessly indulged by Sir Julian's lavish hospitality, which included, he decided wryly, as much wine as he suspected was consumed over an entire month by Vince and Olivia entertaining dinner guests at Sheridan Place.

Excellent vintage no doubt, but it had shot his powers of clear thought to blazes, completely dulled his wits. And he desperately needed to think.

Now that George's identity had been revealed, he remembered the scene in the drive with the two boys and one bodyguard. The missing bodyguard was in all probability George's, the man who came to his room and wished to tell him something before his speech that evening.

'A matter of life and death.'

He felt sickened with remorse. Doubtless the bodyguard wished to confide some vital matter concerning Luxoria. Luxoria had always meant Amelie, now it also stood for George.

He groaned out loud. Perhaps he could have saved the man's

life too. An accident, falling out of a window indeed! It was too banal for serious consideration. Doubtless that was why Inspector Crane was on the scene so smartly.

Would he ever forgive himself for not appearing just five minutes late on the platform in the dining hall at Glenatholl?

Matters were serious enough without this new incident, he thought, remembering Julian's first-hand account of political unrest in Luxoria, which even before Amelie's visit to East Lothian had been fast deteriorating towards revolution. What those intervening years had been like for her he did not care to imagine, or the situation which had led, as Julian hinted, to her desperate consideration of abandoning centuries of independence and placing Luxoria under Germany's protection. As Julian had suggested, this was doubtless the reason for her attempted assassination at her husband's instigation.

In the light of his present knowledge, Faro longed for an excuse to arrive at Glenatholl, see the lad again, talk to him, even ask some questions. Was he aware that his mother might no longer be alive. How much had they told him of her 'accident'?

The picture of his tears, of being consoled on the drive by his companion and the other bodyguard shouting that it was forbidden would remain etched in Faro's mind forever. But sense reasserted itself over emotion, as it had done throughout his life. Whatever happened, the last person who must ever know the true facts regarding his birth was Prince George of Luxoria.

As the carriage approached the railway station through the streets of Perth, being unable to spot a newspaper vendor was a further frustration and anxiety. Faro wanted only to be back in Edinburgh as quickly as possible for a bulletin regarding Amelie's condition. Inactive and helpless, patiently awaiting developments had never been a strongpoint in his character or a virtue to number among his nobler characteristics.

7

The carriage set him down in the station forecourt in good time for the Edinburgh train. Walking briskly back and forth along the platform to ward off the chill east wind, he observed a stationary railway carriage on a siding, seemingly deserted and without any engine in sight. Faro had no difficulty in recognising it, despite the lack of any distinguishing marks, as the royal carriage which would be attached to a normal service train between Ballater and England. With no longer the least nostalgia for having often sat in that carriage during his service with Edinburgh City Police, he watched curiously as a figure descended and quickly disappeared, hidden by the other side of the platform.

Faro wondered idly which member of the royal family was on an incognito visit in the neighbourhood. The Edinburgh train steamed into the station and Faro was about to climb aboard when a figure rushed panting on to the platform, recognisable as the man he had seen leaving the stationary royal carriage.

The guard was waiting to wave his flag, and obligingly holding the door open for the latecomer, Faro's foot was on the step when he was taken aback to discover that instead of a grateful acceptance of his help, the man seized him round the waist and dragged him bodily back on to the platform.

'What on earth? What do you think you are doing? Release me at once!'

'Inspector Faro, is it not?' panted the man.

'It is indeed, if it's any of your business. Now kindly allow me to board the train.'

Out of the corner of his eye he saw the guard with the whistle at his lips, the flag in readiness. His mouth had dropped rather open and he looked like a man who felt he ought to intervene but didn't quite know the right words or gestures required. However, Faro's assailant, for such he seemed, nodded briefly in his direction and at the same time produced a card and thrust it before Faro.

Faro groaned. He had seen it before many times. It bore the royal signature. The code-word uttered at the same instant brought his immediate attention to Her Majesty the Queen's command.

'You do understand, sir. Bear with me, if you please. I will explain and you can catch another train. I assure you this is of the utmost importance.'

And still holding Faro's arm firmly, as if instant flight was intended, he nodded again to the guard who, thankful that his intervention was not required, blew his whistle. Faro watched helplessly as the train steamed out of the station without him, and with an exasperated gesture pulled his arm free of the man's grip.

'I am very sorry, sir. Captain Reece, at your service.' This, with a respectful bow. 'Now if you will be so good as to follow me, I will explain. My carriage is outside.'

So it wasn't to be the royal train to Ballater, after all. That was a relief, thought Faro. Following Reece out of the station, he demanded angrily, 'What in hell's name is all this about? Perhaps you are unaware that I am now retired. And that means I am no longer responsible for taking care of Her Majesty's affairs. There are other senior detectives and here in Perth I understand there is an excellent police force, who are perfectly adequate to deal with such matters.'

Reece did not appear to be listening. Ushered into a waiting cab in the forecourt, Faro consulted his watch impatiently. 'Will this take long?' he demanded. 'The next train is in two hours' time and I should like to be on it. There are urgent matters in Edinburgh requiring my immediate attention.'

Reece stared out of the window, craning his neck, a gesture which suggested even to the uninitiated that he feared they were being followed.

'Captain Reece, I am addressing you. Have the goodness to give me your attention.'

With a sigh, Reece sat back. 'I will do my best to accommodate you, Inspector, but once I tell you what has happened, perhaps you will change your mind.'

The man's sombre manner was unmistakable. The fact of the royal carriage and his sudden emergence suggested a crisis.

'Her Majesty – ' Faro began.

Reece shook his head. 'No. Her Majesty is in no danger.'

'May I ask where you are taking me?' Faro looked out of the window. The carriage had turned into a minor road. He noticed landmarks from the route he had travelled the day before.

'We are going to Glenatholl College, Inspector.'

'Glenatholl, for heaven's sake!'

'No!' was the solemn reply. 'For Her Majesty's sake.'

Such flippancy further angered Faro. 'Indeed. As I was there only yesterday, as you are no doubt aware, could I not have been informed of what was the trouble? It would have helped considerably with my arrangements.'

'Helped, sir.' Reece laughed shortly. 'You couldn't have helped yesterday. It hadn't happened yesterday.'

'What hadn't happened?'

'Since you left there has been a kidnapping. One of the pupils was kidnapped last night.'

The stationary railway carriage in the siding at Perth suddenly slotted into place. 'A royal pupil?'

'Yes indeed, sir. We were here in readiness to escort him to Balmoral when it happened.'

'And who, may I ask, is this lad?'

'The heir to the Grand Duchy of Luxoria. His life is in the greatest possible danger.'

Faro felt as if he had been struck in the chest by a sledgehammer. He could not breathe for a moment, as Reece continued, 'Perhaps you have not seen the newspapers? There has been an attempt on the life of the boy's mother who is Her Majesty's goddaughter.'

He shook his head. 'This is not the work of some political fanatic, the whole future of a kingdom is at stake and secret plans were ready to have him returned immediately to Luxoria if – ' Reece sighed. 'If his mother should die. You understand, Inspector.'

Faro was speechless, shocked into silence.

'The Headmaster will tell you everything. When he mentioned that you were still in the area, a very fortunate coincidence, we knew we could rely on your help.'

Faro was no longer listening. Numbness was receding, his mind raced ahead, his suspicions confirmed regarding that accident with an open window.

'A matter of life and death.' Dear God, why hadn't he listened?

The bodyguard's accident had been deliberate murder. Desperate to warn someone, he thought a detective would be the proper person. And his attempt to save Prince George had cost him his life.

Perhaps even now... No! kidnappers did not kill immediately. They demanded ransoms for their hostages.

But that thought did not console him. He could see a door opening before him, moving away from local crimes into the world of international politics where he was a stranger – where lives were cheap when kingdoms were the prize.

Faro shut his eyes against the terror of what lay ahead.

8

Despite Reece's sombre warning, Faro told himself again and again that if the kidnappers had wanted the boy dead they would have killed him in Glenatholl. A ransom, that was it. It had to be a ransom. But the thought did little to console him as the cab swept down the college drive and emerged through the rhododendrons in front of the house.

In the Headmaster's study anxious faces turned towards him, the other bodyguard and Anton, George's companion.

Could it be only yesterday that the boy reciting Mark Antony's tribute to Caesar had been informally introduced as George? No title, no identification.

That the Grand Duchess Amelie had chosen to send her son to Britain – no, to Scotland and only forty miles from Edinburgh – to be educated was an appalling coincidence. Doubtless she had her own reasons. Had these included the hope, a mere whisper, that fate would provide a chance meeting? Other than four words added to the newspaper announcement of George's birth, she had never communicated the dangerous secret that linked their lives.

Faro tried to suppress the turmoil of emotions that seized him. He must concentrate on the fact that there had been a royal kidnapping and obviously, his sinking heart told him, George was in mortal danger.

'If you please, Anton, tell Inspector Faro exactly what happened,' said Headmaster Banes. The boy looked scared and moved nearer to the bodyguard, addressed as Dieter, as if for support.

'George received a note that a friend wished to meet him at the walled garden, near the gazebo.'

The Headmaster sighed. 'These are forbidden areas unless the boys are escorted.'

'The gazebo near the statues of the Roman senators?' queried Faro.

All heads swivelled towards him. 'You know the area, Inspector?'

'Indeed, yes, Headmaster. I found myself there on my way through the grounds yesterday.'

The Headmaster looked disapproving and faintly suspicious. 'You were unable to procure a hiring cab at the railway station? We did offer,' he added reproachfully.

'I did take a cab but I decided to walk from the gates as I had time in hand,' said Faro, anxiety making him sound more irritable than usual. 'And I met the missing boy there. He was alone. Please continue,' he said to Anton, annoyed that he was suddenly the one being interrogated.

Anton shook his head. 'I told him he must not go, especially – especially since the accident to Tomas, his servant.'

'The unfortunate young man who fell out of the window?' asked Faro.

Anton nodded. 'George was fond of him. He was very loyal.' The pieces were fitting together perfectly for Faro even before Anton went on. 'I was against it but George thought this meeting might have something to do with what happened. He – he – '

Turning, he gazed at the Headmaster. 'He believed that Tomas might not have had an accident.'

'Explain, if you please,' demanded the Headmaster stiffly.

Anton took a deep breath. 'George believed that Tomas had – had been pushed out of the window.'

'Outrageous!' was the roar of disapproval. 'Of course it was an accident.' And to Faro, 'The boys read too many adventure stories, I'm afraid. We try to keep such drivel from them, but the books are smuggled in by the servants.'

Anton gave Faro a despairing look. He did not care to contradict the Headmaster.

As for Faro, events were rapidly building up to an ominous certainty in his mind that the bodyguard's death and George's kidnapping were connected. And in view of what he had been told of secret plans to annexe Luxoria to Imperial Germany, he had little doubt that these two sinister events in Perthshire's elite public school were linked with the attempt on Amelie's life at the Kaiser's hunting-lodge.

'He was very upset about Tomas and wanted to tell Mr Faro,' Anton interrupted his thoughts. 'A policeman might have helped.'

Faro stared at him, unable to say a word. He groaned inwardly at this information of another who had believed in him and he had failed, adding to his remorse for the man who had needed his help and had been rejected.

Worse was the terrible feeling that had he listened, he might have averted this potential disaster. Tomas must have been aware of a plot to kidnap George, and he had been murdered for that knowledge.

'Inspector, a word, if you please.'

The Headmaster drew him aside. 'I expect you have heard the grave news from Germany concerning the boy's mother, the Grand Duchess.'

'I have. But did the boy know?'

'Not from us. We were told to keep it from him, not to distress him without cause unless – unless the worst happened and then, of course, he would have had to be told and sent back home immediately. This kidnapping puts a very different, a very serious, complexion on the matter,' he added darkly. 'I'm afraid the information has leaked out and this is a deliberate attempt to prevent George returning to Luxoria. Be as discreet as you can with your enquiries, sir,' he said, leading the way back to the little group. 'Please continue, Anton. Tell the Inspector all you know. Everything, every detail no matter how unimportant it may seem to you.'

Anton nodded, and thought for a moment. 'The note suggesting a meeting was on his mother's personal stationery. He misses her very much.'

Another pang smote Faro as Anton went on. 'I wanted to go with George. I pleaded and promised not to tell Dieter,' he nodded to the bodyguard, 'but George would not listen. So I decided I'd follow and see what was going on.'

'That was very foolish, but very brave of you, Anton,' said the Headmaster proudly.

Anton shrugged. 'Thank you, sir. At first I thought nothing was going to happen. Then a rough-looking man, like a gypsy, came from behind one of the statues.'

'Gypsies, eh?' the Headmaster nodded. 'There are a lot of them about the district.'

'This man came out and was talking to George. He obviously wanted George to go with him, but George was shaking his head.

I couldn't tell what he was saying. Then another man came and they grabbed him and carried him away.'

'Carried him?' Faro put in quickly. 'Was there no carriage?'

'Not that I could see, sir.'

Faro thought rapidly. No carriage was very unusual, and considering the scale of the grounds, suggested that George might have been hidden locally. But before he could elaborate on the theory, the Headmaster's frown in his direction indicated that this was an unnecessary interruption.

'Surely George was putting up a struggle. Surely he would not give in readily to such treatment,' he said sharply as if regulations regarding behaviour *in extremis* were sternly laid down in the college curriculum.

Anton shook his head. 'I think they had tied his hands and feet. I could not be sure, though, I wasn't close enough to see exactly what was happening.'

'Of course, of course. You are not in any way to be blamed for your actions, which were quite courageous in such horrifying circumstances,' was the smooth reply. 'Pray continue.'

'I did not know what to do, sir. I thought about following them and then I thought – I thought it would be better if I raced back and raised the alarm, told Dieter. He would know what to do.'

'Quite correct, Anton, you behaved admirably,' said the Headmaster. And to Faro, 'The police were informed immediately. They alerted Captain Reece here. He had arrived in Perth with the royal train to take George to Balmoral Castle, as a guest of Her Majesty.'

'I have already told Mr Faro,' said Reece impatiently. 'All was in readiness. He had been invited to spend a weekend shooting on the moors before the family disperse and return to London.'

'What are the police doing?' Faro demanded.

'They are searching for the gypsies, according to Anton's description,' said the Headmaster, 'since he was the only witness of the kidnapping.'

'I would suggest they start their search nearer home. In the grounds, for instance.'

'Indeed? And what brings you to that conclusion, Inspector?' demanded the Headmaster.

'Anton did not see a carriage. Presumably the kidnappers could not risk a strange carriage being brought into the grounds, possibly stopped and questioned.'

Banes nodded and put in quickly. 'Correct, Inspector. That is our rule. The lodge-keeper at the gate deals with such matters. With our reputation for having foreign royalty as pupils, we get our share of the curious, you know,' he added, not unpleased at such notoriety.

'And since the drive is a mile long, Headmaster,' said Faro, 'it seems unlikely that a struggling boy, bound hand and foot, would not have caught the attention of someone, the lodge-keeper or a gardener. They could hardly risk that. So I would earnestly suggest that a thorough search is made of the estate and any outhouses. Presumably they will be awaiting the right moment for transporting him elsewhere.'

There were noises outside, the door opened and George, dishevelled and scared-looking, rushed in.

Faro had to restrain himself from rushing over and seizing the boy in his arms. Afterwards he realised he had lived through what were some of the worst moments of his life, wondering if the boy was in danger, or even dead.

At George's heels was Inspector Crane, looking very self-satisfied indeed. Faro extended his silent thanks and gratitude to him.

George looked around bewildered, as if he could not believe he was safe again. Squaring his thin shoulders, he assured the Headmaster that he was none the worse for his experience and was escorted from the study to be delivered into Matron's care by one of the masters. Begging the Headmaster's permission to leave, Anton trotted after them, obviously eager and anxious to be with his friend.

With no opportunity to question or even speak to George, Faro took Crane aside and asked what had happened.

'We found the lad, tied up and blindfolded.'

'Where?'

'He wasn't far away.'

'He was in the school grounds?' said Faro.

Crane frowned. 'Yes. But how did you know that?'

'An inspired guess, since there was no carriage involved.'

Inspector Crane nodded. 'Very astute of you, sir. Very astute.

We actually found him in the old stable block which was part of Glenatholl House before it was extended into the college.'

'At least he's safe. Were there any clues to the identity of his captors?'

'Not one. However, our investigations continue.' Crane shook his head. 'The gypsy encampment has gone. Packed up, nowhere in the vicinity. We shall of course track them down.'

'You still believe it was gypsies?' said Faro who had never put much store by that particular theory.

'We only know what the young fellow, Anton, told us.' He sounded unconvinced. 'Actually we have no records of suspicious persons about the area. The gypsies might steal a few clothes from drying lines, but they are mostly poor ignorant craiters, few can read and write well enough to be able to concern themselves with international politics.'

'Have you taken the accident to the prince's bodyguard into your calculations, sir?' Faro interrupted.

'Of course. But there is no evidence to suggest foul play. An unfortunate coincidence.'

Faro was no believer in coincidences. 'Earlier that evening, he wished to talk to me. I now believe he had some vital information.'

Crane stiffened. 'Had he indeed? The proper authority for such information is the Perth Constabulary, Inspector.' Without waiting for a reply, as the Headmaster approached, he said quickly, 'A bit of a storm in a teacup. Boys will be boys, sir. All's well that ends well. I'll leave it with you, Headmaster. Naturally we'll continue our enquiries and if we find any significant evidence we will let you know.'

And that cliché didn't quite fit the occasion either, as far as Faro was concerned. If the attempt was genuine for all its confusing details, then all was far from well and far from ending. He had an unhappy intuition that it was just about to begin.

9

Faro followed Inspector Crane to the door. 'I should like to see this place where the boy was found, if you will direct me to it.'

Crane gave him a sharp glance. 'You would be wasting your time, Inspector.'

Faro bowed. 'Allow me to be the judge of that.'

Crane sighed. 'It has all been taken care of,' he protested. 'Believe me, there is nothing to see. Just an ordinary old disused stable. You have my word that my men are searching every inch of it for any evidence. So far there is nothing.'

Faro was not to be put off. He was determined to carry out his own investigation.

Watching Crane departing, somewhat grumpily, Faro observed Reece hurrying across the gravelled forecourt, his manner urgent.

'Exactly the man I want to see,' he said. 'I have received a message from Balmoral. Her Majesty has decided that you are to take charge of the boy, see him safe to Luxoria. The royal train will take you to Dover.'

Faro began to protest but Reece swept aside his interruption. 'There is concern that the death of the prince's bodyguard, Tomas, who was attached to our own secret service, might not have been an accident. He was very loyal to Luxoria.

'Her Majesty said there is no man she would rather trust. "I have put my own life in his hands many times." Her very words, sir,' he added reverently.

'I keep remembering that occasion at Glen Muick. They still talk of how you saved her from assassination.'

That time was long past and belonged to a younger, more enthusiastic Inspector Faro, who had not yet tasted the sweets of retirement. And flattery would get Reece nowhere, he decided.

'It isn't difficult, sir,' Reece pleaded. 'There are quite excellent trains, the Orient Express goes through Germany,' he added eagerly. 'You can pick it up in Paris at Gare de l'Est and get off at Stuttgart as the nearest stop to the Luxorian border. They will send a train to meet you.'

He made it sound like a picnic day at Musselburgh, thought Faro, seeing all his easy life of sitting in the garden at Sheridan Place and teaching Jamie to play chess evaporate like mist on a Highland hill above Balmoral.

Regarding his doubtful expression, Reece continued. 'There will be a substantial reward, recognition for royal services from Her Majesty personally,' he added with a significant pause.

Was he hinting at a knighthood? It was an offer which Faro had already declined, much to his stepson's chagrin, as the last thing he had ever wanted or desired.

'As you know, Luxoria is very close to Her Majesty's heart. Anything remotely connected with her late husband, the Prince Consort, is deified. And the Grand Duchess was very closely related to both of them.'

Faro had heard all this before and he wasn't listening. He had been commanded and he could not refuse a royal command without some legitimate excuse, like ill-health or sudden infirmity.

He sighed deeply. He might as well do his best to please Her Majesty, once again. For the last time.

And quite suddenly, as Reece rattled on nervous and eager at his side, Faro's mind began to present a consoling sequence of not unpleasing pictures. Once they reached Germany and he had seen George and Anton safely delivered to the Luxorian border, then he could travel on to Heidelberg. And Imogen. Not a bad thing at all. In fact, the more he listened to Reece, the more it appealed as he realised this was the chance of a lifetime, never to be repeated. The first and last chance he would ever have of spending time with his – with George – of taking a lifetime of getting to know the lad in a few precious days.

And that, come what may, was the deciding factor. He was ready to take on any odds for this unexpected hand destiny had offered him.

He had never expected to see Grand Duchess Amelie again. Now he would return her son to her. If she lived, please God. If she did not, then George was heir to Luxoria.

A wave of paternal pride swept over him. A secret that could never be divulged, but how he would relish hugging it to his heart for the rest of his life.

And so it was all arranged by Reece with military precision.

On the following morning, once George had had time to rest and recover from his ordeal, the royal carriage at Perth Railway Station would be linked with the express from Aberdeen which would convey both boys and Dieter to Edinburgh. There Faro would join the train at midday.

The travellers would include Helga, a servant at the school suggested by Dieter himself. She had left Germany some years earlier and was anxious to return to her now widowed mother.

'It is an admirable arrangement, necessary to have a maid's services. Helga will attend to the laundry and take care of the personal ablutions of the two boys,' the Headmaster told Faro.

Before leaving Glenatholl to catch the Edinburgh train, Faro insisted on inspecting the old stables where George had been found.

He invited Dieter to accompany him and the bodyguard stood around looking bored and rather cross as Faro examined the faintly discernible footprints, for the weather at the time of George's kidnapping had been dry. That was unfortunate. But Faro realised from the evidence that Anton's description of George's captors had been correct. One was a large man wearing heavy boots, the other smaller. The lack of a carriage and the use of the old stables seemed to confirm that Crane's suspicion of a practical joke by the boys was correct.

He wished he could believe it.

In Sheridan Place, hastily repacking his valise to include a passport and his revolver, which he prayed he would never have to use, while bravely fending off Mrs Brook's anxieties about how many shirts and sets of underclothes and socks he might need, Faro told Vince and Olivia that something very important had happened.

'I am going to Germany immediately.'

Olivia's immediate reaction was delight at this news. Her face brightened and her expression said more clearly than any words that she believed Faro and Imogen were planning to marry at last. He could only guess at her disappointment as he told Vince of his plans to escort the heir to Luxoria back across

Germany. In the interests of sparing Vince and Olivia unnecessary – he hoped – anxiety, he made no mention of the events at Glenatholl which had brought this about, beyond saying that it was Her Majesty's wish.

Olivia looked pleased and proud at that, but Vince, whose chief concern was always his stepfather's welfare, protested.

'Do they know whether the Grand Duchess is still alive? The newspapers have been remarkably silent about the extent of her injuries.'

On his arrival in Edinburgh Faro had visited the special and highly secret department of the City Police whose business was the acquiring of such information.

'They knew nothing. No news was good news, or so they told me,' he said consolingly.

'Are you sure you want to be involved in all this, Stepfather?' asked Vince, unable to keep the anxiety out of his voice.

'I have very little option, lad.' Faro shook his head. 'Even I cannot ignore a royal command.'

'But she knows you are retired,' Vince protested.

'Yes, indeed. How very unthoughtful,' said Olivia. 'A great strain on you.'

'Wait a bit!' Faro protested. 'I'm not exactly decrepit.'

'Olivia is anxious, as I am,' Vince put in sternly. 'Besides, how do you deal with anything when you don't even know the language?'

Faro shrugged. 'I will cross that particular bridge when I come to it, if ever.'

Vince sighed. 'I do wish I was going with you, Stepfather.'

'Since you don't know the language either, we would both be in trouble,' said Faro. While appreciating their concern, his patience was running thin.

'I would very much like to meet this prince,' was Olivia's tactful rejoinder.

'And so you shall, my dear, when you see me off tomorrow,' said Faro, glad of her diversion.

They drove him to the station the next morning, where a very wide-eyed Olivia was ushered into the handsome royal carriage which looked so dark and unassuming from its exterior.

She curtsied to the boy, who took her hand and bowed. Anton did likewise, as did Dieter, while Helga curtsied nicely.

Olivia was charmed by George and so was Vince, in spite of himself and his fears. Already he had his suspicions that he had not been told the whole truth and that his stepfather was embarking on no ordinary assignment. Reading between the lines, a matter he had become skilled at in their early days, Vince guessed shrewdly that if some person or persons did not wish the heir of Luxoria to set foot in his native land again, then Faro's mission was perilous indeed.

As they watched the train steam out of the station, Olivia said, 'What a charming boy. I have never met a prince before and George is such a very English name.'

'But it owes its royal origins to the Hanoverians,' said Vince leading the way back to their carriage.

Olivia emerged from her cloud of euphoria. 'He doesn't look in the least foreign, not like the boy Anton. George looks more like, well, a Viking.'

'Precisely,' said Vince drily, for the resemblance to Faro was unmistakable and he hoped no one in Luxoria was aware of the outcome of the Grand Duchess's visit thirteen years ago. How after many barren years the birth of a premature princeling had followed her reconciliation with her husband.

Olivia looked at him wide-eyed. 'You think – oh, surely not – ' And with a gasp of astonishment, 'You mean – '

'Exactly,' said Vince, opening the carriage door. For once he preferred to be a man of very few words. 'And we would be well-advised to keep such thoughts to ourselves, my dear.'

10

The royal carriage allocated to the travellers was comfortable but not luxurious. With the Queen's spartan attitude towards waste and extravagance clearly evident, it resembled a small parlour and only the rigidly anchored seats and table indicated that this was a fast-moving vehicle subject to the vagaries of speed on a railway line. As their journey did not include overnight travel, a bedroom was not at their disposal. The carriage, although part of the train, was private and inaccessible to other passengers boarding at the stations they passed through.

Berwick, Newcastle, Durham, York and so to London where they would be shunted on to a siding to await another train which would deliver them to Dover. There the wagons-lits' specially commissioned ferry for the Orient Express would carry the passengers across the English Channel to Calais and then the luxurious and famed Club Train would take them direct to Paris and the Gare de l'Est, where the next stage of their journey began.

It sounded simple enough, a smooth-running plan efficiently activated by royal commands issuing from Balmoral courtesy of the telegraph service. Faro hoped it worked, content meanwhile with the opportunity to acquaint himself with his travelling companions, in particular young George.

He was not by nature a nervous man, in fact he carried a lifetime's guarantee in the records of the Edinburgh City Police of being reliably robust in the face of adversity. However, in this instance he exercised extreme caution over the efficiency of arrangements in which he had not been personally involved. Any unscheduled halt of the train and his hand flew by habit and instinct to his pocket for the reassuring presence of the revolver concealed there.

Once, just beyond York, a great hustle ensued, with men rushing alongside the train, shouting at one another up and down the line. Dieter also carried a weapon and Faro noted his reaction was identical. Both men exchanged glances, with one thought in mind, aware once again of the compartment's few hiding places for the two boys should the worst happen.

There seemed nothing worthy of comment but George had interpreted what might be happening outside. He had also observed the two men's gestures towards their concealed weapons and said in a matter of fact way, 'If there is trouble, I think it would be best if Anton and I lay down on the floor, out of sight.'

'I don't think it will come to that,' said Faro looking at him admiringly. A cool head, twelve years old and no signs of fear. Well done, George.

He looked round the little group, brave indeed. He had expected that the woman Helga might have trembled just a little, but she showed no signs of emotion. All was calm. Nerves of steel.

Afterwards he was to remember the significance of that incident and how George was the only one who anticipated danger.

A guard appeared at the window on the line below them and explained the sudden halt. 'We're off again. Just a cow wandering along the line.'

Anton gave a sigh of relief and sat back in his seat. Perhaps he had been scared after all, as he said to George in German (which Faro only partly understood, but got the gist of) that it was as well that the Inspector and Dieter were armed, for one never knew.

Until the wandering cow incident, Faro had not seriously considered that any attempts would be made to stop George from leaving the country. Now he realised he had responsibility for George and the enigmatic Anton who, he gathered from Dieter, was a remote cousin who had been chosen to accompany George to Glenatholl. 'In case he was lonely and needed a boy of his own age, speaking his own language and from his own background,' Dieter explained.

Admirable sentiments, thought Faro, and a splendid opportunity for a paid companion. In the circumstances it seemed inevitable that Anton should also be returned to his own country, although Faro decided he could have been forgiven for wishing to remain in Scotland and continue the expensive education that being companion to the heir of Luxoria had given him.

Anton gave little away. There was a watchful, guarded air about the lad which discouraged Faro's attempts at conversation. Was he homesick and anxious, or devoted to George? Both, or neither? Whatever Anton's reasons, there was a distance, perhaps an instinctive resentment as his sullen glance often rested on his cousin. With little difference in their ages, it was understandable that Anton should be envious of the younger boy's privileged position.

Regarding Dieter, Faro could only speculate. He did not like the man or enjoy the prospect of his company all the way to Germany. He felt no rapport, no common ground, and knew only that he had met many such bodyguards in his long career. He regarded them guardedly as shady individuals who gave nothing away, and Dieter fitted the pattern, his emotions locked behind an expressionless face.

Yet there was something, Faro suspected, something ruthless behind that cool mask. A mask for the man of instant action, and that should be a source of comfort for here was a man who would kill without hesitation.

Having presumed that the two bodyguards were comrades, once while the two boys were out of earshot in the corridor, he asked Dieter what would happen to Tomas. Would his body be returned to his family in Luxoria after the accident inquest?

Dieter looked at him in surprise, as if such an idea had never entered his head. Without any emotion, he shrugged. 'He will be buried in Perth.'

'Has he no family?' Faro asked.

'None. Arrangements have been made. We have no details of next of kin.'

Faro knew there were reasons for such omissions by men who led secret and highly dangerous lives. He looked at Dieter's cold face. 'Do you believe it was an accident?'

Dieter shrugged. 'Of course. What else?'

Faro ignored that. 'Even considering George's kidnapping? Did that not seem significant?'

'Not at all. What makes you think they were connected? A mere unfortunate coincidence.'

Faro had long since learned to distrust such coincidences. Would Dieter be of the same mind if he knew about Tomas's visit to Faro's room just a few hours before his death?

'A matter of life and death.' He was about to tell Dieter but suddenly he decided against it. He would keep that piece of information to himself.

'People have accidents and get themselves killed every day,' said Dieter, which was hardly consolation.

But killing seemed far from that little group as the countryside and towns flashed by and Dieter opened the connecting door to allow waiters to bring their meals from the restaurant car attached to the first-class carriages.

Helga, a large, solid woman of uncertain age, withdrawn and keeping her own counsel, was another enigma. Faro continued to be puzzled over Dieter's insistence that she should accompany them. She seemed content to stare out of the window, her fingers busy, knitting needles clicking over some garment in bright red wool. Had her presence been suggested by Dieter as a mere kindness, to allow her to return safely to her widowed mother? Such a thoughtful gesture did not quite fit Faro's summing-up of the man's personality. Had she been young and pretty, he might have considered there was a motive, even a relationship between them. But although he was watchful, they remained distant from each other, two people locked in some secret compartment of their own thoughts.

As for Helga's recommendation as a servant, Faro regarded this with the indifference of a lifetime spent fighting off danger with little time and a total disregard for personal comfort. Did it really matter whether the boys had clean shirts and underwear for such a short journey? Helga spoke only to Dieter. Faro did not exist, while the activities of George and Anton were studiously ignored.

Apart from the two boys chattering together, there was little conversation in the group. And that was in German, of which Faro recognised only occasional words. As Dieter and the boys always addressed him in excellent English, it was then he made, a sudden decision – that it might be a wise move, considerably to his advantage, to appear, as far as they were concerned, to be completely ignorant of the German language.

The hours slipped past, the boys played cards or read the books they had brought with them to the tune of Helga's clicking needles, while Dieter spent much of his time in the corridor smoking very strong cigars.

Faro had brought *The Mystery of Edwin Drood* which had a special appeal to his own instincts for detection. Unfinished when Charles Dickens died in 1870, it lacked the author's brilliant drawing together of all those seemingly unimportant threads and minor characters in one of his famous endings. Now, as Faro read, he made special notes of any possible clues, deciding that a pleasant retirement task would be to complete Mr Dickens' unfinished task by inventing possible and logical endings of his own.

The last part of their journey was in complete darkness with only the lights of stations and of isolated cottages, under a canopy of bright stars. Tall trees flew backwards out of their path and, illuminated here and there by lighted windows, ghostly telegraph poles threw out metal arms that gleamed moonbright.

This mysterious landscape of the night gave way to the sprawl of the great city of London, a vast spread of eerily gaslit streets of tall houses, overhung by palls of smoke. Lines of houses with tiny squares of windows in their walls, bright as eyes staring out into the darkness, gave tantalising glimpses into rooms warm and welcoming in lamplight. Eagerly, Faro rolled down the window, and the thick smoke of a thousand chimneys drifted into the compartment, the smell of city life and human habitation.

Then London, too, had vanished into the night and at last, yawning and weary, they were in Dover, with the train settling by the pier where the Club Train's ferry was about to depart.

Tomorrow they would be in Paris. By evening the Orient Express would have set them down at Stuttgart. There another royal train would be waiting and Faro's role in the life of George, heir to Luxoria, would be over forever.

It was such a short time, he thought sadly.

II

Following the porter wheeling their luggage towards the Club Train, Faro was impressed by the new stratum of society in which he had been deposited. He was very conscious of his best tweed suit, tweed cap and boots, good enough for Balmoral Castle but very suburban when surrounded by men dressed in the elegance of fur-collared greatcoats and top hats. On their arms were ladies swathed in furs with haute couture outfits, and bonnets especially striking or outrageous which, he decided, he must try to remember in some detail for Olivia's benefit.

Even the air around the platform, as these passengers waved farewell to friends, was redolent of luxury and wealth, expensive cigars mingling with heady French perfumes.

As for Faro, he consoled himself on the grounds of anonymity, that their little group would not be worthy of a second glance in such company. If any had observed them with curiosity, it would be to dismiss their group as a family with two sons.

Perhaps Helga had her uses after all, he thought, and there had been method in including her in the party. Her unassuming attire consisted of a navy blue jacket and matching skirt, with an equally unassuming bonnet. Well-tailored but shabby, her garb had the look of being handed down by some rich employer, giving her the unmistakable brand of a poor female relation or governess, while Dieter's reefer jacket suit and bowler hat provided a nondescript disguise for his profession. Tutor, upper servant...

With the confidence of one who had dealt with such situations every day of his life, Dieter had elected himself leader.

'Leave everything to me, sir. I will make all the arrangements,' he said and gathering Faro's passport and papers, he went off to confirm their booking.

Dieter returned and said: 'I have booked a single cabin. It is best that we remain together. In the interests of safety, you understand. A wise move, I think.'

Wise, but alarming in its implications.

And, at this reminder, looks were exchanged by the two boys, their laughter and excitement giving way to uneasy glances which Faro understood, even while deploring the necessity of that single cabin. If, indeed, they were being followed, it would be very easy to isolate the two boys and the group and staying together offered extra security, with Dieter and himself both armed and ready to deal with any emergency. But the thought of being closeted in a room of ten feet by eight with the constant smell of engine oil and the threat of seasickness remained distinctly unpleasant.

Faro looked at George. The boy was as much a stranger to him as the rest of the group and he wished he could have had more time to discover more about him. For once, Fate was on his side and the Channel ferry crossing provided that opportunity.

From the outset it promised to be a bad crossing with a heavy swell. Almost immediately after the ferry took to the open sea of the English Channel the faces of Dieter, Helga and Anton took on a pale shade of green. Faro advised them to retire immediately to the cabin and 'get their heads down'. They could hardly argue but Dieter, with a handkerchief stuffed to his mouth, looked anxiously at George.

'You should come with us, Highness.'

'No,' said George bracing his thin shoulders. 'I am perfectly well. And I want to stay on deck. I love storms. I don't want to miss the chance of experiencing a rough sea.' Exhilarated by the wind and the sharp movement of the ship, he laughed delightedly at the consternation on the others' faces.

'Are you sure you do not feel just a little unwell?' asked Helga, at last showing signs of concern for their charges.

'I feel wonderful,' said George, throwing his arms wide to take in the sky as the ship gave a particularly vicious lurch. 'Please go below and take care of yourselves. Mr Faro will look after me.'

The three needed no further bidding and lurched towards the companionway in great haste, leaving Faro and George to face the elements alone – and whatever dangers were threatened by the unseen enemies Dieter had predicted were following the heir to Luxoria.

'May I stay out on deck, sir?' George asked.

'Of course.'

'It is the best place, isn't it?'

'Yes, indeed. And here's a corner,' Faro pointed to a pile of ropes, 'where we can sit down and be sheltered from the strong winds. Are you used to these crossings?' he asked curiously.

'Just coming back and forward to school. In the long vacation, when I can see Mother,' the boy added sadly.

'Are you ever sick?' Faro asked.

'Never. Perhaps I have been lucky in the past.' And turning to Faro he asked, 'Why are you not ill like the other grown-ups?'

'I expect that is because the sea is in my blood. My ancestors were Vikings and I was born on an island. All my ancestors went to sea.'

'Where is this island, Mr Faro?'

'Orkney.'

George laughed. 'I have heard of Orkney.' And Faro's heart gave a sudden lurch when the boy added, 'My mother knew someone who came from there, long ago before I was born.'

And studying Faro again he continued, 'She will be so pleased to know I have met a gentleman from Orkney. A Viking too. Yes, you do look like one. Oh, I beg your pardon, sir,' he added, completely mistaking the reason for Faro's confusion.

Faro laughed. 'Not at all. I am used to it. People think Orcadians are Scots, but we are actually from a different race. From the Norsemen, not the Picts.'

'Do you have your own kings and queens, then?'

'Not for a very long time, George. We govern ourselves.'

The boy nodded. 'I would like to go to your island some day,' he said wistfully. 'The idea appeals to me. We never see the sea in Luxoria, we are what you would call land-locked. We have only rivers.'

The sea was settling down, the wind had dropped and the sky above them swayed, a huge black velvet canopy studded with bright stars. From below deck drifted music, a small orchestra for the passengers' entertainment, the sound of laughter, of happy voices. Far away, faint lights bobbed on the horizon, glowworms in the darkness marking the shores of France.

George yawned. 'I am quite tired, sir, but I do not want to go below. I don't want to miss any of this chance of being at sea and I would rather stay and talk to you, if I may, sir,' he added shyly.

Looking at the boy's pale face, which showed more than his brave words the recent ordeals he had been through, Faro said, 'Indeed you may. You may rest your head here, against my shoulder, if you like.'

'Thank you, sir.' And the boy leaned against him gratefully.

Faro closed his eyes, content to have this precious hour, precious moments that some fathers enjoy for a lifetime.

After a while George stirred, yawned and said, 'Do you think I will ever go back to Glenatholl again? I expect Mother will want me to finish my education once she is well again.'

Listening, Faro wondered how long they would be able to keep the truth about Amelie's 'accident' from her son. Surely he would see a newspaper or overhear the dread word assassination.

'Do you like Glenatholl?'

'Very much. At least I did; now I think I am a little scared.'

He shivered. 'Mr Faro, why should anyone want to harm me? I have no enemies. I have never harmed anyone and I had – have lots of friends at school. None of the boys care a jot about – who I am – you know, about Luxoria and that sort of thing.'

And with a sigh he added apologetically, 'A fellow cannot help what he is born and princes and earls are not all that rare at Glenatholl, so why should I be in any danger?'

Faro realised he was thinking about the kidnapping.

'I was really scared. I expect I shall have nightmares.'

This was the chance Faro had been waiting for. 'Perhaps it would help if we talked about it. Would you like to tell me exactly what happened that day?'

George thought for a moment. 'Anton could tell you better than me. He saw it all. I never saw anything,' he added ruefully.

'How was that?' Faro was puzzled.

'It all happened so quickly. One moment I was waiting to meet this mysterious person who had a message from my mother – I know her personal stationery very well. She writes to me often, every week, you see.'

'Do you still have this message?' Faro put in eagerly.

George shook his head sadly. 'No, it disappeared. I must

have lost it somewhere. Perhaps it fell out of my pocket while they were carrying me. I struggled quite a bit, you know,' he added bravely.

The note was more likely to have been stolen and destroyed than dropped during the struggle, Faro thought. And destroyed so that it could not be used in evidence. Especially as it was most likely to have been a clever forgery.

'I knew she was going on a visit to Cousin Willy's hunting-lodge in Germany. He's the Kaiser, you know,' he added casually. 'Mother is your Queen's favourite godchild and the Kaiser is a favourite grandson. They have been best friends for a long time.'

Faro had heard all this from Sir Julian Arles and gently reminded the boy, 'You were telling me about the kidnapping.'

George frowned. 'I was waiting for this person who wanted to meet me and the next thing I knew, something – a cloak I suppose – was thrown over my head, and my arms were fastened behind me with a rope. They lifted me off my feet and a man threw me over his shoulder.'

He thought for a moment, as if puzzled by something.

'I'm sure it was a man. At first I thought it was one of the boys playing a game – a practical joke. I laughed and told them to put me down and pretended I knew who it was.'

'And did you?' Faro asked eagerly. This was a new piece of evidence.

'No.' Turning in the dark, George looked at him. 'I knew it was in deadly earnest when I struggled and fought but it was no use.'

'You said "they"?'

'There was someone with him, running alongside.' George clenched his fists. 'Mr Faro, I was very scared. This was the first time in my life anything dangerous or even unpleasant had ever happened. When I realised it wasn't a game – '

Faro interrupted again. 'A game seems an odd sort of thing.'

George smiled. 'Oh, the boys get up to all sorts of pranks. They love playing tricks on each other. But not this time.' He shook his head. 'I really thought they meant to kill me.'

'What happened next, as much as you can remember, exactly?'

'Oh, I shall never forget. Never. Although each minute seemed like an hour because I was so frightened, I knew I hadn't been carried very far. I heard a door open, I was in a building and they threw me on to the ground. There was straw – I could smell it. I knew it wasn't a game now and I was very frightened and I kept asking, "Who are you? Let me go. Please let me go. If it is money you want, my mother will pay you – anything – anything you ask for." But no one took any notice.'

'I heard the door bang.' Faro felt him shudder. 'I – I tried not to cry, Mr Faro, really I did, remembering the boys and how they would jeer.'

Faro wondered if any would, had they experienced such real-life terror, as George went on.

'But I was very cold and hungry. Then suddenly I knew I must not waste time being sorry for myself. That wouldn't help. I had to be practical and use my energy thinking of ways to escape. It was very difficult with my hands and feet firmly tied, lying there helpless like a trussed chicken.'

He thought for a moment. 'The worst thing of all was their silence. That they had never spoken to me, never answered my questions or told me why I had been kidnapped or what they were going to do with me. That was worse than anything, not knowing. That and the silence.'

'You never heard them speak?' Faro asked curiously.

'No. Not once. Not a word. Not even whispers among themselves.'

Remembering Anton's description of seeing the kidnapper talking to George, Faro found this extremely interesting, for it suggested that Anton had been mistaken about what happened.

George's account was more likely. The obvious and sinister reason for not talking to him was that the kidnappers where known to him, people whose voices he would recognise. And that, in fact, was the very reason he had first suspected that they were boys from his class playing another of their practical jokes.

'Anton said there were two men.'

George nodded. 'That is so. The older man carried me but there was someone else running alongside.'

'How do you know that?'

George frowned, thinking. 'The man had strong arms, a broad chest. Tall. The other one was smaller.' He shrugged. 'Perhaps even a woman.'

'A woman?'

'Yes. Although they didn't speak to me or to each other, I heard their footsteps. The man who carried me was heavier-footed than the one who ran alongside, lightly, quickly – like a woman or a smaller man.'

Faro marked down favourably that the boy had inherited the useful asset of observation, despite his terror. Meanwhile there were many more urgent questions the kidnapping attempt raised. Particularly George's reactions to his bodyguard Tomas's fatal accident at Glenatholl.

He was considering how to raise the subject tactfully without further distressing the boy when a door opened and Anton shot on to the deck, out of breath and distraught.

Terrified!

It needed only one glance at his face to tell them something dreadful had happened.

12

'I have been searching for you, everywhere,' Anton shouted. 'I thought you might – might be dead!'

'Dead!' George looked quickly at Faro. 'In English, Anton, so that Mr Faro can understand.'

Flustered and shaking, Anton repeated slowly to Faro what he had said to George. 'I thought he might be dead.'

George laughed. 'Not at all. Here I am having a fine time with Mr Faro. Have you recovered from the seasickness?'

'Recovered!' Anton screamed at him. 'Don't you understand? I almost died out there. I was attacked. Someone tried to – kill – me!'

It was George's turn to look alarmed. 'What do you mean? Who would want to kill you?' He laughed uneasily. 'Anton, you must be mistaken.'

Again Anton turned to Faro and said slowly in measured tones. 'Someone has just tried to push me overboard.'

At his companion's dramatic announcement, George gave a horrified gasp. 'Anton – no!'

'Yes. It was like this. I was feeling better, not so queasy and as Dieter and Helga were still asleep, I decided to have some fresh air. It is horrible being in a tiny cabin with sick people. I thought I would come up on deck and look for you but I turned dizzy again and leaned against the rail. That was when someone grabbed me.'

'What was he like?' asked George. 'Did you see his face?'

Anton hesitated. 'No. But I think – ' he hesitated, 'yes, definitely, a big strong man.'

And Faro's mind flashed back to the description of George's kidnapper as Anton said, 'He crept up, took me by surprise.'

Again Faro thought of the scene in Glenatholl's gardens that George had just described.

'He had a stick, he raised it to strike,' Anton continued. 'But I was fortunate. At that moment the ship lurched, it threw him off balance and I ran away as fast as I could.' He paused. 'That is why I am so out of breath.'

Before Faro could ask for more details George, who was clearly very doubtful about this little drama, asked, 'Are you sure he meant to kill you, Anton?'

'Of course,' was the angry reply. 'How could I be mistaken about that?'

'It could have been the ship lurching at that moment that threw him off balance so that he bumped into you.'

The voice of reason, thought Faro, amazed at George's calm and quite logical interpretation.

'No,' Anton shook his head firmly. 'I am perfectly sure he meant to throw me overboard.'

'But why, Anton? Why should a complete stranger threaten you so violently?'

'That is easy. Because he thought I was you,' said Anton triumphantly. And at George's horrified exclamation, 'Yes, you, George! We are much the same height and in the darkness, with my back turned to him. You see, I am wearing a cap and your cape – here.'

As he held it out, George regarded it wide-eyed.

'I picked it up to come on deck. Helga was using mine as a blanket and I didn't want to disturb her, Dieter was also asleep, as I told you. Now, what do you think of that, George?'

Dazed, George shook his head.

'So it is true, Mr Faro,' said Anton sternly. 'Someone is trying to kill him. They have followed us and they are here on this ship.'

Faro inclined to George's interpretation, since the alternative was very sinister indeed. But if Anton was not dramatising an accident then the killer had bungled his opportunity. He had run out of time for a second attempt, as the ferry was arriving at Calais.

Just then an announcement was made that passengers were to remain on the ferry until morning due to the breakdown of the Club Train on its way from Paris. There were cries of dismay and alarm at this news, though passengers who had booked cabins gave a sigh of relief and were not at all sorry to retire and continue their journey the following morning.

Faro was glad of Dieter's foresight and as the two boys raced ahead down the companionway he seized the opportunity of telling the bodyguard about Anton's alarming experience.

Dieter shrugged. 'He has mentioned it,' he said in a voice devoid of all emotion.

'And what were your conclusions? Do you think it was, as he believed, meant for George?'

Again that shrug of the shoulders. Dieter spread his hands wide.

'Who knows? It might have been an accident, but we must remain vigilant at all times. Expect the unexpected, as they say in your country,' he added as they reached the cabin where Helga and the two boys were waiting.

Full of a solitary sleeper's apprehension and resigned to spending a crowded night in a small space with relative strangers – all but George, for he was no longer included in that category – Faro was pleased to find that the four bunks in the cabin were at least roomy and comfortable.

'Where is Helga to sleep?' he asked.

Dieter's shrug indicated indifference to this matter. 'I believe she has found accommodation among the other servants travelling with their employers.'

The two boys were obviously very tired but brightened up considerably at being given a complimentary meal in the elegant ferry restaurant.

At last they retired and Faro hoped sleep would be possible since not all the travellers were weary. Most were in high spirits, already exhibiting every intention of whiling away the hours until morning with wine, women and an abundance of song.

As for Faro, he was surprised to find that despite his misgivings about the crowded sleeping arrangements in the tiny cabin, he slept very well. No dreams or nightmares. No predictions at all of what the future held. No more danger than if he had been on a journey to Germany to meet Imogen and spend Christmas in Heidelberg.

But Jeremy Faro's optimism was in vain. And it seemed that his guardian angel was having an off day or his normally reliable intuition was once more letting him down badly and had taken early retirement.

They were awakened at daybreak by a waiter bearing a light repast of coffee and croissants, with fruit juices for the two boys. This was offered with due apologies as the passengers would receive a proper *petit déjeuner* once they boarded the Club Train waiting at the rail terminus by the ferry.

Their luggage already transferred to the baggage car, the five travellers made their way across the quayside, with the smell of the sea still encompassing them and the shrill cries of seabirds, who were particularly attracted to ferries after the breakfast hour.

A porter ushered them into a six-seater compartment and soon they were under way, on the first stage of their journey across France where, unfortunately, the landscape was blotted out by heavy rain.

The boys and Dieter played cards, Helga frowned over her knitting, counting some complicated pattern, and Faro returned to his unsolved mystery of Edwin Drood.

At last the Club Train steamed importantly into Gare de l'Est railway station and the passengers were set down alongside the sleek gleaming teak exterior of the Orient Express.

This was the moment the two boys had been waiting for.

'I love trains, Mr Faro,' said George, clapping his hands and jumping up and down. He and Anton had to be restrained from tearing along the platform by Dieter dashing after them, grabbing their arms and muttered a warning in German. Something about causing embarrassment among the passengers. Whatever it was, it had some effect on George, who continued to regard Dieter with an odd, puzzled expression.

The spontaneous excitement and exuberance of two young boys faced with this wonder of the age, travel by train, was well understood by Faro. When he was young and trains were in their infancy, the thought of tearing through the countryside at fifty miles an hour was a daring prospect, not for the timid-minded.

Her Majesty, who now accepted trains as the most convenient means of travelling between London and Scotland, had originally refused to expose her royal person to such unnatural speeds, quite against what God had intended for those He had anointed to rule over ordinary mortals. At last prevailed upon to risk a short trial journey to Stroud and emboldened by escaping unscathed, in the summer of 1879 she ventured across the newly-built Tay Bridge. In December it collapsed, taking 75 passengers to their death in the river far below.

Faro realised that this new generation would have very different attitudes to experiments with travel, if the two boys were any indication. Wild with excitement at the sight of the huge train steaming gently on the platform, George ignored Dieter's restraining hand and, turning to Faro, he said apologetically, 'I do adore trains. This is the most exciting moment in my whole life,' he added solemnly.

And Faro prayed fervently that was so, that nothing more hazardous lay ahead than a smooth-running uneventful train journey across France and Germany to the Luxorian border.

He was well-pleased with their compartment: comfortable seats padded against the motion of the train, to be adapted into small beds for the further comfort of passengers travelling by night, mirrors on walls of marquetried wood panels, curtains on the windows, a small table let down from the door frame for refreshments and an adjoining screened washbasin and water closet, much to the delight of the two boys.

'This is more luxury than we have in Glenatholl,' George pointed out.

The guard checked their tickets, followed by a porter wishing to stow away their hand-luggage and somewhat surprised that the older gentleman in the party preferred to keep his valise at his side.

Soon the two boys were bouncing up and down on the seats while staring out of the window at the platform crowded with onlookers watching out for the famous, or saying farewells to friends. Once or twice Dieter tried in vain to entreat the boys to remain seated, not to be vulgar was how Faro's limited German translated his words. But even Dieter had not the heart to quell their enthusiasm. Indeed, looking at the man's slightly flushed countenance, devoid of its usual calm, Faro suspected that he too was suffering from Orient Express excitement.

Suddenly, as the train prepared to depart, he realised that Helga was missing.

13

Faro turned to Dieter. 'Helga – where is she? Surely we aren't leaving without her?'

Faro's last sight of her had been trailing behind them as if she did not wish to be associated with the two boys' exuberant behaviour. It also suggested that she might be keeping a lookout for the ladies' toilet facilities on the platform.

Now Dieter shook his head. 'Did you not know, Mr Faro? I thought Anton had told you.' He darted a sharp glance at the boy, who merely shrugged at this matter of no importance.

Dieter gave an exasperated sigh. 'Helga has not been feeling very well, the crossing upset her badly. She is not a good traveller and she decided that she might be going down with a fever.'

'A fever?' Faro exclaimed. He found that hard to believe, Helga had looked perfectly healthy to him.

'Indeed yes. And a fever on the Orient Express could be a great embarrassment to us all, especially to other important travellers,' said Dieter, nodding towards the two boys who no longer had interest in anything but the train steaming out of the station. 'Cholera, you know,' he whispered.

Indeed, Faro did know. Cholera epidemics were the scourge of Europe, the haunting fear of every traveller on a long journey into foreign lands. There was a clause Imogen and he were now accustomed to encountering in all railway timetables, in very small print so as not to cause undue alarm: 'These schedules are issued, cholera permitting. The company does not accept responsibility for any illness incurred by its travellers during transit.'

'Helga is in a constant state of anxiety about her health, even when she is quite well,' said Dieter. 'She suffers from her digestion.'

That, thought Faro, was one answer to her rather flustered manner on the platform.

'The journey has been difficult for her,' Dieter went on, 'so she decided it would be advisable to spend a few days with her grandmother, who lives here in Paris, to recover before continuing her journey to Germany.'

Faro wondered when the silent and withdrawn Helga had imparted all this personal information to Dieter. Listening to the man as he talked, watching him closely, Faro decided he could hardly argue, although Helga had seemed robust enough on the Club Train journey from Calais, recovered from her seasickness and content to sit in a corner with her knitting. A smooth tale, well-prepared, he thought, but was it the truth? Again his aversion to the man brought a cold feeling of distrust, a twitch of his old intuition again.

And the sinister fact remained, what had caused Helga to so abruptly change her mind?

Once more studying Dieter, he made a mental note that he must never relax vigilance, that this man who had appointed himself their leader was an unknown quantity, a ruthless man, one who would not think twice about killing an adversary or of getting rid of someone who was no longer of any use to him, their presence an inconvenience. Especially if he was being paid well to do so.

The train was now gathering speed. Faro was helpless to do anything. He could hardly raise an outcry about a missing passenger and insist on the train returning to the platform while he went in search of Helga.

He bit his lip, frustrated. True, he owed her nothing, her attitude toward him had been indifferent, even faintly hostile, but he could not shake off the fear that some misfortune other than a suspected fever had prevented her from joining the train and continuing the journey with them.

'I wish Helga had told us of her intentions,' he remarked to Dieter, in a tone of stern disapproval.

Dieter grinned at him, a cold mirthless parting of his thin lips. 'She informed Anton of her change of plan.'

Confiding in Anton also seemed rather unlikely, thought Faro.

'You must understand that her English is very poor,' Dieter explained. 'She would have found it difficult to explain to you why she was leaving us, and perhaps feared that you might have objections.'

'Why should I have objections?'

Dieter shrugged. 'You might wish for a maid to look after us. Most gentleman in your position would expect such services. For the laundry and so forth.'

'I hardly think we will need the laundry on this train,' Faro said coldly. 'I imagine all such matters are well in hand.'

'I am sure you are right, Mr Faro,' was the smooth reply. 'But look at it this way. Is it not to our advantage and more convenient, as you will surely see, to have four males sharing a compartment – for safety?' he added emphasising the word. 'A lady's presence would have been difficult. We would have had to engage a separate sleeping compartment for her.'

'I had presumed you would have thought of that,' said Faro. 'Surely the train provides places for lady's maids and nannies travelling with their employers.'

Dieter gave him an angry glance. He did not like being questioned. 'I would have found accommodation for Helga once the train had started,' he said shortly. But was that all? Had Dieter regretted his impulse to bring her along, overcome by some crafty measure of thrift that Faro knew nothing about?

The man was an enigma, he thought, as Dieter shrugged and looked out of the window, indicating that the matter was closed.

But was it? Faro continued to have pangs of conscience about Helga, wishing he had taken more notice of her and that he could believe Dieter's story had some elements of truth in it.

The boys announced that they were hungry and when Dieter responded by saying they should all go directly to the restaurant car, they raced ahead and George cannoned into a crusty old gent.

'You should teach your son better manners, sir,' the man said to Faro.

Faro pretended not to hear, the significance of the remark lost upon him as he gazed at the elegant restaurant car. The walls were padded in Spanish leather, the ceiling painted in Italian stucco, and at tables set with linen and silver, *petit déjeuner* was being served. Studying the menu he was unaware of Dieter's puzzled gaze changing into sudden enlightenment.

There were wine glasses and George, tapping one with his finger, said solemnly, 'Real crystal, Mr Faro, like we have at home.'

Faro smiled, for crystal was one of Luxoria's famous exports. It would have seemed an extravagance considering the possibilities involved in a swaying train, the kind with wooden seats and no facilities, crowded with people and all too often with their animals too – trains that he and Imogen were used to in their travels across Europe – but here was a machine from the world of the future, gliding along the railway lines so smoothly. Imogen would be so envious when he told her about it. He thought wistfully that some day in the future, if they saved enough money, they might manage a very short journey on the Orient Express.

Having observed Faro's anxious reaction to the possible fate of crystal glasses, George said, 'This carriage, like our sleeping car, is on bogeys, did you know that, Mr Faro?'

Faro shook his head. The only bogeys he knew anything about were of the supernatural variety beloved of Celtic myths.

'Bogeys make travel much safer as they allow the wheels to swivel independently of the carriage and this gives a smoother ride round bends,' was the knowledgeable explanation.

Faro smiled. 'You know a lot about trains.'

George laughed and said proudly. 'I once met Monsieur Nagelmachers who created this Orient Express. He came to visit Luxoria when I was quite small – four years old. He is a Belgian and King Leopold, who loved travelling on his trains, and was a great friend, came with him. The King was cousin to your Prince Albert, and liked visiting my mother.'

King Leopold was another of that great sprawling royal family of Europe, all of them related, near and distant, to Her Majesty Queen Victoria.

'Monsieur Nagelmachers told me all about trains, and he gave me a tiny model which I always carry with me. I'll show it to you sometime.'

Faro looked across at Anton listening expressionless to this conversation with nothing to contribute. And he guessed that George's not-so-privileged companion probably had less happy experiences of travel, similar to his own.

As for Dieter, he was positively animated. With an air of excitement he leaned forward, stared fascinated at George, then at Faro and back again, a smile twisting his thin lips.

Returning to their compartments, those passengers who were journeying across Europe with hopes of enjoyable continental scenery were in for a disappointment. The weather had deteriorated since they left Paris. Rain streamed steadily down the windows, obliterating a landscape which, from very brief glimpses, Faro found flat and disappointing, used as he was to the more romantic undulating hills of Scotland. Vast tracts of land dotted with sentinel lines of poplar trees and rows of dry-looking sticks planted with mathematical precision stretched mile after dreary mile, sticks that in the proper season would blossom into vineyards, their harvest served as wines famous across Europe in every high-class hotel.

Finding it difficult to concentrate on the problems of Edwin Drood, Faro turned his attention to his fellow passengers.

Dieter leaned back in his seat with his eyes closed, apparently sleeping, since he had brought nothing, not even a newspaper, with which to while away the hours. Occasionally his eyes flickered open, he yawned and went into the corridor to smoke one of his strong-smelling cigars.

After an altercation when Anton was accused of cheating and George seized the playing cards and set them aside, the two boys sulkily resumed reading the books they had brought with them. Faro was pleased to see that although Anton was reading in German, George had a copy of *Treasure Island* by Robert Louis Stevenson.

George sometimes glanced across at him, frowning. There was a word in dialect he wasn't sure about. When Faro explained, George asked, 'Do you know Mr Stevenson?'

Faro shook his head. 'No. But my stepson was at the University in Edinburgh when he was studying law.'

'He lives in Edinburgh?'

'Not any longer. His health is very poor and he plans to live on an island in the South Seas.'

George smiled. 'Will it be as nice as Orkney, do you think?'

Faro laughed. 'I'm sure it will be much warmer.'

Anton, once again not included in the conversation, suddenly put his own book aside with an irritable gesture and, picking up the pack of cards, began to shuffle them.

'Another game?' he demanded in German.

'Very well, if you promise not to cheat this time,' was what Faro understood as the gist of George's reply. 'Will you play with us, Mr Faro?'

'No, thank you. I'll continue with my book.'

But somehow his efforts to solve Mr Dickens' fictional mystery had evaporated in the face of a much more present mystery.

What had happened to Helga? His thoughts kept returning to her. And because his life's work was a search for clues in apparently unconnected events, he took out paper and pencil and wrote down:

1. Attempt on the life of Amelie. Possible connection with:
2. The fatal accident at Glenatholl of George's bodyguard Tomas.
3. George's kidnapping and rescue.
4. Anton's attack and escape on the ferry. (Note: A big strong man was described on both occasions. At Glenatholl, indications were that he had a companion. A smaller man or a woman?)
5. Helga's disappearance. Where did she fit into this curious pattern of events? And, more important, why had she been brought along in the first place other than as a gesture of kindness? Was there a more sinister reason? Had she been disposed of permanently?'

He was too preoccupied to realise that Dieter had also found a vital clue to the secret of Faro's identity. It had taken Helga with her woman's intuition to hint what was now strikingly obvious and Dieter toyed happily with thoughts of President Gustav's reward for this particular piece of information.

14

Faro's thought pattern was destroyed by the entrance of a waiter announcing luncheon in the restaurant car. The perfect antidote to possible boredom, though passengers had breakfasted only two hours earlier. Obviously this constant serving of meals to while away the hours was one of the spectacular luxuries of the Orient Express, a boost to flagging spirits, regardless of the weather beyond the windows.

The two boys cheered. They were always hungry and had to be restrained from yet another headlong dash down the train.

At last they were seated and an imposing menu set before them, calculated to tempt even the most jaded appetite: *foie gras* served with Vienna rolls, smoked salmon, steak *tortellina* and an extravagant range of vegetables.

Faro looked anxiously at George and Anton since this was somewhat different from the homely fare even important visitors at Glenatholl encountered. He was pleased to see that the two boys tucked in heartily, undeterred by such a sophisticated meal, and how their eyes brightened at the sight of a rich chocolate *Sachertorte* served with thick cream.

The waiter was not at all put out when Faro looked askance at their demands for second helpings. He smiled and said, in very good English, 'It is a pleasure. So many of the young ones travelling with their parents refuse the fare we have on offer and make a great fuss at every meal. Nothing ever pleases them,' he concluded with a weary sigh.

'When do we arrive in Strasbourg?' Faro asked.

'In one hour.' The waiter looked at the rainstreaked windows. 'However, we may be running a little late as I understand they have had a fall of snow.'

'Surely it is early for that?' said Faro.

'These things happen, sir.'

As they returned to their compartment, the outlook was very bleak indeed, the grey landscape obliterated by heavy rain. The approach to the railway station on the outskirts of the town was through a huddle of poor dwellings, tiny hovels crushed together, Faro imagined, by a ruthless builder, interested only in profits and with scant regard for human comfort. The houses were so close to the railway track that every passing train must have rattled them to their flimsy foundations. From windows lacking glass and covered in dirty rags, white faces of children stared out wide-eyed at the magnificence of the Orient Express as it thundered past, a creation from a world beyond their wildest dreams.

Remembering the luncheon they had just enjoyed, several courses of huge and elaborate helpings, Faro thought of the plates removed from tables, many with their contents either half-eaten or untouched. They would have provided rich sustenance for those starving families bordering the railway sidings. He felt disgust at the extravagance, although these were familiar scenes he and Imogen frequently encountered in the slums of great cities, and they never failed to stir in him feelings of guilt, the indignation of a social conscience at the unfairness of the distribution of the world's wealth.

'Strasbourg! Strasbourg!'

The Orient Express glided to a halt alongside the platform and Faro rolled down the window, determined to take this chance of a breath of air.

As the clouds of steam diminished he looked towards the departing passengers. There was one he recognised. A figure in a navy-blue jacket and skirt, with an unmistakeable shabby bonnet, hurrying towards the exit.

'Helga!' he shouted. 'Helga! Wait!'

The woman half-turned, glanced back briefly and disappeared in the crowd.

'Helga!' Faro shouted again.

Dieter looked over his shoulder. 'What is wrong?'

'That was Helga,' said Faro. 'Didn't you see her? She's just hurried towards the station exit.'

Dieter stared at him. 'It cannot be. She never boarded the train. I told you she left us at Paris to stay with her grandmother.'

'I tell you it was her.'

'You must be mistaken, many servants wear the same sort of outdoor garments as Helga. They are not unique by any means.'

The boys now wanted to know what had happened, what all the excitement was about. The three talked in rapid German, impossible for Faro to grasp and interpret.

As the whistle blew and the train began to move, Faro knew he was once again rendered helpless, in a situation he could do nothing about.

The train gathered speed and he sat back in his seat, frustrated and angry, certain that he had not been mistaken, that the woman he had seen was Helga. He was certain, also, that Dieter had seen her and lied. Otherwise, how could he describe what she was wearing? Faro hadn't described that to him.

Now the question was why? Why? Faro did not like being tormented by illogical reasons. His instinct would have been to race after the woman, who had always been an enigma, and question her. Her disappearance raised burning issues, in particular what she was doing on the train after all and why Dieter had lied about her staying in Paris if he was not somehow involved in the deception.

Seeing Helga again aroused one of those imponderables which had long intrigued Faro – the reason for her presence in the first place. At least knowing that she was still alive removed one of his hidden fears about her disappearance, that something more permanent than a digestive upset had removed her from the train. He was consoled that he could dismiss the sinister thoughts regarding her fate that had plagued him since they left Paris. But that did nothing to settle his growing suspicion that Helga might have been involved with the kidnappers at Glenatholl and, even more disturbingly, the fatal accident to George's bodyguard Tomas.

He tried to remember the man, who was certainly more lightly built than Dieter. Helga was a big strong woman, and as a servant would have had the most ready excuse for persuading Tomas that a window was jammed, and then pushing him out of it.

If that was so, then there was an undeniable link with the attempt to push Anton overboard on the ferry. She might have been pretending to sleep in the cabin and followed him out on deck. Faro remembered the boy's uncertainty, his exact words. 'Someone – I think it was a man – '

Such also had been the description of George's kidnapper. In neither case had the face of 'a big strong man' been seen. George was grabbed from behind, lifted bodily. In the darkness Anton saw only a shadowy figure, a stout stick raised to strike him. In the darkness big strong Helga could have been mistaken for a man by a frightened boy. And Faro also remembered George's idea that one of his kidnappers might have been a woman, since her footsteps were lighter.

Faro's thoughts were interrupted by the arrival of the *chef de train*. 'There was a telegraph message waiting for us at Strasbourg for Herr Dieter. We should have had it when we arrived in Paris but it came too late.'

Dieter read it and said to George, 'It is really for you, Highness. The Grand Duchess, your mother, is home again from Mosheim. She is safe and well and longing to see you.'

George took the telegraph and read it out to them again.

'Such good news,' said Dieter. 'Is it not?'

'May I see?' Faro asked. The message had been transmitted from Paris earlier that day to await arrival of the Orient Express at its next point of call. Unfortunately the time stamp was illegible.

George was delighted. 'I am so glad.'

Faro was having similar thoughts. He had been afraid that news might arrive that Amelie had died of her injuries in Germany. At this rate he might safely conclude that his journey, his royal command to restore George to his kingdom, would end when he saw the boy on to the Luxorian train at Stuttgart.

He was glad, relieved in fact. He had little desire to go into the home of Amelie and George. Some of this was self-preservation. He dreaded a meeting with the President, with a guilty feeling that if he were seen with George their unmistakable likeness might raise grave doubts in the President's mind about his own paternity. Gustav was not a man, by all accounts, who would take that kindly and Faro realised that the possibility of leaving Luxoria unscathed would be remote indeed. He would meet with an unfortunate accident, be eliminated. And George. Nor would President Gustav have any remaining scruples about Amelie.

It was a grim picture and Faro suspected that the secret was out already. Once or twice he had seen Dieter watching George and him with a curious expression. After seeing their reflections together in the compartment mirror opposite Faro avoided sitting next to the boy. Perhaps he was overreacting and his safety lay in the fact that Dieter would never imagine the Grand Duchess of Luxoria in an intimate relationship with a commoner. Especially an Edinburgh policeman.

Casting aside his gloomy thoughts and observing George, he was greatly consoled by the boy's joy and excitement at the prospect of being reunited with his mother. By a bitter twist of fate, he had unknowingly met his real father but their time together was brief, already almost over. The secret was safe, never to be revealed. Indeed, it was better for all concerned that they were unlikely ever to meet again.

The detective in Faro sighed. Already he was forced to mentally draw a line under Tomas's accident and Helga's disappearance, as well as George's kidnapping at Glenatholl. A few hours more and he would never know the answers to those unsolved mysteries. Although he had reached some conclusions, they would remain interesting theories only. It was very irritating, but he was aware that he had reached a dividing line and the time had arrived when he must set aside a lifetime's habit of thinking like a detective.

As Imogen often advised, he was too ready to make a crime out of the most innocent happening. 'After all,' she had said, 'the world is littered with unexplained things and weird coincidences.'

Faro was not convinced, believing that an explanation could be found for everything, if one looked hard enough. But the memory of Imogen's words made him smile. He would have a lot to tell her, so much to discuss about George and Glenatholl and the Orient Express.

Suddenly he was content to look ahead, glad to be embarking on the next stage of his journey. He had come to terms with the inevitability of parting with George. Once the Luxoria train departed with the boy in Dieter's care, he would send a wire to Imogen and be on his way to Heidelberg.

He had it all planned.

It was not to be.

15

Before sending a message to Imogen, Faro required a reliable timetable. No doubt this would be available at Stuttgart railway station.

When he mentioned this Dieter seemed pleased at the prospect of their journey's end and said, with more enthusiasm than usual, 'It is possible that the guard will have timetables since the Orient Express passengers often have to link up with other trains.'

'Good,' said Faro. 'I'll take a walk along the train. See if I can find some information about trains to Heidelberg.' He was feeling restless as well as in desperate need of exercise after all the rich fare he had consumed.

'May I come with you, sir?' asked George.

'Of course.'

'I should like to see the rest of the train.'

'Me too,' said Anton.

The two boys hurried ahead of Faro, chattering excitedly, while Dieter trailed in the rear.

Walking along the corridors, they were greeted by other passengers similarly engaged in this very restricted activity, the only exercise available on the great train.

A door ahead of them opened and amid shrieks a tiny dog rushed out barking and dragging a ball of wool entangled in its paws. As the dog's owner appeared, shouting to it to stop, Faro stooped down, grabbed the little creature's collar and returned it to the middle-aged lady, who was volubly expressing her gratitude in German.

Suddenly he realised that the ball of wool was familiar. A ball of red knitting wool.

'That belonged to Helga!' he said sharply to Dieter.

Dieter said nothing, merely shook his head and gave a despairing sigh.

'I tell you that is her wool. Ask the lady where her dog got it from.'

'I cannot do that,' Dieter protested.

'Of course you can. Do it!'

There followed a conversation of what seemed like interminable argument and length. It was very difficult to follow but Faro gathered that the lady thought he wanted the wool for some reason and freed her pet from its entanglement, eager to hand it over.

Faro got only the gist of it. 'Ask her where her dog found it?'

The woman clearly thought this Englishman was quite mad and Dieter said, 'The dog has had it since before they left Paris, so it could not have belonged to Helga. She would never have been parted from her knitting.'

'She could have dropped it,' Faro insisted.

Dieter gave an exasperated sigh. 'Red is not an unusual colour, Mr Faro. Many women the length and breadth of Europe will be knitting garments in that colour. This is a mere coincidence. I should advise you to be calm, sir.'

Calm indeed! Here was Dieter making him sound like the village idiot. Damn!

Again that frustration of not knowing the language, but Faro was sure the woman was pointing and saying that the dog had found it. Someone lost it. He heard the word Strasbourg. Left the train?

Certain that Dieter was lying, Faro groaned. If only George hadn't dashed ahead. He could have translated.

Finally, with a rather angry look in Faro's direction, the woman dismissed them and returned to her compartment, clutching the dog and firmly closing the door.

Aware of Dieter's long-suffering sigh, Faro knew there was nothing more he could do. The guard appeared and he asked for a timetable to Heidelberg. 'I do not have one, sir, but we will be arriving in Stuttgart shortly.'

Why should he care what had happened to Helga? He would never know anyway, since this journey on the fabulous Orient Express was almost over for him, something of a wasted experience, since he realised he would remember little but his own frustrations.

Ten minutes later they were approaching Stuttgart, gathering together their luggage, as they prepared to wait on the branch line where the Luxorian train would collect them.

A tap on the door announced the *chef de train*. 'Sirs, I have bad news,' he said, handing Dieter a piece of paper which he read, his face expressionless.

'What is it?' demanded Faro anxiously.

Dieter sighed. 'The storm we have come though has done widespread damage. There has been a landslide. The royal train will be delayed for a few hours until the line can be cleared.'

'I have a suggestion, sir,' said the *chef de train*, eager to be helpful.

'In English, if you please,' said Faro, determined not to miss any of this vital information.

'Yes, sir. About ten kilometres distant there is an alternative route. The old railway line to the Luxorian border which was closed as unnecessary when the Orient Express took over. It is now used only for freight trains.'

'And?' said Dieter.

'We pass by, a mere half kilometre from the old station. It would be possible to halt there and for you to disembark. It is just a short distance to walk over to the siding, which you will be able to see from the train.'

Dieter frowned, clearly put out by this new suggestion, and Faro decided that knowing even less about the terrain he had better keep his thoughts to himself. Dieter was leader of the party, decisions were in his hands.

'What sort of station facilities are there?' he asked.

'None, sir. It is no longer used. They need to keep the line open as the freight trains move a lot slower than our express train. There is a waiting-room, and a porter in attendance. It will be for only a very short time,' he added encouragingly.

As he was speaking, the great train came to a halt. 'Over there, sir, you can see the siding.'

There had been a fall of snow and the black-and-white world, with a wood and a slight hill, was a very unappealing sight.

'It looks like the middle of nowhere,' whispered George.

It did indeed.

The siding had long since ceased to be dignified as a railway station. The Orient Express would have passed it by without being aware of its existence. The recent heavy snowfall did nothing to soften the bleak dreariness and isolation of a tiny hut alongside the platform, the waiting-room of the *chef de train*'s somewhat extravagant description.

Steps were provided to set them down on the track.

The *chef de train* was full of apologies. He was very polite but, to anyone carefully observing his expression, hardly able to conceal his impatience to get his train safely under way again. And not only for the delays to his scheduled timetable. There was another much more important reason: safety.

And that was uppermost in his mind at this moment as he looked anxiously down the track at the lovely gleaming length of his train. He did not know the identity of the two boys, but guessed that the party must be important Luxorian nationals to be able to afford such a journey. He did not want trouble from some irate official in London, so he would make ample provision that they did not go hungry while they waited.

Beside their luggage, a large picnic hamper appeared. 'This with our compliments, sir. We hope it will make your waiting more pleasant.'

What the Luxorian nationals did not know, and the *chef de train* did not care to brood upon, was that this was a notorious area with greater dangers to life and limb than a heavy snowfall and going hungry for a few hours. There were brigands, notorious killers who would have shot a man for considerably less than the picnic hamper and a few pieces of luggage.

He was already looking over his shoulder as he talked, praying that this wild and apparently empty countryside would not suddenly erupt with whooping gun-firing horsemen, tempted to descend on his precious Orient Express by the prospect of so many treasures within their grasp. In this dangerous territory the freight trains carried guns and the guards went armed. On his train, so civilised and fashionable, there was nothing so vulgar as an armed guard, no soldiers with a gun-carriage at the ready. The thought of his passengers made him want to weep. The ladies, such wealth, such jewels. Such pickings.

Already conscious of illustrious countenances bearing irate looks staring out of windows and standing on the train's steps, demanding to know what the delay was all about, he realised he had lingered too long already. He looked at the little group with their luggage and the picnic basket. Two young boys, he thought sadly. Then he remembered he had daughters that age. Not privileged girls, but ones who would need good dowries.

Should he warn the two men of the possible dangers that lay ahead, just out of sight perhaps? If anything happened to his train he thought of all those other illustrious passengers who would would not hesitate to bring an action against La Companie Internationale. He shuddered, thinking of the tears and tirades of his wife, the miseries of his children should he be held responsible, brought before a company tribunal, down-graded or worse, dismissed.

No. He must not linger. And bowing quickly, he boarded the train and left their fate in God's hands. He hoped.

16

Faro watched the train disappear snail-like into the gathering nightfall, its smoke a series of pale exclamation marks against the darkening sky.

Left stranded by the empty railway line, he felt suddenly angry and resentful. He should by now have seen George and Anton safely aboard the Luxorian train in the custody of Dieter and, with a telegraph sent to Imogen, be waiting on a platform in Stuttgart for the Heidelberg train. He looked in exasperation at the little group for which his responsibility was not yet ended, the two boys scared and vulnerable.

Faro considered the landscape with a jaundiced eye. As far as he could gather, they were the only humans visible in a desolate land, a world in mourning, where spring's rebirth was a forlorn hope in the wilderness which nature had forgotten.

At his side, Dieter wearily picked up the valise and the picnic hamper. The two boys had swiftly deserted the luggage and, waiting for someone to tell them what to do next, were pelting each other with snowballs.

'It will soon be dark,' said Dieter. 'We should get settled for the night. Delays in this area can be lengthy. We must not expect too much.'

'Then we had better see what the building over there can offer,' said Faro with little hope as they set off in the direction of the old railway siding.

They stumbled over the rough ground. The recent heavy snowfall, unmarked by human footfalls, might have appeared beautiful in any other context. Nothing, however, could soften the bleak dreariness of the landscape around them, broken by one solitary building. By no stretch of imagination could this small wooden hut be dignified as the waiting-room of the *chef de train*'s description, Faro thought grimly.

They pushed open the door. By a flickering stove, a dejected-looking porter, with only a red and rather dripping nose visible above the swathe of shawls in which he was huddled against the cold, picked up a wavering lamp to inspect the new arrivals.

Perhaps expecting an influx of would-be passengers, he went to the door and, peering into the gloom, he raised the lamp and shook his head by way of acknowledgement, since greeting seemed a gross exaggeration for that expression of woeful melancholy.

'The Luxorian train?' Cupping his hand to his ear, he answered Dieter's question and stared up and down the line. 'No, Excellencies, I have been told nothing about any engine from Luxoria. It is not on my station schedule,' he added sternly. 'We deal only with freight trains.'

Dieter resumed a detailed explanation in German which Faro gathered related to the landslide emergency. The porter clearly understood not one word but was intent on argument. Exasperated, Dieter turned to Faro.

'This is getting us nowhere.' And turning back to the porter, 'Perhaps I can telegraph Luxoria and let them know that we are here and waiting for the train to collect us?'

The man shook his head triumphantly at that. 'No, Excellency, you cannot. For the simple reason that we don't have one. It broke down years ago and was never replaced.'

'Then where is the nearest office?'

'Two kilometres down the line.'

Dieter translated this new disaster briefly for Faro's benefit.

'I will go,' Dieter added finally. 'I must let them know where we are.'

'Let me come with you,' said Anton.

'No. You stay with Mr Faro. It isn't far and I will be back as soon as I can.'

Faro admired the man's courage. He did not fancy the inactivity of waiting but someone had to remain with the boys. He was painfully conscious of his limitations in this emergency, helpless to deal with the intricacies of sending telegraph messages in a language only half understood in a German zone with a difficult local dialect, if the porter was anything to judge by.

'There must be houses somewhere not too far off,' said George.

'What makes you think that?' asked Faro hopefully.

'When we were playing in the snow out there, we heard dogs barking, didn't we Anton?'

Dogs? Faro and Dieter exchanged anxious looks. Guessing that it was more likely the distant howl of a wolf pack, Faro followed the bodyguard outside. 'You will take care.'

Dieter looked towards the woods, a thick black impenetratable mass. 'Yes. But do not trouble yourself on my account. Wolves will not attack me. I will borrow the porter's lamp. Fire will keep them at bay. And I have a gun. I will be quite safe.'

'I think you should wait until daybreak.'

'And spend all night just waiting, doing nothing?' Dieter laughed harshly. Faro understood that this emotion was one they shared and any further argument was useless. With George and Anton, he watched Dieter walking down the track until the swinging lamp was swallowed up by the darkness.

Inside the tiny hut the two boys huddled close to the stove, while the old porter applauded his good fortune in sharing the travellers' hamper of excellent food. The only item which he recognised instantly was cold roast chicken. But his palate happily accommodated all the new tastes, the like of which he had never before experienced and had little hope of ever doing so again. And such wine too!

At last he bedded down on what was little more than a straw pallet in a corner farthest from the door. The comfort of the travellers was not his concern. Wrapping his voluminous cape around himself, he was soon snoring and Faro wondered if he had a home somewhere and what had brought an old man long past retirement age to such a comfortless existence.

Yawning, the two boys looked helplessly at Faro as he considered two long wooden benches facing each other on opposite walls in what must have been a cold and inhospitable waiting-room even in its better days. At least the porter had indicated that there were plenty of logs to keep the fire going all night, mostly old sleepers from a broken-down platform.

'We must be thankful for small mercies,' Faro told the boys, setting Anton to sleep on one bench and George on the other. 'We are well-fed and warm. We will survive until morning very well indeed.'

'Where will you sleep, sir?' asked George.

Faro indicated a wooden chair.

'You may have my bench, sir. I will sleep there.'

Faro smiled. 'Thank you for the offer, but as it is five feet long and I am over six feet tall, I think it is better adapted for your needs than mine.' He nodded towards the chair. 'I will do excellently in that.' He refrained from adding that he would not be able to sleep until he saw Dieter safely back.

And so he began his vigil. The two boys were silent, probably exhausted, and he hoped asleep, for outside the barking they had mistaken for dogs became unmistakably wolves howling.

It grew noisier, hungrier and bolder. And nearer.

After a while, George sat up. 'I cannot sleep, Mr Faro. I am too excited. Seeing Mama tomorrow, I expect. I can hardly believe it. I am so glad to be going home again. I never realised it until now. I do wish you could meet my mother, sir. You would like her very much.'

Faro did not doubt that as he nodded politely.

'And she will like you and want to thank you for bringing me safely home.' Pausing, he looked at the book open on Faro's knee. 'But I am disturbing you, sir. I have finished *Treasure Island*, I enjoyed it but real life is much more exciting, isn't it?'

Faro could only agree to that too. There were few moments in most boys' lives, and he hoped there would be none in this particular lad's existence more exciting and dangerous than the present one of being stranded in an old railway-hut with a starving wolf pack howling outside the door.

'I should like to read more books by Mr Stevenson,' said George. 'Has he written anything else I might like and find interesting?'

Faro did not think there were many books more exciting and interesting than *Kidnapped* which had a curious parallel in George's life and his own at this very moment.

'It is the story of a man and a boy on a terrific adventure and the friendship that grew between them in danger. Mr Stevenson, someone wrote, had a genius for friendship. And he knew what he was talking about, he has a young stepson.'

'I should like to read that book, sir.'

'Then I shall send you a copy as soon as I get back to Scotland.'

'Oh, thank you, sir. I shall look forward to that.'

'Some of their adventures are in the Highlands. You'll enjoy that part, I'm sure.'

George sighed sadly. 'And I will keep it to remind me of my time at Glenatholl.' He looked at Faro. 'I do wish I had the chance to see your islands, Mr Faro, your Orkney.'

'So you shall when you come to Britain again.'

But he knew, and he thought that George also knew, how remote the possibility was of his return to school or even to Scotland in the foreseeable future.

George looked at him. 'I would be greatly obliged, sir, if you would tell me a little more about the Vikings.'

'I will gladly.'

And so, by the embers of a dying stove that cracked and sparked as Faro fed it more logs, with George at his side, he retold stories from the *Orkneyinga Saga* of the Norse chieftains, of Vikings and trolls and mermaids.

And of how his own grandmother was reputed to be a seal woman. 'She had webbed toes and fingers and people said she had magic powers of foretelling the future. She came from the kingdom of the sea, so folks believed.'

George listened enthralled as Faro told him the legend of the seal woman, not his grandmother this time, one who was taken in a fisherman's net and, falling in love with her captor, shed her skin and became mortal. They married and had children. Then one day she found, hidden in an old chest, her seal skin. When she took it in her hands, the sea called her home again.

He looked down at George, his head resting against his shoulder. He was breathing deeply, fast asleep and Faro pushed back his hair and kissed his forehead gently. As he did so he whispered in his heart the words he must never utter aloud, 'Goodnight, my son – my dear son.'

As he was settling him on the bench, George opened his eyes momentarily, sighed and with a shiver closed his eyes again. Faro, fearing that he was chilled, threw his Ulster coat over him and returned to his wooden chair and Edwin Drood.

With so many mysteries of his own since he had begun the book, he found his concentration wandering.

Where was Dieter? Why was he taking so long?

Determined to keep vigil, to stay awake until he returned, he read a few more pages.

Sleep seemed impossible as the old porter's snores deadened even the wolves' hungry howling outside the door.

17

Sometime around daybreak, Faro awoke from a bad dream. For a moment he had not the least idea where he was, then every aching bone in his body reminded him that he had spent the night sitting upright on a hard wooden chair.

The faint light from the window revealed that the two boys still slept and the porter snored as gustily as ever.

But Dieter had not returned.

The fire was dead ashes, the room bitterly cold, and ice had formed on the window pane clouded by the sleepers' breaths.

Faro opened the door and walked along the snowy platform. Animal pawmarks everywhere indicated that the wolves had been very active, hungrily pacing back and forth outside the door.

He shuddered. Why had Dieter failed to return? What had become of him? Faro stared down the track in the direction the man had taken, certain now that he could not have survived. He had fallen victim to the wolves or some other dire misfortune.

Faro shook his head sadly, full of sudden remorse, never having thought it possible that he would long to see the man he had instinctively disliked. And, it now appeared, quite irrationally distrusted.

Obviously the personality of a killer also had in it the necessary thread of fierce courage required to face the inevitable. This was no new discovery for Faro. In a lifetime of dealing with hardened criminals, he'd often found that no man is totally evil. The human soul has its redemption clause.

He walked back into the hut, a haven in comparison with the hostile landscape outside. The porter, still swathed as he had slept, was already relighting the fire, grumbling to himself as he did so.

The boys had awakened and announced that they were very hungry. As they went outside to relieve themselves, George said cheerily, 'Come along, Anton, remember the rules in Glenatholl. We would have been ordered in the absence of water to use the snow to wash our face and hands.'

They did not linger over their ablutions and returned indoors shivering as Faro opened the picnic hamper. He had not expected it to have to last another day and was glad to see that the contents had been generous and there was still bread and cheese remaining from the night before.

Strangely, perhaps because of his hidden fears, he wasn't hungry and settled for coffee, which the old porter brewed up on his spirit stove.

'Where is Dieter?' asked George anxiously. 'We must save something for him. Shouldn't he be back by now, sir?'

Faro tried to sound casual and reassuring. 'I expect he decided it was safer to stay near the telegraph office until daylight.'

'You mean because of the wolves?' asked George quietly.

Faro looked at him.

'We saw their footprints outside, a whole pack, by the look of them.' He sounded scared and Faro realised that he had underestimated the boys' imaginations. Dogs, indeed!

'I imagine Dieter thought it was too dangerous to walk back in the dark. Perhaps he had to wait until the telegraph office reopened this morning to send his message. I expect he'll arrive any minute now with the train. Just think, this time tomorrow you will both be waking up in your own beds,' he added with a confidence he was far from feeling.

He smiled at Anton, silent, asking no questions, curiously withdrawn from their anxiety about Dieter. And watchful. Watchful was an odd word to use for the boy's complete lack of emotion, which had concerned Faro in the earlier part of the journey and now worried him more than ever. After all, Dieter was his bodyguard, which suggested that his standing in Luxoria must warrant such an appointment.

As for George, he regarded Faro with an expression of faint disbelief. And no wonder. The boy could count and the train that should have been with them last night was now ten hours late.

As for himself, he was feeling the full force of the predicament of being in a foreign country in an area where his basic knowledge of German, which he had been at pains to keep concealed, was utterly useless, too basic to deal with any emergencies.

He looked despairingly at these two boys – fourteen and twelve and he was entirely responsible for seeing them safely to

Luxoria. Not in his wildest dreams had such an idea presented itself.

As the boys finished eating and rushed out to play in the snow, he watched from the window, afraid to let them out of his sight for a moment. The porter smoked a fierce pipe and totally ignored these unwelcome sharers of his hut's hospitality.

Another hour ticked by and still Dieter did not appear, nor did any trains. Occasionally the distant noise of an engine had them alert and listening, rushing to the door, only to watch with considerable frustration the passage of an express train thundering down the main line.

Faro had come to a decision. If by the end of the day neither the Luxorian train nor Dieter had put in an appearance then he would have to try to find some way to get himself and the boys to Stuttgart. He hoped for some inspiration, that some bright idea would come to him of how one stops an express train without endangering the safety of the passengers or getting killed in the process.

Then suddenly he heard it. A sound from far off, but not in the direction of the express trains. This one was coming from over the hill.

A train's engine?

He listened, and saw the boys look up from the wooden board they had turned into a sledge and were using on a snowy mound.

'The train – the train – at last.'

'No.' Not a train. Rifle shots.

The porter appeared at the door, shouted something incomprehensible to Faro and waved urgently to the two boys. Whatever he said, they needed no second bidding and raced through the snow to the hut. The porter pulled them quickly inside and closed the door. He was trembling.

George turned to Faro. 'He says it is not the train. It is the brigands.'

Brigands. Dear God.

If confirmation was needed the rifle shots were nearer now, mingled with the sound of horses, and yells and shouts which made the wolves' howling during the night an attractive alternative.

The porter was speaking to George again.

'Translate?' Faro demanded.

'He says they are like buzzards watching for carrion. They will have been watching us and know how few we are. They must have seen us leaving the train yesterday, seen our luggage – guessed there would be rich pickings.'

Faro wanted to ask why they had waited so long. Why didn't they attack during the night? George continued to translate the porter's terror into English.

'When the Luxorian train didn't arrive, they must have guessed we were stranded.'

Faro glared at the porter and put a finger to his lips indicating that he had said enough. He didn't want the boys to be any more terrified.

George looked scared. 'What will happen to us?' he asked Faro.

'We two will be all right,' Anton put in quickly. 'No harm will come to us. We will be taken hostage.' He put a comforting arm around George's shoulders. 'They don't kill children and we will be valuable to them. Not like adults.'

This was the first comment Anton had made and Faro realised he meant well although his remark clearly indicated that Faro need not expect to be so fortunate.

As for hostages, they might well be valuable to the brigands but not quite as Anton believed.

For one thing, they would have no idea of the importance of the two boys, that one was heir to the kingdom of Luxoria. Brigands did not move in the circles of diplomacy, or know anything of subtle bargaining with royal households.

Faro shook his head. He would die fighting, but no one could have any doubt of the fate of two well-grown boys if they were captured, or of the naivety of Anton's words. They would not be killed, since two strong healthy boys were useful to boost the brigands' numbers and fighting strength, which was frequently depleted by running battles. Rifles would be thrust into their hands and they would be told how to use them and made to fight alongside the brigands. There were other unpleasant things likely to happen to Anton and George among such men that Faro preferred not to think about.

The shouts, din of horses and rifle shots indicated that they were close at hand.

'What do we do, sir?' asked George, biting his lip but trying to sound brave.

'We fight them off, of course,' said Faro.

'But there are only three of us,' said Anton.

'And one with a gun,' said Faro grimly, producing the revolver he had never expected to use.

The porter who saw his action grinned and gave a crow of delight. From under his voluminous cape he produced a rifle and waved it vigorously.

Saluting Faro, he said to George, 'I had the honour to serve in the Imperial Army of the Kaiser fighting the French when I was a lad.'

George translated and said, 'If anything happens to either of you, I can use a rifle. I learned how when I was at Balmoral with the shooting party last year,' he added in casual tones. And with an apologetic smile at Anton, 'Sorry that you didn't get the chance as well, but you were just with the beaters.'

Normally Faro's eyes would have widened at the idea of an eleven-year-old using a rifle on the grouse moors. How soon did the royals begin teaching their young the art of slaying wild animals!

But there was not a moment to lose. The shots and yells were outside. The platform vibrated and the little hut shook to its foundations with the sound of horses' hooves.

Faro's last thought before he went into action was of the Four Horsemen of the Apocalypse.

Was this what it was like to die?

18

Telling the boys to lie down on the floor well out of range of window and door, Faro broke the window with his revolver, took careful aim and cheered as one of the brigands gave a groan of pain and slumped in the saddle.

The platform cleared instantly. But surely one wounded man was not enough to scare them off.

Cautiously, Faro looked out of the window again. Gathered at a little distance a group of twelve horsemen were drawn up together. They were not quite as he had pictured a band of villainous desperados. There was a military precision about the group despite the red bandanas tied around their foreheads. Their horses, no motley collection of stolen animals, had the sleek well-groomed look of regimental steeds.

As he watched, the men were gathered around one man, conferring or awaiting instructions. The leader suddenly emerged and rode forward swiftly towards the hut, alone and carrying on his rifle a white flag.

'A flag of truce!' yelled George. 'We are saved!'

He ran forward but Faro stopped him. 'Wait. I'll go first. You translate for me, George.'

As he opened the door, the horseman with his white flag rode on to the platform. He did not dismount.

He looked at George, his expression puzzled for a moment, then at Anton who was standing close behind him.

'You – ' he pointed. 'You boy – '

Anton stepped forward.

'Come here!'

Anton went over to the man, head up, and Faro marvelled at his bravery. The man leaned over, said something inaudible and, seizing Anton around the waist, lifted him bodily on to the horse.

Anton stared back at them, bewildered, and Faro guessed too terrified even to protest, to cry out.

'Anton! Anton!' George screamed as he watched his friend being carried back to the group. Then to Faro and the porter who was watching open-mouthed, 'Don't you see, they're taking him hostage. Why didn't either of you kill that man? You could have at least taken a shot at him,' he sobbed.

Faro did not reply. He was watching the group, already riding fast, disappearing across the hill. Then he said gently to George: 'You know we couldn't do that. We have to honour the white flag and if we had fired, we might have hit Anton, or they might have killed him in revenge.' He put his arm around the still-sobbing George.

'Dieter will be back shortly. He will know what to do.'

It was little consolation and he didn't believe his own words. Neither did George.

'He isn't coming back,' George said shortly. 'I think Dieter is dead.'

There was nothing more Faro could say. At that moment, he too was certain that they had seen the last of Dieter.

Still with an arm about George's shoulders, he led him back into the hut. The boy was trembling, his face white with fear, but trying to keep his voice calm, he asked: 'What will we do now, Mr Faro? What is to become of us?'

Faro had no answer to that. But there were a lot of questions that required answers. There were things in this particular puzzle, this dire and dreadful adversary which was death itself, questions with answers that did not make any sense at all.

He simply had to think. And fast. Because whatever the nature of those horsemen who had taken Anton hostage, time was running out. If George was to survive to reach Luxoria, there was not a moment to lose.

Inside, the porter was gathering together his few possessions. Waving his arms about, he shouted to George and ushered them outside. As they watched he seized their luggage, dragged it outside and locked the door of the hut, turning on them a face of furious indignation.

Faro began to protest but George translated. 'It's no use, sir. He says he's an old man and he's not going to be at the mercy of brigands. He has never experienced anything like this before, they have always left him alone and now he is not prepared to risk his life. He is going back to his village, four kilometres away, and the railway can find a younger man to deal with their freight trains and be shot at.'

It was quite a speech and the old man strode off without another word or a backward glance, leaving them helpless beside their forlorn pile of luggage.

Faro looked at the railtrack winding away into nowhere. The landscape was empty, but somehow menacing. The brigands had vanished, yet he felt the prickle of unease, an intuition that he knew better than to ignore, that the danger was by no means over.

Death was close at hand.

'Pick up your bag, George.'

'I'll carry Anton's,' said George. 'I can't leave it behind.'

Faro tested the weight. It wasn't heavy. 'I'll take it,' he said and with little idea where their next meal would be coming from, he gathered the remaining food from the picnic hamper.

'Now let's get away from here.'

As he started off down the line, George asked, 'Where are we going, sir?'

'We'll head towards the telegraph office, find out about trains.'

'Shouldn't we wait for a while, just in case – '

In answer a violent explosion split the air behind them. Faro threw George to the ground and sheltered him with his body.

The great whirlwind of noise was followed by an eerie silence. Cautiously Faro raised his head. Where the hut had been there was only a mass of shattered smoking timber.

'Someone blew it up, Mr Faro,' George gasped in a shocked frightened voice. 'We might have been inside.'

Faro regarded the ruin grimly. 'That, I think, was the general idea.'

'It wasn't the porter, surely. He seemed such a nice old man.'

'No. It wasn't the porter.'

'But he must have known.'

'He didn't, George. He wouldn't have put our luggage outside and locked the door if he'd known the place was going to blow up.'

'But how? Who?'

Gazing anxiously at the horizon, Faro said, 'Let's keep going. We shouldn't linger, in case they come back to inspect the damage.'

Seizing the bags, he walked rapidly down the line.

'Was it an accident, sir, do you think?' George asked hopefully.

When Faro shook his head, he said: 'You think it was the brigands. It was as well they got Anton out first.'

Faro stopped in his tracks and said 'Exactly, George. And that, I am afraid, was the plan. We were the target – and the old man, if he had been foolish enough to stay around.'

'What will they do to Anton now?'

'I don't think we need worry too much about Anton. Nothing is going to happen to him.'

'But they kidnapped him. He'll be a hostage.'

They had been walking for some time before Faro decided it was safe to stop by a curve in the railway line, well out of sight of the pile of rubble that had been once been a railway waiting-room. There were some boulders by the side of the track and Faro said, 'Let's sit down here for a moment.'

George sighed. 'I don't understand, Mr Faro. We both saw that man with the white flag come and take Anton.' He shook his head. 'We saw it with our own eyes – '

Faro remembered that well-dressed, smartly turned-out band of brigands with their fine horses and military precision.

'They kidnapped him, sir. Took him hostage,' George continued.

'That, I'm afraid, is what we were meant to think. Think back, George, were you near enough to hear what the man said to Anton as he lifted him on to the horse?'

George shrugged. 'I thought he was telling him not to be afraid – that all would be well. Something like that.'

'Exactly. Nice soothing words. Not quite what one would expect from a savage blood-thirsty brigand.'

George thought for a moment. 'Actually, he had quite a nice voice, sir. Well-bred, you know.'

Faro nodded grimly. 'And I would have expected Anton to struggle more and for the man to be a little more convincing, rougher in dragging away a frightened and unwilling victim.'

George didn't answer and Faro continued, 'That wasn't the way you reacted with your kidnappers at Glenatholl, was it now?'

George shook his head. 'No. I fought and kicked and struggled.' Wide-eyed he stared at Faro. 'You mean – you mean, it was all pretend?'

'I'm pretty sure of that.'

'But why did they do it then? And what will they do with Anton?'

'That, my lad, is what I want you to tell me.'

'I don't understand.'

'I want you to tell me everything you know about Anton. Who is he, for instance, this vague cousin who was sent to Glenatholl as your companion?'

George was silent for a moment, then he shrugged. 'I'm not supposed to tell anyone, ever.' He looked up at Faro. 'You see, Anton is actually my half-brother.'

'Your *what*?'

'Yes, our father is President Gustav, but we have different mothers.'

At last, thought Faro, a lot of things were becoming clear, not exactly crystal, but well on the way.

So Anton was the President's natural son, the boy who had been an infant when Amelie came to Edinburgh, childless. His mother was the President's mistress, the reason why he wanted rid of Amelie, to marry her... And declare their son Anton legitimate. The heir to Luxoria.

'Well, well,' he said and George stared at him when he burst out laughing.

'Are you pleased, sir?' George smiled. 'He really is very nice when you get to know him. And he is very fond of me. He has always behaved just like an older brother should. Protective, you know.'

Faro thought grimly that there wasn't much protectiveness about leaving his little brother in a hut to be blown to smithereens. If, that was, he had known in advance what was in store for them from the so-called brigands.

But although knowing Anton's real identity at least provided some of the answers to the questions that had been plaguing him, it still didn't provide any ideas about what they should do next. And worst of all was the certain knowledge that his German wasn't up to coping with this particular kind of situation.

As if George had read his thoughts, he said, 'When we reach the telegraph office, sir, I am going to send a wire to Uncle Karl – he is Mama's most trusted servant and he will have returned to Luxoria with her. He has lots of influence with people who can help.'

'He is not her equerry?' asked Faro sharply, remembering the first victim of the assassin who, according to Sir Julian Arles, had taken the bullet meant for Amelie.

If that loyal servant was dead, then their last hope was indeed gone.

19

George laughed. 'Oh no, sir, Uncle Karl is much higher than that. He is a statesman as well as a soldier. He holds the rank of colonel in the Kaiser's Death's Head Hussars.'

'Is he also one of your President's men?' Faro could not bear to say 'father'.

'No,' said George firmly. 'He hates him because he has been very unkind to my mother, you know,' he added with a candour well beyond his years.

Faro did know, but his eyebrows raised a bit at hearing that piece of intelligence from the boy who believed the President to be his father.

'But Uncle Karl – Count Karl zu Echlenberg,' he added proudly. 'will make sure the train comes for us. And that we are safe.'

Faro had already taken that missing train into his calculations. Seen in the light of the last twenty-four hours' events, the landslide excepted – if that piece of information could be trusted – had there ever been any intention of sending the royal train? He could see the President's hand clearly directing the whole operation, the ambush at the railway merely a device to rescue Anton, his own son, and destroy Amelie's child.

Faro had little doubt that the plan had been worked out well in advance. Starting with the Grand Duchess Amelie's assassination while she was in Germany, the trap was then laid for George to be summoned home from Britain, and annihilated before he reached the frontier in an unfortunate accident!

Faro himself, whom the President had never heard of, as well as any other appointed bodyguards of George, would be regarded as expendable.

The plan was emerging clearly now.

After a brief time of national mourning, President Gustav would marry his mistress, Anton's mother, and take over dictatorship of Luxoria, declaring their son as the next heir.

Even an unskilled politician like Faro could recognise that this was not only a personal vendetta, but behind it was the fact that Kaiser Wilhelm II was a long-term friend and supporter of the Grand Duchess and, what was vastly more important, he wished to bring Luxoria under the vast and ever-growing umbrella of Imperial Germany.

When Faro had agreed under duress to Her Majesty's request that he see her god-daughter's son back to Luxoria, he had knowingly entered into a situation involving political intrigue. Remote from any he encountered during his duties as a detective with the Edinburgh City Police, this was a development beyond his wildest nightmares or experience.

Realising the enormity of his personal involvement, he was tempted to blink rapidly, as he did in bad dreams, a technique he had perfected in childhood to wake himself up. Alas for his hopes that he would open his eyes and breathe a sigh of relief, find that it had all gone away and he was back in his comfortable bed in Sheridan Place. That was the dream, but this was cold reality.

Here he was, sitting by a railway track, a foreigner in a strange land, with him a twelve-year-old prince, the heir to a kingdom, whose safety was entirely in his hands and whose real identity he must never reveal, much as he longed to shout out the truth.

He looked at the boy. They were both cold and hungry, prey to wolves and the President's secret army who would hunt them down once they knew that they had survived the explosion.

That vital link with the world of sanity and safety, the telegraph office, still lay far down the railway track somewhere out in that desolate landscape, haphazardly dotted with sticks of dead-looking trees and boulders that a little imagination might turn into crouching brigands. They could have been sitting on Mars, Faro thought, but for the occasional very distant and frustrating emblem of civilisation, an express train thundering into Germany, towards Frankfurt and Heidelberg. And Imogen Crowe.

While he wondered sadly if he had seen Imogen for the last time, he told George encouragingly not to worry.

'I have been in worse situations than this,' he said cheerfully.

'Have you really, sir?' asked George.

And Faro was glad he was not called upon to name one. At that precise moment he would have found it difficult even to remember anything of greater peril. True, he had fought villains in plenty in his long career. But on his own territory, where he made the rules; where he knew the terrain and the language; where people understood him and his requests to official channels were dealt with promptly; where Chief Inspector Faro was respected, obeyed. But here in this alien land Chief Inspector Faro did not exist. Here he was merely Mr Faro, a retired policeman who nobody knew, escorting the heir of Luxoria to his home.

George leaned against him, trying hard to be brave and not to shiver. Pretending not to notice, Faro produced the bread and cheese. They were in deadly peril, but as Faro sat with his arm around George's thin shoulders, he knew that, in the seemingly unlikely event of his survival, this was the memory he would take out and treasure every day for the rest of his life.

George ate hungrily. If this was a dreadful ordeal for himself, Faro thought, how much worse for a lad who had been protected and cosseted all his short life and had always been quite clear about where his next meal was coming from? A lad who had never faced anything more threatening than a badly-thrown cricket ball in Scotland and had just survived a well-directed bomb.

'I suppose I had better get used to things like that,' said George through a mouthful of bread, nodding back the way they had come, where the acrid fumes of gunpowder still lingered in the air.

'There is a lot of it about in Germany just now, don't you think?' he added with that curious way of seeming to know what was going on in Faro's mind.

Faro stood up, dusted down the crumbs and gathered the valises. 'We had better not be too sorry for ourselves and get to that telegraph office before we start getting hungry again,' he said, watching George wrap a piece of bread and cheese in a rather grey-looking handkerchief.

'No need to keep that – eat it if you can.'

George looked at it longingly and shook his head. 'I would like to, sir, very much. I could eat a horse, as we say at Glenatholl. But I think I'll save it, just in case.'

'I'm sure we won't need it. We'll be seeing that telegraph office any minute. It can't be far away now,' Faro said encouragingly.

They had walked only a further hundred yards when they heard a sound. Not a train's distant vibration, but the sound of hooves – and close by.

'The brigands,' whispered George.

Worse than brigands, thought Faro, trained soldiers with orders to kill.

Looking round for cover, he seized George and dived behind the very inadequate shelter of a dismal-looking shrub.

They waited. The hoofbeats drew nearer...

'Listen!' said Faro.

'There's only one of them,' whispered George.

'And I think I can deal with that,' said Faro grimly. With more confidence than he felt, he took out his revolver and prayed that he did not miss, knowing that he had only a few bullets left.

The rider approached and Faro prepared to take aim.

A voice screamed at them.

'George! Mr Faro!'

'Anton!'

And George leapt out of his hiding-place as Anton jumped down from the horse.

The two boys embraced.

'Thank God you are safe,' said Anton and there was no need for translation of that into English.

'I thought you were both dead.'

Anton brushed his tear-filled eyes.

Faro stared in amazement, for he had never thought the lad capable of such emotion, or indeed, of any emotion at all.

'How did you escape?' asked George.

Surprises weren't over for Faro, as Anton's next move was even more out of character. He dropped on one knee, seized George's hand and said, 'Highness, you are my liege lord as well as my half-brother. I am your faithful servant until death. That I do most solemnly swear. Before this man,' he nodded towards Faro, 'who is a witness to my oath of allegiance.'

And George placed his hands upon Anton's head as one day, God willing, he would do in the Cathedral at Luxoria.

Anton stood up. The solemn moment was past. He dusted down his already grubby knees and looking suddenly rather self-conscious, he tied his horse's reins to a tree stump and in a breathless voice said, 'Do you mind if I sit down for a moment?'

George took out his handkerchief, and shook out the bread and cheese.

'I saved this for you – just in case.'

'Thank you. I'm so hungry.'

As Anton seized it and started munching gratefully, Faro, regarding this curious scene, felt as if it was suddenly out of context. Their little trio had been miraculously removed from sudden death by a railway track in an outlying district of Stuttgart but if he blinked suddenly, he felt he would find himself instead witnessing the aftermath of a cricket match in the grounds of Glenatholl College. He groaned inwardly. What would he not have given for that to be true.

As for what still lay ahead, he dared not even try to imagine.

20

Watching Anton approvingly as he demolished the last crumbs, George said, 'We were so worried about you. We thought you were being held to ransom, didn't we, Mr Faro?'

'How did you manage to escape?' Faro asked. 'And with such a splendid horse.'

Anton sighed. 'I might as well tell you both the truth.'

'What do you mean, the truth?' demanded George.

'That I never was in any danger really. It just had to look that way, as if I was being taken hostage.' Biting his lip to hold back the tears he turned to Faro and said, 'You have no idea, sir.'

'I think I have,' said Faro. 'George said that he thought the man who seized you whispered to you that you were not to be afraid.'

'That is true,' said George. 'That was what the brigand leader said, wasn't it?'

'That is what he said.' Anton shook his head. 'But they were not brigands.'

'I realised that,' said Faro. 'They were soldiers, weren't they?'

'Yes.' Anton stared at him in amazement. 'Members of my father – I mean, the President's private army. I recognised a few of them, a crack regiment.'

Faro remembered the sleek horses and the red bandanas that had struck a false note as Anton continued: 'It was all set up to –' he paused and looked anxiously at George,

' – to save me. When I heard that they had planted a bomb under the rubbish at the railway hut as they rode in to get me –' he gulped and took a deep breath.

'It was meant to kill you, George. And Mr Faro and the porter too, I was horrified. I knew I had to warn you before it was too late. They had no idea that I knew what they intended, they had even given me a horse.'

Pausing, he looked at them and laughed proudly. 'They didn't expect me to try to escape and thought that a boy would

441 THE FINAL ENEMY

be delighted to have such an excellent horse, be proud to ride with them.'

'Have you any idea where they were heading?' Faro asked. 'Where they were taking you?'

Anton shook his head. 'I think they were there only to escort me to the royal train. It is on its way here now.'

That, at least, sounded hopeful, thought Faro as George cheered.

'I rode like the wind back to that horrible hut,' Anton continued. 'When I was still quite far off I heard the explosion, my horse was terrified and after trying unsuccessfully to unseat me, he tried to bolt. But I got him under control. I thought I must have lost the way then I saw – saw all that was left of where we had stayed, just those smoking ruins.'

He looked at them both as if he still couldn't believe his eyes and then clenching his fists he buried his head in his hands for a moment. 'You can't imagine how I felt. It was dreadful, dreadful, the worst moment in my whole life.'

Turning, he looked at Faro. 'I am sorry, sir, you must think me an awful cry-baby but I really thought you were all dead. I had to steel myself to search for – for – well, you know – '

He shuddered at the memory. 'Then I started shouting, kept on shouting your names over and over, in case, by a miracle, any of you were still alive among the ruins. It seemed like hours later when I realised that if you weren't under – all that – then you must have got out in time. And you'd be walking down the track towards the telegraph office.'

He grinned. 'And I was right. Here you are. Safe!'

Safe! Perhaps, but for how long, thought Faro, seeing the two boys beaming with delight.

Personally he wouldn't put too much hope in the chances of safety until the moment that elusive Luxorian train put in an appearance and he saw the two boys delivered into safe hands and on their way home. Only then could he relax and think of the next stage of his own journey.

'What about Dieter?' George was asking.

Again Anton shook his head. 'I don't know. I don't know if he's even alive. They certainly haven't killed him or captured him because when I asked, they just shook their heads and said nothing. I thought, it might even be that he is in the plot to – to – ' He shrugged. 'He would never have told me, because he knew I would never agree to anything if he intended hurting George.' And turning to Faro, he said impulsively; 'Or you, sir. You have been so good to us on the journey. You've thought of everything. You're kind to George too.'

He took a deep breath. 'The other night, when I was supposed to be sleeping,' he said shyly, 'I was listening to you telling George that story about an island where you once lived. I knew whatever happened you would never let any harm come to him. Or to me. Although I was sometimes afraid that you had guessed, sir.'

'Guessed?' asked Faro.

'Yes, sir. You know, about that business on the ferry crossing,' he said shamefacedly.

'I thought it very unlikely,' said Faro but did not add that it had opened up an interesting new line of thought. 'Now if you are ready, shall we start walking again?'

Picking up his valise, George said in shocked tones, 'Are you telling us, Anton, that it was all lies? About being attacked and someone trying to throw you overboard?'

Anton sighed wearily. 'Dieter told me to do it. He said it was a practical joke, just to give Mr Faro something to think about.'

'He certainly did that,' said Faro acidly as George gasped, 'A practical joke! I don't think that was very funny.'

Anton shrugged. 'Dieter thought Mr Faro having been a detective might have worked one or two things out – '

'Like George's kidnapping at Glenatholl?' asked Faro and when Anton nodded cautiously, 'There were some curious things about your story, Anton. Your version of witnessing the incident didn't quite tie up with George's account. You said you saw him talking to a man you described as gypsy-looking but George told me no one spoke to him.' He paused to let that sink in. 'You realise there was a very good reason for that.'

Anton frowned as Faro went on. 'You know perfectly well what I'm saying. If George's so-called kidnappers had spoken then he might have recognised voices which were very familiar to him. Particularly yours.'

Anton shook his head. 'There never was a kidnapping attempt really.'

'You mean – you and Dieter arranged it all between you?' George interrupted. 'What a beastly thing to do, Anton.'

'I didn't much like it but Dieter persuaded me. He said it just had to look that way so you'd be sent back to Luxoria. He had been told that the President believed you would be in danger if you remained in Scotland. He thought it was a brilliant idea, especially after Tomas's accident. When I protested, he told me there had been an attempt on your mother's life, here in Germany but that I must not tell you because you would be terrified.'

'Was it true, about Mama?' George put in sharply.

He sounded panic-stricken and Faro said, 'You have the message from her, from the train.'

George sighed with relief. 'Of course. Of course.' His face darkened suddenly. 'What really happened to Tomas? Did Dieter push him out of the window?'

'I think perhaps he did, although he never admitted it.'

'But why should be – or anyone – do such a thing to Tomas?' George demanded.

'I imagine the reason was that he was afraid you were in some real danger that you knew nothing about,' said Faro.

'Dieter planned the kidnapping,' Anton explained. 'He told me that it was the President's wish and that he would be very angry if I did not obey.' Anton stopped and looked at Faro questioningly.

'Yes, Anton. Mr Faro knows – I've told him that we are half-brothers.' George shook his head, bewildered, as Anton said, 'I still cannot believe it. A father wanting to murder one of his own sons. It is just too awful. How could any father do such a thing?'

To Faro, however, the answer was grimly obvious. The secret was out. President Gustav had somehow found out the truth, and knew that George was not his child. It explained a great deal and put both George and himself – if he and the President ever had the misfortune to meet – in deadly peril.

George had returned to the Glenatholl incident. 'Something that puzzled me was that I seemed to recognise the footsteps of the other kidnapper. Now I realise why they were familiar. They were yours, Anton.'

'I am truly sorry.' And Anton sounded very repentant. 'But I have now taken the oath of fealty before a witness,' he nodded towards Faro. 'And I have promised to serve you loyally and never lie to you again.'

Anton's account had fitted some of the pieces together, but for Faro there were still unanswered gaps. Had it really been necessary to make George appear to be in deadly danger so that he could be withdrawn from Glenatholl and returned to Luxoria to be disposed of in his own country?

Perhaps that was only the most logical reason if his mother the Grand Duchess was no longer alive. But according to the telegraph message received on the train, she was alive and well and waiting for George in Luxoria.

'What about Helga?' Faro asked. 'Was she a part of Dieter's plot too?'

Anton shook his head. 'I don't know anything about her. Honestly, sir, I wasn't even aware of her at college. We never associated with the servants, of course. I don't remember seeing her and she wasn't very friendly, was she? She didn't want to talk to us or play cards on the journey to Paris.'

'She certainly did not look like a person with a fever, either,' remarked George the observant. 'She looked quite stout and healthy.'

'Do you know, I thought that too,' said Anton. 'And as she was going to Germany, it did seem odd that she left us in Paris,' He frowned. 'Unless she knew something from Dieter. Something he had told her or wanted her to do for him.'

'It could be that she was to send the wire to the Orient Express in Strasbourg,' said George, voicing the dire possibility occupying the forefront of Faro's mind. 'But Mr Faro was certain he saw her leaving the train there.'

'I might have been mistaken,' said Faro who had no wish for George to continue on his own grim line of thought that the wire from his mother was a fake. 'I only saw Helga's back view. I didn't see her face and as Dieter pointed out, perhaps quite rightly, a lot of servants wear the same sort of clothes.'

'Maybe she went to find out about the missing train – ' George began.

'Listen!'

A faint sound far off, growing steadily nearer.

What was this? A new danger? That fear was clearly visible in the scared looks the two boys exchanged.

21

Under their feet the track began to vibrate. Distant puffs of steam and there, a hundred yards down the line, a train was fast approaching.

They waved. The driver saw them and blew on the whistle. Never had a sight been more welcome to Faro and the two boys than that of the engine of the State Railway of Luxoria as it braked to a halt.

Of more modest proportions and considerably less impressive than the Orient Express, the Luxorian engine was painted in the national colours and bore the royal flag. With a tall stove-pipe chimney in highly polished brass as well as the usual pipes, tubes and valves, exterior cylinders and brass-rimmed wheel-splashers, its open cab had a tiny roof which housed the driver and fireman in a space so small as to seem totally inadequate against the elements.

The head of the State Railways, in full ceremonial uniform, leapt down from the front carriage and bowed low to George. 'Welcome home, Your Highness.'

Acknowledging the man's greeting, George whispered gleefully to Faro: 'We're safe, safe – ' sounding as if he couldn't quite believe it.

Their luggage stowed aboard, Anton gave a sigh of relief.

'At last,' he said, grinning at George, and stood aside with a bow to let Faro precede him into the carriage. Lacking the extravagant furnishings of the Orient Express it was nevertheless comfortable, a blissful haven after their recent ordeal.

'Isn't it wonderful?' said George bouncing up and down on the plush chairs.

The railway official, consulting an important-looking gold watch on a handsome gold chain, assured his royal passenger that they should reach the border in less than forty minutes. The watch snapped shut, the signal was given to the waiting guard and after some strains, jerkings and renewed steam they were off at a steady pace down the line.

'Soon we'll be home. Just think,' said George, 'won't it be wonderful, Anton? All our familiar things again, there waiting for us.'

Staring out of the window, the two boys lapsed into German as they talked excitedly of horses, and games and the archery field.

Suddenly aware of Faro again, Anton smiled. 'Tell him, George, you are better than the English Robin Hood.'

George shook his head. 'He is exaggerating.'

'No, I am not. I've seen you.' And to Faro. 'Archery is our national sport.'

'In the Middle Ages,' George said, 'Luxorian archers were famous and fought as mercenaries with many European armies. They went on the Crusades too.'

'The President prefers guns and soldiers,' said Anton grimly.

At this reminder of what might lie ahead, Faro wished he could share the boys' excitement and confidence in the future. It seemed absurd that he could not shake off the growing certainty of danger still to come.

He found himself staring out of the window anxiously scrutinising the horizons for any signs of movement. That twitch of unease remained that they had not yet seen the last of this bleak and threatening landscape.

His two young travelling companions had no such misgivings. With all the resilience of youth they had recovered from their recent ordeals and begged to be allowed to ride on the engine.

The guard was summoned to escort them and Faro was delighted to enjoy a little peace and quiet in the very comfortable carriage. Though not as elegant as the Orient Express, it had attractive features and a very distinctive style. The wooden panels were hand-painted with highly decorated scenes that he associated with travel in Europe. Swiss-style houses and mountain peaks covered in snow, with edelweiss predominant on their sunny slopes.

He was delighted to lean back in a comfortable chair unobtrusively anchored to the floor by the window, and a few moments later the carriage door opened to admit a splendidly uniformed waiter with a food-laden tray. Fresh coffee, warm croissants, ham and cheese. A selection of good things for any man's breakfast, especially one as hungry as Faro at that moment.

The young gentlemen, he was told, had elected to have food brought to them on the engine. They did not wish to miss any of the journey.

Faro was surprised to realise he understood every word. The waiter smiled. Then Faro remembered that English was the second language of Luxoria and that even minor officials would be well-versed in the language.

He watched the passing landscape as he ate. Although there was still little colour, there was less snow than he had expected and a marked improvement had taken place in the terrain. Meadows, vast orchards, with deciduous forests on the hillsides' lower slopes, changing into conifers as the trees ascended. Vineyards and glimpses of twisting rivers and water mills. Here and there the turret of a castle frowned down from within a deep forest. There was an odd familiarity about the scenery. He had a sense of *déjà vu*.

Suddenly he knew why. This area reminded him of Royal Deeside. He laughed out loud. No wonder Prince Albert had chosen Balmoral and been so very much at home there. When His Royal Highness felt wistful, by narrowing his eyes and imagining those tall Scottish pine forests above the River Dee replaced with vineyards and a twisting river from his homeland, he could have been in Saxe-Coburg again.

'We will be arriving at the border in a short while, sir. We should be inside Luxoria within the hour,' the waiter told him, coming to collect his tray and take any further orders.

The head of the State Railway appeared, bowed and announced, 'We are still in Germany at present, sir. We were given special permission to cross over on this minor branch line, now closed except for freight trains, to collect our very important royal passenger.'

To Faro's enquiry regarding sending a telegraph to Heidelberg, he was assured that there were always such facilities available at the border post.

So he relaxed in his comfortable chair for a while longer, viewing the landscape as it flashed by, a constant source of interest. He must remember any particular details that Imogen would want to know about.

It would be such a delight to be with her again, he thought, forcing her image to the front of his mind to obliterate the sadness of the inevitable parting from George. He was aware that there was not the remotest possibility of ever seeing his son again, of watching the boy become a man and eventually the ruler of Luxoria.

He sighed. He must guard against over-indulgence in sentiment, remembering always with gratitude that he had shared a few precious days of the boy's existence and had been instrumental in returning him safely to his mother. As for himself, he would be the practical traveller once again, taking an ordinary service train back to Stuttgart. A telegraph to Imogen would have her meeting him in Heidelberg.

He smiled at the thought of how surprised she would be and of the great adventure he had to relate to her. Was the time now ripe to tell her the truth about George?

How would she react?

The sound of the train rhythmically chug-chugging along was very hypnotic. He would rest his eyes just for a moment.

Perhaps he slept. Suddenly he was aware that he was no longer alone. Confused, he opened his eyes, to find Dieter looking down at him.

22

'Dieter!'

The man smiled. 'Mr. Faro, I am sorry to disturb you. You were looking very peaceful. I am very glad indeed to see you safe and well. And the two boys – I am sorry I was not here to welcome you.'

Faro stared at him. 'When did you board the train?'

'Some time ago, Mr Faro. You must excuse me but, like yourselves, I was very tired by all my travels.' He sighed deeply. 'After giving orders that the boys and yourself were to be well looked-after, I said I did not wish to be disturbed until we were in sight of Luxoria.'

With a thin-lipped smile he added, 'They took me at my word. I fell asleep and I am afraid you came aboard unobserved.'

Faro listened to him, not believing a word of it. He remembered the boys shouting, the welcome. 'You must be a very heavy sleeper,' he said.

'Oh I am, very,' Dieter said smoothly. 'I had little chance of rest after I left you. I had to make my way to the telegraph office and – it was very trying – I found it was closed until morning. I had to wait all night and then there were many complications that I will not bore you with.'

'I take it that you were not attacked by brigands? We feared that you had been taken prisoner by them.'

'Brigands!' Dieter gave a start of surprise. 'You saw brigands at the railway hut?'

'We did indeed, and Anton was taken hostage.'

'Anton!' His eyelids fluttered briefly and again Faro suspected that his surprise was feigned. 'I gather that since I am told both boys are enjoying the ride on the engine at this moment, Anton took no ill from his experience.'

'He managed to escape. Apparently they did not make him prisoner and, in fact, he thought he recognised them as some of the President's guards.'

Dieter shook his head, a somewhat unconvincing gesture. 'That is a very odd happening. Why should the President have Anton taken prisoner?'

'Why indeed? His own son,' said Faro drily.

That broke through Dieter's calm. 'Er, Anton told you that?'

'George did.'

Dieter shook his head and said gravely, 'It was to be kept a secret, Mr Faro, for obvious reasons. Anton is illegitimate but his father is fond of him and wished him to accompany his own son to Scotland. You realise it would have been very degrading both to the President and to Anton for his fellow-pupils to know his true background.' He shook his head and continued. 'Especially knowing how the other boys would react to such information. They would have made his life unbearable.'

'Do you know what happened at the railway hut to George and myself and the porter?'

'No.' Dieter frowned. 'I presume, like myself, you made your way to the telegraph office.'

'We were doing so when the hut was blown up.'

Dieter blinked as if in disbelief. 'Blown up! How dreadful. Who would do such a thing?'

'The same soldiers who took Anton.'

'But why, Mr Faro? Why should they do that if it was Anton they wanted?'

'The explosion was planned deliberately. But first they were to make sure that Anton, their main concern, was safe.' With a pause to let that sink in, he went on: 'You are an intelligent man, Dieter, you know something, I am sure, of the devious workings of Luxorian politics. Surely it is obvious to you that, whoever was in charge of this hostage-taking and destruction of the railway hut, George was the real target.'

'I cannot imagine such a thing, Mr Faro,' Dieter said coldly. 'And your reasoning is beyond me.'

'Then might I ask you to consider some more of my reasoning, as you call it. May we talk about Glenatholl for a moment?'

'Glenatholl?' Dieter frowned as if he had some difficulty in remembering the place. 'I do not follow you.'

'First of all, I would like to discuss the accident to George's bodyguard Tomas.'

Dieter shrugged impatiently. 'I have already told you that it was an unfortunate accident that could happen to anyone. He fell out of the window. I thought you knew that, Mr Faro. You were on the premises when it happened.'

Faro smiled grimly. 'You did not know then that Tomas came to see me just before I gave my lecture. He had some urgent secret information, concerning George.'

Dieter looked uneasy. 'And that was?' he demanded sharply.

'We will leave that for the moment,' Faro said smoothly. 'I should like you to tell me instead about Helga and why she pretended to be leaving us in Paris when I saw her on the train at Strasbourg.'

'Mr Faro,' said Dieter wearily. 'She did leave us at Paris.'

'What about that ball of knitting wool?'

Dieter held up a hand in protest. 'We have gone into all that, Mr Faro. I can only insist once again that you were mistaken. As I told you at the time, it could not have been Helga. She was ill and wished to stay with her grandmother.'

'Very well. Tell me, how well did you know Helga?'

Dieter spread his hands wide. 'Hardly at all. I hardly remember her from Glenatholl. She was a servant and I had little to do with the domestic staff. I had exceptional duties looking after Anton and George. I was not interested in Helga, if that is what you are asserting, Mr Faro, I simply accepted what she told me.'

'To return to Anton. He has confessed all about George's kidnapping.'

'Has he indeed?' Again that flicker of uncertainty in the man's expression. 'I presume he has told you that it was really his idea, a practical joke to play on George.'

'A curious practical joke. Like the one on the ferry. To pretend someone tried to throw him overboard.'

Dieter made no denial, just a weary shrug of indifference. 'The kidnapping was a wager from the boys in his class. Anton insisted that I must help him if it was to succeed.'

'That was not quite Anton's version,' Faro interrupted. Dieter looked startled. 'But do go on.'

'We were to leave George in the old stable overnight.'

'With no regard to the dangers to his health, lying bound on a cold floor for hours,' Faro, said indignantly.

Dieter laughed grimly. 'He is a very strong child. Well used to the rigours of sleeping out all night. One of Glenatholl's more spartan exercises is camping in the hills, survival in the open air with only one blanket. What I did not know when I agreed to what seemed a harmless schoolboy's prank was that Captain Reece and the royal train would be arriving that day to take George to Balmoral.'

'Did Anton know?'

'I am sure he did. George tells him everything.' Another weary sigh. 'Mr Faro, you are always searching for reasons. I put it to you that Anton had a very good one for pretending that George was kidnapped.'

'And that was?'

'Jealousy, Mr Faro, just plain jealousy. Surely that must have occurred to you, seeing them together. Anton was jealous of George being invited to a shooting-party at the home of your Queen. Left out because he is his father's natural son, unacknowledged whereas his half-brother is the rightful heir to Luxoria. Anton's mother was a German actress while George's mother is the Grand Duchess Amelie, a relative of the late Prince Consort and god-daughter of the Queen of England.'

He paused. 'Surely you can see Anton's motives in all of this? And I would say, although I have no experience of children, it seems perfectly normal that now and again Anton wants to prove he is as good as George in every way. You have already mentioned another example of his passion for practical jokes, you saw it on the ferry going to Calais.'

'Were you involved in that too?' Faro asked.

'No. That was one he thought out all by himself. But he confessed later that it had just been to scare George.'

'Not quite the story he has told us, that it was your idea, to test my powers as a detective,' Faro said.

Again no denial came from Dieter, who was watching him carefully. 'Perhaps it is difficult for a foreigner – and a policeman from another country – to understand how things work where kingdoms are at stake.'

Pausing a moment, he said slowly, 'I do not think you have fully realised, Mr Faro, that Anton has a lot to gain, worth fighting for and telling a few lies for, if George should meet with a fatal accident. Bearing this in mind I would advise you not to trust him or listen to all he says. He pretends to be a good friend to George, but – ' he shrugged, 'Anton is a very good actor, he can be very convincing, even shedding tears.'

And Faro remembered that extraordinary emotional scene on the railway track and earlier his tearful Prince Arthur in the scenes from Shakespeare entertainment at Glenatholl.

Who was he to believe? The answer was taken from him by a sudden interuption as the door was flung open as the boys rushed in. They were as taken aback as Faro had been to see Dieter there quite unharmed. As he told them what had happened, the train began to slow down.

George ran to the window. 'Luxoria! Hurray, Anton, we are home!'

The train had stopped. The guard came in and, before he said a word, Faro knew something was wrong.

23

'Why have we stopped?' Dieter demanded of the guard.

'There is a change of plan, sir.'

Brushing the guard aside, the head of the State Railway appeared. Bowing, he said, 'We regret the delay, but we have received an urgent message that the train is not to proceed until further notice.'

'What do you mean, not proceed?' demanded Dieter.

Another bow. 'The royal train is to remain here.'

'Remain? For what purpose?'

Not only Dieter looked angry, the two boys were very upset indeed. As for Faro, he felt only despair that his intuition had been right. It had all been too easy and his happy sigh of relief that his mission to Luxoria was over had been somewhat premature. The whiff of danger in the air was not only due to the steam rising from the stationary royal train.

'I am sure we will not have long to wait, sir,' said the official.

Faro looked out of the window. A small cloud of dust on the horizon revealed itself as a band of horsemen rapidly heading in the direction of the train.

At his side, Anton and George exchanged alarmed glances which Faro shared. Had the so-called brigands caught up with Anton for escaping and stealing one of their horses? Or was George their target? This time, surely, there would be no mistake.

Dieter looked over their shoulders and turned quickly to the railway official.

'I insist that the train proceeds through the border. At once. That is the President's command.'

The man shook his head. With considerable dignity he replied 'I regret to say, sir, that, as you are probably aware, our President's commands are not applicable while our locomotive is resting on German soil.' Drawing himself up, he saluted and added, 'These orders are direct from the Imperial Headquarters and it would create an international incident should I have the temerity to ignore them.'

'Damn your orders,' said Dieter through clenched teeth. 'Obey mine! I am in charge here! Perhaps this will persuade you to change your mind.' And taking a revolver from his pocket he flourished it in the face of the astonished and now terrified official.

Faro only got the gist of what was being said, but it was enough for him to seize Dieter's wrist. 'Why don't you wait and see what is happening out there? Surely a short delay won't make any difference.'

The troop of horsemen was nearer now. Faro sighed gratefully. Those black-and-silver uniforms could never have been mistaken for the red bandanas of Anton's so-called kidnappers.

'Get this train going! Immediately!' shouted Dieter, at the sight of the new arrivals, and Faro had to grasp the arm in which Dieter held his revolver as the reason for his anxiety became clearer.

Were the Hussars intending to kidnap the Luxorian train? Was that why he was so upset? Faro wondered, as he watched the leader of the troop leap on to the engine.

His footsteps came towards them. The door opened to reveal a colonel, splendid in black and silver and wearing a shako with the skull-and-crossbones emblem. It was the uniform of the Death's Head Hussars, Kaiser Wilhelm's crack regiment.

The boys ran towards the newcomer and yelled in unison, 'Uncle Karl!'

The Colonel roared with laughter, put an arm around both lads and sternly nodded towards Dieter, who was still holding the revolver he had been using to threaten the railway official.

Stretching out his hand, the Colonel said sternly, 'You will not be needing that any longer, since you are almost home. You are not in any danger.' He bowed. 'You may cross the border and proceed into Luxoria.'

Dieter took a deep breath. 'Excellent! Perhaps you would care to tell me what all this delay is about. Or is it just an idle moment for a family reunion?'

The Colonel ignored him and bowed towards Faro, clicking his heels. 'We have not been introduced,' and to George, 'Perhaps you will do the necessary.'

Beaming, George introduced Faro to his uncle, adding proudly, 'Mr Faro saved both our lives, Anton and me. We owe it all to him, Uncle Karl. Will you please see that he is properly rewarded?'

'Of course.' Another clicking of heels produced a weary sigh from Dieter.

'May we now proceed, Colonel? With your permission.'

The Colonel regarded him solemnly. 'You may proceed, by all means, sir.'

'Thank you.'

'I have not finished. I have said you may proceed into Luxoria, with the royal train.' He paused. 'Alone.' And cutting short Dieter's protest, he added, 'His Highness and Anton are to remain with me here in Germany.'

'What!' Dieter demanded angrily. 'I have my orders to deliver Anton personally to his father.'

The Colonel shook his head and Dieter shouted, 'You will answer for this. He is the President's son.'

The Colonel smiled. 'He comes with me by his mother's wishes, who still has legal custody of their son.' At Faro's puzzled expression, he explained. 'She is my sister, and Anton my nephew. Is that not so, Anton?' he asked gently.

'Yes, Uncle Karl. But I wish to stay with George,' he said moving closer to the boy he believed was his half-brother.

'Please, Uncle Karl,' George added.

Dieter could hardly conceal his fury. 'Very well. We will see what the President has to say about this. Meanwhile, I am to return George to his mother the Grand Duchess, who is eagerly awaiting his arrival in the royal palace.'

The Colonel shook his head. 'You have been misinformed. The Grand Duchess is still in Mosheim at the Kaiser's hunting-lodge where she has remained since her accident.'

Dieter looked even more angry. Touching his pocket, he said, 'I have here a telegraph saying that she is well and awaiting George.' He turned to the boy. 'You read it.'

It was George's turn to look bewildered. He shook his head. 'How do we know it was from her, Dieter? Anyone can send a telegraph message. Helga could have sent it when she left us in Paris.'

Faro gave him an admiring glance. The boy was sharp and the full measure of the plot to separate him from his mother was now beginning to emerge. The reason for Anton's so-called kidnapping to get him safe to the President. And when Gustav knew that George had survived the journey and the bomb attempt, Faro feared that his days would be numbered once he set foot in Luxoria.

'Are we ready to leave?' asked the Colonel. 'Very well, if you care to look out of the window, Anton, you will see that the Imperial train is approaching on the line behind us. We just transfer from one to the other.'

With their luggage gathered together, the boys and Faro jumped down on to the track. An angry-faced Dieter watched them from the window and the Colonel went over and spoke to him briefly as the train gathered up steam to cross the border into Luxoria. Not even Anton gave Dieter a backward glance or offered a word of thanks to his ex-bodyguard.

The Imperial train was waiting for them some hundred yards down the line. The carriages were painted dark blue and ivory outside; the Kaiser's drawing-room carriage, as Faro was soon to discover, was magnificent in upholstered blue silk with crystal chandeliers that tinkled like musical chimes as the train moved smoothly on its way.

Such delights were of no interest to George and Anton who insisted, with Uncle Karl's permission, that once again they ride on the engine, a much grander locomotive than the one they had just left, with engineers and footplatemen in tall hats and frock coats.

The Colonel relaxed in the chair opposite Faro. Removing his shako, he took out a gold cigar case. Faro declined the offer. At that moment he would have given much for a pipe of tobacco and a dram – or several – of an excellent Scotch whisky.

He was intrigued by the magnificence of the Colonel – the uniform, the splendid moustache, the famous Prussian 'peg-top' haircut. The lightest brightest blue eyes now regarding him with equal curiosity and ready to crinkle into merriment could, he did not doubt, also turn to ice. Even on this, the merest acquaintance, Faro felt that beyond the bravura there lurked an honest man, one he would trust with his life. It was the same instinct that had made him dislike and distrust Dieter from the very outset of their journey.

After some polite exploratory conversation in which the Colonel continued to regard him with that friendly but curious intensity, it became clear that he had reached the same deadly conclusions about the President's actions regarding George's future.

'I presume that the fake telegraph regarding his mother, sent to the Orient Express, was arranged with one of the man's fellow-conspirators. Once the President had him back in Luxoria, he would be useful as a hostage.'

'A hostage?' asked Faro. 'I don't understand. It seems to me that he would want to get rid of him more permanently.'

'By no means, though that might have come later. First he planned to use George as an instrument to give the President enormous bargaining power over the Grand Duchess – and Luxoria. He knew that Amelie would give anything – anything – '

He paused and added what Faro already knew. 'It is my opinion that she would sign any agreement to save her only son. Even to handing over the country and forsaking all future rights of George as heir. That is how much the boy means to her.'

'And the Grand Duchess's health?' Faro put in carefully, trying not to sound too eager for the news he longed to hear.

'She is recovering. The spray of bullets which killed the two servants hit her near the right lung. Her life was despaired of, but with the Kaiser's excellent doctors, although she is still very weak, she has a good chance of survival.'

The Colonel paused. 'There is another matter of Luxorian politics which you might not be able to understand, another reason for George's bargaining power. It has long been well-known amongst those of us who are close to the Kaiser – myself included as a lifelong friend – that he wishes to annex Luxoria to Imperial Germany.'

'So I have heard,' said Faro. And when the Colonel's eyebrow raised a little at that, he added, 'We have our sources of secret information too.'

The Colonel laughed. 'Of course, a senior policeman in the service of Her Majesty Queen Victoria. Stupid of me!'

'I begin to see your reasoning, Colonel.'

'Excellent! Proceed.'

'The President could use George's future to force his mother to refuse the Kaiser's wish for annexation with Germany.'

The Colonel shook his head. 'I think you are oversimplifying matters a little, Mr Faro. George has no "future" as far as the

President is concerned. He is expendable, since the President wishes to have his natural son Anton as heir to Luxoria.'

'But surely George is his legitimate heir?'

The Colonel smiled. 'Ah, now there is a point! Suppose we ask why Gustav should want to destroy George, the son of his marriage, forced perhaps but legal, to Amelie.'

Leaning forward, he raised a finger. 'The answer is very plain, surely – ' Pausing, he laughed, 'especially to a detective of your powers, Mr Faro?'

'I don't follow you,' said Faro, trying to look blank despite his fast-beating heart.

The Colonel shook his head, and said triumphantly: 'George is not his child.'

They were interrupted by the arrival of a waiter bearing some excellent schnapps. Not quite Faro's preference but, at that moment, strong enough to down in one gulp and hopefully still the anguish of hearing what the Colonel had to impart.

'Permit me to let you into a secret, Mr Faro.'

24

Pausing, the Colonel looked out of the window. 'This secret goes back a long time and is a very personal one.'

Sighing, he smiled. 'I have been in love with Amelie for a very long time. But to go back to the beginning, Wilhelm – the Kaiser – and I were childhood companions. I knew all his secrets. He told me how he had met this wonderful lady while visiting his grandmother Queen Victoria at Balmoral.'

He paused. 'I believe you know it well, Mr Faro, and that you are a trusted intimate of Her Majesty.'

Faro bowed. 'Hardly that, sir. I have been a useful servant only, on many occasions.'

The Colonel laughed. 'Ah, like John Brown, perhaps. The servant who taught her to enjoy your Scotch whisky in her tea.'

And Faro smiled wryly at another reputation ruined by crossing the English Channel. 'No, sir. I am a policeman – a detective – I was on hand on several occasions when there were threats to her life.'

'Ah, yes – assassination attempts like the one on Amelie?'

Faro nodded. 'Very similar.'

'And you were able to avert them. A pity you had not been present at Mosheim.' Again that intense look. 'I understand that you were also responsible for Amelie's safety when she visited Scotland some years ago.'

'I was.'

The Colonel smiled. 'Scotland has a fascination for us, a beautiful country. I once had the honour to accompany Wilhelm. He loves his grandmother, a rather formidable lady, according to Bismarck.' Pausing, he asked, 'Did you ever meet His Imperial Majesty?'

'I never had that pleasure.'

'A pity, for he is a remarkable man. Not only as my good friend but as a statesman and a soldier. Someone once said of him that he is eager to impress everyone. That he wants to be the bride at every wedding and the corpse at every funeral. He is a great raconteur, few can match him telling a story. And physically too.'

His face darkened momentarily as he continued. 'He has overcome a physical disadvantage that is not publically referred to,' he touched his left arm delicately, 'to become a great horseman. You must be wondering why I am telling you, a stranger, all these things, Mr Faro. The reason is very obvious. Compare this man with what you know of Amelie's husband, President Gustav.'

He shrugged. 'The man is a savage, a moral degenerate. Would it surprise anyone that Amelie, a beautiful cultured woman, would prefer His Imperial Majesty to such a fellow?'

Faro listened, fascinated now. They had come some distance from George's parentage, but was the Colonel hinting that he thought that Wilhelm was the boy's father?

'We were all a little in love with the unhappy Grand Duchess that Wilhelm had brought into our small circle. We all wished to see her free of such a marriage. My own reasons were intensely personal. My sister Melissa was born with the gift of a voice, she defied family tradition by going on the stage. Gustav saw her, charmed her by some means unknown to the rest of us. Perhaps his savage background had a sexual fascination after her gentle upbringing.'

He stopped and sighed again. 'Who knows? She was young, beautiful, ambitious and with a passionate nature. She became his mistress and Anton was born. As his own marriage was childless after many years, he decided to be rid of Amelie, and marry my sister.'

He shook his head. 'For me this was a very difficult situation personally. I was in love with Amelie.' Smiling gently, he added, 'And I still am. I have been faithful to her for many years.'

Pausing again, he regarded Faro. 'I am telling you all this because there is a mystery which has long intrigued me and one I hope you might be able to solve. It is rather personal, but I gather from your dealings with Amelie's godmother, your Queen, that you are a man of discretion, a man who can be trusted with secrets.'

He looked at Faro as if expecting some affirmative and when there was none, he went on. 'As you know, Amelie went to

Scotland all those years ago to seek refuge from Gustav. Her life was in constant danger. There had been attempts to poison her to clear the way for Melissa who, of course, would not listen to any of us. She adored Gustav and wanted to marry him, have their child legitimised and made his heir.'

With a shake of his head, he added bitterly: 'She has learned the truth about Gustav, but all too late. But that is another story. When Amelie returned to Luxoria, it was for a reconciliation with Gustav and I am afraid my foolish sister was distraught when this resulted in a child. Immediately her own relationship with Gustav began to fall apart. She had served her purpose and now she was no longer needed. There were other younger, prettier girls he could take as mistresses and she returned to her neglected career.'

'Had he any other children by these unions?' Faro asked.

The Colonel smiled. 'Your question interests me exceedingly, Mr Faro. We are obviously thinking along the same lines. But he has no other offspring than Anton, that we are aware of.'

Pausing, he looked out of the window. The landscape had changed, in Faro's eyes confirming the reason why the Prince Consort had found Deeside so attractive.

The Colonel said, 'We will soon be at the end of our journey and I must make haste since the two boys will be returning to the carriage and we may have no further chance of an intimate conversation like this. And I will go on never knowing the answer to this little mystery.'

'How do you think I can help you, sir?' asked Faro, knowing that four simple words could clear up the mystery of George's birth, four simple words that would never pass his lips.

The Colonel put his fingertips together and regarded Faro gravely. 'In your short acquaintance with Amelie, was there anyone in Scotland with whom she might have had a temporary infatuation?'

Regardless of his fast-beating heart, Faro said: 'I cannot answer that. We met only briefly during a visit to her friends in East Lothian, near Edinburgh.'

'Then there might have been someone at this place?' the Colonel asked eagerly.

Shaking his head, Faro said truthfully, 'I hardly think that would be possible. There were no suitable or eligible men from my acquaintance with that family.'

The Colonel looked disappointed and, frowning over his schnapps, Faro felt uncomfortably aware of his penetrating gaze. At last he shrugged.

'Perhaps I am all wrong, what you call "barking up the wrong tree".'

Faro pretended to be puzzled. 'You have said yourself that there was a reconciliation, so why shouldn't George be the President's child?'

'Because, Mr Faro, Gustav has found out the truth.'

'I don't understand,' lied Faro, who understood perfectly.

The Colonel spread his hands wide. 'All the evidence is confirmed by things that have happened lately. The assassination attempt at Mosheim – who else would want to be rid of Amelie, who else realises that this annexation with Imperial Germany would topple the President from his power?'

Faro's thoughtful expression suggested that he was considering this possibility. 'But if this is such a well-kept secret, about the child, how could he have found out?'

The Colonel shrugged. 'Who knows? In a moment of terror or desperation, perhaps Amelie confessed the truth. Certainly his behaviour towards George – Amelie is terrified of what might happen to the boy – seems to confirm that the President is now aware that the boy is not his son.'

Pausing to let this sink in, he added, 'I have known and loved Amelie for a long time. I have asked her to marry me, knowing it was unlikely although my blood is better than that of her President. In Germany the Junkers are country gentry, a noble class of landowners formed in the Middle Ages. They do not correspond to any other society in Europe. We belong to men who are not too proud to join their estate workers during the harvest but are proud of their right to carry a sword for the King of Prussia.'

He smiled. 'So I have always loved Amelie, always hoped that she perhaps loved me a little. But one day, when she was staying at Mosheim, she told me that although she was grateful she could never return my affection. And she hinted – just a mere hint – that there was someone else. Someone she had loved from the first day she met him and would love to the very last day of her life.'

He shook his head, as though still bewildered. 'It was a great shock to me. I had never suspected such a thing.'

'Perhaps the Kaiser?' said Faro helpfully, just to ease the tension.

'No. I am sure of that. We have talked of Amelie's little mystery, Wilhelm and I. He is somewhat vague and at one time I suspected they might have been lovers, very briefly.'

'You might be right,' was the cautious response.

'No,' said the Colonel emphatically. Leaning forward, he subjected Faro once again to that intense gaze. 'The secret lies in your country. Someone she met, someone we know nothing about, a brief love for a mysterious man her heart still aches for. Whoever he was, that man is undoubtedly also George's father.'

The train was beginning to slow down. The Colonel sat back and gave him a brilliant smile. 'We are almost at our destination. Come along, Mr Faro. We have only minutes for you to solve my mystery. Surely, before we part, Scotland's greatest detective must have some clue to offer about the man's identity?'

25

Faro was spared any further interrogation regarding George's parentage as the train slowed down.

'Ah, we are there!' said the Colonel.

Faro looked out of the window. The terrain with its pine forests and undulating hills and river did not immediately suggest the outskirts of a great city.

'Stuttgart?' he said.

The Colonel laughed. 'No. But this is where we leave for Mosheim. Unfortunately a railway line does not yet exist but it will in time. It is on the list of the Kaiser's projects but he has been persuaded against it by the Kaiserin since once royal associations make Mosheim popular with the masses, their privacy will be destroyed.'

Faro wondered how he could politely take his leave of the Colonel and insist on continuing on the train to Stuttgart. The Colonel had observed his bleak expression and realised that he did not look very enthusiastic at this change of plans. 'You do not wish to accompany us?'

Faro smiled. 'I was hoping to take a train to Heidelberg. I am meeting a friend there.'

'A lady, perhaps?' The Colonel gave him a teasing glance. 'A romantic meeting?'

Faro's enigmatic smile was rightly interpreted.

'Can this impatient lady wait a little longer? I believe the Grand Duchess is very anxious to see you, to thank you personally for bringing George to her.'

This piece of news made Faro groan inwardly. Meeting Amelie again, with George at his side, was something he had hoped to avoid.

'It is inconvenient, yes?' asked the Colonel anxiously.

'A little.'

'But we will only delay your journey by a few days,' he insisted. 'And Mosheim is a place you should see. It dates back to Roman times, indeed the remains of a Roman settlement have been found here. Once it was a monastic town.'

But Faro wasn't listening any more. How could he find a valid excuse to decline Amelie's invitation? Did she know he was coming? Would she be equally embarrassed? What would it be like for those closest to her to meet him?

He cursed the resemblance between himself and George, evident to even a casual observer. Anyone seeing them together must guess the truth. Remembering the shock of seeing their reflections, he wondered whether others were as observant. He was certain that Dieter had guessed, or was that the workings of his guilty conscience?

'I had hoped to send a telegraph to my friend from Stuttgart,' he told the Colonel, who laughed.

'If that is all, Mr Faro, I can assure you it will be taken care of. We have excellent facilities on board the train. The Kaiser has thought of everything for his passengers' and his own comfort.'

Pausing, he added, 'I wish you to stay also. I have enjoyed our short acquaintance. And I am secretly hoping that a meeting with Amelie will jolt your memory regarding her visit to your country and the people she met. Perhaps it might provide some clues to the mystery concerning George.

'I also hope that you will have a chance to call upon my sister Melissa when you are in Heidelberg. She will want to meet the good man who looked after her son so well on the journey from Scotland.

'I have to make arrangements for his future, since he is unlikely to return to the Scottish college. I think perhaps the military academy but Melissa would rather he chose a less warlike career. He is like her and wishes to be an actor, which seems a very strange choice for a male from an old Junker family.'

Faro smiled. 'I can assure you he would do very well. He has a natural ability, from what I observed in the Shakespearean scenes put on by his school.' He explained that he had been a guest at the school on that occasion.

'Is that so? Then your judgement is indeed a recommendation to bear in mind, Mr Faro. The boy is young enough and with his mother's career, which is doing so well at present. She must leave his education in my hands as his legal guardian. I have little to do with children, I am afraid.'

Faro pushed to the back of his mind the darker side of Anton's acting ability that Dieter had stressed. The ability to shed tears at will, the screen for telling outrageous and convincing lies.

At that moment, the door opened to admit George and Anton. As George rushed over and sat down at his side, Faro felt again the intensity of the Colonel's disconcerting gaze.

Fortunately the two boys were full of questions. George was telling his uncle that he was longing to see his pet falcon again. There was a small menagerie at Mosheim, Faro gathered, kept for the Kaiser's shooting guests.

Steps were provided for the party to leave the train and in the small station precinct a carriage awaited to take them through the town and on to the Kaiserhof.

The Colonel pointed to a hillside with a dark forest. 'That is our destination, Mr Faro. It was once upon a time a Franciscan monastery, quite secluded. You will see it in due course.'

The drive through the town was picturesque enough for anyone's taste, thought Faro. There was a fairy-tale look about the ancient half-timbered houses leaning towards each other across narrow cobbled streets and the wide market-place dominated by an equestrian statue of some early benefactor staring reverently towards a handsome and equally ancient church, unmistakably a one-time fortification. The atmosphere of Mosheim recalled illustrations from the children's stories of the Brothers Grimm. Here was a place where anything could happen, wildly romantic and remote as a distant planet from stern-faced Scottish streets where tight-windowed grey houses paid careful tribute to respectability.

The passage of the royal carriage was enhanced by the ringing of church bells. They were not to greet young George of Luxoria however but to call people to Mass.

Leaving the town behind, the horses began their strenuous upward climb on the last stage of the journey, along roads twisting up through the forest. Looking down, Faro saw a water-mill and a twist of river far below the treeline, the houses and church now reduced to the dimensions of a child's toy village.

Suddenly the forest cleared a little to reveal glimpses of a small castle, romantic and quite unreal.

So this was the hunting-lodge, the old castle Wilhelm's parents had discovered and renovated long ago in an area allegedly teeming with wildlife. Faro hadn't seen any. They remained prudently invisible, shy creatures like deer and fierce ones like wild boar.

The Kaiser had invested in strong gates for privacy and behind them a drive swept towards the front of the house. The boys leaped out of the carriage and dashed up the steps to the front door.

It seemed that there were other visitors present since a small army of carriages lined the drive. Faro, not looking forward to the unavoidable encounter with Amelie, was thankful that with others present, this would be a formal occasion.

The two boys had already disappeared inside the lodge and a waiting footman ushered the newcomers into a waiting-room, through a hall with walls overburdened with trophies of the hunt.

Deer, wild boar and eagles in glass cases stared down on them. Stepping cautiously across a fierce-headed tiger-skin rug, Faro felt depressed by the presence of so many dead things.

Watching his expression with some amusement, the Colonel said, 'Wilhelm tells us that your Balmoral is like this.'

'It is indeed,' said Faro and left it at that.

An equerry arrived, bowed and greeted the new arrivals. 'Her Highness is resting at present. She has been told of your arrival and will receive you shortly.'

The Colonel indicated chairs and ordered schnapps. As they sat by the sunny window Faro was not kept long in doubt of the identity of those other important visitors, who were just leaving.

'Count von Bismarck,' said the Colonel.

And Faro caught a glimpse of the legendary man of German politics, immensely tall and imposing as he came down the steps. Noticing the Colonel at the window, he saluted him gravely and, stepping into the leading carriage, drove off, followed by his retinue.

The Colonel sighed. 'A pity we didn't arrive earlier. I am sure he would have enjoyed a meeting with you. He is also a friend of Amelie, I expect he has business with her regarding Luxoria. Honest Otto they call him, since he has acted as broker between the European powers. He has built up a web of alliances and even enjoys a good press in your native land. When he met your Queen Victoria, he was very impressed. Told everyone: "What a woman! There is someone I could have dealings with."

'Twenty years ago, he made it his business to win over the German princes and created a unified Germany with Berlin as the capital. The Reich has become Europe's largest state, dominated by Prussia. And it is always growing. Bismarck is a Junker like myself and that helped him achieve greatness, so some say.'

With a deep sigh he added, 'Alas, poor Bismarck.'

'Why do you say that? He doesn't sound like a man who needs anyone's pity.'

'Not on the surface, but I know a thing or two. Wilhelm isn't happy about him. They do not see eye to eye, Mr Faro. Bismarck is a politician of the old school, anti-socialist. Wilhelm has more modern ideas of extending our social security system. I am afraid when it comes to open warfare between the two, Bismarck may have to go. He will accept the inevitable with great dignity and Wilhelm will make it all very polite. That it is time for him to take honourable retirement.'

The door opened. A woman appeared, leaning on her servant's arm; a woman with regal presence, tall and slender, quite lovely, Faro thought, but with the fragility of crystal.

Her eyes sought him out, smiling.

He went forward and, bowing, realised that his image of her all these years had changed. It was like an out-of-focus painting, the colours of which had been disturbed, their margins blurred.

He looked up, confused.

She smiled at him. Her eyes were undeniably all that remained of his memory of the Grand Duchess Amelie.

'Welcome to Mosheim, Inspector Faro,' she said and held out her hand.

26

Amelie was used to hiding her emotions. That intimate glance of recognition and adoration faded swiftly and formality took its place.

George ran to her side, led her to a sofa and sat with his arm around her. They talked together for a few moments, laughed and kissed while the Colonel answered Anton's numerous questions about sport and shooting and pet animals. Faro suddenly found himself in the midst of a family circle from which he was excluded by more than his inability to follow the voluble German of this reunion.

Glad to retreat to the window and look down on the track through the forest towards the distant town, he knew he had served his purpose, his mission fulfilled. George was safe home again and he longed to be released, to breathe freely with no more anxieties in his life than catching the next train to Heidelberg.

Watching the little group, he was relieved that meeting Amelie again had touched no chord of lost love. His brief role in her life had been over long ago, played out almost before it began.

Was Amelie experiencing the same feelings of relief, ignoring him completely, involved only in the joy of having her son at her side again? Aware of his isolation, the Colonel approached.

'Perhaps you would care to retire for a while, Mr Faro. A room has been prepared for you.'

Faro shook his head. 'That is most kind, but I will not be needing it. I intend to leave shortly if you will provide me with a carriage to the railway station.'

The Colonel smiled. 'We cannot permit you to leave us so soon, Mr Faro.' And watching Faro's expression, he said, 'You must be our guest until tomorrow. My sister is arriving with a friend and you may perhaps travel back direct to Heidelberg in their carriage.'

He beamed. 'Will that not please you, no more trains for a while, Mr Faro? Besides, we wish to have your company for a little longer. We do not wish to lose such a good friend and one deserving a well-earned rest after his travels.'

Smiling, the Colonel regarded him. 'A room and a bath at your disposal – surely that is tempting. And a suit of clothes,' he added tactfully. At that Faro became aware with some embarrassment of his dishevelled appearance, which had not perturbed him in the least until then.

'There are always clothes in readiness for guests. Shooting parties are liable to be rained on, or have guests fall into muddy rivers,' the Colonel smiled.

At least he did not mention being subject to assassins, Faro thought, rubbing his chin and conscious that he badly needed a shave. A bath and a change of clothes would be welcome before meeting Imogen again, he decided, thanking the Colonel for his thoughtfulness.

The Colonel bowed. 'You are most welcome. It is a pity you will not have a chance to meet the Kaiser, he is absent at this time on a visit to Potsdam. He will be sorry to have missed you, since you are a devoted and trusted servant of his grandmother.'

How they liked to dwell on that, Faro thought as he was ushered through the hall with its hunting trophies, stags and wild boar, whose fierce gaze relentlessly followed his progress up the staircase.

Inside the room they were replaced by walls hung with gilt-framed hunting scenes. Two of Mr Landseer's paintings of dead animals and birds suggested that they had originated from Balmoral, fond birthday gifts from devoted grandmother to favourite grandson.

As he closed the door, Faro once again found it depressing to be surrounded by so much dead and dying. The room was warmed by a closed stove and the huge canopied bed was at least inviting. On it, in readiness for his use, lay clothes and fresh linen. Handsome grey breeches and a jacket trimmed with hunting-green, complete with sportsman's hat, the uniform of the hunting-guest, he thought, appreciating an entire wardrobe of accessories.

He was delighted to find a full tub in the dressing-room, steaming warmly and ready for his use. Thankfully stripping off, he sank into it gratefully and decided that this was luxury indeed, peace and quiet and a hot bath. He closed his eyes.

He awoke with a start to find that beyond the window the sky had darkened. It was now late afternoon. Seizing the voluminous bathrobe, he went back into the bedroom. A footman appeared, followed by a valet with razor and soap, a business-like towel over his arm.

Invited to sit in a chair, Faro enjoyed one of the few occasions his life had offered the luxury of what was in middle-class Edinburgh a pleasant daily visit from the barber. However, when a week's growth of beard was removed he felt suddenly naked and vulnerable.

It had also removed his last hope of disguise; his likeness to George was there for all the world to see.

He smiled sadly at his reflection as he dressed. A likeness most fathers would have been proud of, but for him a cruel twist of fate, and potentially fatal for himself and others.

Trying to thrust aside such gloomy thoughts, at last attired in his borrowed suit – which fitted very well, apart from being a trifle too short in the sleeves and a trifle too wide in the breeches – he was considering whether or not to wear the hat with its ridiculous feather when a tap on the door announced the Colonel.

'Ah! The new suit indeed becomes you, Mr Faro.' But Faro felt his gaze was more concerned with his now smooth and beardless countenance. If the truth came out on this visit, would the Colonel once again come to his aid?

'Amelie sends greetings. She will dine alone with George this evening.'

That was a relief, Faro thought.

'She is still very frail, you know,' the Colonel continued. 'Wilhelm's physicians have done their best for her, but she may always remain something of an invalid. Our other visitors are expected shortly. My sister and a friend from Heidelberg, as I mentioned to you. It may surprise you to know that Amelie and Melissa have formed a deep friendship, united by the cruel treatment of Gustav. At one time Melissa hated her. It was not reciprocated since if truth were told, and it seldom is, Amelie was relieved when her husband took a mistress. All that is past now, Anton and George and their respective mothers are firm friends, united by misfortune.

'Now you must excuse me as I have matters to attend to in Mosheim. Tedious, but there it is. I must apologise for leaving you to dine alone, but you will be well taken care of, I can assure you of that. Perhaps you would care to dine in your room here?'

Faro considered that prospect very agreeable. The thought of being waited upon by an army of servants alone at the huge dining table he had glimpsed across the hall, surrounded on all sides by the reproachful gaze of dead animals, had little appeal. And he recognised, not for the first time, the need for solitude, time to sort out all that had happened since he had left Edinburgh.

Silent-footed servants arrived. The lamps were lit, the stove replenished and it was with a feeling of great comfort that he sat down to the huge platter of food set before him. Roasted meat and vegetables, wine and rich dessert of chocolate and cream. Delicious! But he was to pay a price for this over-indulgence. His stomach, used to spartan fare, and little of it in the last few days, rebelled. He went to bed, fell asleep and awoke in such agony he was sure he had been poisoned.

His mind raced ahead. That was it! He had been invited to dine alone and someone had taken the opportunity of putting poison in the wine. Someone in President Gustav's pay.

Then common sense took over. He realised these symptons were those that had haunted him all his working life. Bad eating habits, acquired in long days with the Edinburgh City Police, had resulted in a digestive system which was one of Vince's cautionary tales. Would that he had Vince at hand instead of merely the packet of digestive powders in his valise.

He took one and decided dismally that it was useless and his suspicions had been right. A second dose and he began to feel relief as he lay back on his pillows thinking of the mad imaginings a simple attack of indigestion could bring.

Poison indeed!

But although he told himself he was being foolish, he was haunted by uneasy dreams and awoke next morning feeling slightly under the weather, with an inability to rid himself of that spine-tingling awareness of danger which had little to do with his faulty digestive system.

But who would want to harm him here, of all places? Looking out of his window at the front of the hunting-lodge, he realised this was the very place where the assassin had struck; where two of Amelie's servants had been slain and she herself almost fatally wounded.

Breakfast was brought to him. Coffee, warm bread, butter, ham and cheese. But he ate little.

He went downstairs, his feet echoing on the boards. The lodge seemed uneasily deserted and he almost jumped when a door opened to admit the Colonel.

After the usual polite questions about whether he had slept well, to which Faro gave polite but untruthful answers, he was told there was a message from Amelie.

'She wishes to show the kind policeman who did so much for her in Scotland one of her favourite places here in the Odenwald – once an old woodcutter's cottage that the Kaiser had restored and gave to her as a gift long ago. It has been a retreat for George and herself. She has already left with the two boys.

'There is a horse for you, ready saddled. The track is well-marked – I will direct you. It is less than a quarter kilometre away.'

Faro was in a quandary. Naturally the Colonel presumed that all men of any substance rode, knowing little of the circumstances of Edinburgh policemen. And Faro hated to confess that he had had little opportunity for equestrian pursuits since his boyhood days in Orkney as he followed the Colonel to the stables.

A horse was led out to a mounting block.

'He belongs to Anton. A gentle beast, well-behaved,' said the Colonel, patting the animal's neck. 'Thoroughly reliable,' he added as if aware of Faro's apprehensions.

Mounting was easier than he expected after so many years, and Faro moved off, watched anxiously by the Colonel. Trying to appear like an experienced horseman, he realised that with the Colonel's usual tact, a boy's horse had been selected for an indifferent rider.

As he proceeded up the track, taking his time, trotting slowly and carefully, a shot rang out. It was close by and Faro had a confused thought that there must be a shooting party, perhaps some of the servants bringing down game for the larder.

Another shot, closer at hand. The beast neighed, terrified, as Faro felt the wind of a bullet close to the horse's mane. It had narrowly missed him but was enough for the beast to rear.

Faro was unseated, lost his reins and fell to the ground. Stunned and winded by the fall, some instinct told him not to move. Whoever fired that shot, he was the target.

As he lay inert, as if he had been hit, he tried to decide on the next move.

Suddenly everything was becoming sickeningly clear to him. Perhaps this whole trip to Mosheim had been arranged. A trap for him, now that the truth about George's parentage was out. And with such a deadly secret and its political consequences, he was never to be allowed to leave alive.

Cautious footsteps were approaching. He was lying curled up, vulnerable, on the ground.

The terrified horse had vanished back down the track and Faro knew that death was very near. He was totally unarmed. His only hope lay in his killer believing he was dead.

He saw a pair of boots, well polished. The butt of a rifle. A kick at his ribs. A grunt of approval.

As long as his killer believed he was dead. If he could spring into action before the man had a chance to raise that rifle and fire again.

This time there would be no possibility of missing.

At point-blank range.

The man leaned over him, breathing heavily...

27

Like a coiled spring, Faro unwound, seized the man's legs and threw him to the ground.

Dieter!

Taken by surprise, Dieter lost his grip on the rifle, which began to roll away down the slope. Faro strove to hold his attacker and at the same time reach the rifle, but Dieter was younger and stronger and Faro realised that he was no match for him. A sudden blow in his stomach had Faro retching, falling away, rolling, his gathering momentum halted by a boulder which cannoned into his side.

He felt the agonising crack and the next moment, Dieter was standing over him, the rifle pointed at his head.

'Mr Faro, you never learn, do you? Yes, I am going to kill you, make no mistake about that this time. I have my orders.'

'I thought you went back on the train to Luxoria,' gasped Faro, fighting for breath and playing for time.

'I jumped off and made my way here – and here I am. This is our last meeting, you shall die here, and I shall have carried out my part in the the plan.'

'What plan?'

'Mr Faro, it was never intended that you should leave here alive. Especially when the truth was known.'

'What truth? I don't understand.'

Dieter gave him a thin-lipped smile. 'Everyone who has seen you with George must have guessed the truth. There are many disguises a man can have successfully, but when his offspring is his image – the President guessed some time ago that George was not his child. And now I think everyone who has seen you together knows. You are not a fool, Mr Faro, you must see that you have walked into a trap. You are a marked man, too dangerous to remain alive and I have orders to kill you.'

Faro sat up, each breath an agony.

'You can get to your feet if you wish. That will not help you. But you may choose how to die. There on the ground like a dog, or like an Englishman, bravely facing the firing squad,' Dieter added mockingly, clearly enjoying the situation.

'Thank you for your consideration,' said Faro, rising to his feet unsteadily, incapable of making any sudden moves, and without any hope of taking Dieter by surprise again.

Faint and dizzy with pain, certain that his ribs were cracked, his shoulder agonising, perhaps broken, he leaned weakly against a tree for support. He knew that there was no escape, only a few minutes remained of a life that was almost over.

What a way to go, he thought bitterly. That he of all people, with all his experience, should have walked into such a trap! There was no comfort in knowing that this trap was one no father could have resisted when the bait was his own son.

Dieter seemed in no hurry to kill him. Was his leisurely manner regret? Faro did not think so. More likely a sadistic enjoyment of having his victim helpless before him.

Occasionally he glanced beyond Faro down the track, his face expressionless. Who was he expecting?

Whoever it was Dieter did not seem perturbed or anxious and Faro realised he need not entertain hopes of a last-minute rescue party. Tempting fate, he said, 'Well, I am ready. Get it over with. What are you waiting for?'

Dieter smiled grimly, shrugged. 'I am in no hurry. You have been very clever, Mr Faro – indeed there were times I almost began to like you. To feel that we had much in common, the paid policeman and the paid bodyguard.'

'Or the paid assassin,' Faro put in sourly. But curiously he had sometimes felt aware of their similarities. Could it be that Dieter had finer feelings that might be appealed to? Even at this moment, could he be persuaded to let his helpless victim live?

'What happened to Helga?' Faro asked. 'Did you kill her?'

Dieter laughed. 'Helga! It was Helga you have to thank for realising immediately that you were George's father. She saw the likeness – a woman's intuition, of course.'

'You did not kill her for that.'

'I did not kill her at all. As far as I know she is in Germany with her family.'

'But you needed someone to send the telegraph to persuade George that his mother was in Luxoria.'

'Correct, Mr Faro. You have hit the nail on the head, as they say in your country. And I was speaking the truth when I told you she had never boarded the train with us,' he added reproachfully.

'And talking of trains,' Faro put in. Even now certain that he was to die within the next few moments, he felt impelled to know the truth.

'When you disappeared from the railway hut to risk wolves and worse to go to the telegraph office, I presume that was all part of the plan.'

Dieter smiled. 'I knew that the President's crack regiment was somewhere in the vicinity in readiness for the arrival of the Luxorian train. I thought of an excellent way of obeying orders that would greatly please the President for it was most economical. First they must kidnap Anton so that he would be safe.'

'And plant the explosives for the rest of us, was that it?' said Faro grimly.

Dieter nodded. 'Exactly. A time-saving measure.'

'To kill an innocent child?'

Dieter's expression did not change. 'Alas, the innocent often die with the guilty – such matters are not for me to decide, indeed they make little difference in my profession, one way or another, Mr Faro.'

He shrugged. 'George will die sooner or later, the President will see to that. And you have always been expendable.'

The man's cold-blooded dedication appalled Faro. What hope was there of mercy from such a man?

Suddenly there were sounds. A rider approaching fast up the steep track.

A rescuer after all, Faro thought hopefully. Until he saw relief on Dieter's face. And realised that this was the moment he had been waiting for.

Still covering Faro with the rifle, he motioned him into the open. Looking over his shoulder, Faro saw the Colonel dismounting and shouted, 'Thank God you arrived in time.'

But the Colonel ignored him and turning to Dieter, said in German, 'I heard a rifle shot. I thought it was all over.'

Even as Faro thought he had misinterpreted the fatal words, Dieter bowed. 'Mr Faro eluded that one. I thought you might want to deliver the *coup de grâce* personally.'

The Colonel shook his head and Faro stared at him unbelievingly. So he, too, was part of the plan.

Dieter shrugged. 'No? Very well.' And raising the rifle. 'Farewell, Mr Faro.'

And Faro closed his eyes. Goodbye, George. Goodbye, world.

He heard the explosion. But he was still alive.

Dieter was lying on the ground. Dead with a bullet through his forehead.

Birds were screaming overhead and there were other sounds, faint voices echoing far-off.

The pistol in the Colonel's hand was turned towards him.

Suddenly the sky fell in on him and the darkness of death once more enfolded him.

28

He was being torn apart by wild animals, one of them was ripping off his shoulder.

Faro screamed and opened his eyes to find he was propped up on a bed in the hunting-lodge. An elderly man, presumably a doctor, was bending over him, tying a bandage across his chest. Behind him stood Colonel Karl zu Echlenberg, the man he had trusted. The man who had ordered his execution.

The doctor spoke a few words to the Colonel, bowed and left them.

'Your ribs are broken but our good doctor has set your dislocated shoulder. The pain of it made you pass out. It was as well you were unconscious when we carried you back. Very painful – I am sorry about that.'

'It could have been worse,' was Faro's laconic reply.

The Colonel sat down by the bedside, shook his head and said, 'I could not let him kill you. Even had I wished to do so, it was too late,' he added wryly, 'since George and Anton had appeared on the scene. They had been on the archery course, heard the shots – '

'Then it was true – what Dieter told me.'

The Colonel nodded. 'That you were never meant to leave Luxoria alive. To bring George back and then you were to be disposed of.'

'What was it to be? What had you in mind?' Faro asked bitterly.

He smiled grimly. 'A convenient accident, Mr Faro. This is just one of the sad facts of political necessity. You are not a foolish man, surely you can realise that.'

'Did Amelie know?' Faro put in anxiously.

'Of course not,' was the scornful reply. 'She would never have allowed any harm to come to you. Perhaps if she knows that I spared your life, she will be grateful.'

Faro said nothing. He had no emotions to spare for a lovesick Colonel who had sacrificed a family life for a useless infatuation for the Grand Duchess Amelie of Luxoria.

The Colonel was looking at him wistfully, obviously hoping for a consoling response but all that Faro could say was, 'I don't think one should mistake gratitude for love or that any man would want a wife on such conditions.'

There were more urgent matters on Faro's mind. 'And the Kaiser? Did he know?'

The Colonel shrugged. 'I think not. But perhaps he suspected something was in the wind and that was why he diplomatically absented himself. He seemed anxious not to meet you, Mr Faro. I know him well and this is not quite in character, especially since you are a close and trusted servant of his beloved grandmother.'

By whose orders he had been instructed to return George to Luxoria, Faro thought coldly. He was beginning to suspect everyone in this plan to dispose of him, even Her Majesty the Queen.

The Colonel was saying, 'Wilhelm has no reason to hate you, unlike myself. As my rival for Amelie's affections, you have long been the unknown man who stood between us and I have hated your image and would gladly have you dead. But if I destroyed you it would not make Amelie love me and I never give up hope that someday she may.'

He smiled sadly. 'And then I did not know you, but now we have met and I have put a face and body on this hated rival. Then there is George, whom I love like my own son. In Amelie's many difficult times, when she has sought refuge here, I have felt that I stood *in loco parentis*. I was in a quandary. I could see the boy had formed an affection for you, as well as my nephew Anton. You had saved their lives.'

He spread his hands wide. 'But what could I do? The arrangement had already been made.'

And Faro remembered the scene he had witnessed, the brief tense words between the Colonel and Dieter as the latter apparently departed with the train to Luxoria.

'Dieter was to return, make his way to Mosheim and kill you. I could not do it myself, although I have killed of necessity in battle, I have never taken any man's life dishonourably. But Dieter is a hired assassin. It is merely another job of work with him.'

Leaning across, he put a hand on Faro's arm. 'But you are safe now, Mr Faro. You have my word as an officer and a gentleman. Now perhaps I can help you into these – ' he indicated a shirt and jacket on the chair nearby.

'Another new suit,' said Faro wryly.

'There are wardrobes of them here in the hunting-lodge, as I told you. Besides, those ones were required elsewhere,' he added grimly.

At Faro's puzzled glance he continued. 'There is a mill-race you will remember passing on the way up to the old woodcutter's cottage. By now it will have received Dieter's body in your clothes. By the time it is recovered, it will be unrecognisable as the policeman from Edinburgh. And President Gustav will be satisfied, having received secret information that his orders were carried out.'

'What of Dieter – won't he be expected to return to Luxoria, now that he is no longer needed as Anton's bodyguard?'

The Colonel shrugged. 'Dieter would not be welcome. He failed in his mission to return Anton to his father and to eliminate George. His services are expendable and since it is in the nature of hired killers to come and go without anyone expecting explanations, no awkward questions will be asked.'

And with a swift change of subject, he leaned forward and held up the shirt. 'But this, I am afraid, is going to be awkward – and painful.'

It was.

When the last button was fastened, a tap on the door announced George and Anton.

George rushed over to him. 'Are you all right, sir? We were on the archery course waiting for Mama to arrive.'

Faro glanced in the Colonel's direction, who shook his head. Amelie waiting to receive him in the woodcutter's hut had been part of the well-laid trap.

'We heard the shots and decided to have a look, especially as there isn't supposed to be any shooting up there,' said Anton.

'You must come and see our archery course and my falcon,' said George eagerly. Then looking across at the Colonel, 'Mama is waiting to see Mr Faro, Uncle Karl.' And to Faro, 'She heard that Anton's horse had thrown you. Please don't tell her what really happened. She might be frightened.'

'I cannot believe it,' said Anton. 'Dieter must have gone mad to have attacked you like that, Mr Faro. And after saving all our lives, too.'

Faro could think of no answer suitable for the boys. 'I was very thankful that your uncle arrived in time,' he said with a grateful smile in the Colonel's direction.

'It was dreadful,' said Anton. 'I had never seen anyone really dead before, Mr Faro. Just pretend in plays.'

'It was just like one of the adventure stories they try to keep from us at Glenatholl. But this was real blood,' said George with a shiver.

'Where is your Mama waiting?' the Colonel put in quickly.

'In the salon. She is not allowed to climb stairs until she is properly well again.' And remembering Faro's accident, 'Can you walk, sir, if we help you?'

'You're very kind, George, but I think I can manage. It's my ribs that are cracked, my legs are fine.' And he added to himself, 'somewhat shaky though to find I am still in one piece.'

When they reached the room where Amelie waited, the Colonel said to George, 'Your mother wishes to talk to Mr Faro alone.'

'Very well, sir,' said George, sounding a little disappointed and looking at Faro as if he did not wish to let him out of his sight.

'You must tell her all that has happened, Mr Faro, since we left Glenatholl. She will want to hear all the details. Leave nothing out. Everything – remember!'

Not quite everything, thought Faro. There were some things George must never know.

29

As he entered the room, Amelie looked up from the sofa where she was sitting. This time there was no formality. She indicated a place beside her and took his hand.

'My dear, I am so sorry. Karl tells me you had an accident with Anton's horse and you have cracked ribs. Is it very painful?'

Faro smiled bravely and she went on, 'What a terrible thing to happen when you have just arrived. The boys' mounts are chosen for their reliability. Something must have scared your horse.'

Faro decided to go along with this version of his accident. 'The animal wasn't to blame. I lost my stirrups. I'm afraid it is a long time since I was on a horse,' he said truthfully. 'There wasn't much call for it in my particular line of business.'

Touching his shoulder and assured that it didn't hurt, which wasn't entirely true, Amelie smiled and said, 'Dear Jeremy, I don't know where to begin. I owe you so much. But first of all, and most important, thank you again for bringing George home safe to me.'

Pausing, she looked into his face intently, as if memorising every feature. 'I can hardly believe you are here with me. I am scared to close my eyes in case I open them and you have disappeared,' she smiled sadly, 'as so often happens in my dreams. Now you are really here and I wonder if you can guess how many days of my life I have dreamed of this moment,' she whispered, patting the sofa. 'Of sitting here like this together and sharing an hour with the man who saved my life so long ago.'

As he began to protest she said in a low voice, as if they might be overheard, 'It is true, Jeremy. If George had not been born then I would never have survived Gustav's determined attempts on my life. But all that is past now.'

Closing her eyes, she sighed deeply. 'Now I can pretend for one perfect hour that I am not a Grand Duchess, but merely an ordinary housewife.' A wistful smile, 'Perhaps an Edinburgh policeman's wife and we are spending a holiday together travelling in Europe.'

Faro hadn't the heart to tell her that such things were beyond ordinary Edinburgh housewives, especially those on a policeman's salary.

Lifting his hand, she held it against her cheek. 'I can hardly believe that you are so unchanged by the years. Sometimes I have tried to remember your face and found I could not do so. That worried me; you meant so much to me and yet I had forgotten what you looked like. I could no longer bring your face to mind, as if I had an image of you that had faded away.'

Guiltily Faro recognised this experience as similar to his own, but for a vastly different reason – a deliberate attempt to eradicate all memory of that brief fateful visit of the Grand Duchess Amelie.

'There has not been a day in my life when I have not thought of you in the past thirteen years, Jeremy. Thinking what time it would be in Scotland and what you might be doing at that moment. And all the time railing against my destiny.'

Again that deep searching gaze into his face.

'Always saying if only – if only I had not been born a Grand Duchess, I could have made all my dreams come true. I could have been with you forever.'

And Faro listened sadly, wishing for her sake that he had been in love and that he could honestly share her emotions. Wishing he could say just once that it had been the same for him. For that was what she expected, as her right.

But it had never been so. Would it have been different if she had not been royal? Had some caution reasoned against loving someone far above him? Just as she must have always known that to love an Edinburgh policeman was a waste of time.

Acceptance had been easy for him. He had never loved her. That night of madness and passion long ago had never seemed part of his real life. Yet it had resulted in a child, ironically a now beloved son he could never claim as his own.

'I have talked to the Colonel,' he said trying desperately to get the conversation on to less emotional ground. 'I am glad you have such a friend.'

She sighed. 'I expect he told you that he loves me. Everyone knows about that. Such a good kind man, a great friend, but how could a Grand Duchess marry a mere Count?'

Or a policeman, thought Faro. What an intolerable existence it would have been. To be passionately in love – at the beginning – believing he could spend the rest of his life in her shadow in Luxoria. How love would have soon faded, changed into resentment.

'I have had one consolation through the years,' Amelie said, 'when I look at George. And he grows more like you every day. So I have always had a part of you, a mirror in him.' She sighed deeply. 'I would not mind dying now.'

'You must not talk of dying, Amelie. You have much to live for.'

She shook her head. 'Not now that I have seen you again. I have often thought I would give the rest of my life for one more hour together. Maybe God has been good and heard my prayer,' she whispered.

And Faro remembered the bullet that had lodged close to her heart and the odds on her survival, as she added, 'The future of Luxoria is settled. That was why I came here to Mosheim this time, to make the final arrangements. Willy is to take care of everything.'

'What of President Gustav?'

She shrugged. 'He will be helpless against the might of Imperial Germany. And I have Willy's assurance that he will take good care of my people. I trust him, for he is a man of his word. Once, when we were in Balmoral, his uncle the Prince of Wales said that William the Great, as he called him, needed to learn that he is living near the end of the nineteenth century and not in the Middle Ages. Willy never forgot that. He was determined to prove him wrong. He did not care for his uncle, a feeling that was reciprocated.'

'How will your own people react to this annexation?'

'Agreeably, I think. They love me, they hate Gustav. They will believe that anything I choose for them is the right thing. Luxoria is a poor country, bled by his indulgence and extravagance. With Willy she will blossom and live again, share a new economy.'

She smiled. 'My people like him very much, you know, and they will learn to trust him. He has visited Luxoria many times, as my old friend, purely social visits. Willy is so popular with the people, a charming man – do you know they turned out in their thousands to watch his carriage pass by, to cheer him. How Gustav hated that!'

'And what of George's future in all this?'

'That is all decided. Willy will take care of his education until he is old enough for his official role.'

'But by then Luxoria will be part of Germany,' Faro reminded her gently. 'So it will be in name only, surely?'

'I do not think George will mind in the least. He has never cared for the prospect of ruling a country. He seems to have inherited other ideas of what he wants to do with his life.'

Faro let that pass as Amelie went on, 'Please tell my dear godmother when you return to Scotland that I leave my little country in her grandson's excellent keeping.'

Faro knew the chances were remote indeed that he would be able to approach Her Majesty with such a message.

'Your Queen will be pleased with our decision,' Amelie continued, 'because that was what her beloved Prince Albert, my very dear uncle, always wanted for Prussia.'

A clock struck the hour, slowly, solemnly.

Amelie sighed. 'If only... if only. Are they the cruellest words in any language? Soon it will be time for you to leave. For us to part,' she looked at him calmly, candidly. 'I think we are unlikely ever to meet again.'

She leaned forward and kissed Faro on the mouth. He held her close, briefly, wishing he could say and mean the words she longed to hear.

'This is our real parting, dearest Jeremy,' she whispered. 'Our official one will be, alas, much more formal. But there is someone else I want you to meet, if you would – ' she indicated the bell-pull.

A moment later the door opened to admit a vision of elegance: a large-eyed, large-bosomed woman, swept dramatically into the room, looking as if she had just stepped off the stage. She ran swiftly to Amelie and kissed her. Anton was close behind his mother, their likeness immediate.

She had not seen Faro and, following Amelie's whisper, turned to face him.

Amelie smiled. 'This is Melissa, Karl's sister.'

And Gustav's late mistress, thought Faro, as the vision bore down upon him.

'So you are – ' her eyes widened as she turned and looked at Amelie. Then she laughed, a deep-throated laugh. 'How could anyone be mistaken?' She wagged a finger at him. 'I have heard all about you, Monsieur Faro and there is someone here dying to see you.'

She called out, 'Enter!' and the door opened to admit another woman, tall, slender, auburn-haired, green-eyed. And in Faro's eyes, the most beautiful woman in the world.

'Imogen!' he gasped. 'What on earth are you doing here?' he asked, holding her hand formally but longing to gather her into his arms.

Laughing, she indicated the woman talking to Amelie. 'That's Lisa, the opera singer friend I told you about.'

'Such a small world!'

'Sure now, isn't it just? Too small for comfort sometimes. Too small for secrets too.'

Faro ignored that arch smile, as she looked at him searchingly. 'Well now, Faro. And what have you been doing to yourself? I hear you have cracked ribs.'

'Trouble with a horse,' he murmured.

Imogen laughed. 'Life is full of surprises, Faro. All this time and you never even told me you could ride a horse. Not one of your accomplishments you've ever cared to discuss with me, like some others that are now seeing the light of day.'

Ignoring her teasing smile, Faro said, 'But what are you doing in Mosheim?'

'I came with Lisa. We've been in Munich and are on our way back to Heidelberg. She wanted me to meet Amelie, who I understand loves Scotland and had a very interesting holiday there once, about thirteen years ago. That was before we met, of course,' she added primly.

If she expected a reply to that, she wasn't getting one.

'Amelie talks of nothing else to Lisa,' she went on with a sideways glance over at the diva. 'Lisa is leaving immediately, she's singing Beethoven's *Fidelio* in Heidelberg. This is just a fleeting visit.' She paused, looking at the little group chattering, oblivious of their presence. 'I can go with her if you're planning to stay on for a while.'

'No!' said Faro sharply. 'I'm not staying.' He took her hand. 'I want – desperately – just to be with you again. To have you all to myself and that means without Lisa. The Colonel was to send you a telegraph at Heidelberg – that I had arrived.'

That pleased her. 'And me not even there. A good thing your plans were delayed.' She looked at him impishly and nodded towards the door. 'The other lad is waiting for you. I saw him as I came in. Said he wanted a word.'

In answer Faro went over to Amelie and Melissa, bowed and held out his hand. 'Goodbye, Amelie.'

He hoped she was not going to cry for her voice trembled as she said, 'Please see George before you go.'

Melissa took his hand in a strong grip. 'You are not really going to leave us so soon, Mr Faro,' she whispered. Her eyelids fluttered seductively. 'We have only just met.'

Faro bowed. 'I hope to see you again – in *Fidelio*.'

George was waiting for him. 'Mama said you must go. That you couldn't stay for a while.' He had none of his mother's restraint, none of that adult world of dissembling had touched his childish sorrow at losing Faro.

'It's so unfair.' And putting his thin arms around Faro he sobbed. 'You should have been my father. You who are so good and true, not that – that – beast, who ill-used my mother, and Anton's mother too. I hate him and would give everything in the world to call you father, to say that word just once.'

It was said, it hung in the air between them. Too late Faro's hand covered gently the boy's mouth. 'No, Highness, no,' he whispered. 'You – we – must never think about it.'

And George threw his arms around Faro again. 'It is you I will love as a father, your image I shall carry when I'm a man. You, I will try to be like. I want so much for you to be proud of me.'

'That I am, George. And will always be,' said Faro as he hugged the boy to him, stroked his cheek then gently released him. And he thought that the pain in his heart at this parting was greater than any physical agony he had ever suffered.

'We will meet again – some day. Promise!' George whispered.

'No, lad. I can't promise you that, but I can promise I'll never forget the bravest prince that ever lived.'

'May I write to you, then?' George asked, fighting back the tears.

'Of course. I would be honoured. Goodbye, lad.'

'Goodbye – ' and the word, the ever-forbidden word followed him in a whisper. But Faro heard it.

Imogen was waiting for him outside, his battered valise at her feet. As they walked into the winter sunshine, she took his arm, aware that his emotions were running high, that this man who rarely wept was very close to it now.

'That's a fine young lad. We had a chat. A very interesting encounter. Do you know, he reminds me very much of someone – ' she added archly. 'If only I could think who – or, more important, when and why.'

Faro looked at her sharply, wondering how much she had guessed or been told by Lisa who was Amelie's confidant.

She squeezed his hand gently, stood on tiptoe and kissed his cheek. 'I'm glad I came and met Amelie at last.'

It was a sign. She knew. But his secret was safe with her. She knew her own place in his life was unchallenged and would remain so.

'You must tell me all about your adventures. All of them, I mean. Leave nothing out,' she laughed.

'Sometime – maybe,' he said wearily.

She smiled up at him. 'Whither now, Faro?'

'Whither indeed. I wish I knew. Meanwhile, I think the next train to Heidelberg.'

And the two, both exiles of a sort, walked arm in arm towards the waiting carriage.